Dark Spores

Dark Spores

Stories We Tell After Midnight
Volume 4

Edited by

Carol Gyzander

&

Rachel A. Brune

ISBN: 978-1-952388-15-6 (print)
978-1-952388-16-3 (ebook)

Original Cover Art & Design by
Lynne Hansen

Many thanks to Ravyn Crescent,
Crone Girls Press
Online Content Strategy & Marketing
Your work was integral in the success of the Dark Spores Kickstarter campaign!

Published by
Crone Girls Press
Crone Girls Press Trade Paperback Edition December 2024
Printed in the USA

Our immense gratitude to the members of the horror community who backed this project on Kickstarter and made it a reality. We are proud to be part of such an amazing, nurturing community of horror readers, authors, artists, and fans.

Contents

Mushrooms in our Blood:
Foreword

Clay McLeod Chapman

Back in January 2021, there was a news story slowly emerging from the topsoil of the internet: a 30-year-old man injected himself with a home-brewed cocktail of magic mushroom tea. He filtered his concoction through a cotton swab before administering it.

Mushrooms. Injected. Into his veins.

True story.

For the next couple days, he became increasingly more lethargic. Waves of nausea constantly washed over him. His skin grew jaundiced. Before long, he was vomiting blood.

Something was happening—*changing*—inside of him.

Fermenting.

Two days after he first injected himself, this man was brought into the ICU. Full-on multisystem organ failure. His liver and kidneys were shuttering. He was put on a ventilator due to the fact that his lungs weren't working. Respiratory failure. Everything internal to this man was collapsing. Quickly. *What in the hell's going on?* The doctors had absolutely no idea what they were dealing with. They promptly performed a blood test and...hold up.

What do we have here?

A fungal infection. Our patient tested positive for the microbe *Brevibacillus*. A particular contamination was found present in his bloodstream, stemming from *Psilocybe cubensis*. The doctors had never seen something quite like this before. Not this severe.

Mushrooms in his blood.

Growing.

Sporror is having a moment right about now, yeah? It has been lying dormant over the decades on our bookshelves, reviving itself every so often with a fresh outcropping of fun fungal fiction. We're all aware of megahits like *The Last of Us* rippling through our streaming services, along with (my personal fave) *Mexican Gothic* by Silvia Moreno-Garcia or *What Moves the Dead* by T. Kingfisher cropping up on everybody's TBR pile. But the determined literary truffle hunter knows this subgenre has been around for ages, whether it's "Grey Matter" by Stephen King or *The Woodwitch* by Stephen Gregory. Deep cuts such as "The Voice in the Night" by William Hope Hodgson or *A Scent of New-Mown Hay* by John Blackburn are personal treasures. So many. Too many. What pleasures this niche offers! So many stories, spawning their own substrata of a particularly patient but persistent horror subgenre.

Here's a new crop sprouting up as we speak...

The stories you find in your hands now are in of themselves fruiting bodies—spores of a different sort—ready to spread their own particular terrors. Consider this anthology something of a spore sac. The pod bursts the moment you open it, spreading each and every one of its distinctive microscopic particles all over you. Into you. You inhale every story. They get into your system. They take root while you ruminate. Then they take over.

That's what the best anthologies do, right? Take over? Change you from the inside out? *Dark Spores* is an infection on the reader's mind. It stands alongside collections like *Fungi*, edited by Silvia Moreno-Garcia and Orrin Grey. These anthologies, ecosystems of mushroom horror, are in communication with one another, speaking an ancient language our ears can't hear, our minds can't decipher. I'm a firm believer that sporror, unlike any other subgenre, is in conversation with itself. I'm imagining their mycelium burrowing through our bookshelves, creating an interconnected system below, where we can't see, all the various threads tethering them together and communicating in some fungal language. The only way to understand what they're saying is to let them in. Inhale every last story. Let these tales hijack your mind. Take root. They convert you into the sustenance they need to survive. Alter us from the inside out. Then, and only then, will we truly comprehend sporror.

You may be the one devouring these stories, but at the end of the day...who's truly devouring who? You? Or them?

It would take a literary practitioner of a higher caliber than myself to classify all the creeping taxonomic categories of sporror that you have in hand here, but rest assured, there are so many different flavors to imbibe in *Dark Spores*. Think of it as a garden of fungal delights. Editors Carol Gyzander and Rachel A. Brune have harvested the best of the best. Each story has its own flavor, its own aroma...but all with a specific intent: To get under your skin. Then sprout. Then spread to the next reader. And the next...

Are you willing to share this collection with someone else? Spread the word, as it were?

What is it about sporror that's so terrifying? I guess it depends on the reader, but for me, it's something akin to infection. The presence of something within ourselves slowly taking over. You are not the same after you read it. And sporror is nothing if not patient. It has all the time in the world to affect you. It's been days since I finished reading this collection, and only now am I feeling the deep-rooted effects this collection has to offer.

It won't let me go...and here I am, telling you about it. *Recommending* it.

Or should I be warning you?

Remember that man? The one who injected mushrooms into his veins? I discovered his story while doing a little digging for the novel I was working on at the time: *Ghost Eaters*. It truly was a moment of truth being stranger than fiction. He was eventually released from the hospital. The doctors prescribed him a strong antibiotic in order to eradicate the fungal infection filtering through his bloodstream. He went home, "cured" of his contamination.

The news story essentially ends there, but if I'm being frank, that's where the horror truly begins for me. This man now has to live with the persistent whisper of something foreign to his own body still lingering in the furthest reaches of his bloodstream, latent and patient. A spore. A seed. An invader. How long before the mushrooms grow back?

It is only a matter of time, isn't it?

Just imagine all those sleepless nights, left awake with the notion that there is this cancerous organism simply biding its time, waiting for the day where it finally grows back.

Sprouts.

That's the true terror of *Dark Spores*—for me, at least. The knowledge of its inevitability. No antibiotic can rid yourself completely of that feeling, that slow, all-encompassing dread that it's still there in your bloodstream, in your mind, on your bookshelf, dormant but never dead, waiting. Biding its time for the next life cycle to begin.

The collection in your hand is a fruiting body. I want to warn you to tread carefully—open slowly—for fear that it might burst and spread, but I'm pretty sure it's too late by now.

You're infected already.

ABOUT THE AUTHOR

Clay McLeod Chapman writes books, comic books, YA/middle-grade books, as well as for film and television. His upcoming novel, *Wake Up and Open Your Eyes*, hits shelves on January 7, 2025. You can find him at www.claymcleodchapman.com.

Swamp Fever
Jamie Lackey

EVERYBODY KNOWS that you have to cover your mouth and nose whenever you go down the valley or you'll get swamp fever. A bandana's usually good enough as long as you don't do anything too strenuous. Alls we ever do is go down fishing, or maybe frog hunting, or sometimes, I'll take my grandma's old canoe out and gather the elderberries that grow out along the creek toward the beaver dams.

I heard that one of the neighbor boys fell into the water once, and his bandana was gone when he came up, spluttering. His own mother pushed him back under and held him down. There's no treatment, and swamp fever is too dangerous to let run its course.

And once it's run its course, it's too late to do much about it.

My whole family, we're always real careful, not because we're scared of dying, but cause none of us want to be like my grandpa.

When he was young, my grandpa wanted to join the army, to fly planes and come back a hero. Instead, he had to stay home and tend the farm. He got so mad about not getting to do what he wanted that he walked barefaced right down to the swamp, breathing the unfiltered air right down deep into his lungs, and stayed out there all night. Course, he didn't tell anybody about that. He's always kept his secrets close to his chest.

Now, frogs and herons and fish and even cats and dogs can breathe the swamp air just fine. But when people do. Well. That's a whole other thing.

The spores hanging in that muggy air don't catch in other creature's lungs. Don't spread their mycelial fingers through their nervous systems and change them, taking everything that was warm and human about them and rotting it from the inside out.

Course, I don't think my grandpa had much warmth to him even before he decided being human wasn't worth it if he had to stay home and couldn't follow his dreams.

He got my grandma in the family way before she knew what he'd done, and then she was stuck with him. And since she didn't want to be stuck with him alone, they had a slew of kids.

I asked my grandma once about her dreams, about what she wanted before she got married and settled down on the farm. We were in her kitchen, making no-bake cookies from an old Better Homes and Gardens cookbook, and the room smelled like melting butter and cocoa. "I'm happy with how things are," she said, not even glancing toward the dark living room where my grandpa was sitting. "I love you kids, and maybe I should have made different choices, but I can't be sorry." She handed me the wooden spoon. "Now stir this."

I've seen old pictures from before the change was obvious. When he still had skin instead of the gray chitin that covers his body now. When he still moved around instead of lurking in his easy chair, when he saw with his eyes instead of sensing temperature and chemical changes in the air around him.

But I wasn't alive for any of that. I've only known him as he is now.

The swamp fever gives him powers, lets him charm strangers and manipulate their minds so they can't see him as he is. I'm not sure if we're immune from being around him so much or if there's something genetic he handed down.

I used to have nightmares about waking up with gray creeping up my fingers, about my hair falling out and my eyes getting cloudy. Still do, sometimes. But it hasn't happened to my dad or my aunts or uncles, so I don't really think it's likely.

I can't ever tell if he wants any of us to follow in his footsteps or not. With the swamp fever, not with the farm. It's pretty obvious how much he hates the farm. Won't let anybody take care of it the way we should. He sold off the cattle years ago, tells us to plow less and less of it every year, lets the barns fall into rickety, dangerous disrepair, and runs the machinery without maintenance till everything falls apart.

And down in the valley, the swamp spreads. More and more beaver dams pop up, keeping the water still and fetid. Sometimes, I think I can just about catch a sweet, earthy scent, even through my bandana. I worry about the breeze carrying spores to our front porch. I've taken to sleeping all wrapped up in my covers like a cocoon, wearing my bandana most times I'm not eating.

I'd avoid the swamp altogether if I could, but we need the fish and the frogs and the elderberries. None of us can get a good job, since Grandpa told everyone around that we were lazy and useless and they believed him, and moving away would take money that none of us have.

Of course, he tells us that we're lazy and useless to our faces, too. And fat and stupid and all kinds of things that aren't true, but sometimes feel true anyway just because we've all heard it so often and because he says it with such authority.

My grandma tried leaving once, but she didn't have any money either, and I think she was more susceptible to his powers than the rest of us. She started fading away after that, bit by bit.

I bet it'd be easier, not caring about anyone but myself, basking in the admiration of strangers and crushing my family with chains of obligation and need.

I'm sure we've all thought about it. About walking down to the swamp and giving up on being people. After all, not a one of us is able to go after our dreams. We're all just trapped here. He won't let us go, even though he says he never wanted us, and he'll probably outlive us all.

If I walked out into the swamp, maybe I could beat him at his own game. Maybe I could distract him while everyone else clears out his bank account and gets away.

But that probably isn't what I'd do. Because I wouldn't be me anymore. I'd just be another him.

So we put on our masks and put up hay and make elderberry wine. We bake cookies and catch fireflies and tell each other that he's wrong. We have each other, even if we don't have much else. And we all know that any sacrifice is worth it, as long as we don't end up like him.

ABOUT THE AUTHOR

Jamie Lackey lives in Pittsburgh with her husband and their cats. She has had over 200 short stories published in places like *Beneath Ceaseless Skies*, *Apex Magazine*, and *Escape Pod*, and she has a novella and two short story collections available from Air and Nothingness Press. She has also self-published a novel, two novellas, a novelette, and three short story collections. In addition to writing, she spends her time reading, playing tabletop RPGs, and hiking.

The Epigeous Dead
James Chambers

THE CORPSE-THINGS FRUITED from the damp earth on a Tuesday morning. A dozen sprouted in a ring around the graves in the oldest, most tree-lined part of the cemetery.

Two days of thunderstorms and drenching rains—then they rose, organic effigies swaying in the wind, arms outstretched to the sky, heads back, mouths wide as if in glorious, silent song. Pale crimson pulp replaced rotted flesh, molded to dry skeletons. Tattered Sunday-best outfits fluttered from twisted limbs and torsos. Bone gleamed through bare spots in their makeshift skin. The rising sun painted the figures gold as their bulbous heads tilted under the burden of their resurrection. Sunken black pits, once home to eyes, gazed out through clouds of flies.

I slumped behind the wheel of my car, so shocked by the sight I felt only a pang of frustration at the maintenance crew's pickup truck blocking my exit from the section that held Beatrice's plot. Not that anyone at work cared if I showed up late—or at all. After the past six months, no one nagged me anymore about missing reports and unreturned phone calls. I could sit in my office all day, and no one would knock at the door, so why not sit and watch the laborers back their truck up along a narrow row between grave markers, its reverse signal shrilling crudely. I flicked off my car radio and rolled down my window while I waited.

A strange, musty perfume drifted into my car. It reminded me of Beatrice's favorite scent, trapped forever under a crystal rose topper in a half-full glass bottle on her dresser, furred with dust. A voice called my name—or, at least, it sounded like my name, a phonetic doppelganger that flickered in my brain, and no one around to have spoken it other than the work crew.

I nudged my car onto the pavement's edge, then got out to lean against the hood. The cemetery peace soothed my nerves, raw and rattled from sleeplessness. I'd come to rely on it as much as my morning coffee to get through the day. The scent of recent storms still lingered in the air despite the cloudless sky. All around me, granite and marble touted the names of those laid to rest, but in this historic part of the cemetery, time and weather had stripped clean most of the details the way time steals good memories.

When the pickup truck cleared, I could've gotten back in my car, gone back about my day, gone to work, but the gnarled figures captivated me. They looked ready to spring to life. The sound of my name brushed my senses again, faint and teasing, and I realized it wasn't the figures holding my interest but the sound that seemed to emanate from them. An airy susurrus swirled over their heads like the flutter of moth-wings, growing louder, more distinct as the trio of sullen laborers put on brave faces and approached the risen. They carried shovels and picks and dragged green landscaping barrels, ready to destroy, remove, and discard.

The lead man—bald and mustached—lifted his shovel and prodded what resembled a middle-aged woman in a disintegrating navy blue dress and pearl necklace. She bobbed, her head tottering almost comically, then quivered.

I didn't understand why the men seemed so unperturbed by the figures. Maybe they'd seen others like them. Maybe they thought kids had erected them as pranks. Maybe they were part of a new, gruesome style of memorial. Or maybe the men just didn't care beyond the task of clearing them out.

The bald man poked the woman-thing again. The flutter-whisper gathered in growing vibration. I glanced around for a machine creating the palpable thrum rising from the ground through the soles of my feet, up my spine, and needling into my brain, but no vehicles other than my Infiniti and the pickup truck—neither running—were in sight. As the hum grew, the other two laborers cringed and covered their ears. I clamped my hands over my own, but it did nothing against the intensifying shrillness that seemed to spring from within my skull. The aural illusion of my name persisted, rippling out of white noise like a sonic sprout budding from cacophonous soil.

Again, the bald worker poked the woman-thing, trying to topple her, digging the shovel tip in a couple of inches deep—and in reaction the sound erupted into a soul-chilling scream, a crushing banshee wail of total despair and inescapable fate that gouged into my awareness.

Then the woman-thing exploded.

She burst like a puffball mushroom, dousing the laborer in a mist of vaguely pink dust. Reeling from the eruption, he tripped and fell flat on his back, then clawed at his throat, choking, his face coated with magenta powder, red puffs of breath wheezing from his mouth.

The other workmen stood frozen in fear until one snatched a face mask from a toolbox in the bed of the pickup. Tugging it hastily over his mouth and nose, he dashed in and dragged the gasping man away from the cloud, which, after a few seconds, settled thickly onto neighboring graves. Of the woman-thing, only chunky, fibrous remnants of her feet remained, fragmented on the loose earth.

The eleven others quivered and hummed. In their phantom sound, I listened to my name, its syllables spoken with the soft sweetness of familiarity disrupted by the harried voices of the workers yelling at me to get in my car and go, that they were closing the cemetery, even as they rushed their fallen friend to the pickup. They didn't care enough to look back, though, as they sped away toward the mausoleum on the east side of the grounds. The morning breeze swept my face with a touch of the day's oncoming warmth. The sun surmounted the tree line. The corpse-things' shadows spider-legged across the grass and grave markers—and somehow, from somewhere, came the sound of my name. I closed my eyes and held my breath and heard it again, not with my ears, though, no, but as if the syllables resonated within my skull. Lips tight, vertigo creeping upon me from lack of oxygen, I sifted the sound cloud, swimming blind through a lake of radio static, searching for a clear signal.

"You hear them," a man said.

His coarse throaty voice snapped me out of my reflection. I opened my eyes and resumed breathing.

"What they telling you, man?" he said.

Maybe six feet tall with a wiry build, rich, brown skin, and short, graying hair, the man tilted his head and squinted as he looked me up and down. His eyes showed so little white, his sockets resembled those of the corpse-things. A threadbare, gray, three-piece suit draped his bony frame, suggesting weight lost since its tailoring. A red tie like a streak of blood hung from his neck. He held a faded gym bag in one hand.

"Who're you?" I said.

"Name's Roman. C'mon, man, what do they say to you? Tell me."

He stepped forward, his stance threatening. Maybe he spied the bags under my eyes and sized me up for easy intimidation, but I had nothing to lose, no one to care about or care about me.

"What's it to you? Fuck off. Mind your own business," I said.

I walked onto the lawn, among the graves, toward the circle of corpse-things. Roman hurried after me, his footsteps padding grass.

"Whoa, hey, sorry, man, don't be like that, just chill a minute, all right? You don't want to go messing with those things," he said. "Just tell me, do they know your name?"

I stopped mid-stride. This close to the corpse-things, the air crackled with their presence. Not turning around, I said, "What if they do?"

"Oh, yeah, they do all right. I see it now." Roman sidestepped around me beyond arm's reach. He waggled his finger at his temple. "It bops around inside your skull, right? You don't hear it, but you *hear* it. You're close to their world. Someone on their side wants to touch you."

"Whose world?" I said. "You know what these things are? One of them blew up in a guy's face, doused him in pink powder."

"Yeah, that guy's fucked. He got a full dose. Those are spores," said Roman.

"What, like plants?"

"Nah. Fungi. In the right conditions, they grow fast, spring up overnight then wait to cast their seeds into the world. I tried to get out here last night before anyone messed with them, but the energy was wrong, very foul, the connection unstable. If I'd come, they might've sucked me over to their side. Had to wait for the daylight. Didn't think anyone else would get out here so damn early."

"What the hell are you talking about?" I gestured at the corpse-things. "Those things are alive?"

"Hell, no, they're not alive, not the bodies, anyway. Wouldn't be any good to me if they were. But the fungus, yeah, that's a living thing, and I spent a lot of rough years cultivating it just right. Why're you here so damn early, man? Don't you have better places to be?"

A shudder trembled through me. Without meaning to, I glanced toward the quarter of the cemetery where Beatrice lay only a few months interred.

"Oh, I see, you're grieving, wondering if you're really still living or if maybe you died right along with whoever you lost—a child, a wife? Someone unbearable to part with. You're still hoping it's a nightmare you might wake up from even if you wake up dead. You're not dead, though. You're as alive as me and every other poor sucker on God's green earth, although you most certainly walk in the valley of the shadow of death."

Roman's hard stare softened as he released a long breath.

"Listen, none of this is meant for you. Best thing for you to do is go home and enjoy the days you got left, know what I mean? That guy who got a face full of spores is one of the first, but there'll be others.

Maybe someone'll figure out how to stop it. Maybe not. Won't be my problem. I'll have what I want long before then."

"Stop what? You're not making sense," I said, then the pseudo-sound recaptured my attention. A voice in the circle called my name and obliterated the world outside my head. It compelled me to move. I shoved past Roman, closer to the broken circle. Roman hustled after me, urging me back, ordering me to keep out. His words meant nothing now that I recognized who was calling to me: *Beatrice.*

Not her voice, no, but its cadence and weight. A telepathic intrusion into the nerve centers of my brain. A conjuring of sound without its physical presence. As I neared the ring, the pulpy details of the corpse-things obtained clarity. No one could ever mistake them for living people, but they possessed an energy I didn't understand. Their mouths opened on throats like tunnels that seemed to drill through their core, straight into the earth, far underground, tapping into the deep, hidden places down there, into the Underworld—where something stirred.

Roman tackled me before I breached the ring's perimeter. I crashed, my head missing the edge of a granite gravestone by inches. The fall broke me out of the spell that had overcome me, leaving me disoriented as Roman rolled me onto my back.

"You don't belong here! You hear me? This is mine! *I* dug the grave-yard soil. *I* planted the spores in the shriveled voids where hearts once beat. *I* made the blood sacrifices. *I* cried out to the dead—and they will answer *me*! Not you. Do you understand?"

Finding unexpected strength in my anguish and confusion, I shoved Roman off me then clambered to my knees and stared into the circle. Grass and soil pulsed. Earthen clods broke then rolled upward and aside to expose tendrils that became fingertips that grew to wrists then arms and, in minutes—with the surreal progression of time-lapse photography—half a dozen more corpse-things fruited from graves inside and outside the circle of the first risen. Their jaws sagged on pulpy joints. From their gaping mouths flowed sub-aural screams that ran through me like acid, leaving me with hopeless tears streaking my face.

Roman, having retrieved his gym bag, approached. I jumped to my feet and backed away, ready for another attack, but he shook his head.

"Nah, man, I ain't going to fight you no more. You're part of it whether I like it or not. But you got to listen to me, understand? I can't let you screw this up." Desperation strained Roman's voice. His lower lip trembled. "You got no idea what I did to get spores of *Auricularia auricula mortem* and *Calvatia gigantea corpus*, the rituals, spells, and sacrifices it took to bind them, how many years I've given to this, the goddamn blood on my hands, so, no, you ain't taking this from me. You stay, you do what I say. Otherwise, get the hell out of here right now."

Beyond Roman, my Infiniti looked so far away, ephemeral and ghostly, my body ached at the thought of walking the distance between. The un-sound of my name still reverberated in my head, a perfect mimic of how Beatrice used to say it.

"I don't think I could leave now if I wanted to," I said.

"They got their hook set deep in you," said Roman. "You breathed in some."

"What does that mean? What's happening to me? You some kind of magician?"

"Some kind, yeah." Roman opened his gym bag, pulled out a small folding shovel, a long-bladed hunting knife, a human skull, and a three-foot section of spine with the bottom few vertebrae sharpened to a point.

"What the hell is that?" I said.

He tossed the bag aside and entered the circle. "C'mon, I'll show you."

The whine of sirens haunted us. Over my shoulder, lights flashed by the mausoleum. Emergency vehicles and police cars traveled the cemetery pathways. I heard and saw it all through a curtain of static. Outside, everything occurred in fast forward. One second, a police cruiser appeared in the distance, the next it sat parked by my car. If Roman noticed the activity beyond the veil, he ignored it.

At the center of the circle, he knelt and stabbed his knife into the earth of one of the old graves. Time had robbed the stone of its identity. In a database somewhere, maybe, the name of the person interred there remained on record. In that moment, though, only Roman knew whose remains he disturbed, and from the savage way he stabbed the ground, I guessed he held strong feelings about them. He plunged in the knife, carving the first line of a three-foot square of topsoil and grass.

"Who'd you lose?" he said.

"My wife," I told him. "Cancer. She was fine one day. Woke up in pain the next. A few months later, I held her hand as she died."

"How long ago?"

"Six months."

"And every day since has felt like another six months, right? That's her calling you. She's the one down there who knows your name," he said. "It takes time for the dead to forget. They still want to taste life when they're freshly deceased. If they latch onto your presence, like, say, you visit their grave every morning, they can touch you, but you'd never know it. You'd just be all fucked up—can't sleep, can't eat, can't find purpose anymore, can't barely get through a day, because they're sucking that taste out of you, hanging on to what they lost, and it only fades when they let go. You ever lose someone you love and feel at peace? That's 'cause they didn't fight it. They let go fast. Sonsofbitches who go willingly like that, you want contact with them, you got to dig." Roman stabbed the soil with rising fervor. "And dig." Stab, slice, inches added to the square. "And dig." Earth grating steel blade. "And *dig*."

The square completed, Roman shoved the knife flat under an edge and levered it up. He slid the shovel beneath then discarded the knife. Working the shovel head around, he pried loose the slab of sod then flipped it over, revealing the rich, black soil beneath it, shot through with webs of wriggling, lacy white fibers. From outside the circle, voices shouted warnings I barely heard through the static still buzzing my name like a drum beat.

"And if you want to talk to the really old ones, the ones who died and moved on a long, long time ago, the ones who selfishly took all their damn secrets to the grave and stole with them everything they ever promised to leave behind for you, well, then, digging just ain't enough. You got to plant, you got to reap, you got to force them to listen—and make them answer." Roman lifted the spine stake with both hands. Golden wires and black twine held it together. Carvings of symbols and words covered the vertebrae. With a grunt, he drove it deep into the soil. "You got to make yourself a direct line."

The sharpened bone plunged into the earth several vertebrae deep and penetrated the fibrous mesh. The risen corpse-things quivered and screamed. The ropy, white threads—the mycelium of the fungus that had forced them to the surface—vibrated. Roman set the skull atop the spine. Its jaw cracked wide, and it shrieked. The sound crashed through me. I clung to the buzzing echoes of Beatrice saying my name. Roman sat on his haunches, raised his hands, then cut gestures in the air while his fingers formed strange configurations. Did he not hear the skull scream? Or was he so accustomed to the sound, it didn't disturb him?

When he finished his gesticulations, he jammed the web between the thumb and index finger of his left hand into his mouth and bit through it, drawing blood, sucking it in, and then spit a gory gob onto the skull's forehead. The foamy red liquid dribbled down the face, dripped between the teeth, into a phantom throat, onto the mycelium and soil.

"You got to reach deep and pull them to the surface," he said.

In moments, fungus sprouted and roped up the vertebrae, entwining and embracing it, growing into a pulpy, empty-eyed sheath around the skull. It grew ear-like appendages. Roman leaned in close and whispered something into one of them. A question? A request? A curse? I couldn't hear what he said except for two words, spoken with venom: "*You promised.*" I could barely hear the cries of the police and workmen kept outside the circle by the aural emanations of the dead.

Roman rocked back and waited. Beatrice called my name.

Could I really talk to her? Tell her all the things gone through my head since she died, all the interminable seconds, minutes, and hours without her? How could she hear me? I spoke her name over the static. No reply. I said it louder, shouted it, screamed it. Nothing. Not even Roman seemed to hear me, his gaze steady on the quivering, fungus-padded skull.

Its jaw shifted, and with a light in his eyes, Roman leaned forward to listen. A pink puff of spores blasted from between the skull's teeth. It covered Roman's face, coated his open eyes, filled his nostrils, mouth, and ears. He stiffened, muttering "Yeah, oh, yeah, that's it, I knew it, I knew it, oh, thank you, thank you so much," then he fell to his side, rigid, staring at nothing.

The skull screamed again. Ripples of motion popped all around me. Corpse-things fruited from every grave. The police and laborers shouted as the pulpy masses ejected themselves from the earth under their feet. Gunshots cracked. Corpse-things burst. Dusty, pink clouds filled the air. Those who inhaled them fell, choking.

Paralyzed by uncertainty, I watched the circle spread itself wider through the cemetery. The exposed mycelium at my feet throbbed with the nacreous light of decomposition, a peephole into a vast, growing network that connected the dead and linked our world to theirs, a network Roman had cultivated, planted, and reaped—then abandoned when it had served his purpose.

Far across the manicured lawn, beyond dying, graveside floral bouquets, stone markers, and winding roadways, I looked to Beatrice's grave, where the earth churned, and dull, faintly red fingertips emerged, prelude to a head, to shoulders, a torso, a body I knew better than my own and had held tighter and tighter in our final days together as if I could cling hard enough to keep it in this world forever. My name echoed through my head.

"Beatrice," I replied.

I left the skull, left Roman and the innermost span of the circle, and began the long walk through whatever strange world Roman had summoned as the top of Beatrice's head breached the soil in an obscene mockery of birth, or rebirth, and she rose to meet me, her new, fungal ears eager for my whispered words, her newly fruited lips waiting to answer me with a dusty kiss.

ABOUT THE AUTHOR

James Chambers is the Bram Stoker Award® and Scribe Award-winning editor and author of *A Bright and Beautiful Eternal World, On the Night Border, On the Hierophant Road,* the original graphic novel, *Kolchak the Night Stalker: The Forgotten Lore of Edgar Allan Poe,* and editor of *Under Twin Suns: Alternate Histories of the Yellow Sign, A New York State of Fright,* and *Where the Silent Ones Watch.* His website is www.jameschambersonline.com.

Appetizers
A Quincy Harker, Demon Hunter Short Story
John G. Hartness

DINNER WENT WELL, right up until the waiter tried to kill my uncle during the soup course. Which I guess means it didn't go well very long at all. But that's how it goes when you're a demon hunter having dinner with the most famous vampire in history, I guess.

My name is Jonathan Quincy Abraham Holmwood Harker, and I'm the son of Jonathan Harker and Mina Murray. You might have heard of my parents, from a little book written at the end of the nineteenth century by Bram Stoker. Basically, my dad did some work for a mysterious European count who turned out to have some odd dietary restrictions, and that led to him and my mom both being nibbled on by vampires. When that happens, apparently your DNA gets jacked up, and you end up with super-powered part vampire babies. Like me.

Their DNA wasn't tweaked enough to extend their lifespan, but it sure did some odd things to mine, since I'm alive and kicking a century and change after my birth. Nowadays, I live in North Carolina with my friends, my fiancée, my cat, and my "uncle," for lack of a better word. That uncle goes by Lucas Card nowadays, but when my father worked for him, he was better known as Count Vlad Dracula.

Yeah, he didn't really die like Stoker wrote in his book. And when it became obvious that I was not like other children, Luke took an interest in my life. He followed me around for a little while, and eventually became almost a second father to me. Except instead of giving him ties for Father's Day, I give him bags of O-Negative.

On this particular night, we were out together for a nice dinner, celebrating the end of a long and brutal case that spanned multiple states and left a ton of corpses littered across the Eastern U.S. Luke had heard about a new Romanian restaurant opening up in Charlotte, and I wanted to try it out. Luke agreed to come along, mostly to be judgmental about all the historical things they got wrong, but he did want to try their *ciorba de persioare*, a meatball soup I'd seen a few places but never tried. Luke doesn't eat much, subsisting primarily on a liquid diet, but he can manage a few meatballs now and then.

The place was empty when we arrived, and the little old lady at the hostess stand jerked awake when the bell over the door jingled. We had our pick of tables, so I chose one in the middle of the room so both Luke and I would be able to see the door. I thought briefly about someone coming in from the kitchen, but decided that since most of the people that want to murder me wanted to do it in a big, flashy way, they weren't gonna sneak in through the kitchen and knife me in the back. They were more the "stand in the street with a bazooka" kind of murderers.

We settled in and ordered a bottle of nice Shiraz from the waiter, a middle-aged guy with Eastern European features, a little pot belly, and slicked-back black hair in a widow's peak. As he walked away, I leaned over the table and said to Luke, "That guy's stealing your look, isn't he? All he needs is a cloak with red velvet lining to be you."

Luke gave me a look loaded to the eyebrows with disdain. "I have never, in my life or death, worn a cloak with a red velvet lining. I told that to Lugosi, and I have told you multiple times."

"Yeah, but it's still funny," I replied. Pushing Luke's buttons was my favorite pastime, and one I excelled at. A hundred years hanging out with someone will insure you know where their weak spots are.

"What can I get for you gentlemen this evening?" the waiter asked as he materialized out of thin air near my elbow. He was good, this chunky innocuous-looking server. He just popped up whenever he was needed, refilling water and taking orders. This place was definitely going up in my estimation.

"We will both have the *ciorba de persioare*," Luke said. "Feel free to spice it as authentically as possible. I spent many years in Romania, and I miss it."

"Anything else?" the waiter asked.

"Not right now," I said. "We wanted to try the place specifically for the ciorba."

He nodded and vanished, and Luke and I returned to our conversation. The restaurant remained deserted, and I started to wonder if we were in either a mob hangout that everyone else was scared to step into, or some place with such bad advertising that literally no one but Luke knew it existed.

Our soup came, and it was delicious. I hadn't spent any significant time in that chunk of Europe, and my father certainly never went back after his adventures there, so ciorba was not something I'd known before, but it was excellent. It was thick with vegetables and massive meatballs, and was heavily seasoned with pepper and garlic.

I noticed Luke's nose twitching, and smiled a tiny bit. "Too much garlic?" I asked.

"No," he replied. "Although I am not fond of garlic, this is different. Something..." his voice trailed off and he froze in his seat. This wasn't a metaphorical freezing, like someone had surprised him. No, he locked down completely, moving nothing but his eyes, and I saw something there that I'd never seen before—panic. Luke, Count friggin' Dracula, was *afraid*.

I sprang to my feet, noticing for the first time that my muscles were tight, like I was in the throes of a full-body cramp. I stumbled, then fell back onto my butt, sending my chair across the floor with a clatter. I felt paralysis creep along my limbs, a sensation I'd known before and very much did *not* enjoy. I'd been turned to stone by a medusa a couple years back, and it was one of the least pleasant experiences of my exceedingly long life. This felt a little like that, except I could move if I concentrated on doing so. But my arms and legs were heavy, like I had thick resistance bands strapped to them, and I moved at maybe quarter speed at best.

Luke was completely frozen, however, unable to even speak. I could only think how terrifying that would be, and how fatal if he had to breathe to survive. I guess sometimes hanging out with dead people has its advantages. I mean, it's not like he could get any deader. At least, I hoped not.

"Is the soup to your liking, gentlemen?" The waiter appeared at the table, silent as ever. His mild expression had been replaced by a nasty, leering grin, and the little old lady hostess stood beside him with a huge wooden stake and a wicked smile of her own.

Fuck. I thought. We'd been set up. This whole restaurant, their shitty marketing, the abandoned dining room, the authentic Romanian soup...it was all a lure to get us here so they could drug and murder us. Or maybe just me. Or maybe just Luke. When you've been around as long as either of us have, and dropped as many bodies as we have, it's a coin toss as to which one of us any given rando wants to kill.

"Who are you?" I asked, using another chair to drag myself almost upright. My words were slurred, but the waiter got the point. I sat on the chair, my arms and legs tingling like they'd been asleep for hours. I could move, but only very slowly and with great concentration. I needed to keep this guy talking until I could figure something out.

"I'm Bill. Bill Feero," he replied. "I don't expect that name to mean anything to either of you. This is my nonna, Marina. I don't expect her name to ring any bells, either. After all, she was just a babe in arms when you slaughtered her parents, my great-great-grandparents, and left her to freeze in her crib that night outside of Bran."

I'd never been to Bran. I was only pretty sure, because I'd lost a few years in the middle of the twentieth hartncury to a berserker rage that left a swath of Nazi corpses across Europe a mile wide. But if Nonna Marina was as old as she looked, she was more than a babe in a cradle in the forties. That made this definitely Luke's old sins coming back to haunt us. And he had several centuries' more sins to haunt than I did. I caught his eye, and he blinked once, acknowledging that he knew what the man was talking about.

"Wasn't me," I replied, employing the time-honored "Shaggy defense."

Feero's glare drilled into me. "I don't care about you. You're just collateral damage. Some poor asshole who went to dinner with the monster that murdered my great-great-grandparents. I almost regret that you're going to die, too."

Nonna Marina tugged on his sleeve and whispered something in his ear, and he smiled. "Never mind. Nonna just reminded me that if the mushrooms worked on you, then you're a monster, too. So, you can die just like this murdering piece of crap!" He pulled a stake out of his belt and raised it over his head for emphasis.

Just for the record, this never looks as impressive as people expect it to. Usually, it leaves people looking like a Statue of Liberty impersonator rather than a badass, and this was no exception. It didn't help his cause that he wore a pressed white shirt and a waiter's apron, not exactly a costume designed to strike fear into the hearts of men. In fact, he kinda made me think of The Penguin from *Batman*, except way taller than Danny DeVito.

"Wait!" I said. "What was that about mushrooms?" The whole time I was thinking to myself *this is never gonna work. There's no way you get this guy to monologue enough for you to burn whatever is wrong with you out of your system. That only happens in movies.*

Except this time. Bill the Murdering Waiter tucked his stake into a pocket of his apron and leaned over to grin at me. "*Mycetinis scorodonius*," he said.

"Bless you," I replied. I speak a little Latin, but all I got outta that was that it was probably some kind of mushroom, and I already knew that.

"They call it Vampire's Bane," Waiter Bill continued. "Most people think it's just because it smells like garlic, and vampires hate garlic, but that's not all. There are properties in the scorodonius that react with certain antibodies in human blood, and they react most strongly with blended blood, blood that didn't come from a single source."

That's not something that a human would be likely to discover, since humans make their own blood. Except in cases of transfusions, humans will always have single-source blood. Vampires, however, get their blood from multiple donors or victims and it's processed through their magical digestive system, so their blood is a blend of multiple types. No idea why it was working on me, since I didn't drink blood on the regular. But the point was to keep him talking, not poke holes in his theory. "How the hell did you ever figure that out?" I asked, noticing that my words were clearer now, less slurred.

My muscles were reacting better, and I could feel my strength returning. I focused my will internally, and whispered, "*Mundare*," sending a cleansing spell running through my body. My veins felt like I was flushing them with rubbing alcohol, but I could tell the spell was working. If I could keep this asshole talking for a few more seconds I might survive.

"I'm a chemist, you moron. I've spent my entire career working on these mushrooms, developing new uses for them in medicine and agriculture. Once I had the formula perfected, I poured my life savings into this restaurant for Nonna, so she could watch me avenge our family, slaughtered for no reason other than a monster's hunger. So she could be proud of me as I slay the legendary Count Dracula!" He brandished the stake again, looking even more ridiculous the second time. So apparently Luke had killed this dude's family back in his more predatory days, back when he didn't have a blood bank on speed dial. Back before there were blood banks. Or speed dial. This family knew how to hold a grudge.

"I've always been proud of you, my dear boy," Nonna Marina said, reaching up to pat him on the cheek. "Now stop babbling and kill these two. We have to dispose of the bodies and get ready for our real grand opening next weekend."

Nonna not only knew how to hold a grudge, she was *brutal*. Luke seemed to still be frozen, but as I glanced at him, I saw his pinky twitch, just a little. He was breaking free, too. Maybe Waiter Bill's recipe needed a little more in the way of Vampire's Bane in it. Or maybe he was no better a chemist than he was a criminal mastermind. Either way, it was go time.

Bill stepped forward, raising his stake over his head, and it was time to see how well my own little plan had worked. I leaned forward and jerked my feet under me, springing out of my chair. Or at least that was the plan. I still didn't have all my strength back, and the cleansing spell I'd used had apparently done a little too much cleansing on my blood, because I felt seriously light-headed. I crashed into the table and sprawled face-first across the damned thing instead of leaping over it to knock Waiter Bill down and out. It was enough to save Luke, though, because the table slid into both him and Bill, toppling them both to the floor.

I heard a shriek and rolled to my right just in time to see a wooden stake slam into the table where my torso had been half a second earlier. Nonna Marina had full-on crazy eyes now, and swiped at me with her sharpened stick like she was the Fifth Musketeer or something.

"I really don't want to punch an old lady," I muttered, hopping back to avoid another wild slash at my midsection. Nonna Marina snarled at me and lunged, the tip of her stake scraping across my ribs.

"But I will." And I did. I punched the great-grandma right between the eyes, dropping her to the floor like a sack of demented, revenge-starved potatoes.

"Nonna!" Waiter Bill cried from the floor. He abandoned any thoughts of killing Luke then, turning his full attention to me. Which is what he should have done from the start, since I was the one who could move enough to stand and speak, and was thus the bigger threat. Admittedly, most chemists aren't taught combat threat assessment, so I couldn't fault him for his mistake. But I could damn sure take advantage of it.

Bill charged me, and in a normal fight, where I had my full faculties, I would have ended him in three seconds. A quick side-step, a chop to the back of the neck, a severed spinal cord, and then home for takeout. But with my blood still all jacked up from less-than-magic shrooms and my legit magical cure for mushroom poisoning, I was at way less than my best. I managed the sidestep, but missed on my shot at his neck, barely managing to slap-shove him further away as he rumbled past.

He picked up a huge bread knife from a nearby table and spun around, coming at me again. I called up power and shouted *"Repello!"* Bill flew back eight feet and landed ass-first on a round four-top laden with flowers, Chianti, and silverware. It all crashed to the floor around him, and I looked over at Luke, who was dragging himself across the floor. *Okay, he's burning this shit out of his system pretty quickly, too. A few more seconds and we should be in the clear, as long as Nonna doesn't pop up with a flamethrower or some such bullshit.*

Bill scrambled to his feet, just in time to see me standing upright, glowing purple magic wreathing my hands and a snarl on my face. "You know the worst part about this?" I asked the now-frozen waiter-cum-murderer.

"What?"

"I liked the soup. Now it's ruined for me. Because you had to get bent out of shape over something that happened a century ago."

"He ruined my Nonna's life! He murdered her parents! She lived in an orphanage! It was awful!"

"I'm sure it was. But that was a long time ago. He's changed. He doesn't go around murdering people anymore. He's one of the good guys now."

Waiter Bill pointed past my shoulder. "That's what you call a good guy?"

I turned, and let out a sigh when I saw Luke's face buried in the side of Nonna Marina's neck. He was draining her dry, probably to replenish the blood polluted by the mushrooms. Vampires gonna vampire, I guess. "Well, shit," I said. "Okay, he's *usually* one of the good guys."

I turned back to Waiter Bill, but he wasn't at the crushed table anymore. He was almost right on top of me, his stake pointed right at my heart. "Bad move, Bill," I said. "I never said *I* was one of the good guys." I raised my fists, pointed them directly at Waiter Bill, and blasted him with everything I had. A wave of purple energy streaked forward from my outstretched hands and slammed into his chest, blowing a hole clean through the man, vaporizing skin, muscle, bone, and the wall twenty feet behind him. Before his corpse collapsed to the floor, I could see the kitchen through the hole in his torso. Then he fell in a *splat* of ick and viscera.

I looked at Luke, who was done with his meal of Nonna Tartar and wiping the blood from his chin, and said, "Next time, we're getting takeout."

ABOUT THE AUTHOR

John G. Hartness is the founder and publisher of Falstaff Books and the author of multiple series, including *Quincy Harker, Demon Hunter, Bubba the Monster Hunter,* and *The Black Knight Chronicles.* He lives in North Carolina with his wife and two judgmental cats.

Flesh, Fungi & Farewell
Gwendolyn Kiste

Iᴛ's long after midnight on the streets of the city when a man guarding a red door invites me inside the club.

"They're waiting for you," he says and motions me toward the darkness yawning at the end of the hall.

I peer into the shadows, wondering why it feels suddenly like the shadows are peering back at me. "I don't even know what this place is," I tell him, but the man only shrugs.

"That doesn't matter," he says. "Not here anyway."

I do my best not to roll my eyes. It's the kind of answer that isn't an answer at all. No doubt this is part of some silly promotion for a club nobody's ever heard of. That's why I shouldn't listen to him. I shouldn't even hesitate, not for a moment. All I need to do is keep on walking down this lonely street and head back to my even lonelier apartment.

But it's been a long day, longer than most, and I could use a drink. A martini, maybe. Something dry and bitter to burn up my belly and make me forget.

"You're sure it's safe?" I ask the man, and he nods back at me.

"You'll like it," he says. "I promise."

Without another word, I head into the darkness. At the end of the hallway, I'm expecting a curtain or another door, but instead, there's a narrow stairwell that descends into the gloom for what feels like an eternity, only a few dim lightbulbs to guide my way.

My hands tremble against the railing as I glance over my shoulder. It's not too late to turn back. But that's what I always do, cowering from everything. I'm the one who never takes a chance on anything, my life preordained from the time I was sixteen. Straight A's in high school, straight A's in college, a job in an accounting firm the week after graduation. I was the girl brimming with promise. Now, it's twenty years later, and I'm starting to wonder what that promise ever got me.

At last, I reach the bottom of the stairway, but there are no eager patrons to greet me. No music and no bar either. There's just another corridor, the ground spongy beneath my feet. I kneel down and run my fingers across it. A fistful of dirt crumbles at my touch. In a city built of concrete and mortar, there should be no earth waiting like this in the shadows. My head spins, and I suddenly hear her voice echoing everywhere.

"You never believe in anything, sweetheart," she'd tell me.

I almost smile at the thought of her. I almost shed a tear, too. The one I always knew would get away. She and I met on this same street five years ago, a couple of lonely hearts wandering after midnight.

"I've never seen you here before," she said to me, as though she'd already witnessed the whole world and was bored with it.

"Well, you've seen me now," I said, everything in me desperately hoping to see her again.

That's why I was walking here tonight, pretending I could recreate the past. Pretending I could conjure her out of the darkness.

With my head down, I venture further along the corridor, the melody of faraway voices ringing in my ears. This is madness, and I know it, but a part of me is almost giddy about it. Thanks to my job at the firm, my life is an endless stream of numbers and calculations, everything about me hermetically sealed off from the world. I'm the road not taken, and she was the only risk that ever managed to cross my path. That's why I never wanted to let her go.

We moved in together far too soon, but I never minded, not when she pranced barefoot on the hardwood floors, barely touching the ground, all whimsy and wildness. She used to grow mushrooms in every closet of our apartment, only letting the light in for a little bit each day.

"What's the point?" I asked her.

She smiled at me. "What's the point of anything?"

I would stand back and watch her, marveling at the way anything she touched would blossom. Or at least anything that lived in the dark. That was the trick of it. She was best at night, the glint in her eye sparking once the sun went down.

"My little vampire," I used to say, my hand on her cheek, but even then, I knew she was something far more complicated than that.

There's a pair of long curtains in front of me now, and with the voices closer than before, I brush the fabric aside to reveal the ballroom within. It's bustling and bursting, the lights dimmed low, the bodies writhing on the dance floor. It's nothing like I expect. The guests are all wearing intricate masks, their real faces hidden beneath the revelry. And there's something else, something I have to squint in the dark to notice. Everything's made of velvet here—the walls, the suits, the gowns. It's a soft room in soft light, and when I breathe deep, the scent of forests and freedom fills my lungs. The throng of people pulses closer around me, but even in a crowded room, she's the only thing I can think about.

"Bryn," I murmur, as if that's all it takes to make her materialize in the middle of the mob. It's a fool's errand, of course. If she wanted to be with me, then she would be. But that's not how it went. It's been almost a month since she left, disappearing in the dead of night, my own personal phantom.

To be fair, I probably had it coming. I barely even glanced up at her anymore, consumed with the facts and figures of my day job. For the past year, she would linger in the doorway of our bedroom, watching me, those pale eyes never blinking.

"You can't see me," she whispered, "even when I'm standing right in front of you."

I tried to argue with her, tried to tell her how much I adored her, but we both knew she was right. I wasn't very good at being in love. I wasn't very good at much, not when it came to her. She always scared me a little, in a way I could never quite fathom. How she lived her life by the skin of her teeth. Once, after we'd been together almost a year, she took me foraging upstate, a dainty wicker basket at her side, her filthy fingers plucking fungi from the earth like she was only picking flowers.

I loomed nearby, not helping, not wanting to get my hands dirty. "How do you know which ones are poisonous?"

She tilted her head as if considering. "You learn to tell the difference," she said, a sly grin on her face. "And you learn to hope for the best too."

That night, she made us a mushroom omelet for dinner, and I nearly gagged on every bite, convinced it would be my last.

"Don't you want to see where I come from?" she asked afterward while we were lying in bed, tangled up in the dark.

"Sure," I told her, but there was a slight tremor in my voice, that lingering fear that she wasn't at all who I thought she was. That's probably why she never took me home to meet her family. *If* she even had a family. I never bothered to ask.

Now that she's gone, I wonder if that was the right thing to do. Sometimes, I wish she'd told me everything. Sometimes, I think the only reason we lasted as long as we did is because she didn't. There are secrets in this world that are meant to be kept.

But maybe I don't like secrets anymore.

All around me, from speakers I can't see, there's a distant sound like white noise, like the room is quietly singing to us. It's not music, not exactly, but it's still beautiful in its own way.

I blink once, and from among the anonymous crowd, a lithe figure drifts toward me. She's wearing a disguise like the others, the face of a fox, but she seems like someone I know. I shake my head, telling myself she's no more than a stranger. I tell myself she's not really Bryn.

I wait until she's closer before I exhale a small laugh. "I'm the only one not wearing a mask."

"You're not?" She tilts her head. "That's odd. I thought you were."

And with that, she wanders back into the crowd, moving like a ghost, like something not quite real. I track her every movement, even though I don't know why. We pass a row of waiters arrayed in velvet suits, each of them carrying a different tray of hors d'oeuvres.

Mushroom pate smeared on sesame seed crackers. Stuffed mushrooms sprinkled with parmesan and pepper. Tiny pots of gray soup that you can slurp down in an instant.

This place is far fancier than I was expecting, and I feel suddenly like the piece that doesn't fit. But this woman does her best to make it seem like a second home. We dance for hours, her hands guiding me from one side of the room to the other, the crowd parting like the Red Sea at our command. There's something beneath us in the earth, the ground uneven at every turn, but it's too dark to see what it is, and in her arms, I don't even care. In this moment, she's a singularity, the universe wrapped up in the shape of her.

The hours disintegrate around us, the crowd drifting back and forth, their gazes quietly following us until, beyond reason, I can sense it. Outside, it's almost morning. Almost time for me to return to my life, my job, the world.

"I should go," I whisper.

She only shakes her head. "You still don't understand."

Dread clots in my chest. "Understand what?" I ask.

She leans in closer, her skin smelling of earth and promise. "I told you that you couldn't see me, even when I was standing right in front of you."

Bryn. She takes a step back from me, but I won't let her go, not this time.

"Are you an illusion?" I ask, and she can't help but giggle.

"What if you're the illusion instead?"

The question hits me hard, because I don't know the answer. With the crowd murmuring a little louder now, my head goes dizzy again, and I lean against a nearby pillar to steady myself. That's when I feel it beneath my fingertips, soft and strange. The walls and the suits and the gowns aren't made of velvet at all. They're made of mold, shimmering and alive. My throat closing up, I stumble away, and the vague light shifts just enough that I can see what's been beneath our feet all night.

Mushrooms. They're everywhere, growing faster by the moment. That's the music I'm hearing. It's the room coming to life from every angle, blossoming in real time.

The throng of guests moves closer, and I hold my breath as all their masks slip off at once. They're watching me now with those same pale eyes as hers.

I should run. I should scream. After all, they're not stopping me. She's certainly not keeping me here. None of them are. They're simply standing back and waiting.

All at once, I understand it, the way this choice is up to me. It always has been. That's why Bryn stuck around for five years, patiently hoping that I would see what's always been right before my eyes.

Bryn's the last one to take off her mask, smiling at me the way she used to. "Is this what you want?" she whispers, and my knees buckle as she runs her fingers through my hair.

"Yes," I say, and that's all it takes.

My vision blurs, the room going gauzy and gray around me, as she reaches down and plucks a mushroom from the earth.

"You're finally ready to see where I come from," she says and pops the fungus into my mouth. It melts on my tongue like butter.

One after another, everyone in the room closes in around me, scooping mushrooms from the ground, forcing them between my lips, gorging me until I'm bursting at the seams with this place. Bursting with everything she is and always has been.

"How do you know which ones are poisonous?" I ask between gluttonous mouthfuls.

Bryn beams at me. "You learn to hope for the best," she says, and for the first time, that's more than enough for me. The others fall back, but she keeps feeding me, and I devour every bite of what she offers, something writhing deep within my blood and bones.

"That's a good girl," she says, and as the darkness envelops us, I pull her closer, my skin shifting, my body at last in full bloom.

ABOUT THE AUTHOR

Gwendolyn Kiste is the author of *The Rust Maidens*, *Reluctant Immortals*, *Boneset & Feathers*, *Pretty Marys All in a Row*, and *The Haunting of Velkwood*. She's a Lambda Literary Award winner as well as a three-time Bram Stoker Award® winner. Originally from Ohio, she now resides on an abandoned horse farm outside of Pittsburgh with her husband, their excitable calico cat, and not nearly enough ghosts. Find her online at gwendolynkiste.com

Dead and Forgotten in Manhattanville

Nicholas Kaufmann

THE FOLLOWING IS the rough draft of an investigative article titled "Dead and Forgotten in Manhattanville," written by Kristine Groff for The New York Times Magazine. It remains unpublished after the death of the author from a respiratory illness in 2024.

The blizzard that walloped New York City this February is already the stuff of legend. With the streets blanketed by eighteen inches of snow, followed by frigid temperatures that kept the hard, dangerous ice underneath from melting for at least a week, the city that never sleeps found itself grinding to a halt. Schools were closed. Garbage wasn't picked up. Ambulances couldn't reach those who needed them.

One New Yorker who could have used an ambulance was Adelaide Meyer. Shortly after the blizzard, she was found dead in her Manhattanville apartment, just shy of her 91st birthday. Given her age, her neighbors assumed her death to be from natural causes, but in truth, no one could be certain since her body wasn't examined by a medical professional. It wasn't even picked up by the Office of the Chief Medical Examiner, the city agency responsible for taking away the dead when there's no funeral home involved, as was the case with Meyer, who had no family to take care of such arrangements.

"I tried calling funeral homes directly to come and get her," says Dante Accardo, the superintendent of the building Meyer lived and died in, "but they won't come without the right paperwork, either from the family or the city."

It was, without question, the OCME's responsibility. At first, they couldn't get to Meyer because of the severe ice conditions on the roads. Then, once the thaw came and New York City sprang back to life, they still didn't come. Adelaide Meyer was forgotten by the city, a life of nine decades that fell through the cracks. Accardo moved her body to the apartment building's basement while he waited for the OCME to come. He's still waiting.

What does the building's landlord have to say about a dead body being stored in the basement? "It's not a landlord, it's a management company, Best Choice Residential," Accardo says. "So far, they haven't done squat about it. They have their big fancy office down in Midtown, and as long as the rent money keeps coming in, they don't care what happens up here."

Accardo's phone calls to the OCME went unanswered. When the *New York Times* called, we were told there was a sizeable backlog, but they would send someone out to pick up Meyer's body soon. How soon? They refused to say.

Manhattanville is a small neighborhood in West Harlem, located between 122nd Street and 135th Street, bookended by the Hudson River on the west and Adam Clayton Powell Jr. Boulevard on the east. The neighborhood dates back to 1806 when it was an independent village founded by wealthy Quaker merchants. Looking at the five-story apartment building at 314 West 127th Street, in the heart of Manhattanville, it would be easy to imagine it dates back just as far: a cracked and peeling concrete exterior, rusted fire escapes, and a front door that looks like it once had paint on it, many years ago. Inside, the building is filled with single-bedroom apartments, two per floor, with floorplans that would be considered spacious by the highly compressed standards of today's new constructions.

Once a free-standing building—one of the last in the city—this relic from the early days of New York is now flanked on its east side by a new co-op three times as tall, a narrow infill building usurping the alley that used to stretch alongside the length of 314. Now the two buildings, old and new, stand flush, wall to wall. New York City lots are valuable land. None stand empty forever. Luckily, the alley on the west side of 314 remains untouched, although one wonders for how much longer.

This is the building where Adelaide Meyer died.

One resident, Stewart Sanford, a 46-year-old accountant, tells me Meyer wasn't found for at least a week after her death, maybe longer. "It was the smell that tipped everyone off," he says. "When they finally went into her apartment, they found her sitting in her chair by the window. She'd been dead so long she was stuck to the upholstery. I heard that when they tried to take her out of the chair, the skin tore off the backs of her arms and stayed there."

"That's bullshit," comments Natalya Shvartsman, a 29-year-old executive assistant. Shvartsman is the one who alerted Dante Accardo to the smell coming from Meyer's apartment. "Addie was nice," she says, using her nickname for Meyer. "I used to help her out sometimes, just with carrying groceries or lifting packages that were too heavy for her. I was worried when I hadn't heard from her in days, and then when the smell came, we all kind of knew what happened."

She was present when Accardo used his master key to open the apartment door. Sanford's story about Meyer's skin peeling off her arms may have been "bullshit," but he was right about one thing. They found Meyer in her favorite chair, an upholstered wingback positioned at the window.

"She loved to sit by the window. She'd do it all day long, just sitting in the sun," says Shvartsman. One would expect that daily ritual to have changed when the new building went up next door and cut off the sunlight that used to come through Meyer's window, but Shvartsman says nothing changed. "She kept sitting there all day anyway, more out of habit than anything else. She died in that chair. When I saw her..." It takes Shvartsman a moment to gather herself. It's clear this is a memory she'd rather not relive. "At first, I thought someone had placed a lace sheet over her body, but then I saw it wasn't lace. It was mushrooms. White mushrooms with tops that looked like delicate latticework. They were growing all over her body."

"It's absolutely possible for a fungus to grow on a dead body," says Neil Stolley, lead mycologist in the Hunter College science department. "Also on a living one."

Stolley's expertise is in parasitic fungi, and his lab at Hunter is currently set up to study the effects of *Massospora cicadina*, an especially nasty example, on a group of cicadas from 2024's rare double brood emergence. Within a glass enclosure, dozens of big, winged cicadas cling to carefully positioned artificial tree branches. Some of the insects are missing the bottom half of their bodies, their absent organs replaced by a white plug of fungus. This, Stolley tells me, is how the *Massospora* reproduces. Its microscopic spores infect the cicada as it emerges from the ground, flooding its brain with psilocybin, a powerful hallucinogen produced by some fungi, while at the same time, the fungus grows its hyphae—thin, stringlike filaments—throughout the cicada's body. "These filaments are the true fungus," Stolley says. "Mushrooms are just a fungus's fruiting body, the method by which it spreads its spores when it's time to reproduce."

The *Massospora* essentially turns the cicada into a puppet from within, using those internal hyphae as marionette strings. The fungus eats through the cicada's nether regions to replace it with a plug of spores, which it then uses to infect other cicadas by shaking the spores onto them, repeating the cycle. One cicada in the enclosure has lost more than its rear end, however. It has such a big plug of spores that all that's left of its body is the head, the wings, and two of its legs, leading me to wonder if it's even truly alive.

"It's definitely more fungus than cicada now," admits Stolley. "They all are. They look like they're continuing to do regular cicada things, but it's the fungus that's controlling them. It's part of the *Massospora*'s trap to lure more cicadas and keep the cycle going. Fungi are one of the oldest organisms on land. They were around long before us, long before the dinosaurs. They're cunning and manipulative. They've had millions of years to evolve and adapt to new environments and find new ways to spread their spores."

Would that include spreading them to dead human bodies? Stolley confirms that if the conditions are just right—for instance, a dark, warm place—a fungus could indeed grow on (or inside, where the hyphae would be) a human body. In fact, fungi have even made their way into the funeral business. Mushroom burial suits are a hot new item, in which the deceased is interred in an expensive biodegradable burial shroud made from fungus spores. Unlike the *Massospora*, which has its own twisted use for the insect bodies it infects, these fungi help decompose the body, removing any toxins and safely returning it to nature, ashes to ashes, dust to dust.

In the case of Adelaide Meyer, Stolley says, "Fungi and mushrooms don't just spontaneously generate. The spores would have to come from somewhere first. If she was as homebound as it sounds, my guess is the source would be somewhere in her apartment."

Only Dante Accardo has the key to Adelaide Meyer's apartment, and he has no qualms about letting me in to look around. He's made it clear that if this article will finally get the city to do its job, he'll help however he can. Inside, I'm surprised by how warm the apartment is. It's barely thirty degrees outside, but the apartment is sweltering, thanks to the steam radiators. They're old, like everything else in the building. "Turn 'em off and you freeze, turn 'em on and you boil,"

Accardo says. It's a story many New York City residents know by heart.

The electricity has been shut off since Meyer's death, but apparently, she rarely had the lights on anyway. Accardo could tell from the meters that she hardly used any electricity at all, just a little in the evenings until she went to bed. Before the new building went up right outside her living room window, enough sunlight came in during the day that she never needed to turn on the lights. After the building went up, her habits didn't change. She sat where she always sat, only now it was in the dark. It's a sad thought, this old woman sitting alone in the gloom. Was Meyer depressed, suffering from mental illness, or just a creature of habit unwilling to change her behavior after so many years? No one knew her well enough to provide an answer.

The wingback chair by the window is visible in the light coming from the hallway outside the apartment, but it's the window itself that draws the eye. It's like something out of an art installation commenting on overdeveloped urban settings. Right outside the glass pane is the cinderblock wall of the building next door. There's not even an inch of space between them. The sunlight Meyer enjoyed sitting in for so many years has become perpetual night. If it weren't for the visible white lines of mortar between the cinderblocks, the view might as well be the infinite blackness of space.

In real estate lingo, her window is called a "lot-line window" because it exists right at the edge of the lot. It's within the rights of the owner of the adjacent property to one day erect a building that comes to the edge of their own lot, effectively blocking the window. When that happens, the responsibility falls on the management company to seal up the former window in compliance with building and fire codes, but clearly, that didn't happen. "This building needs a *ton* of repairs and renovations, but Best Choice Residential only cares about cashing checks," Accardo says.

Another tenant, Lucia Gonzalez, 51, who lives in the apartment directly across the hall, pokes her head in to yell at us that we shouldn't be in Meyer's apartment. While Accardo goes into the hallway to assure her it's all right, I use the flashlight app on my phone to inspect the wingback chair further. There's no sign of any skin that tore off Meyer's arms when they removed her body, but all over the upholstery are small, slightly fuzzy white spots with darker spots at their center, reminiscent of irises and pupils. Mold? Spores? Are they responsible for the mushrooms growing on Meyer's body, or did they come from those mushrooms? There are more white spots on the rug around the chair, and even more on the walls. Up high on one wall, near where it joins the ceiling, are dark stains signifying longtime water damage, and there sits the culprit: a cluster of mushrooms growing out of a crack in the plaster. They're white with long caps that hang low over their stems and look like delicate, lacy skirts. (Later, showing Neil Stolley photographs of the mushrooms, he would identify them as akin to the *Phallus indusiatus*, also known as the veiled lady, but they're missing the conspicuous greenish-brown bell-shaped caps at the top, where the spores would normally be kept. Without that cap, Stolley can't be sure how this fungus reproduces.)

A dizziness comes over me in Meyer's apartment, an unexpected lightheadedness akin to standing up too quickly, but Gonzalez's urgent voice from the hallway breaks the spell: "Just make sure you're not still in there when it gets dark! And keep that door locked!" She's gone before I can ask why.

When I point out the mushrooms sprouting from the wall to Accardo, he gives a one-word response that can't be printed here. He promises to call Best Choice Residential about it, but we both know what that will amount to.

Accardo claims to have moved Meyer's body down to the basement on his own. He didn't want Natalya Shvartsman, who was with him when he entered the apartment, to have to touch the body. "It was no trouble," he says. "I wrapped Addie in a blanket and carried her down. She was light as a feather."

The stairway to the basement is at the back of the first floor, not far from Meyer's apartment. Behind a hastily mounted chain that spans the width of the stairwell entrance, with a handwritten sign hanging off it that reads "Do Not Enter," an ancient and rusting flight of wrought-iron steps descends deep into the darkness below. Adelaide Meyer is still down there.

Accardo refuses to let me see her. "It would be disrespectful," he said. "I don't mind letting you poke around the apartment, but you should leave that poor old lady alone."

Natalya Shvartsman doesn't share Accardo's sentiment. She wants Adelaide Meyer's story to be told and agrees to bring me down into the basement the next evening after work. The wrought-iron steps go remarkably deep into the ground below the building, more than the depth of a single story. It's impossible to walk quietly on the stairs; each footfall clangs and echoes in the darkness, making me worry Accardo will catch us in the act. The basement itself is frigid, which has helped the body keep while it waits to be picked up. The overhead light Shvartsman turns on illuminates a shape under a blanket on the wooden floor. That strange lightheadedness comes over me again. I have to hold the wall for a moment until the dizziness passes.

As Shvartsman leaves, apologizing that she doesn't want to see her friend Addie like this, I stoop to examine the blanket. It has the same small, fuzzy white spots on it that I found in Meyer's apartment. The form underneath is meager, slight. The body of a 90-year-old woman who never left her home, never left her chair, only now trading one dark space for another. Before I can lift the blanket to confirm that Meyer's body really was covered in mushrooms like Shvartsman said, Accardo comes clamoring down the stairs. There's no excuse I can make. He's caught me dead to rights. Accardo wants me out of the basement—and the building. I follow him back up the stairs, and for the first time, I notice fuzzy white spots on the skin of his wrist.

Dead and Forgotten in Manhattanville

I may be *persona non grata* at 314 West 127th Street as far as Dante Accardo is concerned, but not Lucia Gonzalez. Adelaide Meyer's neighbor from across the hall finds me outside the building, having just been kicked out, and taking pity on me, she invites me into her apartment. It's the mirror image of Meyer's, but because it's on the west side of the building, the living room window has an unobstructed view of the alley outside. It's not much, but unlike Meyer, she still gets sunlight. I ask Gonzalez what she meant when she told us to be out of Meyer's apartment by dark and that the door should remain locked.

"Addie goes back to her apartment at night, usually late," Gonzalez says. "It's true," she insists, seeing the surprise on my face. "I'm the only one on the first floor, so I'm the only one who hears her coming up the basement stairs. I watch her through the peephole in my door. She stands in front of her apartment door, turning the knob, trying to get back inside, but she can't because it's locked. Then she goes downstairs again. The whole thing lasts about five minutes."

As far-fetched as it sounds, Gonzalez is certain it's Meyer. "The first time, I thought she was wearing some kind of lacy veil over herself, but then I realized the veil isn't separate from her, it's *part* of her. It's growing *out* of her. But I've known Addie a long time. I know it's her. I stay quiet and wait until she leaves. It's best not to bother spirits. You leave them alone, they'll leave you alone."

Why would Meyer come back every night to try to enter her apartment? Gonzalez doesn't know, but hazards a guess. "Addie was 90 years old and she lived in that apartment for most of her life. It's the only place she knows. Who knows, maybe she just wants to get back into that damned chair."

Over a pot of tea Gonzalez insists on making for us, as if she hadn't just told me a dead woman walks the halls of her apartment building, I try and fail to get any more information out of her. She's more interested in showing me pictures of her family. As the night stretches on, I feel that familiar lightheadedness come over me again, a slightly giddy feeling. Lifting my teacup to my mouth, my hand leaves a smeary trail in the air behind it. Scanning the walls and ceiling of the apartment, it doesn't take long to find fuzzy white spots on the yellowing plaster. The spores have spread from Meyer's apartment, and if I'm not mistaken, they've brought something extra with them. I've never done shrooms, so I don't know what it feels like, but I suspect what I experienced before in Meyer's apartment and in the basement, and now in Gonzalez's apartment, are the effects of psilocybin.

With a furtive look at the clock, Gonzalez tells me it's getting late and I need to go. She rushes me into the hallway outside her apartment, then freezes. "It's too late," she says. Before I can ask what she means, I hear the slow clang of footsteps on the wrought-iron stairs. Someone is coming up from the basement. The bottom of the stairs, deep beneath us, is lost in darkness, but a murky shape begins to take form, climbing the steps at a halting, deliberate pace. I can't make out any details; their face is blocked from view by the "Do Not Enter" sign hanging from the chain at the mouth of the stairwell. In the shadows, I can just make out a lumpy, stark white hand on the banister.

Gonzalez hurries me out the door of the apartment building, then slams the front door closed. There's no window in the door, no way to see what's happening inside. I hear Gonzalez's apartment door slam, and then nothing. I'm shaken by what I've seen. By *two* things I've seen.

The shape in the stairwell, yes, but also what I saw as Gonzalez pulled the front door closed again, her sleeve drawing back to reveal the same fuzzy white spots on her arm that Accardo had.

In the days that follow, I leave repeated messages for Dante Accardo begging him to let me back into the building, but he doesn't call back. I manage to reach Natalya Shvartsman, but she doesn't want to get in any more trouble with Accardo than she already has. "Good apartments are hard to find in New York City, especially for what I'm paying," she says.

I can't stop thinking about the form in the darkness of the stairwell.

The strange lumpy masses on that pale, white hand. They were mush-rooms, just like the ones growing out of the wall of Adelaide Meyer's apartment. I may very well have hallucinated it thanks to the psilocy-bin-laced fungal spores I inhaled in Gonzalez's apartment, but the metallic clang of footsteps on the wrought-iron stairs was real. *Someone* was coming up those stairs.

Almost a week after my last visit to 314 West 127th Street, I receive a call from Shvartsman with surprising news. Lucia Gonzalez passed away. "It came out of nowhere, some kind of respiratory thing, I think. They found a lot of mold in her apartment," she says. "When the ambulance came to take Lucia away, I asked them to take Addie's body from the basement, too. They checked downstairs and told me the body was already gone. Someone must have finally come to pick her up." Was she able to confirm that with Accardo? "I haven't seen him. No one's seen him in days. He's in his apartment, sick with the same thing Lucia had."

Gonzalez's apartment is on the first floor, across from Meyer's. Accardo's apartment is on the second floor. The fungus is spreading up through the building. "I'm thinking of moving now. It doesn't feel safe here anymore," says Shvartsman, who lives on the third floor. I tell her that's a good idea. However, before she leaves, could she let me into the building one last time?

At the bottom of the wrought-iron stairs, in the basement once again, I hug myself against the cold. It's even more frigid down here than I remember. Adelaide Meyer's body is gone. The blanket that once covered her has been tossed to one corner. Everywhere, on the floor, the ceiling, the walls, are those telltale fuzzy white spots with dark centers, like unblinking eyes, eyes that never stop watching you.

Meyer's apartment, Gonzalez's apartment, Accardo's apartment, the basement—how much of this building has been infected by the fungus? Or rather, at this stage, how much is left that *hasn't* been?

A coughing fit comes over me, and I have to step away from Natalya Shvartsman for a moment, bending at the waist because I'm coughing so hard. It's nothing new. I've been coughing for days now. "Sounds like you've got whatever's going around," Shvartsman says.

At the far wall is a short flight of stone stairs leading up to bulkhead doors that have been left open, the source of the bitter cold in the basement and the likeliest exit for Meyer's body.

The door opens onto a vast courtyard behind all the buildings on this block, a minefield of dumpsters, garbage bags, old mattresses, discarded couches, and assorted other refuse, all coated in snow. The snow on the floor of the courtyard is slush now. What looks like a single pair of visible footprints leaves the basement and arcs through the courtyard to the alley on the west side of the building and then to...who knows?

It's possible I'm misreading the number of footprints. There could be more, lost in the melting snow, left by a whole troupe of people from the Office of the Chief Medical Examiner. Shvartsman didn't see the body get collected, but that doesn't mean it didn't. Dante Accardo might have been informed about the pickup, but he's in his sick bed and not entertaining visitors—especially not nosy investigative journalists he's already kicked out of the building once before.

The fungus-spore eyes gaze at me from all over the room, fixing me with their stare. They whisper a different story to me. One about the veiled lady Gonzalez saw outside her peephole and the shape I saw in the stairwell.

If a dead woman could climb the basement stairs every night to try to get back into her apartment, could she also climb the much shorter flight of stone steps and push open those bulkhead doors? Would a ninety-year-old woman be strong enough to do that herself? Is that even what she is anymore, or has she become something else? Continuing to do regular cicada things, as Neil Stolley might say, despite being more fungus than human now. Leaving bits of herself behind on walls and ceilings and floors wherever she goes. Spreading the sickness.

Shvartsman lets out a deep, throaty cough, covering her mouth. I ask if she's okay, but, still coughing, she waves a hand to let me know she's fine. There's a fuzzy white spot on her palm, another visible below it on her wrist. They're the same as the ones I have all over my body. The same as the ones everyone in this building has, or will have, soon enough. Maybe everyone in Manhattanville. Maybe everyone beyond.

Outside 314 West 127th Street, the snow begins to fall again, dusting the city white, blanketing it like spores.

ABOUT THE AUTHOR

Nicholas Kaufmann is the Bram Stoker Award®-nominated, Thriller Award-nominated, Shirley Jackson Award-nominated, and Dragon Award-nominated author of numerous works of horror and suspense, including the bestsellers *100 Fathoms Below* (written with Steven L. Kent) and *The Hungry Earth*. His short fiction has appeared in *Cemetery Dance*, *Black Static*, *Nightmare Magazine*, *Interzone*, *Cosmic Horror Monthly*, and others. In addition to his own original work, he has written for such properties as *Zombies vs. Robots*, *The Rocketeer*, and *Warhammer*. He is also the co-host, along with science-fiction/horror author David Wellington, of the strange-but-true science podcast *Spooky Science Lab*. He lives in Brooklyn, NY.

Ballerinas of the Earth
Sara Tantlinger

Enter, the corps de ballet
slippery-pink dancers clustered
on crumbling logs where mournful
rhythms howl through the forest,
a broken orchestra of sticky screams.

I buried them here—glistening girls
pirouetting gracefully into the grave,
peach perfume muted by dirt blankets,
skin withered beneath the loam, fruiting
bodies slick with maggoty metamorphosis.

Burgundydrop flesh stretches from melted
pointe shoes, satin turns rubbery,
distending over skulls—smooth blush
caps form helmet-like bonnets, protecting
precious maroon liquid encompassed within.

Each fungi fusion unique as she breathes
through a mixture of lungs and gills,
white spore prints twirling into the air;
ballerinas become mythical, an amalgam
of fae and decayed human, bones rattling

as mushroom girls practice pliés, tiny
hearts still beat as they spark and sparkle,
lightning storms of cellular threads
connecting roots of silky stalks
in an assemblé meant to reshape the earth.

They've traded in bloody toes, but I know
if I slice, just a little, on the pale rosy top
how they will seep for me, stain my fingers
with proof of pain in purplish juices,
the taste subtle and mossy, growing richer.

Bleeding mycena, how they cry for me,
shrieks blend into the orchestra's rising pitch
once again, the performance always meant
to lead them here, sly ballerinas of the soil,
gleaming on my tongue as they ooze and dance.

ABOUT THE AUTHOR

Sara Tantlinger is the author of the Bram Stoker Award-winning *The Devil's Dreamland: Poetry Inspired by H.H. Holmes*, and the Stoker-nominated works *To Be Devoured* and *Cradleland of Parasites*. She has also edited *Not All Monsters* and *Chromophobia*. She is an active HWA member and participates in the HWA Pittsburgh Chapter. She embraces all things macabre and can be found at saratantlinger.com and on Instagram @inkychaotics

The Fourth Girl
Meghan Arcuri

The First Girl

THE FIRST GIRL died before anyone knew what was happening.

We were supposed to be gathering the herbs and lichens for Mother, but I did what I always do when I'm given a chore: sit inside the base of my favorite tree (I call him Max) and daydream.

How could I not?

Max was a giant oak tree, now dry and hollow and dead. And he had a perfect me-sized notch carved out at the bottom where I could sit in silence or escape my family or sleep or make up my own words to the songs of the most recent troubadour to pass through the village and wonder what his next stop might be and would he take me with him and maybe kiss me.

"Theya."

Fredda always interrupted my musings.

"Yes, sister?"

"We're supposed to be getting the lichens and herbs for Mother." The basket she carried was already half-full. "She said Raine and Iris had been sent on the same task so we should gather as much as we can before they get it all."

Where to begin with this.

"First of all, Mother's competitive nature will be the death of her. Her herbs and lichens grow everywhere here, and they grow quickly. We'll be fine."

"You shouldn't speak that way about Mother."

"I know."

My sweet Fredda, although the youngest and the darling of the family, worked hard, did not like to be babied, and—much to my displeasure—was obedient to the nth degree.

How we were related always mystified me.

"But let me get to my 'second of all.'"

Fredda rolled her eyes but did not protest.

"Second of all, Raine and Iris couldn't find their own hands if they weren't attached. We'll be fine."

Fredda giggled. Getting her to laugh was one of my small pleasures in life.

"You shouldn't be so cruel."

"I know."

Raine and Iris were the daughters of the other two witching families in the village: the Baths & the Werths. Two inferior ones, if you ask me, with ours (the Beauregards) being the most powerful. Or at least the most interesting.

"Are you going to help me?" Fredda said.

"When I'm done resting."

"Can I sit with you, then?"

"No."

"Why not?"

"Not enough room."

"I'm not that big."

"You're not that small, either."

"Theya!"

I stood. "We should find those herbs before Raine and Iris do."

"But you just said—"

"I know. But we wouldn't want to disappoint Mother, would we?"

I picked up my empty basket and stood in the opening of Max. He even had a canopy for me (some random fungus, ruffly and white, that grew on his bark), which, in the damp innards of the forest, always provided me a drip or drop of water to taste. I opened my mouth, turned my face skyward, and partook of the few drops falling from the canopy.

"Can I have some?"

"Maybe later."

I led Fredda away from my tree. (And, yes, it was my tree, regardless of what Mother or Fredda or any of my other sisters said. Max had always been there for me. He protected me and kept all my secrets.)

We meandered along, finding what we needed, humming our favorite tunes, sneaking handsful of elderberries every so often. The leaves smushed under our feet, wet from the past month's excess rain. Unusual for this part of the land, but not as unusual as a screaming Fredda.

Which she was suddenly doing.

She knelt in the center of Five Hands Glade, one of the few clearings in the wood always teeming with chamomile and lavender. Two black-booted feet twitched and convulsed on the ground, the smooth, dark leather a sharp contrast to the purples and yellows and whites of the flowers. Fredda's body blocked the rest of the prone one, but as I approached, a tangle of skirts and petticoats, with thrashing head and arms, appeared.

Her face was so red, so contorted, it took me a second to realize it was Raine Bath.

"Raine! Can you hear me?" But Raine couldn't hear me. Or, if she could, she didn't respond.

Fredda tried to touch her, but Raine's body shook too much. "What do we do?"

A rustling on the edge of the glade near a thick patch of lavender and chamomile.

"Hello?" I said.

No one responded, which of course they didn't because if they were an animal, they couldn't, and if they were a person sneaking around, they wouldn't.

"You're faster than me," I said to Fredda. "Go get Mother."

"Will you be all right?"

"Yes."

She hustled off.

Raine choked and wheezed; a white foam spilled from her mouth. Blood dripped from her eyes, now redder than a rose.

Poison?

I gathered some clover, knowing it helped, remembering it needed to be paired with something (though what it was, I had no idea) damning myself for zoning out during Mother's last lesson on antidotes.

Another rustle on the glade's edge.

Even with poor Raine's struggles, I could not stifle my curiosity, and I followed the sound. But like a dream, every time I got closer to it, it moved farther and farther away from me.

"Theya!"

"Theya."

Fredda. And Mother. Though with vastly different tones.

Fredda's held concern. In fact, she ran to me and hugged me.

Mother's tone, however, dripped with...disappointment? Disdain? Some other d-word?

Lips pursed, she cast a glance my way for a millisecond before kneeling by Raine.

"We're too late," she said.

I'd been so distracted by the sounds outside Five Hands Glade and Fredda's greeting and Mother's tone, I hadn't realized Raine's body had stilled.

And worse, a fine, diaphanous web—much like that of the ermine moth caterpillar—covered her entire body.

"Are you sure?" Fredda set down her basket next to Mother. "Theya and I have collected all of this. Can't any of it help?"

"Not unless there's Poultry Root, which there shouldn't be," Mother said. She pointed at my empty basket. "You were supposed to be collecting lichens and herbs...of which there should be more. But I guess Theya had more important things to do."

"Mother. Please." Fredda knelt by Raine again, a tear running down her cheek. "What happened to poor Raine?"

"This is the work of the Angel of Death."

"Who is the Angel of Death?"

"Not a *who*, Theyadora," Mother said, "but a *what*. You know it by its other name: the Destroying Angel."

"But that's one of the Never-Touches," Fredda said. "You taught us about that as soon as we were old enough to walk."

I laughed when Fredda said *Never-Touches*. I hadn't used that term since we were children. Fredda and I would make up songs about the poisonous, deadly flora and fauna we were never to touch.

"You find this funny, Theya?" Mother said. "You find suffocation, explosion of the inner organs, bleeding out the eyes—and sometimes even the skin—funny?"

I didn't bother to answer. She would have accused me of lying, anyway.

"The Baths and the Werths taught their girls the same thing," Fredda said. "Raine knew not to touch them."

"Curious..." Mother poked at the webbing with a twig. "I've never seen it cover the entire body like this."

Then she stood. "I must tell her family." She thrust my empty basket at me. "Finish—or in your case, Theya—*start* collecting the lichens and herbs. And some Poultry Root. You remember what that is, don't you? I mentioned it in our last lesson. Or perhaps you were too busy swooning over the troubadour?" She turned from me and walked toward the Bath's house.

Over her shoulder, she said, "Maybe if you had paid more attention, you could have saved her. Or at least eased her pain."

That stung. But I would never let her know that.

"What's Poultry Root?" Fredda said when Mother had disappeared.

I shrugged. "I was definitely swooning over the troubadour."

The Second Girl

The second girl died because she was stupid.

I know. I'm blaming the victim.

But hear me out.

After Raine died, her family kind of freaked out. They were 100% sure she knew not to consume Destroying Angel mushrooms. They agreed with Mother, too: the webbing was inconsistent with the effects of its poison. So, they went ahead and started throwing around the m-word: *murder*.

Witching families got twitchy with murder on the table. A long history of being hunted and tortured will do that to a bunch of gals. But our ancestors had settled here a long time ago and had remained safe, so the threat of murder shrank in our minds.

The day after we'd found Raine, Fredda and I walked through the village while Mother bought meat and bones from the butcher. We were humming along when Iris accosted us.

"Did you hear?" she said.

"About what?" I said.

"About Raine." She cast a glance over her shoulder, a small smile playing at her lips.

"We're the ones that found her, Iris."

"Oh, yeah." She looked again.

I followed her gaze. A guy stood by the stables among the soggy hay lining the muddy road. He was tall, dark, and lovely. He wore a fur pelt over a leather tunic, but they hinted at broad shoulders and thick thighs. My body reacted to him, but my mind knew better. He was bad news with a capital B (and N), the air about him devilish and mysterious, in a way more dangerous than desirable.

He smiled at Iris, assessing her full form.

"Who is that?" Fredda said.

"He's trouble, is who he is."

"Oh, what do you know, Theya?" Iris said.

"I know trouble. Especially when it comes in the form of a tall, dark stranger with a heavenly face."

"So heavenly," Iris said. She giggled. "But he's not a stranger, you know. His name is Dek, and he's been around for a few days, resting here on his journey between the villages of Leven and Mann."

"You've already talked to him?" Fredda said.

"Of course I have, silly." Iris leaned into her wanton reputation.

"It isn't that far from Leven to Mann. Why is he spending so much time here?"

"Can't a guy change his plans when enchanted?" The male voice, deep and rich and inviting, filled my body.

He'd approached us from behind, all cat-like and stealthy. He smelled like fresh air and...snow? Something fuzzy and purple lined the bottom of his fur, but he stood too close for comfort, so I put myself between him and Fredda.

He kissed Iris's hand. She giggled and bubbled and blushed. Totally pathetic.

She introduced us.

He made no move to extend a hand, but bowed his head and said, "Charmed."

"I'm sure," I said.

He stared at me for a second too long before turning to Iris. "You promised to show me the brook." He held up his leather bladder. "I need to refresh before I continue."

"Of course." She took his hand and led him toward Weeping Sisters Brook.

"Do you want some company, Iris? It's getting dark."

"No, thanks. We'll be fine." And off they went.

"She's such an idiot," I said to Fredda.

But she didn't answer me. Her body had listed toward Iris and Dek, eyes wide and unfocused.

"Lover girl." I snapped in front of her face.

She closed her eyes and inhaled. When she opened them again, she smiled a dopey smile.

"You've got to be kidding me," I said. "You're into that?"

"You're not? He's cute."

"First of all, yes, he's cute. Second of all, he's full of it."

"How can you tell?"

"I just can." It was one of my gifts, though Mother didn't count it as such.

"That's not fa—"

"Let me get to my 'third of all.'"

She rolled her eyes.

"Third of all, you're way too young for that."

"I'm fourteen! Only two years younger than you and Iris."

"Speaking of Iris...we should follow her."

"Why?"

"Because I don't trust Mr. Cutie Face." I walked toward Weeping Sisters. "Come on."

When we reached Iris and Dek, they'd gone to the bank on the opposite side for some dumb reason.

They stood like lovers in a warm embrace, their two bodies melded into one, their hands roaming, their lips dancing and the kiss was long and slow and made my legs wobble and my envy flare and would I ever be kissed like that and he pulled his hand from his pocket and pulled his mouth from hers and smiled a smile so delicious and dark and frightening and her eyes were closed so she didn't see him put his hand to his mouth palm up and purse his lips and blow and she didn't see the white crystalline powder rise from his hand and spiral spiral spiral around her face and into her nose and through her parted lips.

"Iris!" I screamed as loud as I could.

Her eyes shot open as his head whipped toward me and Fredda. His smile became a snarl, and he muttered an oath in an unfamiliar language. Iris's body went slack in his arms, and he grasped her shoulders as her head wobbled, then he threw her to the ground and bolted. He disappeared on the other side of Weeping Sisters, heading who knew where.

"Iris!" I ran toward her, her body jerking and shaking, but Fredda stood rooted where she was. She had the same wide-eyed, slack-jawed expression from before, so I ran back to her and snapped in her face again.

She shook her head, looked at me, then looked at Iris. "What happened to her?"

"Didn't you see?"

"I can't remember."

What the...

"There's no time for this. Go get Mother," I said, and she ran toward the village.

Fortunately, Dek and Iris had chosen one of the more narrow and shallow sections of the brook to cross. I hiked up my skirts and petticoats and waded through.

As I approached Iris, I grabbed a handful of salt from the small satchel I always wore and cast a circle. I muttered the protection and hoped Dek had kept running, the silence a small comfort.

By the time I knelt next to her, the thin, white web that had covered Raine now covered Iris's entire body. And that unlocked the secret of the purple fuzz on Dek's fur: lavender from Five Hands Glade.

Iris had stopped thrashing, stopped moving, stopped breathing. The web covered her mouth and nose, opaque and white but thin enough over the rest of her face to see her eyes: blood red and full of terror.

"Theya!"

Mother stood on the opposite bank with Fredda.

She charged through the creek as if the water were nothing, Fredda following behind.

"At least you used the salt." Mother's contempt stung. I didn't want it to, but it did.

She knelt by Iris's body, put on her pale leather gloves, and tore the web from her face. She pulled and pulled and pulled as a never-ending trail of web, thick and wet, spewed from Iris's mouth. When the last bit surfaced, Mother reached into her satchel and retrieved a small, thick disc, orange with ruffly edges. It looked familiar, but I couldn't quite place it. She put the disc in Iris's mouth and held her jaw shut.

"I have little hope of this working, but it is the only thing to do."

"What is it?" Fredda said.

"Poultry Root."

"It looks like a mushroom."

"That's because it is one." Mother looked at me. "Theya should have been able to tell you that."

We waited a few minutes. When nothing happened, Mother stood and faced me.

"Tell me everything."

I repeated the entire incident, including our brief encounter in front of the butcher's, the lavender, and his oath in the weird language.

"What did he say?"

"Acci."

Her jaw tightened. "The Lockes," she said.

"What are the Lockes?" I said.

"Not a *what*, Theyadora, but a *who*. They are a family from a different age. But they had always been scholars, not rivals of witching families."

"What do they want?" I said.

"I don't know. But they appear to be after our young. We must get you to safety." She stood, giving us a hard stare. "The Angel of Death is upon us," she said with a drama I'd never heard her use before.

I wanted to laugh, but nothing about this was funny.

The Third Girl

The third girl died because I let her.

But I'd been stewing in guilt well before that. Mother knew the exact, right way to weaponize her words.

Why didn't you stop Iris from going with him?

I tried.

You should have tried harder.

Fredda didn't, either.

You're older. I expect more from you. But more and more, I don't think I should.

Obviously, the m-word came up again (*murder*, in case you forgot), so did the h-word (*hunted*), as well as the other h-word (*hide* your witches).

The Locke family? Clan? Whatever? were from a time so long ago, Mother hadn't even bothered to mention them in her teachings (or maybe she did, and I tuned her out).

Our older sisters were safe in the North, their mentor providing ample protections.

But Fredda and me?

Sitting witch ducks.

Mother could not have been clearer about leaving the house (*Do not do it*), but after her blame for Iris, the house felt smaller and smaller as my guilt grew larger and larger.

Not to mention the silent treatment at meals, the doors slammed in my face, and the isolation—was Mother keeping Fredda from me?

So, I holed up in my room, lay on my bed, and replayed the incident with Iris in my head over and over and over. Although I had yet to become a full practitioner—that was a few years away—I found a million ways in which I could've stopped Dek from murdering her. Like casting a circle sooner (*Obviously*) or yelling and screaming and making an ass out of myself (*You have had plenty of practice with that*) or dragging Iris from him (*You are much stronger than her*) or lying to get her to come with us (*You are a very good liar*).

And then I couldn't take it anymore, and I ran from the house.

The rain pelted me in the face because of course it did. Why wouldn't miserable weather match my miserable mood?

I ran behind the house through the wood with the gnarled paths, tripping on roots and loose rocks. I ran through Five Hands Glade—the purple lavender wilting and sagging in the rain—and finally came upon Max and tucked into my notch.

A flash of light in the sky, followed by a low rumble of thunder, followed by a rain so heavy, it blurred the trees and shrubs just outside Max's opening.

A steady stream of water flowed off the canopy of ruffled white mushrooms over the opening, reminding me of my thirst. I stood underneath, opened my mouth, and drank my fill. Then I lay inside my hollowed-out tree in a bed of damp leaves and pine needles, trying to let the sounds of the storm drown out the sounds of my guilt. Fortunately, the storm lulled me to sleep.

"Theya!"

Someone shook my shoulder.

I slapped at the hand and sat straight up.

"Theya. It's okay. It's me." Fredda crouched next to me, a fine mist on her hair. The storm outside had stopped. "You need to come back before Mother realizes you're gone."

"I'm not going."

"You need to. Mother said so."

"You always do everything she says, don't you."

"I'm here, aren't I?'

Fair point, but I was in a foul mood. "Then you'd better get back before she realizes her precious cherub is gone."

"Ouch, Theya."

I didn't want to get mad at her. It wasn't her fault, but sometimes I lashed out because she was the closest, easiest target.

And sometimes I'm awful.

"Look," I said. "It's not safe out there. You'd better get back."

"What about you?"

"Max will keep me safe."

"I could stay with you."

"No, Fredda. I need to be alone. Go back to Mother."

"But The—"

"Go!" It came out louder, angrier than I'd intended.

Eyes prickling with tears, she rushed from Max. I wanted to follow her but I didn't want to follow her, but her muffled yelp made me follow her.

As I rounded Max, the reason for her yelp presented himself.

Dek.

He had not found shelter from the storm. His dark hair clung to his forehead, rivulets of water streaming down his face. He smiled, but it wasn't kind or alluring. It was wicked: all teeth and angles, with a roughly trimmed goatee, wolfish and rabid. His leathers were stained, shiny, and dark; his fur was matted down, drips and drops of water falling off the edges of the pelt.

And he held Fredda—had pulled her into a bear hug, pinning both her arms with one of his. Her eyes were large, her jaw slack. She leaned back into his body, her head resting on his shoulder.

"Fredda!"

Dek chuckled and ran his nose along her hair, her ear, inhaling and licking his lips.

So disgusting.

"What do you want, Locke?"

"So you got curious about me," he said. "I want Witches, of course."

"Why? The Lockes are scholars."

"And scholars like to learn, to experiment. But you have confounded me twice, now. I was meant to bring those bodies back with me."

"Why?"

"So I could split them open."

"Dissection?"

"Tip to tail."

So gross.

Fredda sighed and leaned further into Dek.

"She is lovely."

"Leave her alone."

He shifted Fredda from one arm to the other. As if she weighed nothing. Then he tilted his head and stared at me for too long.

He blinked. "Why does my aura not affect you?"

"Get over yourself."

"I mean my mystic aura. Previous studies have helped us develop it. This one," he nodded at Fredda, "the other two. All three were willing participants. But not you."

"I have no idea."

"It's a shame. You are an interesting specimen for sure. But let's try this."

He pulled his other hand from his pocket, a small mound of white crystalline powder in the palm. He thrust Fredda toward me, and before I could catch her, he blew the powder from his hand.

It spiraled and sparkled and danced. It covered Fredda's face and mouth and nose. It covered my face and mouth and nose. It smelled like the sea and the snow and the sun. I sneezed and spit, brushing the powder from my face.

Fredda fell to the ground, coughing and choking, her body twitching, arms flailing, head snapping back and forth. Blood prickled on her skin like sweat. Crimson tears dripped from her eyes, foam poured from her mouth.

No.

I looked for the orange ruffled mushroom Mother had tried with Iris. The closest thing was the white ruffled one over Max's opening. I plucked some and ran to Fredda.

But as I knelt, her jaw whipped open, and thin, white strands of webbing emerged from her mouth. More and more and more appeared, intertwining as they crawled across her face, her neck, her core, her limbs. Crawling, crawling, until they covered her entire body. Her convulsing turned to shaking turned to trembling turned to stillness.

She was dead.

I screamed, tears streaming down my face, and I fell back on Max among the various debris that had fallen from him over the years, not caring how the sharp, hard edges poked me.

Dek stood over me, motionless. He was so quiet, it startled me silent.

Head tilted, eyes wide, he said, "How did you—"

Without thinking, I grabbed one of Max's thick, fallen branches, jumped to my feet, and thrust it into Dek's neck, yelling like a warrior.

Warm blood spurted on my hand, my face, as Dek dropped to the ground.

"Theya!"

Mother rushed from behind me to stand over Dek. He spasmed, wet choking sounds and bubbles of blood coming from his mouth. Eventually, he stopped moving.

Mother turned to me and held my face in her hands. "Are you all right?"

I was not. I would never be all right.

She pulled down my jaw, looking, smelling, listening. When her internal questions appeared to be answered, she knelt by Fredda.

She did not weep or cry or wail. I'd never seen her do any of those things. She inspected and listened and calculated.

Then she stood.

"I saw what he did to you. The powder from the Angel of Death he blew in your faces, using his conjury to guide it. But I was too far away to stop it." She faced me and stared at me for too long. "How did this fate not befall you, as well?"

"I—I—don't—"

And with a rage I'd never heard from her, she said, "Answer me!"

I couldn't.

She grabbed the ruffled mushroom that had fallen from my hand. "Where did you get this?"

I pointed to Max.

She ran over, inspecting the canopy, inspecting the nook. "The inside is covered with this, as well. It's a cousin to the Poultry Root." She returned to me. "Is this not your secret hideaway?"

I nodded.

"And you were here in the rain?"

I nodded again.

"Your skin must have absorbed its spores."

"I drank from it, too."

She looked at me.

"And you never let your sister join you in there, did you?"

"I—"

"Not once."

I said nothing.

"Selfish." And she stormed away from me.

I couldn't speak around the lump in my throat.

I fell to my knees and wept over Fredda's body.

The Fourth Girl

I am the fourth girl. And even though I wanted the Angel of Death to take me, to replace Fredda with me, to use its choking webs to absolve my guilt, it couldn't.

I would have to find another way.

ABOUT THE AUTHOR

Meghan Arcuri is a Bram Stoker Award®-nominated author. Her work can be found in various anthologies, including *Borderlands* 7 and *Chiral Mad* 3. She served as the Vice President of the Horror Writers Association for over four years and is the recipient of the 2022 Richard Laymon President's Award.

She lives with her family in New York's Hudson Valley. Please visit her at meghanarcuri.com, or on Instagram (@meghanarcurimoran), facebook.com/meg.arcuri, and X (@MeghanArcuri).

In the Dark
Teel James Glenn

The first thing Warren Brant noticed about her was her skin, the alabaster white the poets spoke of, showing in her arms, legs, and cleavage above her dark, red minidress. Then he saw her eyes, two blue beacons beneath a long black shoulder-length haircut that seemed to make her skin glow even whiter.

Warren sipped his whiskey and tried not to stare too obviously at the woman across the dance floor. She didn't make it any easier by the fact that she seemed to be staring at him.

This has possibilities, he thought.

It was when she pulled up a vape pen, took a long sucking hit on it, then spewed out a cloud of vapor around her that Warren knew he had to make a move. He set his empty glass on the bar and tried to make his movement across the nightclub look as casual as possible.

Can't look desperate, he thought. *Can't chase her away before I catch her.*

The thought of catching her and what he planned to do with her when he did caused him to smile. Most of the others hadn't even been discovered yet.

"Hi there," Warren said as he sidled up beside the smoking siren. Up close her skin was even more flawless, the pores invisible, her eyes even more piercing with a lambent inner light that caused him to pause. "I'm Warren," he finally managed to say.

The woman exhaled a little mist around her that seemed to float like a halo and then flowed toward him. She smiled, her thin, painted-on lips parting to reveal blindingly white, perfect teeth. "Hi there, lover," she said in a low, throaty whisper. "I'm Flora."

Warren shivered. Something about her whisper touched his spine like icy fingers, somewhere between a thrill and a sensation of terror. That made him want to have her even more, and for a brief instant, he flashed to what could be—what he would make happen. And what had been with the others. His second shiver was a memory of pure joy.

"I haven't seen you here before, Flora," he said, trying to hold the excitement out of his voice. "And I come here regularly."

"I only get out sporadically," she said.

"Well, tonight is my lucky night then," he joked.

She blew another halo to envelop him, and she smiled again. "It could be," she said.

Bingo! He could not keep the grin from his face and hoped he only looked goofy and in no way sinister.

They talked of inconsequential things while the dance music throbbed in the background. The noise gave him the excuse to lean close to talk, and he inhaled her earthy scent. She didn't giggle girlishly as many of the others had, remaining coolly distant when he joked, and that somehow excited him even more.

After two more drinks—he bought—they mutually agreed to head out into the night air.

After the noise of the club, the city was quiet, the background human and machine noise as calming as bird songs.

The two paused ten steps from the club entrance, and he saw her full form in the yellow streetlight. She wore three-inch heels but still only came to his shoulder and was built on a delicate, yet curvaceous frame. In the better light, he could see that her eyebrows were drawn on, and he realized she was wearing a wig.

God, I hope this isn't one of those cross-dressers, he thought with a flash of anger he had to fight. If they were, he'd make them pay even more than the woman would have paid.

She saw him looking at her, and her seductive smile became a coy one, even shy. "I see you noticed that my eyebrows and eyelashes are both false," she said. "It's not contagious. It's just a condition."

"Like alopecia?" he asked. He'd heard about the condition but never met anyone who had it.

"Yes," she said. "It made all my hair fall out."

"All of it?" he asked, his gaze wandering down and then back to lock eyes with her.

At least it explains the eyebrows and wig, he thought with relief. *That better be true.*

"Yes, there too," she said in a throaty whisper. She blew another cloud of vapor at him as he leaned in to nuzzle her bare neck. He got bold then and kissed her neck, licking along the length of it.

Salty, he thought, and something else, an earthy taste. *Some kind of body oil?*

She didn't push him away; in fact, she leaned into him, then turned to look up into his eyes. "My place is not far," she said in a whisper that was full of promise. "Let's go there."

She didn't have to ask twice. Warren slipped an arm around her narrow waist and allowed her to direct their journey.

He enjoyed the warmth of her body against his side as they walked slowly down the street and found himself becoming excited by the prospect that she had no hair. It would be a novel experience for him. And, frankly, the novelty of what he did to the women was beginning to wear off.

He tried to imagine her throaty whisper forced into a howling scream, and he laughed.

"What's so funny?" she asked as she led him down the stairs to the basement apartment of a brownstone. She opened the door into the dark interior and locked the door behind them.

"Oh, just a private thought," he said, hoping his wry smile was alluring and not off-putting. He noticed an earthy smell in the hall and thought about how many old buildings had mold in them. But that also meant nice, thick walls that muffled sounds like screams.

Flora stopped at a door at the end of the hall, turning back to smile up at Warren. "I like to keep it dark inside," she said. "I hope you don't mind."

"Doesn't matter to me," he said, thinking, *I'll fix that; when I get to work, I like to see the blood.*

"Good," she said as she opened the door. "I wouldn't want to spoil things with bright light."

He slipped in behind her, making sure the door was locked, noting it was good and thick. Maybe even soundproof.

The woman set her vape pen on a table by the door, along with her keys, and stepped ahead of him into the dimly lit main room of the apartment. He could see dark shapes in the corners that he assumed were old-style furniture but little else about the room.

Warren idly picked up the vape pen and decided to take a hit to sweeten the experience to come. He felt his blood rush to the surface, and his pulse quickened. This was the moment just before, the excitement of the fantasy about to become reality. Their pain about to become exquisite.

"I hope you don't mind," Flora said, "but this thing gets itchy." She removed the wig and tossed it aside. At the same time, she slipped the shoulder straps of her dress off and let it drop to the floor.

The effect stunned Warren. He involuntarily gasped. Her skin seemed to glow in the dark room even more than it had in the club.

He tried to draw on the vape pen, but there was nothing there, so he gripped it while he let his eyes rove over the voluptuous figure of the woman. Then he stopped.

"You have—no—"

"I told you I had no hair," she said in a throating voice as she moved toward him with a sensuous, undulating motion. "And there is no point in holding that, lover. It's always been empty." As she spoke, a little cloud of vapor surrounded her face as if she were still vaping.

"But—you have no—!" He backed away until he pressed against the door. *Worse than what could have been there if they were a transvestite...*

"Sex organ?" she said with a sibilant laugh. "Oh, but lover, I do— just not the way you think."

He found himself captured by her eyes, the blue of them now a burning azure flame that held his stare like laser beams. The cloud that surrounded her began to swarm toward him.

He shivered, unable to move. The earthy smell of her and the vapors that enveloped and invaded him seemed to pin him to the door. He saw now that there were no delicate shell-like ears that should have accompanied the alabaster skin, according to the poets. There were not even holes in the smooth sides of her head.

She locked her lips to his and forced the vaporous spores into him. In moments, he could feel the filaments grabbing hold and growing within him.

As he slipped down, his insides were occupied, and the filaments began to grow and entwine, coursing out from his lungs into his blood-stream until they crawled into his brain. Then Warren Brant was no more, just an incubator and food source for Flora's next generation of children.

She smiled as she dragged him into a nice dark corner of the room. "I told you I only came out sporadically."

ABOUT THE AUTHOR

Teel James Glenn has been published in dozens of novels, and his poetry and stories have been printed in over three hundred magazines including *Weird Tales*, *Mystery*, *Black Cat Weekly*, *Tough*, *Pulp Adventures*, *Mad*, *Cirsova*, *Silverblade*, *Heroic Fantasy*, *Blazing Adventures* and *Sherlock Holmes Mystery*.

His novel *A Cowboy in Carpathia: A Bob Howard Adventure* won best novel 2021 in the Pulp Factory Award. He is also the winner of the 2012 Pulp Ark Award for Best Author. And he was a finalist for the Derringer short mystery award in 2022.

His website is: TheUrbanSwashbuckler.com

Lichenthropy
Gregory L. Norris

On the third night of the storm, the lights flickered, winked off, and stayed out, leaving Waldron in utter darkness. The big house on Maple Street sat alone at the end of a long country road, but the top windows of the back bedroom faced town, and he saw that patch of land was unlit beyond the branches, telling him the outage was widespread. He lit candles and waited for the power to return. It didn't. The rain spilled down, deafening at times as it struck the metal roof.

Despite it being summer, a ribbon of cold drifted through the dark house, helped along, no doubt, by the dirt cellar upon which the old manse had been built and the dampness in the air. Along with the lights, his phone was out, so Waldron passed the dusk and early evening reading a book from the back bedroom's shelves by the glow of a sunflower jar candle whose fragrance was almost too cloying to bear. When the words blurred, he shut the book, blew out the candle, and crawled beneath the blankets in the front bedroom. The cadence of the falling rain hitting the old house's roof soon lulled him asleep.

When he woke the next morning, the house sat under a musty gray pall. The power hadn't been restored. The chill still gripped the place, and the rain continued to fall. Waldron checked his phone—dead—and checked it again. A sense of disquiet offered an unwanted embrace. Interruptions in the electricity were rare and never this long. He couldn't recall the phones also being affected. Adding to the malaise was the unexpected iciness he woke to. The inside of the house was like a damp tomb.

Plenty of dry wood leftover from the winter was stacked beneath tarps. He decided to build a fire in the kitchen stove, which would accomplish numerous goals. A fire would banish the cold and dry out the inside of the house. He could also boil water to make tea or brew coffee in the French press. Pulling on his raincoat from the hall tree, Waldron tromped out the kitchen door and into the storm.

The wind screamed around him and turned the rain horizontal. Drops struck his face, icy and painful. He made it to the woodpile. The tarp snapped in the gusts. Waldron removed five stove lengths and started back toward the kitchen door. Eyes aimed low against the storm, he noticed the ground had grown lumpy, as though the earth had sprouted warts.

No, he realized after stepping over and crushing one of the blemishes. The boils were mushrooms forcing their way up from the waterlogged ground. Waldron cast his eye about to see hundreds of similar growths sprouting in the rain. *Thousands.*

A shiver teased the fine hairs at the nape of his neck. He fought it, failed. The chill tumbled down his backbone, shocking him out of his paralysis. Holding the firewood, Waldron hastened back into the house. Not sure why, he locked the door behind him.

There were no close neighbors. The house on Maple Street stood alone. Rarely since inheriting the old manse from an uncle had Waldron locked doors. But after building a fire in the kitchen's wood stove, he went from room to room, making sure that windows were sealed and doors leading inside bolted.

The damp chill lifted. Waldron set a pot on the stove and boiled water from the tap. The memory of the mushrooms—all those pallid growths pushing their way up from the soaked earth—tested his stomach with unexpected nausea. He brewed tea and sipped it black. The elixir worked to settle his queasiness. The lights stayed off, and the rain continued to hammer the world.

With no phone, the stillness inside the house thudded at Waldron's ear. No phone meant no music, no voices, no distractions. No power meant the absence of the constant background hum of electricity no one notices until it isn't there. Almost as unsettling was the not knowing— why had the juice stopped flowing, and when would it resume?

He settled into a seat beside the fire, knowing he'd have to return outside for more stove lengths, and picked up the book from the previous night. The old words blurred in the candle's light, and Waldron realized his ear was crooked in anticipation of hearing the power come back on. But the only sound in the vast house was the cadence of rain striking the roof and windows.

The fire burned down and then went out. Waldron perused the shelves of the refrigerator mostly on memory. The cold was gone from inside the appliance but creeping back into the house. If the power wasn't restored soon, he'd lose everything in the freezer.

He feasted on cheese that tasted particularly sharp and pungent, crackers, and lukewarm fruit juice. As he sat in the kitchen's silence, the candle's light cast strange illusions across the walls. Never before, in his recollection, had the electricity been out this long. The disquietude crept over his flesh at its worst yet, fueled by his sense of isolation, which Waldron rarely experienced inside the house. Until that moment, Waldron had loved his privacy. Now, he felt eyes peering in from the windows and the unwanted glances of unrevealed horrors lurking in the shadows outside.

The night fell early, welcomed in by the storm. Waldron checked the locked doors one final time and headed upstairs, the old book tucked beneath one arm, the jar candle in his other hand. While ascending the staircase, he noticed a dankness in the air, which he at first thought must be mildew until he noticed the stain on the wall. He tracked it up to the ceiling, where a fresh watermark had bloomed. Cursing, he located a pail in the bathroom cabinet and set it beneath to catch the runoff.

Drip...drip...drip...

In the back bedroom, he searched for lights in the distance. Not so much as the flicker of a single candle worked its way through the dark wall of branches and leaves.

Waldron crawled beneath the covers. The air had taken on that note of iciness again, and his flesh prickled. The long gray day had exhausted him, but as he readied to blow out the candle and hide beneath the blankets, he heard it—a single, oaken knock on the front door.

Waldron bolted upright in the bed. He wondered if he'd hallucinated the sound. Crooking his ear, he listened. At first, only the rain was there. Then another knock sounded, inelegant like thunder. Waldron kicked aside the covers, grabbed hold of the candle, and hastened out of the room and through the dark manse, believing some form of help had arrived at his front door. At last, he'd receive news—an update on what had happened! And he could ask for a progress report on when the power would be switched back on.

He passed the new water stain. The candle sputtered at the top of the stairs. After ordering himself to slow down and calm, Waldron descended the stairs.

"Just a minute," he called out. His voice boomed through the dark house.

As he approached the door, another *thump* shook the outside. Waldron stopped on a dime. Up close, his inner voice declared that the sound hadn't been produced by knuckles or even a human hand. As though to confirm this, his mysterious and unknown visitor knocked again. The malevolent quality of that rap against the outside of the door filled him with revulsion. The candle's light flickered as Waldron's hand shook.

Don't open that door!

Thump...

What followed was a rapid succession of hammering punches; an insane staccato that briefly drowned out the rain and left Waldron standing cold and paralyzed in the front foyer.

"Go away," he said in a voice barely there. The hand hammering on the door continued until he shouted the same demand.

The knocking ceased. Then, to Waldron's horror, he saw and heard the doorknob twitch as the unknown hand outside tested it. For a terrible instant, he couldn't remember if he'd actually locked the door. But the sturdy barrier remained shut, and the doorknob stilled. The rain resumed its fury. The long night wore on.

There's someone outside, his inner voice warned. *Someone who's trying to get in!*

His imagination painted the shadows on the ceiling as malevolent horrors while an emptiness consumed his belly. When was the last time he'd eaten? His breakfast of pungent cheese now seemed part of another life and era.

Waldron lapsed into a kind of dream state, not fully awake nor asleep but somewhere in between, lulled there by the ever-present melody of the rain. At one point, he slipped past the precipice and found himself feasting upon a magnificent wall made from candy. The candy wallpaper was fashioned from brightly colored ribbons that tasted of peppermint and lacquered fruit. Waldron licked, and then he chewed, tearing off entire sections of the gilded wallpaper in his bottomless hunger.

Ravenous, he devoured to the point that Waldron's tongue grew numb and the sweet taste soured. When he woke from the fantasy, he found himself in a gray void.

Drip...drip...drip...

His surroundings surfaced from the gloom. Waldron recognized the upstairs hallway and where he knelt beside the new water stain, licking the damp, diseased wall, which now bore a sallow shade of lichen-green.

A bitter, chemical taste ignited in his mouth. Repulsed, Waldron spit and backed away, slopping the bucket over in the process. Foul water sloshed across the hardwood floor. His body tensed. His guts churned. Some unaffected sliver of his consciousness recalled how certain Native American tribes had coated their arrowheads in toxic Wolf Lichen before going into battle. Vomit painted the back of his tongue. Somehow, Waldron choked it down. What was inside him remained there. Swallowing, he composed himself. Outside, the storm without end raged.

Nausea infected his gut. Shivering, Waldron paced the dark kitchen. Lichen was growing on the upstairs walls while mushrooms blanketed the ground around the house. The power was out. The storm surged.

He should hop in the car and drive into town, Waldron reasoned. Only when he stared down at Maple Street from the upstairs windows, he noticed a huge sinkhole had devoured a sizeable chunk of pavement. There'd be no navigating his car over or beside it.

I'll walk, he thought.

Even as his nausea deepened and Waldron worried he'd ingested something toxic from the lichen-covered wall, he knew it was his sole option. With no way to call out and wheels off the table, that only left legs.

As the morning wore on with maddening slowness, Waldron planned his route: down Maple Street to Pleasant, from there on to Main. On Main, he would find restaurants, the town's grocery store, and, most of all, other people.

"*Other people*," he said aloud and noted the foulness of his breath.

The silence inside the house transformed his simple statement into a shout.

He packed his messenger bag with his phone and charger, a pair of clean socks, a change of underwear, and the envelope of mad money he kept in a drawer for emergencies. It contained a thousand dollars. Waldron pulled on his raincoat and grabbed the umbrella from the hall tree. Then, steeling himself, he approached the kitchen door.

He turned the lock and attempted to push it open. The door struck against something solid and refused to budge. This sometimes happened with a significant snow, but never after April. He pushed harder. A sickening squelching sound rose above the cadence of falling rain. Waldron's nausea flared. His revulsion surged back. He thrust all of his weight at the door. Something on the other side snapped. The door pushed open, revealing what had blocked it.

To Waldron's horror, the ground was covered in mushrooms. Their bulbous purple and yellow crowns filled every inch of earth. They'd grown right up to the door and tall enough to hold it in place.

As he stepped out into the rain and over the massacred remains of the mushrooms he'd leveled, Waldron's senses drank in the fetor of rot and slime. Moaning in the voice of nightmares, he scurried over the field of mushrooms and onto the driveway's pavement. Risking a glance behind him, he saw that the insane field of fungus extended beyond the lawn and past the wood line. The mushrooms had even sprouted on the exterior of the house. They were everywhere.

The worry that had pursued him for days like an unwanted second shadow crept silently at his back as Waldron walked down Maple Street.

Something's seriously wrong, he thought while navigating around another rut eaten into the asphalt by the storm's runoff. *This is bigger than I imagined.*

Pain stung at his insides. The foul taste on his tongue intensified. Waldron's vision blurred. He splashed through a puddle, barely feeling his wet feet or the coldness in his sneakers.

A footstep sloshed through a puddle at his back. Waldron's racing pulse galloped even faster. He chanced a look over his shoulder. A dark figure stood on the road several yards behind him. Fear slithered over his flesh. He picked up speed and fast-marched ahead at a dogtrot. The wind whipped past his ear, screaming. His pursuer kept pace. Waldron mumbled a silent prayer and ran. The world blurred around him, as did his thoughts. The foul taste on his tongue worsened. His stomach felt as though it were filled with shards of broken glass.

At one point, his feet slipped, and Waldron pitched forward. The umbrella flew from his hand. His chin struck the unforgiving pavement. Rain spattered his face.

His pursuer caught up. Waldron sobbed. At any moment, he expected the killing blow to be delivered. What else could it be? But that never happened. When he dared to look up, he saw the man leaning down, hand extended in an offer of help.

A pallid, yellow-green hand from a pallid, yellow-green man.

He's covered in lichen, said the voice in Waldron's thoughts. *No, he is lichen!*

To his surprise, no fear came with that conclusion, Waldron realized the burning in his gut had shorted out, and the foul taste in his mouth again reminded him of candy. His hand's pallor now matched that of his rescuer. He accepted the lichen-man's gesture and was soon back on his feet.

The man smiled. Waldron responded in like. He noticed the man's bare arms were covered in what appeared to be tiny mouths, each one slurping up the rain. Removing his raincoat and dropping his messenger bag on the road, Waldron saw similar apertures lining his arms. He'd never wanted children. Now, he couldn't wait for those tiny openings to burst forth with the spores gestating inside him.

Waldron aimed his face at the storm and the beloved rain. Then he and his new friend resumed their march toward town. Along the way, others joined them, and the storm continued to rage across the land.

ABOUT THE AUTHOR

Gregory L. Norris lives and writes at Xanadu, a stately old manor in New Hampshire's North Country, with his giant rescue cat and emerald-eyed muse.

Real Science Shit
L. Marie Wood

It was always so dark.

Tanya didn't know if they had designed the funeral home that way given the nature of the business they were conducting, or if someone thought it was more economical to dim the lights in the hallway when nobody was back there. It wasn't a heavily trafficked spot—that's why Tanya thought she'd be able to sneak back there and scope things out. She waltzed in the door unnoticed; just one of the mourners coming for the Simpson viewing. Or was it the Martins wake? She'd have to make sure to check the door before walking out, just in case some asked her what they thought of the layout or the body...or whatever. Did funeral directors really ask people that?

"How did the body look?"

"Did your loved one look lifelike?"

What a horrible conversation to have with anyone, let alone people mourning the death of whoever was being spoken about. It was morbid, the whole idea that setting someone's face, clothes, and hair for display in their casket was something to be critiqued, discussed like one would the presentation of a meal or a work of art. Tanya didn't want to talk about any of it—not the clothes, the nails, or the flowers. No, not the flowers ever. She remembered a story about a man who had taken some flowers from a funeral–there were so many, so the guy thought he'd take some home, so they didn't go to waste. After he loaded them in his trunk, his car wouldn't turn on. There was literally nothing–no gurgling, no rasping, just silence when he turned the key. When he took the flowers out, the engine turned over like it should. They could keep their damn funeral flowers; they were bad luck.

Ridiculous, when she thought about what she was doing...what she *planned* to do. There had to be some bad juju attached to that, too, she thought. There was no way there wasn't.

But what if they got it right? What if they figured out how to bring people back from the dead for real, not like in the movies where some demonic version of them ran around brandishing a scalpel. What if they figured out how to bring the real person back behaving the way they used to, looking the way they used to? Everybody would want some, would keep it in the medicine cabinets just in case, like Covid tests and aspirin. They would be fucking rich and who would complain about ethics, especially when their parent was revived, when their partner walked away from an accident that should have killed them, their child survived a terminal illness? Who would really care how they did it when it meant life or death for someone *they* held dear...for *themselves?*

No one would, at least that's what Adrienne said. And Tanya believed her. She always believed her, and they both knew it. Never fall in love with a sexy witch.

So, there Tanya was, checking entrances and access. They'd come in through the pedestrian door built into the garage and slip directly into the preparation room. It shouldn't be hard to find the right one; this funeral home only had three. How Adrienne knew that, Tanya didn't know, but she wouldn't have been surprised if Adrienne had been down there before. She was like that, a little creepy, a little edgy. Tanya was into it. She had never known that about herself before, but she was into dark stuff sometimes. Whatever. It worked.

They would come in downstairs later that night, but Tanya was there early to make sure she had properly counted the access points from the floor that mourners used. Tanya didn't want anyone sneaking up on them; she wanted to make sure she knew what door to keep an eye on while Adrienne did what she needed to do.

Two. Tanya counted two doors. The same as last week.

She had attended Mrs. Wilson's funeral that time, sat through most of it before leaving the stuffy room under the guise of finding the restroom. Mrs. Wilson had been old, and her room was full of people ranging from toddlers forced to sit still in itchy clothes to the elderly wheelchair bound. The smell of the flowers warred with the strong perfumes many of the women wore, and the cloying combination made her lightheaded. Tanya looked appropriately dour because of it, so she couldn't complain. When she left the service, she found the darkened hallway empty and tried each one of the doors along it ever so quietly. There were two, both locked. Tanya figured at least one of them had to go to the basement. And it made sense for them to be locked; the funeral home wouldn't want some unsuspecting mourner to end up downstairs with the bodies, now would they? Tanya had even found the casket lift. When she told Adrienne about it, she was dismayed by the glee in her lover's face at the idea of riding it before they left. Tanya warned her off, telling her that they weren't supposed to do that, that they could break it, and then what? Tanya was only kind of sure her logic had broken through.

If it came up again, Tanya would redirect the conversation, bring up the fact that they really should get a fresher body for their subject. The ones at the hospital morgue would be so much better. It would do the trick; Tanya really was serious about that, had brought it up more times than she could count, and she was sure Adrienne was sick of telling her why it couldn't be that way. They'd been over it a million times. The security at the hospital was top notch. There would be no way to get down there to do what they needed to do. There was always a security guard, always someone milling around, and the coroners worked three eight-hour shifts. This funeral home did a lot of pick-ups from there, Adrienne had told her while lying in bed, when sitting across from each other at dinner, while taking a walk in a park not far from where Tanya stood right then. She had said it so many times that Tanya could repeat her argument for her.

"They'd catch us at the hospital, baby, but we can pretty much walk right into the funeral home. As long as we can get a fresh one..."

Tanya always cringed at how flippantly Adrienne said that, how callous she sounded. She always tried to soften her tone, though, and that made Tanya feel warm inside.

"...As long as we find a person who hasn't been embalmed yet, we're fine; we should be able to reanimate the tissue. We'll just go when the youngest son is working–he always forgets to lock the door when he brings a body in, doesn't remember to do it for like ten minutes after he opens the door. By then we will have slipped in and hidden ourselves. He never starts a body without having a drink first, so we just wait for him to lock the door, then go upstairs to make it."

Adrienne knew a lot about his movements, which didn't really sit well with Tanya. Sure, Adrienne had been watching him for a while, but she knew things she probably shouldn't, like the fact that nobody actually lived there full time anymore, that they only sleep there when it's their overnight shift, that he is sloppier with his work than the others, that he's slower. Tanya wondered how she knew so much. She tried not to let her mind wander, tried not to imagine Adrienne there, sharing a drink with the oily little pipsqueak of a man who always wore pants that were too tight and too short to be stylish, but she did. She tried to stop herself, tried not to let her mind run wild. Tanya told herself that going off on a tangent wouldn't help matters, but still, she did.

Adrienne said that sometimes he liked to watch a little TV upstairs with his drink. If he did that tonight, he'd give them something like twenty minutes to work their magic. Tanya knew all this, understood it, accepted it. But Tanya would still make her case as vehemently as she had before if she had to, trying to convince, trying to sway. If Tanya had to take her there, she would make Adrienne work for the win again. Hopefully that would be enough to make her forget all about riding the casket lift like she was at an amusement park.

Two doors, both locked. Fine. She knew where the casket lift was, and the youngest son was working that night. The spores were ready. Adrienne had boiled them all day long the day before and for a little while that day too. She'd worn an N95 mask over her nose and mouth inside a full face mask just to inspect them. When she boiled them, she pulled out some kind of industrial type of mask that sealed around her face and filtered the air. It was cool looking, but scary. Tanya left the trailer when Adrienne started, hadn't slept there last night, had packed a bag and slept in her mother's basement, dodging questions as to why, all of a sudden, she wanted to come home and spend some time. It was mean, she knew it, but she couldn't run the risk that she'd spill the secret, say something that her mom would be able to put two and two together about. Maybe later, when they were all rolling in dough and none of the whys and hows mattered anymore.

Maybe.

Adrienne had come up with the concoction on her own. She had been some kind of science wiz in school, or so she said. When the plan had been hatched, Tanya was fucked out, bliss still slowing her reactions and making everything she heard and saw copacetic. She couldn't care less if the love of her life was having delusions of grandeur about her academic career at that moment, wouldn't dream of reminding her that she was talking about high school when she said school, not college or grad school. To do that might mean Adrienne would take that pretty body away, give it to someone else and cut Tanya off. Tanya wasn't willing to risk never cumming that hard again.

Adrienne used six different types of mushrooms to trigger the spore mix she was looking for. Death Caps, Death Angels, which looked very much like something Tanya had seen growing in a field near her grandfather's house when she was a kid, Autumn Skullcaps and some of the rotten bark it grew on for good measure.

"That red one looks like you could die just from looking at it," Tanya had said as she covered her mouth and hopped away from where it sat on the table. It was bright red, like a fire engine, with little cream specks all over it in a random pattern, almost like freckles. She didn't like the look of it. At all.

"That's Fly Agaric and it's not even the one you should be worried about," Adrienne said with a laugh in her voice, and suddenly Tanya wanted to smile too. She showed Tanya the poisonous ones then, the ones that could put a horse down. "You could eat that red one and you'd probably just hallucinate a little. Eat one of these and your heart would stop before you could get out of this room."

Tanya remembered feeling antsy then, like for once she should listen to the voice telling her to leave and never come back.

"Should we even be sitting here with these?" she said instead. "Could something happen to us by, you know, just breathing in the fumes...you know, the...what're they called..." Tanya floundered unable to remember, terrified that she couldn't remember because she was already under the effect of the poisonous mushrooms and whatever they put into the air.

"Spores," Adrienne supplied as she added the weird, oddly pretty mushrooms to the pot, the simple broth of water and the dried shiitake mushrooms she bought from the supermarket that day at a rolling boil, "and we're ok right now. You can breathe in spores every now and then and be unaffected–we'd have to, like, snort them for a few months to get sick, and even then, it would only give us asthma or some kind of sinus infection."

She sounded so smart. Tanya liked when she talked like that.

Adrienne threw in the last kind of mushroom as the base started to shift in the pot, warming back up to a boil after adjusting for the rapidly filling pot. It looked like a scrunched-up sheet on top of a wide white base. She pulled up the mask that had been resting on her chin. Tanya did the same.

"Now we just gotta let it cook."

They'd made love out back, doing it outside because Tanya was too leery to go back inside without more protection. The light washed Adrienne's body in oranges, reds, golds, and purples as the sun and moon switched shifts, meeting behind Adrienne's back as she gyrated on Tanya's lap. Tanya loved the way the colors of the sunset haloed her head as Adrienne arched her back, how it made the skin of her breasts glow as her nipples reached upward to bask in the waning light. As she kissed the perspiration from her skin, Tanya thought about how she'd do the same thing on the bow of the yacht they'd buy with the money they'd earn once the world found out what they could do, how she'd pull one of those beautiful nipples into her mouth on the rooftop patio of their penthouse in whichever major city Adrienne wanted to live in–New York, Boston, Los Angeles, Paris, Rome...wherever. She thought about telling Adrienne about it, thought about sharing that fantasy, that dream, but she didn't. That goal, Tanya thought, she'd keep to herself.

All they needed now was a call.

Adrienne had insisted they get to the funeral home just after closing even though Tanya thought it was early. They parked down the street and out of view of the windows. There was a video camera there, very prominently displayed, but it didn't work. Adrienne told her as much...it was yet another thing she knew that Tanya didn't want to think about how or why she did. Tanya hadn't wanted to sit there for as long as they would have to to let traffic die down–get all of the mourners out of there, let the workers close up the place, let the street traffic transition from commuting business to quiet evening, let it get properly dark, but what Adrienne said about how anyone seeing them pull up now would forget about them if the car was just sitting there made sense. They would assume whoever was inside had gotten out if they thought about it at all. Smart. Very smart.

She was bored, but it gave Tanya time to think about what they were going to do once they got inside. She tried not to think too much about the way the serum worked, was fine to let Adrienne run with that part of it all, but there was one thing she couldn't get out of her head. Adrienne had been so excited to show her reluctant partner a real-world example of what would happen that she couldn't stop herself.

"It's like that zombie bug thing, you know what I mean? Like when the parasite digs into the bug's brain and takes over. It makes it go where it wants–water source or food, something like that–and then the parasite kills the bug by exploding out of its head like an antenna or something. It's wild, babe. This is gonna be like that, well I mean, kind of. There won't be these fleshy appendages sticking out of people's heads, and we won't be killing them, but the animation of flesh, the control, that's gonna be the shit, I'm telling you."

You can't unhear something like that.

Tanya was all for the rest of it–what it could mean if they really could create something that would help people get up and walk again, the money that would come from the pharmaceutical companies alone would be more than she could ever dream of. But she didn't think she could stay in the room to see the manifestation. She didn't think she could...watch.

And there were other questions, of course, like who was going to control the zombies, how they would eat, how long they would live. When Tanya had brought them up, Adrienne had kissed her cheek gingerly and reminded her they had to take one step at a time.

That made Tanya feel better. At least Adrienne was thinking about things like that, going slow, working things through. Experimenting. Making hypotheses. Real science shit. It made Tanya feel better that Adrienne wasn't just flying by the seat of her pants. She had it under control.

The oily undertaker slipped out while Tanya was thinking about a zombie bug trudging toward water with a fleshy stick poking out of its head, but she saw him when he came back with a body in the back of the van. It was go time.

They used the bushes and the shadows to get to the back door, their approach taking exactly as long as Tanya thought it should, given their dry runs. The undertaker should have made his way toward one of the preparation rooms by now and the door should be unlocked. Bingo and bingo.

Everything was going to plan.

Tanya and Adrienne slipped into the funeral home garage, closing the pedestrian door behind them as quietly as they could, and looked for somewhere to hide.

Shit!

They hadn't thought about where they would go once they got inside, where they would hide until he locked the door and went upstairs for his drink. The room was a rectangle; the garage of the house outfitted with shelves of things they would need to stock a hearse. There was nothing to get under or hide behind–the shelves were flush against the garage walls and any counter space was flimsy and shallow.

They were sitting ducks.

"Shit!" Tanya whispered as she turned toward Adrienne...at least she meant to. The word echoed in her head as the last one she would utter and her mind struggled to keep it, catalog it. Blood gushed from the wound she didn't feel; the bright light that flashed on the back of her eyelids the only indication that something was wrong, something had changed. That and her teeth clamping shut over the tongue, biting off the tip.

"Can't get fresher than this," she heard the oily undertaker say and suddenly understood.

Adrienne's hand smoothed the hair away from her face and, with the last of her strength, Tanya tried to lean into her touch.

ABOUT THE AUTHOR

L. Marie Wood is a Golden Stake Award and two-time Bookfest Award-winning, Ignyte Award- and two-time Bram Stoker Award®-nominated author. Wood is the Vice President of the Horror Writers Association, founder of the Speculative Fiction Academy, an English/Creative Writing professor, and a horror scholar. Learn more at www.lmariewood.com.

The Parasitium
M. Lopes da Silva

JACOB DREAMED of becoming himself again; of transcending the limits of his body, spilling over his previous haunted boundaries to somehow become greater in both the physical and spiritual realms; entangling with others so completely, cell to cell, thought to thought, that he'd never know loneliness again. Never again.

In the slow honey of waking, just before consciousness fully collected, he was happy. Content. But then the sheets suddenly felt all wrong, like giant, flat hands made out of rotting flesh. Jacob unpeeled himself. He sat up. He remembered; he was alone. Riley wasn't there anymore. That's what being alone meant. He sank his fingers into cold pillows. They weren't there. Alone in their bed, Jacob wept.

The trans man wanted nothing more than to excavate his overwhelming loneliness, but every day came with the insistent mental suffocation of never-again, no-more. It pressed against him, driving his skin to tighten like a zip-tie around his own chest, his neck. Propelling him panting out of nightmare-speckled sleep to get up and start pacing through his apartment. He'd pass this coffee table, that chair, and the stories of how the objects got there would come to him. Finding the wooden kitchen chair abandoned on a street and repainting it. Struggling to walk the antique coffee table up the hill with Riley. Inevitably; Riley. Then the tightness would come back: the never-again. The no-more.

Riley was everywhere and yet not there at all. It was exhausting to be haunted by a person who was still alive. Exorcism seemed impossible. Riley's essence secretly possessed all the things they'd acquired together or laughed over or fucked each other on over the years. Riley was in the music playlists they had saved on his phone. In the way Jacob now organized his dishes. In the paint color they'd picked out for the bedroom together (a tasteful, cool-toned lavender). In the coffee brand Jacob now removed from a shelf and added to his hand grinder.

He'd tried to change the order of the dishes, but they kept migrating back to the sensible tiered stacks that Riley had figured out. They'd always been obsessed with ergonomics and design. Habits and the way bodies created little paths of preference. Coffee cup handles tilted at sixty-degree angles for comfort. Jacob frowned at the coffee cup he'd just picked up, suspicious of its angles. He put it down again.

He watched porn hoping to break the cycle of Riley, but they were there in subtle movements: a thumb hooking under a curve of hip fat, the crease of a brow folding in orgasm. He closed his laptop and extricated his right hand from the band of his sweatpants. In the absence of prerecorded gasps, the little noises of the apartment foregrounded: the refrigerator's automated purr, the regular whisper of the tower fan, the buzzing of electricity in the walls. Busy sounds that masked a lonely silence. A silence that would have usually been full of the noise of Riley.

Jacob sat up and reached for his laptop and headphones. He tried to pick out music, but the stuff that felt right made him cry. He shoved the keyboard away in irritation. He thought about looking for a therapist again, but his health insurance was crap, and he intuited that wading through the selection process was a task for a version of himself that wouldn't cry after listening to fifteen seconds of Oingo Boingo's "Elevator Man."

In the sticky mounting heat of late morning, he decided to get a new tattoo. That was something people did when they broke up, right? He was about to text his decision to someone, but after a while spent blankly holding his phone, he realized he couldn't think of anyone in particular to text. It'd been months since he'd hung out with anyone other than Riley. He hadn't spoken to his parents in years, and his brother wouldn't care. Jacob rubbed the flesh of his upper arms, the muscles looser than he usually liked from months of deferred exercise. He already had a moth inked on his left shoulder, a cluster of little animal skulls artfully surrounding his top surgery scars. There was something new going around that he wanted to try.

Jacob scrolled on his phone for a while until he found what he was looking for: a somewhat trendy tattoo parlor with an established reputation for good work. The place was located on Melrose. He sent an inquiry to an artist with thoughts about his vision. Primarily, he'd been charmed by the aesthetic of shelf mushrooms—Keiko's portfolio was rich with oysters and turkey tails and velvety beefsteaks flourishing on diverse limbs and shoulder blades. A forager's delight made flesh.

A narrow environment-controlled tank spanned from the floor to the ceiling next to Keiko's workstation. Behind the glass, different species of mushrooms thrived, almost all of them varieties of shelf mushrooms.

"Where were you thinking of getting your polypores?"

Jacob pointed to the long, angry red dashes of his top surgery scars. The tattoo artist traced them with her nitrile-gloved finger. The sensation he felt there was a kind of sensory static, primarily limited to pressure.

"Can I get them on top of the scar tissue?" he asked.

"Yeah," the artist leaned in, "that should be okay. The only places I can't put them are on faces, and like, anywhere near a spinal column."

"Why is that?"

She inspected a small glass cylinder full of clear liquid and shook it vigorously. "Hmm? Oh, because the hyphae start trying to connect with your nervous system. That's why you had to sign those release forms—it's all in there."

"Then what happens?"

Keiko adjusted a setting on her fungal tattoo machine. "Well, you signed the release forms so I'm about to inject some spores into your body."

"No, I mean what happens if the mushrooms start to connect with my nervous system?"

"You go to the hospital. Right away. Seriously, that's in the paperwork, too. Do you want to read it again?"

Jacob grew hot with embarrassment. He hadn't really read the forms very closely. At most, he'd skimmed the document. "No, that's okay. Sorry."

"You don't have to apologize to me, my dude. Just don't want you to walk out of here with any regrets."

He ended up selecting an umbrella polypore. The friendly clusters of pale, flat-topped fruit in the sample tank already felt like family. The tattooing itself hardly felt like anything at all—his surgery had removed a lot of nerve tissue—and in about forty-five minutes, it was all over.

"Remember to apply the lignin and cellulose ointment to the area every day. That stuff is basically their food."

"Okay. When will they fruit?"

"If you keep them in the dark, or at least stick to dim lighting and keep feeding them well, it usually takes about three to five days. But wait a full month before calling if they haven't fruited yet—sometimes it just takes them a while to get comfy. The pamphlet explains their care, and your aftercare. Basically no antifungal topical soaps, only water or the ointment directly on your polypores. You can come back here for more ointment—that's my sales pitch. Any other questions?"

He wondered what the mushrooms would feel like as they fruited. If their physical presence during the hard days would ease the intensity of his loneliness.

"No, no questions."

"Great, you can pay up front with Mateo. Thanks for coming in today. Feel free to tag me in posts on social media when they start to fruit!"

Late at night, he dreamed of becoming himself again.

Of finding himself like unburying a murdered predecessor, only to restring the violin of his corpse with mushrooms and play it, adagio. Of falling in love with the man he moved to dance. Of falling in love with himself again.

In early twilight, tender hyphae sprouted, unfurling into the hidden parts of his meat, slowly probing muscle with maggot precision. In the middle of his chest, right over his heart, two clusters of roots hidden beneath his skin held each other like hands. Buds of fruit broke through the surface of scar tissue like spring growth cutting through a thaw.

The fruiting was more exciting than he'd anticipated. They were beautiful: clusters like living, fleshy bone lace protruded from his scars. He took pictures and stared at the images on his phone for minutes on end. He gazed at himself in front of a mirror in a way that he had never permitted himself to stare at his reflection before. He couldn't stop looking at the fact of his co-existence, unavoidably inhabiting his body. No longer alone: never-again, no-more. The pressure around his ribcage slackened, rib by rib, only to be replaced by something else.

He wanted more.

He went back to Keiko. At first, he only wanted more polypores: bear bread on his shoulders; sulfur shelf on his thighs; a beefsteak over his heart. But he found himself craving more—he felt like a new world ready for inhabitants—empty and waiting for the first footfall. He just couldn't decide what should occupy him.

Luckily, the tree fungus beetles made the decision easy for him. Drawn by the feast of polypores, the rusty-brown insects settled into the tiny pores of Jacob's bear bread. It was heartening to see them arrive when they did, because around that time the umbrella fruit had begun to wilt. It was natural for them to wilt, and he realized that he should have probably harvested them before the process began, but it was still upsetting to see them go. The umbrella polypores had been his first occupant. His first new friends.

He acquired more: a fistful of ticks, a family of fleas. He let them drink deeply of his blood and nestle into the soft crooks beneath his knees and elbows. He smiled. He gave them red Christmas. Hope was a family, and sometimes that family was one you made, truly.

He was determined he would become a parasitium: a new thing. Forever useful, he would support others. Forever useful, he would never be alone. Loneliness was impossible for a parasitium; it was too fully occupied a thing to be. Everything was about tending to the nature of himself. Benevolent god-planet, he had so many spores and mouths to feed. So much love within him still to give. That he *had* to give: others were counting on him.

He couldn't convince Keiko to add more polypores along his spine, but eventually, he found someone online who would. He met them at a bar and let them inject things into his neck, the music bass-heavy sugar quick on the other side of the walls, and just when he started to realize that maybe he wasn't making good decisions anymore, everything started to get so very beautiful and bright.

Threads intersected and entangled with more organic threads, golden and fine. He knew that polypores usually grew on dying trees, but as he seethed and teemed and crawled along the bathroom floor of the bar, Jacob felt more alive than ever.

ABOUT THE AUTHOR

M. Lopes da Silva (he/they/she) is a polyamorous, bisexual, and non-binary trans masc author and artist from Los Angeles. He writes pulp and poetry, and lectures about the political power of desire. His poetry can be found in *Eye to the Telescope*, *The Dread Machine*, and *Electric Literature*. Weirdpunk Books just released his collection of heartbreaking and exquisite trans and queer horror stories, *Infinity Mathing at the Shore and Other Disruptions*, in March of 2024.

Point Zero
Lee Murray

it dropped in on a lump of rock
that sublimated
a cosmic alien, becoming
air-born, airborne
while the scientists argued triple points

powers-that-be had us mask up
not that again
still, our bodies spored
riddled with cosmic fruit
the same tired arguments circulating

we watched the screen
paralysed by events
apple skins splitting, viscera
disgorging over the floral couch substrate
still we couldn't look away

hurry spreading, deep-deeper, pain, pain, pain, that pierce-bursts, oh god, please, please, the threads weave through and up and out until we're weep-woven and still warping, come, it commands us, this way, this way, this way...

except a strange thing happens
we connect
on some weird level, interlacing
not just us, but billions
warped in post-cosmic enthalpy

we forget about divisions
left, right, and centre
we become, something other
different, yet
still with the all-consuming hubris

languid, I'm struggling to remember
something vital, or maybe someone
only it doesn't matter now

ABOUT THE AUTHOR

LEE MURRAY IS A WRITER, editor, poet and screenwriter from Aotearoa New Zealand, a Shirley Jackson Award and five-time Bram Stoker Award® winner. A *USA Today* bestselling author with more than forty titles to her credit, she holds a New Zealand Prime Minister's Award for Literary Achievement, and is an Honorary Literary Fellow of the New Zealand Society of Authors. Her latest work is NZSA Laura Solomon Cuba Press Prize-winner *Fox Spirit on a Distant Cloud*.

Butterfly Hisses

Tonia Ransom

An off-tune whistle of Beethoven's Symphony #5 rides the leaves blowing in the cool night wind, almost giving the appearance of the greenery shaking its head in disappointment. A harsh whisper interrupts the butchered classic. "Dude. You're too damn loud. If we get caught because—"

Jason scoffs and responds like he's explaining to a child why they can't have cake for breakfast. "We're not gonna get caught. It's not like the police patrol the woods. Besides, it's good to make noise. There's boars and shit out here and we don't wanna sneak up on one of those bastards." His voice rises to a shout at the last few words, definitely chasing any wildlife far away from sour attitude. "If we run up on one of those fuckers, our final screams will live on in those trees," he says like he's got a flashlight under his chin, trying to scare kids around a campfire.

Carson opens his anger-twisted mouth, but Dre interjects before a scuffle can break out. "Jason, he's right. You really are loud as shit dude. It's like you're attacking my ears."

"That's because you're *tripping*, Dre. Everything is loud because our senses are heightened."

"Forget I said anything. Let's just keep walking," Carson says.

Four pairs of feet take careful but heavy steps through the thick underbrush beneath the moonlight, partially because there definitely are boars and other things that would hunt them in the night, but also because their coordination is off. The men have fallen silent, basking in the beauty of the night, enhanced by the shrooms they ate a couple of hours before their journey. The moon shines a little brighter, the crickets sing a bit louder, and the leaves on the trees whisper secrets long lost to time.

"Hey Sam. You good bro?" Dre, never shedding his role of big brother, regardless of what realm his mind is in.

"Yeah. I think so. Stomach hurts a little but that's normal right?"

Dre claps Sam on the back and answers with a chuckle. He gives Sam's shoulder a little shake of pride. "It's amazing ain't it?"

"The stomachache? Hell no."

The men laugh, simultaneously raising their eyes to the sky as if the moon has called them by name. They stare in awe as one, both with themselves and the moon.

"Something's wrong," Sam says, his steps grinding to a halt.

"It'll pass. It's just the shrooms. They can make you feel anxious." Jason says, dismissive as always, but he stops walking. It seems like his mouth forms the words even though he's outside of his body. He might as well have been reading a weather report. "Does anyone else hear that?"

Dre and Carson stop, still as the moon in the sky, stiller than the children of the night alive around them, and listen.

"I told you something was wrong," Sam whispers.

"Shh!" Dre snaps, listening intently. "Is that *hissing*? Fuck, is there a snake out here? Y'all know I don't fuck with snakes."

Jason shakes his head. "Nah. It's...it sounds like screaming."

Carson perks up. "I hear it too." His shoulders fall. "Sounds like a dude. Coughing or choking on something."

"Man, it's fucked up that you were hoping it was a chick in distress so you could play hero," Sam says, playing his role as moral compass of the group. "I don't hear it. I do hear that hissing though. Man, I'm telling y'all something is wrong. We need to get up outta here."

"Don't be a little bitch," Jason says, playing his role of asshole.

"Don't talk to my brother like that, man," Dre says with a warning. He doesn't play about his brother, and everyone knows it. Jason knows this, but he's tripping and forgets his mask, sliding into his true self. The one who, despite being well experienced with psychedelics, is still full of ego.

Mother Mycelium reveals something different to all who meet her, but for some, they keep their eyes closed. Jason's eyes are firmly shut. Wisdom knocks at his door twice a month and he doesn't even know there's a door.

Sam hitches his backpack back up on his shoulder and turns around. "Y'all can stay, but I'm leaving."

Carson steps in front of him. "Dude, chill. It's just a peak. It'll pass. There's nothing wrong, and that hissing and the screaming isn't real. Just a hallucination, like the shit you see, but for your ears. We're almost there. I promise it's gonna be magical. You just gotta stick it out."

Sam's eyes dart around, observing the melting faces of the group. He doesn't want to be a little bitch, but that primitive voice inside of him is screaming at him to run, to get away, to leave this place. He stays planted in his spot until a hiss tickles his ear and makes him jump.

"Dude are you tripping? I mean, I know you are, but I mean are you wigging out?" Dre asks. He leans in toward Sam and whispers, "I heard it too. If you wanna go, we'll go and I'll take the heat."

Sam looks at Dre, a plea welling in his eyes, but he blinks it away and mans up. He's always been the "soft" one, and if he can't hold it together on his first psychedelic journey, he will never live it down. So, he just shakes his head. "Nah, I'm good. Let's go."

Dre hesitates. That big brother intuition telling him it's a lie. Mother Mycelium telling him to GTFO of these woods right now. Not later on. Not in a minute. Right now.

Sam trudges forward, and Dre follows him because if Sam isn't leaving, he's not leaving Sam.

"Glad y'all got that figured out," Carson says and claps his hands.

Sam and Dre walk together in silence, while Jason and Carson chatter loudly about all the shiny things that catch their attention.

"What did you say?" Jason yells, no longer worried about the police catching them, apparently.

"I said that there's an owl up in that tree!" Carson screams in response. "Jesus, I can't even hear it hooting over all this screaming and shit. What *is* that? Is it a *person?*"

Sam and Dre just look at each other, telepathic communication debating whether they want to punk out or not because they both know they should.

"We could say you got a text from your girl asking you to come back," Dre suggests.

"They won't believe that. They'll ask to see it."

"True." Dre pauses. "Man, let's just take the hit to our pride and go."

"Easy for you to say. If you leave, you've got all kinds of heroic memories you can fall back on. Your pride will barely get a scratch. They've been expecting me to not be able to handle this. It took a whole year to convince them to let me try tripping with them. I leave and I'll always be a kid to them."

"Doesn't matter if we're dead," Dre mumbles, hoping Sam didn't hear him.

"Huh?"

Good. He didn't. But maybe he should have. "Nothing, man. I get it. If you stay, I'll stay. Ride or die." Sam and Dre bump fists. "Ride or die," they say together.

Carson yells out, frightening the birds from their perches in the trees. "It's right up here."

"Damn bro. We're not across town. Why you yelling?" Dre says, at his limit with the shouting.

"I'm not yelling, man," Carson says, definitely yelling. "Your ears are just sensitive."

"That's what I said earlier," Jason yells back, shaking his head at the double standard.

"Let's just get there," Dre says to Sam over the hissing in his own ears but keeping his voice low.

Sam looks back at Jason and Carson, who seem to be searching for something. "What are they looking for?" he asks Dre.

"Hell if I know. They've always had this weird connection when they trip. They see the same shit. Hear the same shit. And stay on their same bullshit after they're sober."

"I already feel like I'm...being reprogrammed...if that makes sense," Sam says, his voice so quiet Dre can barely hear it, unsure whether he should have even said it out loud.

"Yeah man." Dre is quiet for a while before he continues. "You still hear it?"

"Yeah. But I think it's real."

"Me too."

"What is it?" Sam asks.

"Hell if I know. Don't think it's a snake though."

The men enter a clearing in the woods, sparkling with wildflowers. In the center, what looks like a very large cigar is planted in the ground. After the final man steps through the threshold between the woods and the clearing, the cigar blooms.

"What the fuck is that?" Jason's screaming now, not out of fear, but wonder.

Carson has his hands over his ears, falling to his knees in pain. He'd swear his ears were bleeding, but when he checks there's no red on his hands. His eyes plead with Jason, who is entirely engrossed in the burgeoning cigar. Carson tips over, trying to turn toward Sam and Dre, tears coming from his eyes.

Dre and Sam are fixed on each other, ignoring Carson's internal battle. "The source," they both whisper together as if they are of one mind.

"What the fuck are y'all hearing?" Dre shouts, hoping they can hear him over whatever hallucination is tormenting them.

Carson is rocking himself now. "Screaming. Pain. Like someone is being tortured." He's full-on sobbing now, his commitment to toughing this out having been swallowed by the screaming.

Jason is approaching the cigar like it's a frightened, growling puppy. Despite the screaming, he's curious about this thing that has unfurled into the most beautiful star he's ever seen, in the sky or on Earth.

"Is that thing hissing for real?" Sam asks.

"I think so," Dre says, then shouts, "Hey man, I don't think you should fuck with whatever that is."

Jason doesn't move away. The star has him in its thrall.

"Seriously man. Leave it alone. I don't know if there's a snake in there or a hive of bees or what, but it's making a strange ass noise."

Carson is suddenly up on his feet, running toward Jason. Dre tries again. "Get the fuck away from that thing! What are y'all doing? I'm telling you it ain't right!"

Dre tries to pull Jason away. Sam stays back, decidedly not fucking with the hissing star.

Jason jerks away, stumbles, and plants his foot firmly in the center of the star.

A black cloud of dust rises up around his foot, encircling his leg, making its way up his body and into his mouth. Jason begins to cough violently, blood spraying everywhere. Carson screams, and the dust abruptly halts its attack on Jason and darts toward Carson like a mind-controlled bullet, shoving itself down his mouth.

When Carson begins to choke, Dre steps back, pulling his brother with him. They both cover their mouths and hold their breath. Do they leave their friends and save themselves, or do they stay and die in solidarity?

For them, the choice is easy. They run.

The dust is deeply uninterested in Sam and Dre, but it begins to eat Jason and Carson alive from the inside out. They're still coughing up blood, but now bits of their lungs shoot out of their mouths too. Tears of blood flow in rivers down their cheeks, and they just stare at each other, sharing a final moment, their eyes finally open to Mother

Mycelium. Before the light leaves their eyes, they both know they were hearing the future. Their own anguished cries lured them to their demise.

Sam and Dre return to the clearing in broad daylight. They have to be sure what they saw was real. And if their friends are still alive, they have to get them help.

But the clearing is empty. Empty except for a cigar buried in the earth. The only thing that confirms their experience is the thick layer of black dust encircling the cigar, two body-sized mounds curled up and facing each other.

This time, Mother Mycelium is quiet, quiet as Mother Earth, for even the cicadas and birds are as silent as the dead.

Sam and Dre walk away, understanding that Mother had to clean house and vowing to keep learning and growing until they, too, become dust.

ABOUT THE AUTHOR

Tonia Ransom is a horror writer and World Fantasy Award-winning creator of horror podcasts *NIGHTLIGHT* and *Afflicted.* Tonia has been scaring people since the second grade, when she wrote her first story based on Michael Myers. She lives in Austin, Texas. You can follow Tonia @missdefying on all the socials. *Risen* is her debut book.

The Cycle of Consumption
Rebecca Rowland

"WHAT TIME IS IT?"

The detective waits a beat before sliding his arm from under the interrogation table and glancing at his wrist. "Almost six-thirty." He chuckles softly, and it comes out much smarmier than he intended, but Arnold Sands is exhausted. He's pulling overtime, covering a hot August Saturday, and the station has been overrun with arrests. Every holding cell is full. His partner, Jerry, used the excuse of grabbing a coffee in order to step out and let him run the "good cop" routine, but he has yet to return. Arnold suspects he's likely face-down on the cot in the locker room, catching a few winks. Bastard probably won't be back for an hour, Arnold thinks.

Pauline Foster swivels a bit in her chair, but her gaze remains locked on the plain-clothed policeman. "Will you be bringing me dinner, or does my court-appointed attorney do that?" She smiles, a broad grin that overtakes most of her face, squeezing her already smallish eyes to slits. The skin beneath her eyes isn't exactly sallow, but something about its color makes Arnold uneasy. "I'm feeling a bit... peckish," Pauline explains.

The irony is suffocating. "Are you, now?" Arnold leans back on his chair, but he keeps his face neutral. "Got a hankering for a bit of Beef Wellington, by any chance? I understand there are plenty of leftovers in the evidence lab. I could fetch you a bowl."

Pauline's grin relaxes a bit, but she still appears pleased. Affable, even. "I'm a vegetarian, Detective. We've already discussed this."

"Why make a dish for your church's potluck when you don't plan to eat it yourself?" Arnold asks. It's the fifth time he's posed this question since they brought the woman in that morning, confiscating her Crock Pot after the precinct received multiple tips regarding its suspected nefarious contents. Pauline's refusal to eat meat might explain her overly pale complexion. Maybe she is iron deficient. Her skin appears almost gray beneath the fluorescent bulbs. "Seems curious, is all. Like they say, you should never trust a skinny cook."

Pauline raises an eyebrow. "Seems a bit excessive, actually," she says. "An overweight cook would suggest a lack of self-control. Gluttony, perhaps. An over-indulgence in physical things." She pauses. "Humans have become obsessed with *things*, consuming them. That's why we call ourselves consumers."

"Sounds like a throwback to the hippie revolution," Arnold says matter-of-factly. "Are you a Communist?"

"What year is this, again, Detective? I mean, do you want to ask me if I smoke 'the reefer' too?"

"No," Arnold says. "I'm just making conversation."

Pauline waves her hand dismissively. "Communism, Socialism, Anarchism: what's the difference, really? Humans have overstayed their welcome on this planet, turned it into a junk pile, a garbage heap. The smarter species will overtake us eventually, and all of our nonsense about politics will be..." The engulfing smile returns. "In the wind."

Arnold eyes the door. He knows he should switch gears, have the woman ready for booking before Jerry returns. He can dump the paperwork on his partner and be home in time for dinner and watch the Sox game if he plays his cards right. He recently installed a wall-sized flat screen in his living room. "Why vegetarianism, Pauline?" he asks. He keeps his tone casual.

Pauline reaches behind her head and scratches at the back of her neck. "I don't know," she says. "I never did like the consistency of meat. Don't like the feel of its stringiness in my mouth."

"Not grilling burgers and dogs on the barbecue this summer?"

Pauline smiles—politely, this time. "Portobello mushrooms can be a fine substitute."

Arnold's jaw clicks before he responds. "I don't think I could be satisfied with a diet of only plants."

Pauline leans forward, suddenly more interested in the conversation. "Actually, mushrooms are neither plant nor animal. They are in a genus all their own. And," she raises her eyebrows conspiratorially, "scientists believe fungi are closer in biological structure to humans than they are to vegetation. We may even share a common ancestor."

Arnold scoffs. "Explains some of the shiitake that show up as my 23andMe relatives," he quips, but Pauline's face does not change.

"Have you ever heard of the fungus *Cordyceps*? Since the pandemic, scientists have been studying its possible uses as an antiviral. It reproduces by inhabiting a caterpillar, killing it, then feeding on the dead tissue that surrounds it." Pauline takes an excited breath. "*Ophiocordyceps* is a very similar fungus, and one species of it is used in Chinese medicine to treat renal and liver disease. And yet..." Pauline leans her head closer to the table as if encouraging an invisible team to gather in a huddle. "And yet, when it infects a moth, it takes over the insect's bodily functions. Turns it into a puppet in the most grotesque sense."

"Makes a puppet out of a moth, you say," Arnold clarifies, trying to keep the boredom out of his tone. He glances at the door again.

"Until it tires of it," says Pauline. "Then, it bursts from the moth's head, obliterating its brain and spraying spores onto its next host. It proliferates like wildfire. One spore can colonize a whole forest."

Arnold pretends to make an entry on his notepad. "You seem to know a lot about them. Mushrooms, I mean."

Pauline seems to consider this. Then, "I know what is needed."

A lengthy quiet settles across the interrogation room.

Finally, Arnold Sands speaks. "When my partner, Detective Casey, read you your rights, you signed a waiver. Would you answer a few more questions for me?"

Pauline stares at Arnold, her face serious. "Of course."

"Did you intentionally poison the Beef Wellington you made for your church's potluck supper?"

"No."

"Did you purchase"—Arnold checks his notepad and slows his cadence to sound out the words—"*Amanita phalloides*, also known as death cap mushrooms, from the Chinese market two blocks from your home?"

"No."

"You didn't purchase mushrooms from the market? It will be easy enough to check, Pauline. The store has a camera system for security."

Pauline's countenance stays neutral. "I did purchase mushrooms, but they were straw mushrooms. Very common in Asian cuisine. And they do resemble death cap mushrooms in appearance, but I can assure you: they are far from poisonous."

"Why not use regular button mushrooms?" Arnold asks.

"Straw mushrooms are much more beneficial to the body," Pauline says, her voice pleasant. "They contain ergothioneine, an antioxidant believed to prevent cancer, heart disease, even Alzheimer's." She reaches behind her head again and scratches the unseen patch on her neck again. When she brings her hand back in front of her, her eyes drift down to her fingernails, examining them. Arnold's gaze follows hers, but he quickly looks away. Pauline's fingertips are covered with a grayish-white substance. It looks almost creamy, the consistency of ear wax.

Arnold controls the shudder slithering up his spine. He has never gotten used to the various hygienic atrocities that skitter into the precinct from time to time: body lice so prolific, it appears that a suspect's facial skin is pixelating; yeast infections so virulent, the stench lingers in the holding cell wing for weeks. He has never seen a suspect scratch this kind of substance from their skin, however. And the sooner he does not have to look at it, the better.

The detective reaches back and knocks on the one-way glass, his signal to anyone observing that he needs a break. At the sound, Pauline looks up from her hands. "I asked about dinner." It's a statement, not a question. Pauline stares directly into Arnold's eyes, unblinking.

Arnold taps his notepad with his pen. "I'll check on that for you just as soon as my partner gets back. He should be here anytime now." At this, he glances at his watch again.

"Am I keeping you from something, Detective?" Pauline asks. "Is the wife waiting at the table with supper?"

"I can be here all night, Pauline. I'm in no rush," he lies.

She leans forward. "You're not married, are you?"

Arnold does not answer.

After a beat, Pauline continues. "You're not married, probably live alone. No pets, not even a fish. Am I right?" She brings one hand up to her collarbone and rubs the ashen hollow above it. A bit of the grayish substance smears onto her skin. "It's just little ol' you, but I bet you reside in one of those three-story Victorians in West Medford, yeah?" She pauses. "Tell me, Detective, what do you do with all that extra space?"

Arnold raises an eyebrow. "Let's get back to the subject. You—"

"Those rooms are filled with *things*," Pauline says, her mouth drawing out the sibilance on the final word. It sounds like air escaping from a tire. "Unused things. Things purchased on a whim and regretted. Things once cherished but now forgotten. Piles of junk you don't touch for months, maybe years on end. Am I right?"

The detective clears his throat. "Well, Pauline, thank you for bringing that to my attention. I'll be sure to get going on plans for a garage sale. But before I do that..."

Arnold's voice catches in his throat. As he is speaking, the suspect lifts her head as if to look up at the ceiling. She bends her head so far back, her face is nearly perpendicular to him. Her neck, the skin chalk white and tinted with the same grayish hue as her cheeks, appears to be tattooed with thin black lines, each of them only a hair in width, extending from the underside of her chin to the top of her torso. Arnold leans forward to get a better look.

They are not ink markings, Arnold realizes. They are slits in her skin: at least twenty of them, a half-centimeter apart. As he watches, the slits seem to fold inward, as if they are—

gills.

Detective Jerry Casey opens the door to the interrogation room, startling Arnold and breaking his gaze. Jerry's eyes are slightly red, and Arnold has seen this look on his partner before: ol' Jerry was taking a few nips from the bottle of Jameson he keeps in his locker. A wave of annoyance washes over Arnold. Something about the room has shifted. He needs to wrap up this interview. Now.

"Miss Foster," Jerry says, his tongue slightly loose, "you're free to go." When Arnold turns to look at him incredulously, Jerry adds, "The lab found no trace of poison in the dinner, and we tracked down the source of the anonymous emails." He turns to look at his partner. "Turns out, Miss Foster sent them herself."

Arnold frowns. "What?" He looks at the suspect. Pauline has lowered her head. Her neck is hiding beneath a shadow of chin and hairdo. She is staring at him, her face void of expression.

"Why would you do that, Pauline? Why set yourself up to be arrested, to be kept in a police station for hours on end?" He taps his notebook with his pen. "Why waste my time?"

Pauline blinks once. "Did you know, Detective, that the busiest time for crime is late Friday evening through Saturday night?"

Jerry stifles a chuckle. "Yeah, Pauline, we're aware. But thanks for the trivia."

"And property crime in particular is at its height at this precise time of the year?" Pauline continues. "Property crime. That includes everything from burglary and larceny to everyday shoplifting."

Jerry is visibly annoyed and raises an unkempt eyebrow. "Listen, Miss—"

"Thomas Aquinas defined gluttony as an exorbitant relationship with physical acquisitions. An over-indulgence," Pauline says, her voice growing louder. "Humans are so fixated on consuming everything on Earth, they don't see their own extinction knocking at the door."

Jerry pulls a chair out and sits down next to his partner. He leans menacingly toward Pauline, pointing a finger at her that nearly touches her forehead. "If you think wasting police time is a form of social protest for your environmental hippie shit beliefs, sister, you are sorely mistaken. You—"

"Oh, no: you are confused." Pauline smiles broadly, her eyes tucking behind her lids again. "There's nothing that can stop it. Humans aren't orchestrating their own demise. They are just too distracted to see that they are slowly being replaced."

Arnold frowns. "Replaced?"

Pauline stops smiling. She places both of her hands on top of the interrogation table, her thumbs folded along its edge as if to brace herself. Her eyes shift from one detective to the other until she closes them, slowly, inhaling a long, deep breath.

She does not exhale.

Instead, the concave space between her eyes pulses, then rips apart. A wide crater opens in her face, breaking her skull and tearing away whitish-gray skin. The terrible cavity grows wider, contorting the rest of Pauline's face into a funhouse mirror reflection even as her jaw goes slack and the muscles of her shoulders and back release, sending her torso forward onto the table. The fissure travels to the back of her hairline, nearly splitting the dead woman's head completely in half.

From the gap erupts a swarm of small, round particles. They pour from the chasm in Pauline's broken skull and scatter like raindrops in a downpour, saturating the air and covering the table, the floor, and Detectives Arnold Sands and Jerry Casey. And when the two men open their mouths to scream, the spores funnel between their lips, implant themselves in the soft, wet membranes of their throats.

And wait.

ABOUT THE AUTHOR

Rebecca Rowland is a Shirley Jackson Award-nominated author who writes too many short stories. Despite her love of the ocean and distaste for cold weather, she makes her home in a landlocked and often icy corner of New England (USA). She is represented by Becky LeJeune of Bond Literary Agency. Follow her tomfoolery on Instagram at Rebecca_Rowland_books or visit RowlandBooks.com.

Fruiting Bodies
Victoria Nations

JAE TWISTED to touch Suze's shoulder, despite the awkward angle. One hand on the steering wheel felt precarious, even with the lighter traffic these days, but it was long enough to feel Suze's bunched neck muscles beneath her long hair. Suze's neck hadn't felt that tight in a long time, maybe since they'd last visited Joanne. The stiffness couldn't be helping Suze's queasiness. The throbbing stalk lying between them was a blessing, but from Suze's rigid posture, Jae knew it wasn't a good time to mention it out loud.

Using a reverent word for the bulbous extra limb that sprouted from Suze's back felt silly, but Jae had thrown themselves into their mother-in-law's language before everything changed. The syrupy words had eventually lightened the outrage that boiled within Joanne's whenever she was faced with the gangly, androgynous person her daughter had married. Jae refused to go back to the beforetimes, when they had to tiptoe into family gatherings hoping Joanne would ignore Jae tailing behind Suze. Of course, sneaking in would be impossible now that the flesh connector kept them tethered. There was no way to balance a casserole when they were already like two dogs tangling in each others' leashes.

Joanne didn't spout off about her daughter's unholy union these days. Suze read her emails over Jae's shoulder and dictated an occasional stilted response as Jae typed back. Joanne kept things light, and Jae responded in kind, sharing stories of house projects and recipes, with nothing about the global upheaval from the past few months. Suze reluctantly agreed that Jae was making headway. Memories of Joanne damning her to a Hell she didn't believe in had swam across Suze's eyes when Jae suggested they visit after all these years, but she didn't refuse.

Seeing Suze's fingers curl into a fist on her stomach made Jae want to reach for her again, but Suze would speak up if she wanted to talk. Jae never imagined a closed fist and stoic face would be a comfort. Before Suze, those were the signs of a gathering storm, the rumble before ugly words rained down from Jae's family, battering them. The barrage had driven Jae to the empty shelter of the streets. But with Suze, they only meant she was bracing herself, readying for the mask to fall from Joanne's face, and her judgement to be unleashed. Jae would soothe Suze's cluster of emotions later, no matter what happened, when they were safe at home and could bundle together with their stalk like a third cat between them.

Suze refused to use Joanne's imprecise language. She'd dazzled Jae when they first met as lab partners, a tall brunette who was already working in a lab and chattered about her dreams of leading one. Suze streaked their petri dishes with yeast and dictated information for Jae to write in the lab report, but Jae kept noticing her curls were streaked with auburn, the same rust color of her eyes. By the time they were pooling their junior scientist and middle school teacher salaries on an apartment, Jae knew Suze's data collection was her way of fighting off chaos. Jae had watched Suze face the recent cataclysm the same way, focused on using scientific terms when the flesh connectors sprouted. Suze tracked all the theories, determined to weigh each on its merits and keep a clear head.

There was the alien cultivation theory, that humans were being farmed as food for extraterrestrial beings. This was the most dismal theory, and its proponents had no evidence except for a doomsayer perspective that humans had to resign themselves to their fates.

Many people believed it was a judgement from God. Their God, in most cases, but sometimes the believers claimed gods outside their belief system were targeting them. Suze rejected this theory because there was no way to measure if a mystical force had visited a final plague on the human race. Jae felt just as ambivalent, and they sent a little gratitude into the Universe that Joanne hadn't mentioned it in her emails. Small gifts and all that.

Jae's favorite was the puffball theory, that an unidentified fungus-like organism had released spores that took hold in humans and sprouted from their bodies. The cellular structure of the membranous cords were human, by all the means science had to analyze them, but the spread pattern fit a puffball model so well that this was the most popular theory. Best of all, it didn't place blame on a specific government or belief system, so anyone could adopt it without feeling responsible. Jae loved this theory based strictly on the term, "Puffball Paradigm," and even Suze's solemnity cracked when Jae repeated it over and over until it sounded ridiculous.

If the growths had only attacked parts of the population, it would have been easy for factions to fight about it, but that wasn't the case. Most people had a growth. Most people, worldwide, were attached to other people at this point, many of them suddenly, when stalks erupted from their body and another's, and roped them together faster than they could get away.

Folks isolated themselves, but the infestation also affected their minds, drawing them together as if chosen. People left work unannounced and got up from a dead sleep next to their spouses. They left their children in parks to walk, drive, and even swim to connect with strangers. The neurological, or possibly psychic, links drove people to fly across the country or walk for miles until they found the person they were looking for. Offshoots of flesh reached out towards one another, grasping, until the two connected. Families were broken in a moment, and people worried the world would rip apart with them.

Jae snuck a glance at Suze. Her shoulders were finally dropping, and her hand wasn't draped across her waist as if quieting her stomach. She brooded, turned towards the window from the massive growth behind her back, but she reached behind her to squeeze Jae's leg. A ghost of a smile made Jae grin back.

When they snuggled under a fuzzy blanket to watch TV, their rope of flesh tucked between them, Jae felt like crying. It would have been so easy to lose Suze. They'd woken up in the middle of the night, jostled awake, thinking the connection growing between them was a cat walking across the bed. When they saw they had merged, a term social media had co-opted to describe the new family structures that were being created, they both had simply scooted closer and gone back to sleep. They were each connected to the person they'd pledged to love until they died.

Now they could carry a cat between them, splayed out on the threaded membrane like it was in a hammock. Sissy loved being carried that way. The big boy cat would be carried everywhere if they would let him, and he purred so deeply their cord sounded like it was growling. Noodle was dubious, ignoring that anything had changed as long as it didn't affect her bird watching on the lanai.

The whole world was in disarray, but their family was still together. They were a weird unit that had to share the shower, learn to adjust bathroom habits, and alter their clothes to fit around their extra appendage, but they got to go through it together, at least. Suze could wonder about the science, and Joanne could continue to be as judgmental as she wanted. Jae knew how lucky they'd been.

And their little family was going to grow. The thrumming stalk had sprouted a branch with a dangling bulb that swelled and retracted as if it held a beating heart. The doctor had found their vessels connected to it, and their combined blood pumping through it. Masses of cells were growing inside the sac, looking almost like a placenta. The doctor warned that there was no information on what the bulb was doing, except growing more complex, and if it were a fetus, the manner of its birth was unknown.

Jae couldn't wait for the day there was movement within it, something Suze couldn't see, but might be able to feel. And when the time came, Jae would help carry it. Right now, the bulb hung rigid and high over Suze's back, but she joked she'd be dragging it like a ball and chain before too long. Jae had already put a stroller together, waiting for the day they could roll it around behind her, the swelling sac tucked in with blankets. It was a shared creation, a little fruiting body, something Jae had never imagined possible.

A word of Joanne's came to Jae as they tested the stroller, making sure it rolled smoothly behind Suze. Grace. Jae felt like they'd been chosen. Their love story, their family, had been given a shining star in the moonless night so many people were struggling through right now.

Humanity was suffering, and had been from before the stalks emerged. Jae wondered if that was why humans had been vulnerable. Random pressures had let some pathogens run wild back in the lab. Exhaustion and ennui. Disconnection and shared ludicrous delusions. They all might have been early symptoms of an infection that humans didn't yet understand, and tipped into a global epidemic by climate change. Salt water moving into previously fresh aquifers. Lead settling sprayed out from old pipes in the cities. Humans had started flaking out from their loved ones before they forged random physical connections with strangers, and just maybe that was the end result of pathology that had been developing for decades.

Or maybe it was aliens.

No one was surprised that people tried to disentangle themselves. People fought with their new partners, as if an emotional breakup would sever their physical connection. Parents hunted for the people who'd stolen their children away with new umbilical cords annealed between them and families they had never met.

Cutting the fleshy connections sent both hosts into shock no matter how quickly the wounds were closed, and death inevitably followed. Freezing, banding, and cauterization caused the same response. People across the globe knelt in the blood of cords they'd tried to chop through, only to have their loved ones die reaching for the stranger they had been split from.

Somewhere between the aliens and religious theories were the folks who saw the merging as a path to unity among people, despite the paralyzing terror it created. Stalks sprouted from bodies with no warning, weird and horrifyingly ugly, splitting their midsections and searching for flesh stalk partners. The pairs bonded instantly, and the tissues merged into smooth, blameless flesh. Some people traveled until they found multiple people, and bonds burst from them to connect into throuples and constellations. The fleshy connections created an intimacy many hadn't thought possible. Despite the pain of merging and the upheaval in their lives and jobs, it was impossible to ignore how the bonded were thriving. Smitten lovebirds looked fruitlessly for someone, or something, to thank.

Violence arose from previous companions attacking the newly bonded, but never from the bonded people. The bonded spoke of a newfound connection that was deeper than belief or devotion. Some said they found happiness for the first time in their lives. And the unbonded, their bodies intact and alone, spoke of an emptiness that could not be filled. Many were lost in the joyous clamor over the new connections, people who seemed to wither away, leaving notes describing an invisible stalk throbbing like a phantom limb, reaching for a mate that didn't exist.

Jae was overwhelmed by their odds. The merging hadn't sent them anywhere but to each other. No wonder folks thought a higher power was moving through things, choosing and selecting, and recognizing a powerful love when it was found. Suze teased Jae about being sappy, of crying about beauty when it was just their progeny pumping hormones through their fused systems. But Suze had Jae tuck their nubbin in between them each night, and she sang to it because she couldn't hold it in her arms. It was precious, the mysterious fruit between them. They could hear it in its strengthening heartbeat, feel it in the toughness of its protective sac.

It was Fall when Jae finally asked if the two of them could visit Joanne. The close of the year was already looking odd for everyone, with people blended together in totally different ways, and folks living in parts of the country that were new to them. Familial traditions of gathering to worship or eating together were being made anew, with each generation pair-bonded to different people, and children scattered to new families and sharing their rituals. Collectively, people were choosing to stay in place and figure it out next year.

Jae laid out the data for Suze. Commercial travel was practically impossible, and driving might be more difficult next year. The little one might emerge before then, and Suze would be even more limited if it didn't. They were already working from home, the tethers making it impossible for the schools and lab to work as they had in the past.

Jae kept quiet about wanting to show Joanne their growing fruit. Happy news hadn't kept Joanne from damning them in the past, and its preternatural nature could startle her into turning ugly. Still, Suze and Jae shared a bond that was stronger than ever, no matter what Joanne had forewarned. And though it was weird and uncertain, Jae wanted Joanne to see something even more beautiful was growing between them now, when connections were more important than ever.

Suze had listened to everything Jae said, and didn't say. Gathering data was her way of finding order in chaos, just as Jae's way was to relinquish control and adapt to the unimaginable. Suze calculated the size when the droop, so Jae could buy a baby sling to help carry, and she agreed to visit Joanne. That night, Suze told Jae they were both gathering data, in their way, reaching out for connections that might be there, waiting for them.

Joanne greeted them at the door as formerly as ever, looking them over before stepping back to let them inside. It was even harder to squeeze by her now that they were roped together. Suze twisted to keep their stalk turned away, but it had become a bulbous bob jutting from her back. There was no way Joanne could miss it. Both mother and daughter walked stiffly into the living room, and Joanne still did not comment, just sniffed to make it clear she'd seen it, her eyes darting between them.

Jae pushed the door closed, wearing the practiced mask they used in Joanne's home. Nothing was happening in a way that Jae thought they could jump in and announce their happy news. Letting others stew until they spoke first was one of Joanne's power moves, something guaranteed to push Suze into a regressive state of stress and Jae to become the peacemaker. The whole world was transforming, but Joanne was just the same.

Just as Joanne's body was just the same. Her T-shirt and shorts hung limp, and there was no connection stalk protruding from her back or side. There were no strangers in the house, merged onto her. Suze and Jae both gawked. Somehow, in the months of superficial emails where they had avoided talking about their stalk, they'd never imagined Joanne would still be untethered.

Jae felt their stomach clench, as if the hormones that made them both woozy in the morning were kicking in. Joanne, still alone, still disconnected after all this. Tears threatened, another symptom of the hormones, but Jae's heart broke for Joanne just the same.

Jae set the casserole on the kitchen counter, Suze following along in the easy way they'd developed since they merged. She let Jae move things around and stow the bag, only pulling when Jae stopped to lean against the counter together. Joanne thanked them in the manner she'd developed over decades, and Jae mimicked Suze's neutral reaction, a school of only two fish monitoring a predator that could attack at any time.

Jae wanted to ask why Joanne didn't have a connecting stalk, but they knew she wouldn't know. She was not the only case of a disconnected human. There were scattered reports across the globe of people who'd never searched for their connection, who'd never had the stalk shoot out of their body and clasp that of another person's. Joanne wasn't alone in her experience. But the implications were tragic.

Did Joanne feel left out, when all of the world was finding their stalk mates, when people were crossing borders and oceans, changing their whole lives to find a partner? Did she feel lonesome that no one had shown up on her doorstep, bursting to be with her for the rest of their lives? Did she resent them, tethered together forever, the way they'd wanted, their unholy union sanctioned by aliens, or God, or the global organism that was remaking humanity into its image. It's not like they'd waited for others to approve their union. They'd just made the connection they needed.

"Mom, we have happy news to share with you," Suze said, and Jae knew she never would have if she didn't feel safe, finally safe, in this house. "We aren't sure what it means. We aren't sure what's coming. But we, Jae and I, wanted to share it with you. Our hearts pulled us to you."

Suze took Jae's hand and turned, the bulbous sac hanging from her back stalk throbbing and glistening in the low wattage bulbs Joanne refused to change. Jae turned with Suze, they were tied together as one, but they could still reach far enough to take Joanne's hand and place it on the sac, so the three of them could feel the heartbeat together.

ABOUT THE AUTHOR

Victoria Nations writes Gothic and weird horror about creatures with emotional baggage. Her work is often set in Florida, as well as other wild, liminal places.

Victoria Nations

Victoria's fiction appears in a number of venues, including *Dark Matter Magazine*, "Nightmarish," and "Fish Gather to Listen." Her poetry has been nominated for an SFPA Dwarf Stars Award and appears in *Magpie Messenger*, two HWA Poetry Showcases, and the Bram Stoker Award®-nominated *Mother: Tales of Love and Terror*.

Victoria lives in Florida, USA, with her wife and son, who indulge her love of monsters.

Devilish Deeds

Candace Nola

THE MOON HUNG fat and full overhead in its net of twinkling stars. As the wee hours of night approached, a cloaked figure moved silently through the forest, partially hunched over by the burden they bore. The figure slipped among the trees like a wraith, following the trail into the deepest part of the forest.

Just as the hour drew near, they approached the cluster of Devil's Fingers that grew there in the decaying leaves and underbrush. Crimson appendages, slick with oozing black, seemed to be reaching for the pale-yellow moon, waving to and fro on the breeze as if greeting their arrival. The putrid scent wafted heavily from the ground as the person turned in a circle, studying the forest grounds. More scarlet tips could be seen in the moonlight, just beginning to burst free from their bulbs.

The stench of death filled the air as the breeze picked up, catching the scent of dank earth, decaying wood pulp, and rotting insects. Carrion may have lingered nearby; the reek was so strong a dozen dead animals may very well be piled there beneath the bony birch trees. The figure removed a hefty sack from under their cloak and a small hand trowel. Then, kneeling on the ground, they began digging next to the newest budding plant poking from the ground.

The hand did not shake as it dug. The breath did not tremble, nor did the knees quake. Only a quiet resignation filled the countenance of the digger as they dug. The breeze fell silent, as if respecting the task at hand. Overhead, only the moon bore witness to the deed, like so many times before. An hour later, they rose, sack empty and black ichor staining their face, hands, and cloak. They turned away, retraced their steps to the trail, and vanished into the shadows.

"Did you know these are called Devil's Fingers?" Ryann pointed at a creepy-looking plant at the base of a tree. The tendrils poking up from it looked red in the low light beneath the canopy of the forest. Bits of sunlight streamed in from above, casting weird shadows on the trees and causing the leaves to glint and sparkle like diamonds from the morning dew.

Mary shuddered as Ryann pointed it out, but she kept her eyes on it as Ryann stepped closer to it. Mary stayed on the trail, not wanting to get her shoes dirty, plus something spelled bad, like dead animal bad. At eleven years old, she was curious, but not enough to want dead animal rot on her shoes.

"Why do you know that?" she asked her, watching her poke at the flimsy appendages that stuck upright from the dirt. "And be careful. Something smells rotten," Mary said, looking around for an animal carcass, or maybe a pile of droppings. She didn't want to step on anything gross.

"It's the mushroom. They smell like dead people," Ryann said. "And I know all sorts of things like that," Ryann said, standing up and wiping her hands on the skirt of her old-fashioned black dress. "Like, did you know when mushrooms grow in a natural circle, it's called a fairy ring? Witches used to use them to cast spells late at night."

"That's not true," Mary scoffed. "Is it?"

"Yup, my nana told me," Ryann said with a grin, "but the witch thing might be wrong. Nana tells me so many things that I may be forgetting, but it is definitely called a fairy ring."

"Well, that's kind of cool." Mary shrugged. "Fairies are nice."

"Not these fairies. They're not like the Tinkerbell kind. These were terrible little creatures, downright nasty when you cross one. Magical, for sure, but not the kind of magic that we would want to know." Ryann smiled as she spoke, brushing a stray curl from her eyes.

"These fairies weren't even pretty to look at!" she exclaimed, pulling a fierce-looking face with narrowed eyes and a snarl twisting her lips. She giggled when Mary rolled her eyes. "Anyway, that's what my Nana says."

Mary smiled and watched Ryann spin around in the middle of a ray of sunlight on the trail ahead of them. She laughed when Ryann's hair spun out, swirling like a lion's mane in a strong gust of wind. Her jet-black curls bounced around her shoulders when she finally stopped, and her bright blue eyes twinkled at Mary. The white ruffled collar of her dress and long skirt made her look like a girl from another time. Mary found her dress odd but pretty, though she much preferred her own ripped jeans and t-shirt. Ryann began chanting, holding her arms out as she turned in a slow circle.

"Every time an innocent dies,
devil's fingers begin to grow,
to creep and point and poke the ground,
until the culprit is finally found,
caught in crimson lies."

Ryann loved folklore and witch's tales. Anything creepy that festered in the dark or lived in the shadows seemed to interest her the most. Mary didn't mind it, not really. She found Ryann interesting, but wished she wouldn't recite the scariest rhymes and stories while they were playing in the dark forest.

"Come on, let's go to the stream and look for more rocks," Ryann said, grabbing Mary's hand. Mary ran along with her, grateful to be leaving the forest behind. Summer was for sunlight, and water, and pretty things, not dark, dirt, and disturbing things.

As they ran deeper into the shadows toward the clearing that led to the stream, Mary glimpsed a trio of those hideous plants that Ryann showed her, each one with crimson stalks reaching for the scant light of the sun. A chill ran down her spine as she thought how much they looked like fingers reaching from the dirt.

A few days later, Mary and Ryann left the backyard to go off on yet another adventure. Happy giggles, swinging sack lunches, and skipping arm in arm. Nana watched them go with a soft smile that curved her lips, but worry tugged at her eyes, making them just a bit downcast. The tall trees seemed to burst from the ground where her backyard stopped, an entire forest suddenly appearing as if by magic. Their house was at the end of the street, and the wooded area started there.

Shadows waited just beyond gnarled trunks and climbing vines. Ivy crept along the ground; wildflowers dotted the space until the soil was swallowed by darkness. The narrow trail led for miles, deep into the murky hills, following the stream far along until it turned into the river, wild and rushing.

Nana knew that Ryann loved the forest more than anything. The shadows that called to her, the dark places to explore. All the smells, and the dank, earthy tang in the air when it rained. The curious plants that grew there and the animals that scurried and skittered in the brush and along tree branches.

Things had been going so well for Ryann now. It hadn't been easy for them both to adjust to the world as it changed around them. Nana could only hope that the good things would continue for them both. The girls had been playing together every day since they met, and Mary had only gotten more endearing as the days went on. In fact, she seemed to like the forest almost as much as Ryann.

Mary had come over early for breakfast with her mother, Darlene.

Darlene had lingered over a cup of tea with Nana as the girls scampered about the house, getting ready to go play. Nana was growing quite fond of Darlene. Raising a child was often a lonely job and having Darlene to talk to helped her feel as if she was doing right. Nana turned away from the pull of the trees and went back inside; there was a cobbler to make.

Beneath the cool trees, the girls wandered along the trails, picking flowers, comparing the petal count, and chanting old nursery rhymes. Before too long, they found themselves back where the Devil's Fingers grew; those crimson stalks poking from the ground, waving and oozing with a tarry black liquid. The stench was horrid, and flies buzzed heavily around the area.

"Eww, Ryann. Let's just go play back at the stream. It stinks here."

"But I like them," Ryann said. "Don't you like them? They're just mushrooms. I think they are beautiful."

"They're kind of gross, though. What is that black stuff? They look like they're bleeding." Mary looked at one, stepping closer to crouch over it, taking care not to breathe too deeply.

"Did you know some people say that Devil's Fingers only grow where dead people are?" Ryann whispered, watching Mary intently.

"No. Why would you want to know that?" Her friend said, turning to look at her. Ryann just shrugged and grinned.

"That's why they smell like death. They're feeding off the dead people that are buried beneath them." Ryann laughed and pulled a spooky face.

Mary just stared at her, then around them at the dozen or so sets of creepy tentacle things that grew from fat ivory-colored bulbs. Some reminded her of weird starfish; others looked like pointed claws dripping thick, clotted blood. Others looked more human, stiff and just reaching from the ground, fingertips searching for purchase among the living once more.

"That's just really creepy, Ryann. I don't want to be out here anymore," Mary said finally, her nose screwed up in distaste. "I think I'm going to go home. The smell is making my stomach hurt, anyway."

"What do you mean? You can't leave yet!" Ryann said, her voice starting to shake. "Nana made us lunch, and we were gonna have dinner again, too. Come on, just wait, we can go to the stream."

Mary gave her a long look, then looked again at the ground. She couldn't keep the grimace from her face as she watched Ryann absently lick the black ichor of the plant from her fingers while she waited for Mary to answer.

"That's okay. I really don't feel good," Mary said, backing away. "I'll just see you later."

"Fine, then. Go home," Ryann called after her. She watched Mary walk a bit faster down the trail, staring after her until the shadows swallowed her. Anger flushed her cheeks as red as the crimson tendrils that tapped and writhed against her ankles as her new friend left her standing alone.

Hours later, Ryann emerged from the woods into the backyard, humming a soft tune. Black stains marred her dress. Dirt clung to her knees, and river rocks clanked softly together in her dress pockets. Nana frowned when she didn't see Mary beside her. She waited on the porch for Ryann to reach the steps.

"Where is Mary?" she asked as Ryann made to walk past her into the house.

"Oh, she didn't want to stay," Ryann said glumly. "She really doesn't like the woods as much as I do."

"Not everyone will, Ryann. We talked about this. It's okay to like different things. Did you ask her to stay? You could have just come back here to play or gone to the stream."

"I asked her to stay. She wanted to leave," Ryann said quietly. "Can I go inside now?"

"Yes, go inside and change your clothes. Clean yourself up. Dinner will be ready shortly."

"Okay, Nana. I'm sorry. I just wanted her to stay." Ryann disappeared inside the house, tears in her eyes and a frown darkened her pretty face.

Nana watched her go, her heart breaking for the little girl. She knew it would be a long night, but hopefully, the cobbler and some good old-fashioned story time might bring back some smiles. She stood for a long while, gazing at the woods beyond the lush green lawn. She felt the shadows calling to her, stronger than ever before. She sighed and went inside to tend to Ryann. She could take a walk another day. There was still much to do tonight.

Later that night, Nana sat with Ryann, brushing the young girl's hair before bed. Ryann had been quiet all evening, and her grandmother could feel her sadness radiating off her in waves. She had always been a sensitive child, and being so isolated all the time didn't help matters much.

"Nana, tell me a story," Ryann said, leaning back against her grandmother as she pulled the brush gently through her still-damp hair.

"Which story do you want?" Nana asked.

"About the forest before, and about the fairies that lived there."

"Ah, the Fae folk and their forest," Nana said, a smile filling her voice. "You always did love that tale."

"I love all your stories, Nana."

"Well, once upon a time, long ago, a fairy queen lived in those woods, deep down in the shadows where the moon shone on a single clearing every night. Every night at the stroke of three, in the darkest hours before dawn, the Queen and the fae folk would gather in the light of the moon to feast and frolic and share their tales. They would sing and dance and tell all kinds of stories to please their Queen. But the fae had a dark role to play by day." Nana finished this part, dropping her voice to an ominous whisper.

"What was it, Nana?" Ryann whispered. "What did they do there in the forest?"

"Well, they had to guard it, keep it secret and safe, but from time to time, they had need of things from the human world. Sometimes, they would venture out for a bit of flint, a special cake, pretty ribbon or thread or needles for clothes. The story goes, if you caught a fairy and let them go back to their forest with the trinket they sought, they owed you a favor, a blessing from the Queen. But if you crossed the fae folk, followed them back to the forest, or told anyone their secret, there would be a sacrifice to the queen for your misdeed."

"What kind of sacrifice?" Ryann asked, almost holding her breath.

"The Queen would make a demand, a penance to be paid. If the evildoer dared disobey, they would meet death that very same night, fed to the forest deep, where the crimson fingers creep," Nana said.

Ryann giggled at the ending rhyme. "Is that all true, Nana? Do the Devil's Fingers really grow where the dead people are?"

"Oh, it's very true," Nana said softly, running her hands through Ryann's soft hair. The little girl leaned closer to her, snuggling.

"I wish the Queen wasn't mean, though. It would be nice if she was nice to everyone," Ryann said sleepily.

"Well, the Queen was very kind, and she was a mother, too. But we have to remember that she had to keep her entire village of fairies safe from humans who wanted to hurt them. It was very long ago, but even then, just like now, some humans were afraid of those who were different," Nana said softly, rocking the sleepy Ryann against her chest.

"Did all humans want to hurt the Fae folk, Nana?" Ryann asked, clasping her arms around her grandmother's neck as Nana scooped her up to carry her to bed. Ryann was much too big to be carried, but she loved it when Nana indulged her anyway.

"Not all humans, no. Some humans understood they just wanted to live in peace like all living things. One night long, long ago, a curious human child chased a fae into the forest, wanting to play with him. The child only wanted a friend, for they were so lonely, living so far from the village where there weren't any children."

"What happened to the human child? Did the Queen catch it?"

"Not that night, because something even worse happened," Nana said. She stooped down and placed Ryann on the bed, tucking her in beneath the covers and smoothing the hair from her face.

"That night, the human chased the fairy child so far that it slipped on the rocks by the riverbank, dashing its head against the stone. He was swept away by the icy waters, never to be seen again. The human child got so scared they ran all the way home and told their mother what they had done."

"Oh no," Ryann said sleepily. "How awful."

"Yes, yes, it was because the fairy child was kin to the Queen. Her own nephew, lost to them because a human had gotten too close, and such a curious child could not be trusted to keep their secret safe."

"And then they caught the human?" Ryann asked, peering up at her Nana, ready to hear the ending. It was her favorite part. Nana shook her head before continuing the tale.

"When the fae folk came pounding on their door after tracking the sweet scent of the human child all the way to the cottage beyond the forest, they found a grieving mother instead, already on her knees and begging for mercy. They took her to the Queen that night, where a deal was struck between two grieving women." Nana smiled.

"And that is what made the Queen kind?" Ryann smiled happily.

"Yes, she showed mercy and grace that night, kindness for another that was not like her. She saw that a mistake had been made, an accident not done from malice, just a simple accident caused by their fear of one another instead of them taking time to understand each other. Seeing a human share a sorrow as deep as her own showed her that not all of them were bad. The woman also learned the same lesson. The Queen showed mercy and gave the woman and her child the protection of the Fae."

"What was the deal, Nana?" Ryann asked.

"Ah, sweet child, you already know the deal the Queen and the lady made. It is late. You must sleep now," Nana said. She kissed Ryann's cheek and rose from the bed. "Goodnight, my sweet, may you have pleasant dreams."

"Goodnight, Nana," Ryann murmured, sleep already drawing her eyelids closed as the top of the hour appeared.

Nana watched her for a long moment, a single tear in her eye, as she removed a single item from the pocket of her apron. Her heart ached as fate let itself unfold once again by her hand.

Later that night, as the moon hung fat and full in the starless sky, Nana slipped out of the cabin with her cloak over her shoulders and a sack at her side. She crossed the yard quickly and vanished into the forest, letting memory lead the way to the trail and beyond. She found the crimson stalks faster than before and found the task at hand waiting for her.

Nana knelt and hefted the bundle into her arms and carried it deeper into the thick underbrush. As before, only the moon was there to bear witness to the deed being done in the darkness of the dead wood. Not a sound came as the trowel dug and scraped and dug some more. Not a rodent or bird, or insect of night disturbed her work.

The moon lit the way home when she finally rose from the earth. Black gore dripped from bleeding palms and stained her skirts. She lifted her sack once more, turned in a slow circle, studying her work before she shuffled her way back to the moonlit path and another small but quiet home just down the road from her own silent cabin at the edge of the wood. With one task behind her and another daunting one ahead, her mind strayed to another dark night so very long ago.

Ryann lay weeping across her lap, her slender frame trembling with fear. Jane heard the footsteps, the pounding across the ground, like a stampede of ponies, but Jane knew what was coming for them. The shouts grew louder, angry and mean. Moments later, knocks came upon the door. Jane fell to her knees on the floor. Hair loose and wild, tears soaking her face, her child hiding behind her, shaking with fright.

The door burst open, and the Queen's General stood on the threshold. His face was leathery and ancient, more wrinkled than the bark of a tree. His eyes glinted from the firelight in the hearth. Fury emanated from him in waves that Jane could feel.

"Give us the girl and we will let you live," came the command, spoken in a cold, furious tone. Soldiers crowded in behind him. Barely three feet high, but muscular and fierce. Spears clutched by weathered hands, arrows at the ready on hand-carved bows. Dressed in shades of green and amber and brown, the forest colors of the Fae folk that dwelled there.

"Sir, I beg of you. I beg the Queen. It was an accident. She meant no harm. They were playing, only playing as children do. Tanner had challenged her to a foot race, all in good fun. Please, sir, please. Let me talk to the Queen! Please, I am begging to be heard!" Jane sobbed, her cries loud and desperate in their small cabin. Ryann cried harder behind her, clutching her skirts.

"The Queen does not deal with humankind. Give me the girl or you both shall die." The General sneered. "It makes no difference to me. You are all the same in your evil ways, hunting our kind for sport. Stealing us away to do your bidding and now, sending your children to kill our own!" The general spat the words at her. "The Queen should wage war against you all, if you ask me."

"Please, sir, we are not all so cruel. Surely, there are those who have done you no harm. Those who know to leave out the tokens you seek and sweets to go with them every night on their steps and their windowsills. There are those of us who seek to protect you. We are not all bad. I only request a chance to speak to the Queen, one mother to another. Won't you please take me to her?" Jane sobbed, hands clutched to her breast, eyes pleading with the small but frightful being before her.

Just then, a hush fell over the soldiers who stood in the courtyard outside, and soft footsteps were heard. Jane blinked away tears, silencing her sobs as the fairy soldiers parted, and there, in their midst, stood the Queen. Dressed in garments of silver and tulle, delicate wings flickering so fast upon her back, Jane could scarcely see them. She gasped in surprise at the beauty of the being, and quickly bowed lower, pressing her forehead to the floor.

"Rise, woman, and plead your case." The Queen spoke, her voice that of tinkling bells upon the softest breeze. A gentle touch fell on Jane's shoulder as she lifted herself to her knees, not daring to stand to full height. Her tears began anew as she began to sob through her words. Jane told the tale of Ryann and Tanner and a child's game gone wrong as Ryann shivered silently at her feet, just behind her. Two fairy soldiers on either side of her held spears aloft, ready to take the girl at the Queen's command.

As Jane's pleading fell to a close, the Queen studied her intently. A hush fell over the crowd as the Queen pulled the child to her feet, then bade the girl look at her. Sullenly, the girl raised her face, staring at the Queen wide-eyed, tears still streaking her face.

"Was it an accident, child?" the Queen asked Ryann. "Speak true or it'll be worse for you and your mother."

"Yes, my Queen. We were racing, laughing. I made him swear not to use his wings so it would be fair, but he tripped over a branch. We didn't see it, but we had gotten so close to the riverbank. He fell." She sobbed, sniffling over her words.

"I tried to grab hold of him, but he slipped. He just slipped from the cliff and his wing tore off. He couldn't fly and I couldn't stop it." Ryann's voice broke on the final words, and her body heaved from the weight of her sobs.

The Queen's blue eyes pierced Ryann's teary ones, staring through her as if looking for cracks in the innocence of her youth. Finally, she sighed and stepped back. "Accidents do happen as all parents know. I see no malice here." She waved the soldiers off, and they started marching out the door of the cabin.

"I am no monster," the Queen said to the weeping woman. "I will forgive the girl, but once and only once. Your tears glisten like mine, are as pure as mine were for my kin. However, there are no second chances. Am I understood?"

"Yes, my Queen, oh, thank you so much. She is just a child." Jane wept, relief in her voice and tears flowing once more from relief rather than sorrow.

"So was my nephew," replied the Queen curtly. "See to it that she stays out of our forest, or you both will pay the price."

Jane remained on her knees, wiping tears from her eyes as she studied the almost mirthful look in Ryann's dark eyes. A look that chilled her to her bones.

Nana shook herself from the dreamlike state she had been in, remembering what had set her on this dark road, then looked around. All was quiet as it should be. All was just as she suspected and had seen many times before. A single light. A soft weeping. Weary footsteps pacing, pacing, pacing. Nana raised her fist and knocked on Darlene's door, plastering a worried smile on her face.

The door opened and the distraught woman fell into her arms. Nana caught Darlene, shushed her, and helped the woman back inside. Nana's hands did not shake, and her voice did not tremble. She closed the door and set about the task at hand, swiftly before the dread could consume her, before the memories could flood her mind once more.

Hours later, Nana emerged from the forest, bone-weary and covered in grime. Only a hint of the moon was left to see her home, her fingers leaving black gore on the doorknob as she twisted it open. Tears coursed down pale cheeks, leaving streaks through crimson stains. She made her way upstairs to Ryann's bed and placed a kiss on her brow.

The next few days passed with Ryann close to home, baking fall treats with her Nana and decorating their front path for the October nights. All Hallows Eve drew near, and Ryann loved this time of year. It was the most special night of all for her, even better than Christmas. Nana worried over her and spoiled her with favorite foods and long walks into the forest. They gathered river rocks and jewel-toned leaves.

Ryann made bundles of branches heavy with autumn leaves, dried cornstalks, and wildflowers for their front fence. Nana ventured out one afternoon to the farmers' market in town and brought home pumpkins and gourds and all manner of treats. Ryann was delighted and immediately set about carving pumpkins and preparing pies. Fall was here, and their humble cottage was full of the wonderful scents and sights of the season.

Just after lunch on All Hallows Eve, a knock sounded on their door. Ryann skipped down the hallway just as her nana reached it to greet their visitor.

"Hello there," her nana said to the figure on the porch.

"Hi! Is Ryann home?" a young voice inquired.

Ryann walked over to the door and peered around her grandmother's side. A pretty girl her age stood on the porch. She had bright red hair bordering on orange, a bright smile, and freckled pale skin. Ryann quickly recognized her as one of Mary's school friends.

"Hi," Ryann said shyly.

"Well, come on in. Don't be shy," Nana said, opening the door wider.

"I just wanted to know if Ryann wanted to play," the girl said. "I used to play with Mary. Since she's gone away, I don't have anyone close by anymore except you."

"Sure, we can go play. Is that okay, Nana?" Ryann said with a sweet smile on her face. "This is Gretchen. Mary used to talk about her a lot."

"Just don't go too far," Nana said. "It's nice to meet you, Gretchen. We've missed Mary too since they moved away."

Gretchen stepped inside and looked around the cozy living room. The warm scent of spice filled the air from the glowing candles and a pie baking in the oven. Gretchen sniffed appreciatively as she followed Ryann through the room to the kitchen.

"It smells wonderful here, like my grandma's house," she said. "She's always baking something yummy."

"My nana just put a pie in the oven, and we were making spiced cider for later!" Ryann said, pointing to the stove where a pot sat bubbling over a low flame.

"My grandma used to make warm cider for us," Gretchen said, "but I'm not sure if I've ever had spiced cider. Is it good?" she asked.

"It's the best!" Ryann said. "We can have some when we come back inside. It'll be ready by then."

"Alright. I'd like that," the other girl said as she followed Ryann outside and onto the back porch.

Nana followed them, wiping her hands on her apron.

"Don't go too far, girls, and don't go to the stream. It'll be too high after all the rain," she called after them.

"Don't worry, Nana. I know!" Ryann called over her shoulder. She flashed a dark smile at her nana, then grabbed Gretchen's hand, leading her into the woods.

Nana lifted a single hand to wave, a sad smile on her face. Another long night was in store, but peace would be at the end, long overdue peace. She stood quietly in the warm embrace of the fall sunshine to listen to the whispers in the wind. Whispers that spoke of fall nights and dark deeds, of anger and sacrifice, of a fairy queen with wrath in her eyes.

Jane hid Ryann beneath her bed, shaking with fright as the marching feet came closer. The howls of the ghouls and their beasts outside made her blood run cold. The soldiers' feet pounded, marching two by two, spears in hand, led by the General in his war cloaks. The Queen led the way, fury changing the ethereal creature into one of black smoke and roaring flame, seething with anger. The wings beat scarlet embers in the night sky as the Queen approached.

Jane fell to her knees as the cabin door burst open. Soldiers flooded inside, surrounding her, searching the rooms. The Queen hovered over the cowering woman. Jane screamed in terror, seeing the ghoulish countenance of the raging fairy queen in the form of a banshee of ancient descent. Tattered shrouds of smoky gray enveloped her delicate form; embers burst from her flaming wings, and her eyes were now black, soulless voids.

"Where is the murderer?" she roared. Her words struck daggers of pain in Jane's skull, and she screamed, bowing face down on the floor.

She didn't need to reply as the General stormed into the room, dragging a crying Ryann. Soldiers surrounded her, each one grasping a trembling limb in their iron shackles. Jane reached for her daughter, screaming for mercy, for help, for anyone to hear them.

"She tried to hide her, my Queen! Kill her! Kill them both!" the General demanded. The soldiers took up the shout. "Kill the girl! Kill them both! Murderers! Murderers!"

"Silence!" the Queen roared, silencing all at once. Even the forest outside ceased to breathe, time stopped. The wind froze. The moment hung there in the silent cabin. Chaos met with timeless rage.

"What say you, woman? Do you beg for your child now? Tell me how she is innocent now! Tell me more of your lies, human!"

"Please, my Queen. She's all I have. All I have left." Jane sobbed. "How could I know what evil she would hide? I swear. I only tried to protect her as any mother would! She carries a black soul, a cursed mind. She is a burden, but she is mine, my only child."

"You. Don't. Know?" the Queen hissed into the frozen air. "You don't know what evil your child has done? What murders she has committed? You are innocent of her crimes, are you? Shall I punish her alone then and leave you to watch her die?"

"No, please, my Queen. Do not take my child," Jane begged. "Take me first, take me instead. Let me serve you until her debt is paid. Please,

I beg mercy, my Queen, if not for her, then for me. From the broken heart of one mother to another, please."

"Serve me?" the Queen sneered, wings beating gently to set the being down, eye-level with the human woman that begged at her feet. "You wish to pay her debt? To serve me to save her soul?"

"Anything, my Queen," Jane said. "I'll serve any penance. Just let her live."

"Your child has slain the fairy kin. Has set the nursery alight this very night. All the babies yet to live were burned within the flames: my prince, my princess, my future bloodline. Gone in smoke and ash." The Queen's eyes glittered coldly in her pale face. She gripped Jane's chin in her skeletal hand and studied her tear-stained face.

"For every soul your child has slain, you will each deliver two more. A mother's life you will take, and Ryann will take her child, to be buried in the fairy wood until your debt is paid. You will age eternally slow, while Ryann remains a girl. The only way to free yourself is for you to take her life," the Queen said, her voice slow and sinister, a cruel and sadistic rhyme that seemed to restart time.

"One night of every year, you can save yourself. On All Hallows' Eve, beneath the forest leaves, cut her throat and bury her deep, where the crimson fingers creep. Then, and only then, will you find eternal peace.

"Is this the debt you wish to owe? To save that murderous child?" the Queen snarled. She hovered again, wings beating furiously in the air as she took flight once more. Smoke swirled around her, scattering ash below.

"Speak, woman, or watch her die slow!"

Jane watched as the Queen held the dagger to Ryann's throat, eyes glittering like jewels as the child trembled and cried.

"Yes!" Jane sobbed. "Yes, my Queen, we will serve."

Nana sighed and shook herself. The memory had held her tight. Jane was gone now, a young mother burdened with the sins of the monster she bore. She was Nana now. Unnatural life lived at an unnatural price, a price she had once begged to pay, had taken its toll, and Nana made a choice.

She stepped inside to the black stone hearth and removed a dagger crusted with jewels. She slid the weapon into her pocket and donned her black cloak. All Hallow's Eve approached. The sun hung low in the darkening sky as tears filled Jane's ancient eyes. It was time to end the debt and put her soul to rest.

She stepped outside and walked to the woods, following the trail. Two little girls waited beneath the trees where crimson fingers crept, but only one would return afterward while Nana wept.

ABOUT THE AUTHOR

Candace Nola is a multiple award-winning author, editor, and publisher. She writes poetry, horror, dark fantasy, and extreme horror content. She is the creator of Uncomfortably Dark Horror, which focuses primarily on promoting indie horror authors and small presses with weekly book reviews, interviews, and special features.

Fun Gus

Pedro Iniguez

Every cut told a story, her skin a book of pain and grief. The crisscross she'd etched into the crook of her arm was from the time her parents got a divorce. The diagonal gash she'd cut into the fleshiest part of her inner forearm was from the time Mark first laid hands on her. As for the vertical cut below her wrist...

Kayla grew tired of staring at the scars and rolled down her sleeves. They were reminders of lapses in judgment. When weakness had taken a stranglehold on her. She stared at the polaroid in her trembling hand. It had begun to fade, diminished to an ugly, dull yellow. A snapshot in time of wonderous days and electric summer nights. In the picture, Mark wrapped his arm around her waist at the county fair as she held the small octopus plushie he'd won at a game of ring toss. Ten years. They'd spiraled down the drain, though she'd refused to see the signs for what they were. The abuse, the gaslighting.

Her phone pinged with another notification. They'd been rolling in all day, and she wasn't sure she wanted to keep up anymore. She considered deleting the app and giving up, but Maritza told her to at least give online dating a shot. A real shot. That it would, at the very least, keep her distracted from the heartache. From certain ideations.

With her free hand, Kayla pulled the phone from her back pocket and stared at her tired, warped reflection on the black screen just before turning it on. This time, she'd matched with some guy five miles away. She looked over his picture. A buzz cut. Neatly trimmed beard. Shades. She scrolled down his profile. He'd been in the Marines and loved deer hunting. That was enough. How they had been matched was beyond her, but she couldn't bring herself to date a guy like that. A person who took pleasure in killing for sport.

She sighed. Maybe it was her. Maybe she was too fragile. A big softy. She'd never find someone like this. Not through a screen. Through an app that took all of a person—their dreams, desires, and fears—and trivialized them into a digital checklist for desperate, judgmental eyes. Maybe she was destined to be alone forever. She felt the tears start to pool under her eyes. She choked back the feelings. No. Toughen up. You can do this. You have to be tough. Learn to love yourself, to accept the fact that you can be alone and thrive.

She set the phone on the kitchen counter, stood over the trash bag at her feet, and let the Polaroid drop into its maw. The last of the reminders and keepsakes. No more Mark. She pulled the drawstrings tight and heaved the trash bag into the garbage bin outside. When she came back, her phone had been blinking. Another notification.

She braced for disappointment and opened her phone. This time, she had matched with another user by the name of Gus Estrada about twenty miles outside of town. This guy was either a bot or had a real sense of humor because his profile picture was a cartoon mushroom. A red cap for a head speckled with white scales and a smile and large googly eyes for a face. His profile listed building model trains as his favorite hobby. He loved anime, and his favorite movie was Miyazaki's Spirited Away. And, apparently, he was an oyster mushroom farmer. That explained the goofy avatar picture.

Finally. It was almost refreshing. Someone so different from the poorly matched suitors the app had been feeding her lately: the truck drivers with the Don't Tread on Me flags as backdrops; the motocross-obsessed fanboys; the roided-out gym bros in tank tops.

Before she'd fully realized what she'd done, her fingers were gliding over her phone's keyboard. She stared at the draft waiting on her screen:

> Kayla: Hi! Looks like we matched up. Nice to meet you.

A part of her wanted to delete the message, the app, forget it all and find another way to cope. To tackle the demons squatting in her head. But she knew herself, she'd just roll into a ball and squirrel away at home all day, sobbing, sleeping, and maybe worse. She needed to break out of her comfort zone. To reject the pull toward the darkness. Maybe just this once.

What the hell. Kayla tapped the *send* button and started to make dinner.

A series of vibrations woke her. Her phone rumbled and moaned on the nightstand like a shivering animal. She squinted at the blinding light as she opened her phone.

> Gus: Hey! Nice to meet you.

> Gus: Sorry I'm writing back so late. I got a little busy earlier.

> Gus: Anyway, feel free to reach out anytime. You seem cool.

Kayla smirked, turned off her phone, and went back to sleep.

The next morning, the darkness had a hold of her and she knew it was going to be one of those days. Where nothing seemed to matter and there was no point in bothering to get up. She called in to work and said she was feeling sick.

The thoughts had crept back like little vermin, gnawing at her mind, torturing her like they always had. The pain was akin to a profound void opening in her chest. An emptiness nothing could fill. Ten years was a long time to invest in a person. It was almost like you'd given a piece of your heart away. Something you could never get back. She eyed her forearm. Wounds that would never heal.

She considered the bottle of sleeping pills on the nightstand. Would it be quick? Like drifting into sleep? Or would the moment be drawn out by excruciating stomach cramps? Either way, she yearned for that darkness to wash over her, make it all go away.

Her phone vibrated.

> Gus: Good morning. Sorry if I came off a little weird last night. I won't message you again, but I wish you the best.

Well, at least this one was polite.

> Kayla: Hey. No worries. Just woke up.

> Gus: :)

She hesitated. She wasn't sure where to take the conversation. It had been ages since she'd spoken to another man outside of work. Mark wouldn't allow her to have guy friends. And she hadn't dated in just as long. She wrote the first thing that came to mind.

> Kayla: So why mushrooms?

> Gus: I'm sorry?

> Kayla: Your bio says you're a mushroom farmer.

> Gus: Yup. They're awesome! They're delicate but resilient. Like me lol

Fun Gus

Kayla: Oh yeah? You must be fun at parties lol

Gus: LOL They call me Fun Gus.

Kayla: Haha. Clever. Fungus. Don't know much about mushrooms. They're like plants right?

Gus: Not really. Sort of. Mushrooms don't produce photosynthesis. The fungus lives underground, feeding off nutrients until we see their fruiting bodies break the soil. Then the mushroom spreads its spores, those germinate into hyphae, then into mycelium, which would be like the roots, and the cycle begins again!

Kayla: Neat lol Sorry if I don't add much to this conversation.

Gus: I'm sorry. Tell me about you! Why are you on this dumb app anyway?

Kayla: I don't know tbh. My friend kinda made me. Just in a rough patch I guess. Trying anything to get my mind off things.

Gus: Yeah same here. Not really sure why I torture myself though. Everyone here kind of sucks lol

Kayla: Amen to that.

Gus: Haha. Listen, I've gotta go tend to my mushrooms. I'm working on a new hybrid strain. Is it ok if I hit you up later?

Kayla: Yeah, that's cool. TTYL.

Kayla didn't hear back from Gus for a few days. She'd begun to wonder if, this time, *she* had scared someone off for a change. Maybe he had picked up on her scent, known that she was irreparably damaged goods.

She pushed the thought of Gus from her head and focused on work, on the day-to-day stuff. Routines, she'd been told, were good for mental health. As soon as she got home from work one night, the phone vibrated in her pocket.

> Gus: Hey Kayla, sorry I haven't messaged you. Something came up. But everything's ok now. How are you?

> Kayla: I've had better days.

> Gus: I know how you feel. Seems like that's been the story of my life lately.

> Kayla: What's going on?

> Gus: Just some stuff I'd probably bore you with. But let's just say I've made efforts to change my life for the better for once.

> Kayla: I could definitely use that mindset.

> Gus: Sometimes you just have to take the plunge into unknown waters to start living the life you want.

> Kayla: You're telling me if I do, I can finally have my cottage in the woods and live happily ever after? Like a fairytale?

> Gus: Yes.

> Gus: And you deserve it.

There came a tingle in the pit of her stomach. She wasn't quite sure what it was, but Gus wasn't wrong, she knew that. Coming from him, someone who'd also been going through the pain, the words resonated in ways they never had with other people. Fuck it. Time to take the plunge. Even if it was a small one.

> Kayla: Hey, would you like to meet up for some coffee?

> Gus: I don't know about that. I don't like being in public places.

> Kayla: I get it. How about you come over?

> Gus: I don't have a car at the moment. Sorry.

> Kayla: Ok. I can go over.

> Gus: I don't know if that's a good idea.

> Kayla: What are you afraid of? I thought you said we should take the plunge. Just coffee. Come on.

There was a lull in the conversation. A drawn-out moment of doubt and anxiety where Kayla found herself repeatedly rubbing her cheek and running a hand through her hair. She was losing him again. After ten minutes, he responded.

> Gus: You're right. It's time I stop living in fear. OK.

Kayla drove north along the interstate for half an hour, watching as the houses gave way to trailer parks until those faded and the woods reclaimed the world. At the mouth of a narrow rural road, Kayla saw a red mailbox, the address Gus had given her hand-painted on its side. She turned right onto a gravel path that terminated outside a dilapidated house nestled in the woods.

When she reached the porch, she found the screen door slightly ajar. "Hello?" she called out. No reply. Kayla let herself in and gagged as a foul stench assaulted her nostrils. An earthy funk. Not quite rot, not quite spunk, but some other musk she couldn't quite pin. Inside, the air was stifling. Almost immediately, she began to sweat as beads of moisture dotted her face.

The house was in disarray: the nicotine-stained ceiling, the pizza boxes littering the coffee table, the flies buzzing in and out of a gash in the window screen, the stack of dirty dishes piled on the sink. Shattered segments from a model railroad track lay scattered on the floor. Large plastic bins filled with soil lined the walls of the living room; beside them, bags bursting with what appeared like white mold and stems sprouting from small tears bearing small blue-gray caps. Oyster mushrooms.

A picture frame sat on a mantle atop the fireplace. She pulled it down. The picture of a man and a woman. All smiles. She knew the look. Of people in love. Numerous fingerprints smudged the otherwise dusty frame. Kayla gave the living room another look over and scowled. This is why Gus was so hesitant. She felt a pang of guilt and second-hand embarrassment for him. She wasn't supposed to see any of this. How could anyone? This squalor was enough to turn anybody off. Instantly, she regretted having come. This was the house of someone who'd hit rock bottom, someone who had been living worse off than she had. She turned toward the door when she heard the clacking of the keyboard in the other room.

"Gus?"

Against her better judgment, she tiptoed up the hallway until she came to a small, dark bedroom tucked away toward the back of the house. There was a tickle in her throat, and she stifled a cough with her hand. Dust and pollen hung on the scant slivers of sunbeams piercing the curtains. She fanned away the cloud of dust lingering near her face.

When Kayla's eyes adjusted to the dark, she gasped, hunched over, and nearly retched on the floor. There, illuminated by the blue light of the computer screen, a large fan-shaped cap crowned a crooked stipe sprouting from the open cavity of a man's temple. It was budding from what appeared to be exposed brain matter. The man just sat in his chair, staring lifelessly at his screen through bloodshot eyes.

Like thin shoots, the mushroom's mycelia sprouted down the man's mouth, crept along his chest and arms, and onto the mouse and keyboard, tapping the keys like human fingers would.

"Gus?" Kayla said, her voice breaking. "Oh my God, is that you?" She shook her head, as if wishing away the nightmare.

Her eyes followed the man's arms, which hung limply at his sides. A handgun lay below his dangling fingers, where the carpet was stained dark burgundy, like spilled wine.

Mycelial threads crept down the man's lower jaw and pulled it open. The tendrils slid inside his mouth and began to flap his purple tongue. The noises that slithered from his orifice were akin to the sounds of wet cement being stirred, a defilement of human speech.

Kayla wanted to turn back, to run for the car, but her legs had turned to useless trunks of meat, her feet seemingly having melted to the floor.

The mushroom-thing's mycelia began to clack over the keyboard, stringing together words on the screen.

Kayla, I love you.

Kayla shook her head. "No," was all she managed to utter as tears streamed down her cheeks.

It's me, Gus. I know this isn't what you expected.

"B-but, you're dead," she said, eyeing the pistol on the floor.

Delicate, but resilient.

"I don't understand," Kayla said, wiping the tears from her eyes. How could she? How could anyone?

Pedro Iniguez

We deserve more than the sacks of flesh we inherited at birth. Join me. You won't feel pain. Not ever again.

For a moment she stood there. The scars on her wrists throbbed, reminding her of all the things that had ever brought her to the brink. Her parents, every failed relationship, her job, the pressures of the world caving in on her. She wasn't cut out for any of it. A tiny voice echoed in her head. Wouldn't life be simpler as a mushroom?

She remembered their conversation. The mushroom breeding, the new strain. This is what he'd meant. She swallowed back the hesitation, the knot forming in the back of her throat. Take the plunge. "What do I need to do?"

Embrace me. Kiss me. We'll be together forever. In our own little house in the woods. Like a fairytale.

Kayla took a timid step forward. The mycelial threads parted Gus's blue lips as they awaited hers. She hunched down and cradled the back of his neck with her hand, her fingers sliding up his disheveled hair. Leaning in, she touched her cheek to his, felt his stubble scrape along her skin. He smelled of musk and mud and rot, and she winced. Gus, or the mushroom, she wasn't sure anymore, leaned in and pressed his lips to hers. They were cold and lifeless strips of flesh. She closed her eyes and felt his tendrils work their way into her mouth and nostrils.

There came a tingling sensation in the back of her head and the world began to blur. Soon, she'd be free from pain and grief. Soon, her fleshy, fertile shell would be host to new fruiting bodies. To a new life. Before she gave herself over to the fungus, she shot the computer screen a sidelong glance. Multiple chat boxes were open, bearing the avatars of several women.

> Maya Wilson: You're different.

> Amanda Klines: I want you so bad. I need to see you.

> Deborah Espinoza: Shoot me your address,
> I'll head over after work!

As her heart skipped a beat, Kayla's eyes darted back to Gus, his pale face pressed against her skin, his lips locked with hers. Her lungs struggled for air as the realization struck. No. This was all wrong. This wasn't love. She'd made another mistake. This time someone, something worse than Mark.

Perhaps she could try to warn the others before it was too late. Before they'd stumbled into the clutches of an online predator. If she could only reach for the gun. She planted both hands on Gus's chest and tried to push away, to break free from his embrace.

But Kayla's head began to throb and flare as thin strands of mycelium budded from her ears. A warm stream of blood trickled down her nose. She heard new voices sprout in her head. Alien thoughts she'd never owned. Like dreams of a family. Of spreading her love and joy with Gus. With as many others as possible. She gave in and let her muscles unwind. The darkness gave way to a bright light behind her eyes. Yes. That was divine. Let the women come. They'd see. This new life that awaited truly was a fairy tale come true.

ABOUT THE AUTHOR

Pedro Iniguez is a horror and science-fiction writer from Los Angeles, California. He is a Rhysling Award finalist and a Best of the Net and Pushcart Prize nominee.

He is the author of *Mexicans on the Moon: Speculative Poetry From a Possible Future.*

Forthcoming, his horror fiction collection, *Fever Dreams of a Parasite* (Raw Dog Screaming Press), and his SFF collection, *Echoes and Embers: Speculative Stories* (Stars and Sabers Publishing), are slated for 2025 releases.

Notho-Pan: A City on Angel Wings

Maxwell I. Gold

I saw that defiled plastic race, rotten and decayed, their mouths filled with ashy fruit-bodies and fungal fractals that stained the sides of their cheeks. Streets in the old city were subsumed by ivory fibers, thick and heavy as they made themselves known revealed from dank nethers beneath nascent foundations; a reminder nothing was forever, except the wings of Notho-Pan. The chorus of asphyxiated cries struggled to be heard betwixt bent stipe-stalks fading into yellow shades, and cloudy spore-songs bubbling across the skin of the mushroomed skies that never seemed to end.

Blood and mucus mixed with the bitter taste of salt and sour dreams clogged my burning throat while the stars, or what I thought were stars, slowly bulged like some mutilated brambleberry-brains until all I knew ruptured around me in a fat, sumptuous cataclysm. Everyone around me, the thoughtless fools who took the woods and whispers for granted, were the first to go, their minds and bodies made sour. Toxic salt gurgled at my feet as if the very earth was pleased to swallow the poor, pathetic city and those who foolishly built their hovels on the back of that Great Mushroom God, Notho-Pan whose hideous wings closed around us, leaving our mouths full of gloom and death.

ABOUT THE AUTHOR

MAXWELL I. GOLD is a Jewish-American prose poet, author, and editor with an extensive body of work comprising over 300 poems. His writings have earned a place alongside literary luminaries in the speculative fiction genre. His work has appeared in numerous literary journals, magazines, and anthologies including *Weird Tales Magazine*, *Spectral Realms*, *Chiral Mad 5*, and many more. Maxwell's work has been recognized with multiple nominations including the Pushcart Prize and the Bram Stoker Awards®.

A Dark Infestation
Ariana Khaim

Ammonia, plastic sheets, mask, goggles, jumpsuit. Vanessa went through the checklist again on this day, just like she'd done every day since taking this godforsaken job.

"You ready?" Marcus asked. He was suited up and carried two jugs of bleach.

"Honestly, I'm never ready," she said with a groan. "Are you sure it's our turn today and not the guys with the holy water?"

Marcus sighed. "I'm sure."

The two of them then left the shack their employers liked to refer to as one of their "guesthouses." There were signs it had been nice once. The dishes were hand-painted, but years of neglect had left them chipped and cracked. The white paint on the outside was peeling. None of that compared to the job site, though.

As they trudged up the hill, it came into view: Wellington Manor. What had once been a gorgeous gothic mansion loomed over the estate. Battlements crested with parapets coated the house. It was adorned with turrets topped with spires and ornate lightning rods. It had once been a sight to behold. Today, as they drew closer, the truth of it became clearer.

The lightning rods were rusted and bent. The battlements and ramparts were crumbling. The windows that weren't shattered were cracked, and the paint peeled to reveal tendrils of black mold.

Vanessa and Marcus masked up a solid fifteen meters before reaching the house. They had started around the same time, and both cleaners, on separate occasions, had made the mistake of drawing near without their PPE and had breathed in mold spores. Both times, they'd wound up in the basement of Samuel and Kara's cottage. The other guesthouse had been converted into a base of operation for the onsite exorcists, complete with a padded room for people who were possessed. They had each spent three days down there listening to them pray and being periodically sprayed with holy water. That's what it took to treat a minor exposure and restore the infected individual's sanity.

The foyer was much like the outside; signs of the manor's former glory were everywhere, from Persian rugs to massive paintings of prominent Wellington family members. All of them were left faded and frayed by the mold.

"Why bother keeping these things?" Vanessa asked, looking at a painting that was now just tattered canvas in an old frame.

Marcus asked, "Why bother trying to keep this whole house at all?"

They were scheduled to work on the third floor. They trudged up the stairs, following a set path that showed signs of the exorcists' handiwork, like bible pages taped to the railing and patches clean of mold.

"Do you think the Torah or the Qur'an would also work?" Vanessa asked jokingly.

"I don't know much about protocols in other countries, but my brother went to Japan recently," he said, tapping on his chest. "He got me this thing called an *omamori*, which has a—JESUS, FUCK!"

Vanessa tensed and looked around. Marcus was staring at a gap in the railing that had been there long before their arrival, but this time, there was an apparition leaning over the ledge. It was a shadow in the shape of a woman. She had her arms spread out as though she were leaning on the railing that used to be there.

"Samuel is losing his touch," Vanessa groaned. "That's the first time I've seen an echo there."

Marcus breathed heavily, which wasn't easy given the mask. "The thing nearly gave me a heart attack."

After a moment, the apparition suddenly fell forward and plummeted to the ground. They heard soft echoes of her screams and a slam. Vanessa craned her neck and peered over the railing without leaning on it. It looked like another black mold patch was forming where the phantom had landed.

She let out a frustrated sigh. "Looks like more work for us."

They only ran into smaller echoes on their way up. That was the term the owners used to describe the apparitions reliving their deaths. Vanessa had been warned about them before signing on, but they'd also reassured her that the exorcists would keep them under control.

Upon reaching their assigned floor, they entered the room nearest the stairs. It was a guest bedroom and one of the few places where no tragedy had struck. For this reason, the Wellingtons had once tried to move all their most treasured heirlooms into the space, but this had attracted more mold, so their treasures had been spread out and the room made into one of the places where the cleaners would warm up. Moving heirlooms to another house ran the risk of spreading the infestation.

They got to work spraying what patches of mold they could find with ammonia and then scrubbing it down. They cleaned and wiped every surface that they could reach. Then they hung up plastic sheets and set out box fans for whatever remained. She wondered how their cleaning fluids would work on a normal mold infestation; everything they used was mixed with holy water, courtesy of Kara. She specialized in sacraments performed on objects, while Samuel focused on cleansing larger areas and exorcizing people.

After that, Marcus and Vanessa split up to cover two rooms. Doing so for these rooms was one of the few pieces of advice from the Wellingtons they'd initially ignored, but not for long. One room was the place where Daria Wellington had murdered her cheating husband,

and her echo became aggressive in the presence of men. The room Marcus worked on had been where her father, Darius Wellington, had died of a heart attack. It was no secret that the man was a lech, and his echo was infamous for groping women.

They were back together for the fourth room, which was also the one Vanessa hated the most. She prayed for an easy day, a day where the exorcists had managed to get as close to clearing out a room as you could in a cesspool like Wellington Manor, but as usual, they heard weak moaning upon entering.

On the bed, there lay the dark silhouette of a woman shakily reaching up toward the other silhouette, which was of a man holding something. There was no echo of whatever he held, but it seemed to fill him with joy as he swung it around and completely ignored the woman on the bed.

The Wellingtons had built their fortune through the coal mines on their property. It had taken a few short years of mining for them to get enough money to build this house. The man who had founded their business, Albert Wellington, had nine children: eight daughters and one son. His wife had passed shortly after giving birth to the male heir Albert had so desperately desired, and Albert himself passed of an aneurysm shortly thereafter. This echo was one of the first reported, and just about the strongest. It would manifest right after the exorcists did their rounds.

The moaning didn't stop until they left the room.

Vanessa groaned and leaned against the wall, panting. "I think I need a break."

Marcus didn't protest. He just followed her as she left the house, counted the distance until she was far enough away that no spores would reach her, and ripped off her mask. Even from so far away, the air around the manor was stale, but the first unmasked breath she took may as well have been the air of Yosemite.

"Why," she groaned, "do they even bother trying to keep this place up? In my hometown, we had a haunting with one echo— phantom—apparition—*whatever you want to call it*, and the owners immediately had the place demolished. Do you know how bad it is for the haunting to start manifesting as something physical like mold?"

"It's not my place to ask those kinds of questions," he said.

"Well, make an educated guess."

Marcus stood quietly and thought for a moment before saying, "Sentimentality. And pride. Only the richest families get to have houses like these, *especially* if they're haunted."

"What?" she asked.

"They think they're like royalty—that they should get special treatment."

"Last I checked, they demolished half of Buckingham Palace to deal with shit like this," she said. "Twice."

Sometimes tragedies happened and a haunting wouldn't manifest, and if it did it could be stopped if it was dealt with early on. Nations invested a lot into looking out for the subtlest signs of a haunting to protect their national landmarks, which were sometimes the ancestral homes of rich families.

He shrugged. "But it's still standing. Besides, the money they pay us is a drop in the bucket compared to what the Wellingtons make in a year. Why not piss away some cash and keep on applying for landmark status? Then taking care of this place practically becomes free."

That stung. Vanessa only kept at this job because it was the best pay she'd ever had. A month where the balance in her savings account went up was no longer a rare treat, but a regular occurrence. Good money to her was pocket change to her employers.

They masked up and returned to the house. They did not like the look of the new patch of mold on the floor, so even though they were supposed to work on the entrance on their next shift, they went ahead and sprayed it down and mopped it up before continuing their work.

The next room they went to was the one Vanessa hated the least: The ballroom. They would almost never see an echo in there after the exorcists had done their rounds. The walls were decorated with gold and the floors were marble, which mold had trouble growing on, and the light outside shone through the large windows, making it the least dreary place in the house.

Given the lack of any signs of mold, they only needed to mop the floors with disinfectant. Sometimes, Vanessa couldn't help herself and tried to dance with her mop, forgetting the stress of her job by losing herself in a Gilded Age fantasy. She mopped in large circles, and imagined herself as an heiress at the height of the Wellington family's glory, when the house was a shining example of opulence and beauty.

Perhaps that's why she didn't notice the echo until she almost bumped into it. When she came close, she let out a small gasp and fumbled with her mop, nearly dropping it. She'd never seen the echo of this room before, so she had trouble recalling it.

There was a woman on the edge of the dance floor. Vanessa could tell by her silhouette that she wasn't a debutante or an esteemed guest, but a maid. Having never seen this echo before, she let her curiosity take over, and she leaned in close. The woman's hair was coarse with a few loose curls hanging free, and the bridge of her nose was wide.

Vanessa had to sidestep out of the way as the woman was yanked away from the fringes of the ballroom to the center of the dance floor by an unseen person. Her movements were stiff at first but became more graceful as time went on. And just as Vanessa began to forget that the woman would die soon, her dance partner picked her up and slammed her into the ground.

The woman sat there, shocked, and tried to sit up, but was then pushed down again. She started clawing at her throat without touching it. She kicked and thrashed, but eventually went limp. Her apparition vanished, and a new patch of black mold formed in its place.

Marcus, who had also been entranced by the display, snapped back to reality and walked over to Vanessa. He grabbed her shoulder and gently shook her. "Come on, are you okay?"

"Do you think that was in the middle of a party?" Vanessa asked. When Marcus said nothing, she added, "She wasn't holding a broom. She was standing straight. She looked like she was from the time before recorded music, but she danced well." She looked at Marcus. "She wasn't alone with him when she was killed."

"Yeah," he grumbled.

"Why?"

The question was followed by silence. Neither of them had an answer because neither of them were monsters.

So, the mold answered them.

The woman's echo emerged from the dark patch but warped this time. Her arms and fingers were longer and crooked, her spine was stretched so she was six feet tall, and her neck was bent at an unnatural angle.

Vanessa was so shocked by the sight that she stood frozen in place. She'd heard about surges in hauntings. They were rare, but they should have realized what was going to happen when they'd seen the phantom on the stairs. Marcus, on the other hand, acted quickly and shoved Vanessa away as the echo reached down toward them. With her out of its reach, it wrapped its arms around his chest, leaving splotches of black mold on his protective suit and mask.

The creature turned to her and hissed, "Because he could." Then, it grabbed Marcus's mask and tore it off before vanishing.

Marcus doubled over, hacking and wheezing. Vanessa took a few cautious steps toward her friend, unsure of what to do. Nothing like this had ever happened before.

That's when Marcus turned and looked at her, his eyes completely black. Vanessa let out a scream. She turned and ran back toward the entrance, only to see that the mold they'd cleaned up minutes earlier was returning, and another echo was emerging from it. She turned around and ran back toward the ballroom. A twisted grin spread across Marcus's face when he saw her, but she acted quickly.

The ballroom windows stretched from floor to ceiling, and many of them were broken. She dove through one, tearing her suit and cutting her arm on a shard of glass. She landed with an ungraceful thud, clutching her mask to her face, before bolting in the direction of the exorcists' house. It was the first time she was grateful for the fact that the manor was on top of a hill.

She'd never sprinted with a heavy mask on before. Vanessa was a good runner. She never skipped a cardio day, but she was already running out of breath. The fact that she was screaming for help at the top of her lungs didn't help.

She counted each step, listening for Marcus between every holler but refusing to look back. She didn't want to see his face distorted by hate. She felt a brief burst of relief when she heard shouting and a door slamming at the base of the hill.

She passed the threshold, ripped off her mask, and threw it behind her, hoping it would hit Marcus and make him trip up, but it had the opposite effect.

She'd overestimated the distance between them. With her arm stretched out behind her, he was able to grab it and pull her to the ground. Vanessa tried to scramble to her feet and simultaneously crawl away, but Marcus grabbed her by the ankles and started dragging her back toward the house. He meant to get her to breathe in the spores!

She dug her fingernails into the dirt as he pulled and screamed, "Why? What will this solve?"

Marcus's response was just a bunch of guttural grunts because that's all that was left of the echoes: mindless, senseless hate.

She twisted, throwing off Marcus's balance, and kicked his feet out from under him before clambering away and diving one more time. She didn't want to block the exorcists' line of fire.

They were armed with what amounted to high-powered water guns filled with holy water. It was a silly idea, but it got the job done, so nobody questioned it. When the water hit Marcus, he collapsed to the ground, screaming and writhing. Vanessa backed away while Samuel and Kara grabbed her friend and got to work dragging him into the padded room. When it was all said and done, the only thing Vanessa could bring herself to do was numbly slog back to her assigned shack and take a long shower.

When she was done, Samuel was waiting at her door. He made her tea and offered her words of reassurance. Vanessa didn't thank him. Instead, she asked, "How is he?"

"There is good news," he said. "We added a few touches to your PPE, but Marcus had a little something extra that helped."

He held up the *omamori,* an embroidered silk bag on a string with Japanese writing on the front. "Normally, a single extra charm doesn't make a difference, but this was a source of joy for him. He might not be too far gone! I'll have to report on this."

Vanessa looked at the charm, a loving gift from a family member, and tuned out most of what Samuel said. He mentioned things about theories and sentimentality and inconsistent studies, but it didn't matter to her. She had her answer.

"It's nothing," she said.

"I'm sorry?" Samuel asked.

"That's what the manor is. Nothing. A lack of love—of light." She held the charm up. "And this is love."

Samuel left her soon after that, and Vanessa went to bed, scratching at the wound where her arm had been cut. It still itched. She'd disinfect it in the morning. Right now, she was too tired to care.

ABOUT THE AUTHOR

Ariana Khaim is an aspiring writer based out of New York City. She was raised by two refugees from Afghanistan who made sure she never abandoned her passion for writing and books, which often overlap with her fascination with the macabre.

WOLD

Jef Rouner

"You're...88.7...with Marshall Nettles. You know this is the truth. You just had to hear someone say it."

Deidre flinched slightly as Zeke let out a yell of triumph when the radio station finally came in. He had been eagerly talking about this moment for the whole two-hour car trip up to Clawspoint. There it was, glowing in electric starkness from the aging display screen of Deidre's Toyota Camry. After two years of listening to secondhand recordings posted on message boards, Zeke was finally in the physical broadcast area of WOLD as Verity Radio went live.

Diedre, in the passenger seat, smiled as convincingly as she could. She both dreaded this moment and was happy it had come at last. This trip was like an unwanted pregnancy, filling up their lives with plans and obligations she would rather have aborted. Much as she loved Zeke, she hoped meeting his hero would get some of this out of his system. It was bad enough riding anywhere with him as he played scratchy recordings of the shows. Now, she had the uncomfortable feeling that the live radio was watching them.

Her sense of paranoia had grown considerably since Zeke started listening to Verity Radio.

"In 2002, not that long ago, folks. Not that long," crooned the earthy voice of Nettles. "American forces in Kandahar, Afghanistan, entered a cave. They had been instructed to aim up if they ran into trouble. Think about how strange that is. U.S. Marines are always taught to aim for the center of mass because it's the surest way to get a hit. I was in the service. I know."

"But these Marines were told to aim up, and it became clear why very soon. According to this letter I received from a soldier, thank you for your service, they encountered giants there in the Earth. Giants, fourteen feet high at least, and covered in leather skins. These giants attacked our forces but were repelled."

Zeke was smiling, his teeth reflecting the red of the setting sun. He made another noise of satisfaction and turned to Deidre.

"He's talking about the Nephilim again!" he said. "Remember those pictures I showed you? The giant skeletons in Wisconsin? The weird heads in South America? Now he's got an inside source with the government. They'll have to answer. We're getting there, babe. We really are."

Diedre smiled wider, nodding along. She was suddenly aware of just how far away they were from anywhere out here in northeast Texas. The closest town, Oakwood, was at least thirty miles away. Dark grew like an infection all around them, leaving empty fields as massive voids of shadow. Diedre had begged for them to come earlier in the day, but Verity didn't start broadcasting until 9 p.m. Zeke wanted to hear it live, under the stars, with the radio waves pulsing through the metal of the car. It would have been poetic if it wasn't so pathetic and disturbing.

"That was the aliens, right?" she asked, hoping she was remembering all the different threads correctly.

"Yes! You remembered! I am so proud of you, babe," said Zeke. "Some people say angels, but aliens make more sense, right?"

"Of course," she said. "How much further?"

The billboard for WOLD had one light still working. Shadow and road dust obscured Marshall Nettles's face. Only his teeth and the whites of his eyes shined in the harsh yellow bulbs. Even with the landmark, Zeke had to slow to a crawl to find the road to the station in the dark. The Camry bucked and skidded on random rocks on the desolate road. If not for the voice oozing out of the radio, Deidre would have assumed WOLD was long since abandoned.

Then there were lights ahead through a tangled copse of dead-looking trees. Zeke carefully maneuvered the car around a few turns until they ended up in a clearing. Once Zeke parked the car, he settled back in his seat with his eyes slightly wet and his mouth in a gaping smile.

WOLD was a squat, metal building that was one drunken step up from a trailer. It looked in no better shape than the billboard at the end of the road, though at least there were more outdoor lights. Rising from the back of the building was a rusty transmission tower approximately four stories high and topped with a blood-colored blinking light. A single, beat-up pickup truck sat in the gravel parking lot, sporting a bumper sticker for Romney/Ryan 2012.

Diedre swallowed a sigh. It was exactly the kind of place she imagined Verity Radio broadcasting from. Zeke, despite seeing the same mediocre building, whispered, "This is so cool." It was further proof that sometimes they simply existed in different realities.

When Deidre slammed her car door, the sound echoed through the surrounding woods like a gunshot. The metal W on the WOLD sign ahead of them shivered, then rotated upside-down with a harsh screech, swinging slightly, then going still. Zeke looked at her with hurt reproach, and she mumbled an apology.

The lobby, such as it was, smelled like candy. Diedre took a step back in shock. She had smelled nothing so sweet and delicious in her life. It made her think of Easter baskets and Christmas stockings. Whatever wax burner or candle made that smell, she wanted a dozen, even if it put money in the pockets of the conspiracy theorist her boyfriend was obsessed with.

Zeke didn't stop as he strode into the room. At a small desk next to a door, a woman sat straight up with an enormous rictus smile plastered on her face. She hadn't reacted at all when they walked in, and she continued to stare straight ahead at the door, even after Deidre closed it. With adorable awkwardness, Zeke swept his cap off his head and held it in his hands as he addressed her.

"Hello, miss," he said. "My name is Ezekiel Wheeler. I called yesterday about visiting the station?"

The woman turned her head slowly to look at Zeke. It made no sound, but it reminded Deidre of an old door gently opening on rusted hinges. Her eyes never seemed to focus on anything, but her smile grew even wider.

"Yes, Mr. Wheeler," she said, her voice deep and melodious. "I'm glad you were able to find us. Mr. Nettles will be happy to see you at the next commercial break. Won't you sit down?"

Deidre took a seat on a very orange sofa. Zeke joined her and took her hand. His own was wet with nervous perspiration. As weird as the whole situation was, she tried to be happy that Zeke was meeting his hero.

Above them, a small speaker played the live broadcast. It was probably there so that Nettles could monitor the commercials while taking a break, but it added to the feeling of inescapability that surrounded Deidre. She had lived with the voice of Nettles for a year now, always on the edge of her consciousness. Zeke played it while gaming, in the car, or cooking meals. Sometimes, he even fell asleep to it, and Deidre swore she could feel the words attempting to burrow through her earplugs, trying to enter her brain and nest there.

"If there are giants, it throws open so many doors," said Nettles on the radio. "What else aren't they telling us? What truths are merely a façade? There are things that aren't human, and the powers that be know about them. They know!"

Zeke squeezed her hand. Deidre had never seen him so happy.

The comparative sanity of a toothpaste commercial startled Deidre. Zeke let go of her hand and stood up like a soldier called to attention. The woman at the desk gestured at the door, her hand unfurling like a flower to point. Deirdre rushed to follow her boyfriend.

The room on the other side of the door was dark. In here, the candy smell was even more prominent, making Diedre's stomach rumble and her mouth salivate. Her eyes slowly adjusted to the gloom, but she put her hand up to feel for the wall and steady herself.

The wall was soft and spongy, and she recoiled immediately. Diedre couldn't see what she had touched, but her fingers smelled like fresh cupcakes and buttercream. The feel, though...the matter on her fingertips was dusty and greasy. She wiped her fingers on her jeans.

By now, her eyes had adjusted, and she could see she was in a small hallway. Zeke had gone ahead, and she jogged to catch up to him. When Diedre turned the corner, she stopped in abject horror.

Marshall Nettles sat in a massive office chair appropriate for a man who had clearly once weighed close to 300 pounds. Now, he was hollowed out and desiccated, his rib cage visible in the glow of an old tri-color computer monitor. The skin on his face was long since eaten away, though his teeth remained as pearl white as those on his billboard down the road. A thick, black mold grew over his corpse, but it was shot-through with vein-like lines of bioluminescence that glowed.

Deidre started to scream but brought her hand up to her mouth to stop it. Her fingertips touched her lips, and she tasted something sweet, like cola-flavored lip balm. Realizing that it was the mold that she had touched earlier, she clamped her mouth shut in fear.

Zeke, however, stood reverentially in front of the corpse in the chair. His eyes shined with fervent wonder. Slowly, he walked forward to the form in the chair, his hand outstretched.

"Mr. Nettles," he said. "I am a huge fan."

The chair turned toward Zeke like a flower seeking the sun. The veiny lines in the mold contracted, and Nettles raised his arm to shake Zeke's hand. Zeke gripped it, apparently with no disgust. Around them, the indistinct sounds of a local concert advertisement played, promising a night no one would forget.

"Good to meet you, Zeke. Very good indeed."

The voice originated from the throat of Nettles's corpse. Diedre saw the infested lungs contract and expand while the vocal cords blinked like fireflies. The voice itself was beautiful, a deep, resonating sound that was a joy to listen to. It reminded Deidre of recordings she heard of Orson Welles, and she thought, *who knows what evil lurks in the hearts of men?*

"This is my girlfriend, Deidre," said Zeke. Afraid to open her mouth, Deidre waved.

Zeke immediately sat in a nearby chair, also overgrown with the mold. Deidre did not understand how he could let it touch his skin and not be repulsed.

"I won't take up too much of your time, sir," said Zeke. "I just wanted to let you know how much I appreciate what you do. The mainstream media, they never cover the stories you do. They don't see what's happening below the surface. There's a big community of people out there, sir, who record your work and make sure it spreads. We know it's important."

The corpse of Nettles shook with a grotesque approximation of laughter, all the while sounding like Santa Claus.

"I know I should get online," he said. "I do have an email address. To tell you the truth, I wish I had someone your age around here to help. Are you good with the internet? You wouldn't be looking for work, would you?"

"Mr. Nettles, that would be a dream come true!"

This was Deidre's breaking point.

"Zeke, babe, look at him!" she screamed. "He's dead! Do you not see that he's dead? His fucking bones are showing. The room is covered in fungus. We need to get out of here. Please."

Zeke's eyes widened, then narrowed like a dog when it sees someone enter its yard. The intensity in his stare struck her like a blow. His lip quivered with hurt like she had just confessed to adultery.

"What are you talking about?"

"You're sitting next to a dead body on a chair covered in the mold that is eating him!"

Zeke shook his head.

"I thought you understood," he said. "Were you lying to me this whole time? Mr. Nettles is literally talking to me. You can hear him. How can he be dead?"

"I admit it's not the cleanest office, young lady," said the body in the chair. "But mold? That's ridiculous. I had this building inspected last month. Are you sure you're alright? Lynette out front could let you lie down on the couch if you need a moment."

For a brief instant, Deidre wondered if she was going insane. Maybe there was no mold, no corpse in the chair. Nettles sounded kind and reasonable. She was probably embarrassing Zeke. The smell was overcoming her. The sweetness took her breath away. It made her want to reach out to the mold and take some in her mouth. Instead, she swallowed and answered.

"I...think I will go outside. I'm sorry. I'm so sorry."

As she walked away, she heard Zeke apologizing for her.

The lobby office was so normal in contrast that it left Deidre feeling dizzy. She walked on stiff legs to the front door like someone trying to mask the fact they were on the way to throw up.

Outside in the humid Texas air, she breathed deep. There was the smell of flowers, dust, and distant cow manure. She could feel the grass poking up around her sandals and began to cry, comforted by the realness of the world.

Deidre got into the car and started it, happy to let the air conditioning blow on her hot face. Then, the radio blared to life.

"Welcome back, listeners," said Nettles. "We have a rare guest in the studio today, a bright young man named Zeke Wheeler, who will be working here starting tomorrow. Good to have young blood at the station again! But before we get him pushing papers, Zeke has a story he wants to tell."

"Thank you, Marshall," said Zeke. Deidre marveled at how low and sexy Zeke's voice was now.

"I used to date this woman. No need to tell you her name. I don't want people to harass her. She was convinced that the world was being taken over by mold. One time, she even yelled at my boss that he was being mind-controlled by mold. Can you believe that?"

"That is serious," said Nettles.

"It never happened until after she got her COVID vaccine. That was the sad part. I tried to warn her that there was something off. You remember how you talked about the whistleblower that caught people putting hallucinogens in the vaccines to make the population easy to control?"

Deidre turned the radio off and drove carefully away down the black, twisting road. Once she reached the highway, she pointed her car back toward Austin and drove as fast as she could. Behind her, the light on the WOLD tower blinked slowly, patiently, as the message spread at its own pace.

ABOUT THE AUTHOR

Jef Rouner is an award-winning freelance journalist from Houston, Texas, who specializes in weird happenings, politics, and extremism. Currently, they are working on a book about Houston cemeteries.

They've written two horror story collections, *The Rook Circle* and *Stranger Words*, and perform weekly flash fiction with the Friday Nightmare on TikTok. In no particular order, they have been a luchador, a hypnotist, a drag performer, and the host of *The Black Math Experiment*.

A Dark Spore Grows in the Rot
Rachel A. Brune

Quartz in the loam, shards of broken rock wall, roots to reach out and trip an unwary traveler—these were all familiar sights on this part of the trail. The narrow dirt path was not as well-traveled as the lower, flatter areas, conveniently available to day hikers looking for a short hit of the nature drug.

Breathing *in-in-in* and *out-and-out*...

In-in-in and *out-and-out*...

Slaps of nylon and thin rubber over the forgiving soil, dark under the canopy of the birches and oak, the flashes and glints off the quartz and white lichen softer now as the sun fought its way over the mountain horizon.

Tremella—Trella to her friends, and the name she used to register for each endurance event—let her breathing carry her up the hill. She could, and often did, run this trail in the dark, after dinner and dishes and all the other chores.

A crack and scurry and some small animal ran off into the underbrush, leaving a patch of daisy fleabane and milkweed shuddering in its path.

Trella squinted as she turned her face back to the trail. The sun pierced the angle of the hill, and she breathed deeply and evenly in her final push to the top of the rise.

In-in-in and *out-and-out...*

Three steps in and two steps out. This had been the rhythm that carried her through every run past her first, stumbling 5K fun run, where her inexperience had launched her almost sprinting out from the pack only to walk, panting and spent, through the final mile.

The slap of her thin soles on the dirt path almost silent. Now the fireflies had started to blink around the sides of the path, tiny glints in the dark as the evening began dropping its cover around the forest. Trella could barely see past the edges of the trail. The white blazes popped in the gloaming, and she sighted to the next one, aiming her steps. Sure-footed, breath in control.

Until she crested the top of the hill and slipped.

And when she slipped, something glinted. There. Not too far back in the woods.

Not a firefly. Not quartz or a blaze or the white-tipped heads of the daisy fleabane.

But a glint that shone, for a brief, silver moment, a little ways off the trail.

Trella stood and dusted off her running shorts. There was a hefty abrasion along her right knee—it had come down on a chunk of granite, and in the fading light she saw the edges where the orange pus was gathering.

But the glint she saw called to her and she stepped once, twice away from the trail, into the darkness, following a call that had no sound but a silver echo where there should be none.

A tiny path, no more than a deer or rabbit run, led her into the darkness. Here, the tree cover broke around a tumble of old, glacial rocks, letting the last bit of light down among the tangles and brake.

The soil had been disturbed. Trella squinted again, still breathing *in-in-in* and *out-and-out*, although she had stopped to puzzle out what she was looking at. Around the disturbance, common white mushrooms had popped up, kissing the edges of the black dirt where they met the detritus of the forest floor.

And in the middle of the disturbance, there lay the glint.

Feeling as if she were violating some unspoken boundary, Trella stepped gently over the soil, avoiding the disturbed area, careful not to step on any of the ferns or mushrooms or live plants. *Leave only footsteps! Take only pictures!*

By now, it was almost full dark, and something pulled at her steps. Some knowledge that this was not where she was supposed to be, that she had things to do once she finished her training run.

But that glint that lay in the center of the disturbance pulled her on, and she picked it up from the middle of the soil and raised it to the evening sky.

How did you get here?

Trella slipped her wedding ring onto her left fourth finger, wondering.

How had it come to rest here in this untraveled patch of disturbed dirt, a short walk off the rarely used trail? How had she not realized it was missing?

Trella struggled to piece together her day. Had she done anything out of the ordinary? She didn't think so.

Wake up, get herself ready for the day, get Brennan up and ready for work, send him off with lunch and a smile, get the kids up and out the door, ice her cheek, makeup on and then sit down for a day of Zoom calls while cleaning the house, then school pickup and dinner and cleanup and chores and then out the door for her run. Only ten miles today. Or was it five? Was today a school and workday? Or were all the days running together, one after the other, punctuated by lacing up her shoes and running into the night, *in-in-in* and *out-and-out*...

And now, this ring. She held up her hand, examining it. It was definitely hers; the white gold had that small scratch on it from the time Brennan had taken it from her and tossed it on the floor and stomped on it. And the tiny diamond chip on the left side was still missing. She hadn't told him about that.

How *had* this ring come to be resting on the black dirt of this patch of disturbed forest floor off the main trail?

Ring on finger, Trella turned back to the trail.

The darkness had become a shroud, thick and comforting and cloaking her in its folds. A breeze pierced the veil, bringing with it sounds of the night around her—the crickets crying out, soft chitters and scutters in the underbrush, the silent symphony of fireflies winking in and out around her.

In-in-in and *out-and-out...*

She'd been in the dark before.

The trail was just ahead, not too far off. Trella calmed her breathing. She was almost home. Just a few yards. Maybe twenty or thirty.

The white trail blazes would pop in the gloaming. She would see them.

The darkness closed back in around her as she stepped carefully away from the clearing. Why hadn't she brought her headlamp? Or the light-up running vest Brennan bought her for her birthday? No, she wouldn't say anything to him about getting lost because she wasn't wearing it. Not if she wanted to keep him from throwing it away.

The trail was not too far now, just a few yards or so. She would keep walking, slowly, steadily.

Her thumb played with the metal band on her fourth finger, worrying at it, until she forced her hand into a loose fist.

Trella went to press the button on her Garmin to switch to her cool down. It would be cutting her run short, but this early in the training season, she could afford to cheat a little. Better than falling and injuring herself and putting herself even farther behind.

Her watch wasn't on her wrist.

Swinging her arms as she walked to help her cool down, Trella deepened her breathing against the first bit of panic.

In...and in... Out...and out...

Where was she?

She tripped over a rock, caught herself against a tree, scraping her palm.

The night sounds paused, then resumed.

Trella wiped her hand on her shirt. There had been something soft and slimy on the tree—a lichen? A slug? Something worse?

Under her feet, something soft broke and exploded with a puff. Trella tried to step more gingerly, but she could barely see to avoid the larger trees, and now under her feet she slaughtered a pack of unseen vegetation—mushrooms? Mountain violets? Plantain weed? Skunk cabbage?

A dark smell like rot rose to her senses, and she swiped at her nose, trying to get it out of her mouth where it settled. It disrupted her breathing, and Trella struggled to calm herself without breathing too deeply of this air that smelled like the festering groundhog carcass a car had left at the trailhead. Death, and maggots, and the rot that reclaimed all the tiny, furry tragedies that littered this back county road.

Where am I?

The trail had vanished, and the dark had claimed the forest. Even the fireflies were thin on the ground. Or had they always been?

Trella realized she was worrying at her finger again, twisting the ring around and around. Should she ask Brennan if he had done something with her ring? Why would he have done something with her ring? But, of course, that was for her to figure out.

Her breath caught.

In—out. In—

Trella stopped. This wasn't the right thing to do, was it? If one is lost in a dark, vast forest, the first rule is to stop and to stay where you are until help comes.

She felt as if she had always been here, in the dark that smelled of dirt and rot, with the sounds of the night dampened and muted around her, and the only light that of the fast-diminishing fireflies.

She had always been here, and she would always be here. If she were to return to her brightly lit, two-story ranch house, to walk in the door and drop her keys in the flamingo dish and say hello to the man, waiting for her, alone—she felt he would stare at her, as if she were some uncanny memory in ghoulish form that must be returned back to the night.

And then, like sand beneath the feet of a drowning swimmer, a light appeared through the trees like a firefly. Only, as she waited, this speck did not flicker out.

Instead, it grew as Trella began hiking toward the warm, yellow glow, drawn to it as if to a long-forgotten, childhood home.

It grew, almost imperceptibly. Even as it became larger, Trella couldn't tell if she was hiking toward an opening in the tree line or if the glow, like the glint she had followed off the path, was teasing her, tempting her even deeper into the woods.

And how could this be the glow of her own windows? Had she hiked so far off the path that she hadn't noticed in the dark the rise and fall of the mountain?

She emerged from the trees, her pale, white hands scrabbling her way through the patch of blackberry brambles that bordered her backyard.

Again, she stopped. This couldn't have been the glow she saw from the forest. Her thumb worried again at her ring. She forced herself to stop. Her skin was peeling around the ring; she could feel tiny bits of it pilling. Maybe a blister?

The front door was unlocked, and the knob didn't slip in her hand. Her sweat had dried. How late was it? No watch, no time...

The downstairs was dark and empty.

What light was it that she'd seen from the forest?

There was an unfamiliar pair of shoes in the rack by the door. Did one of the kids have a friend over? But if they did, where were all of their shoes?

Why did she feel so lightheaded? Her skin was so pale and clammy. She felt cold, as if she'd run much farther and forgotten to properly hydrate and fuel up. A shower. A warm shower was what she needed. She'd take it in the kids' bathroom so she wouldn't wake up Brennan. The kids...

Trella shucked her running shoes off on the rack and headed

upstairs. She paused halfway up to the landing. The smell of rot had followed her. What had she stepped in? Had she fallen in something? She'd have to do laundry tonight. By hand, so she didn't wake him up.

Where were the kids? They weren't in their rooms. Did...

Had Brennan thought she'd be back later? She had cut her run short, but then she'd been lost for what she thought had been a long time. Had he forgotten to send someone home? He had promised. And promised.

And promised.

"'Nita?" A drowsy rumble came from the bed. Brennan shifted. 'Nita the cat, short for Amanita, named by the girls after a character in one of their books.

"No, it's just me," Trella replied. She paused at the foot of the bed. "Sorry, I didn't mean to wake you."

Brennan sat straight up, his face illuminated in the glow from his smartwatch.

Now, Trella could see the second lump in the bed that shifted as Brennan stared at her. Dread pitched her stomach on end.

"What—" Brennan stared at her. Something was wrong with his face. "How?"

He should have been angry, furious. He'd promised, and she'd caught him again.

But this was not anger. The wet in his eyes, the mouth gaping instead of cruel and twisted.

"I got lost..." Trella forced the words out. Why was she having such trouble with them? As if her throat was so dry it had closed up. "It was so...dark."

"I—you can't be here," Brennan stammered. "You can't! You *can't!*"

"Babe, what is it?" The sleepy mumble had a soft, feminine tone, and then a tousled brunette head sat up next to Brennan. The petite woman's face scrunched in confusion, then widened in alarm. "What the fuck?"

As if the woman's voice triggered something in his memory, Brennan's mouth set in familiar rage. He swung his legs over the side of the bed and stood, towering and glaring in the semi-darkness.

"Babe—" The woman stopped herself and pulled the blankets up, covering herself.

"What are you doing here?" Brennan demanded. "You can't—you *can't* be here! You're—"

He reached out and grabbed her, hands gripping her forearm, sinking into her flesh. More bruises, more long sleeves or carefully keeping her arms out of view on the Zoom window.

Trella winced.

Brennan screamed and backed away, his hands holding something that looked like latex or foam or sheets that needed to go to the laundry —something off-white and pale and floppy.

Trella moaned. His hands had sunk all the way through her flesh and pulled away strands of fingers and tendons and bone.

But not red and soft, or slick and wet.

Brennan screamed again, and this time, the woman on the bed joined in, scrambling back until she slammed against the headboard. The smell of rot grew larger in the small room.

Trella sighed, and the soft bits of flesh fell away from her arms. A dark cloud of spores and rot began seeping through her skin as the layers of dermis and muscle and fascia separated and sloughed off.

Her breasts and shoulders and cheeks ripped themselves away, dripping and sliding down her torso. On her knees, still abraded from her fall, orange pustules grew, layering and shaping themselves, running down the fungal skin that scaled off her body, exposing cartilage and veins.

Each part of her grew into multitudes.

And they ran their way through the darkness, spreading and mulching and fertilizing, and when they reached the bounty of flesh and blood, they burrowed into beating vessels and pulsing organs and exploded their nodules into a vast network of orange and yellow and brown mycelium that spread through the rot.

In-in-in and *out-and-out...*

Footsteps in the darkness, slapping lightly against the soil. And in the darkness, where her soles caress the loam, spring up tiny nodules of spores that take root and spread through the rot.

The tiny patch of disturbed soil welcomes her back. The sheer, determined effort of holding all of these parts of herself together lasts until she reaches this one final finish line.

Instead of breaking through the ribbon under the bright sun, she sinks in darkness back under the loam. Her ring, with the scratch in the side and the missing diamond chip, she leaves on the surface. She has no more need of it.

In the house they shared for fifteen years, her husband and his lover strangle on the filaments that grow in their bodies, taking root and mulching their bodies to dust.

And under the dark, in the rot, her two daughters welcome her back home.

ABOUT THE AUTHOR

Rachel A. Brune's first paid writing gig came courtesy of the U.S. Army. After five years as a military journalist, she began writing creatively. Her short stories have been published in *Freeze Frame Fiction*, *The Antihumanist*, and *Dark Moon Digest*, as well as anthologies from Writerpunk Press, Falstaff Books, Tundra Swan Press, and eSpec Books. She is the founder of Crone Girls Press and the Senior Editor of Falstaff Dread, the horror imprint of Falstaff Books. Her short story collection, *Side Roads*, won the 2022 Imadjinn Award.

Of Teeth and Mushrooms
Nicole Givens Kurtz

"How DID Miss Graves end up decomposing in your bathtub?" Detective Emma Carter stuck a piece of nicotine gum into her mouth. She'd picked the worst time to quit smoking. For a homicide cop, there never was a good time.

The recorder flashed its green light. A little past ten in the evening, they'd finally ushered the suspect into the interrogation room. The interview space reeked of tension and body odor. The overhead fixture shot rods of fluorescent light, turning the walls into a harsh urine yellow.

"Mr. Bruin." The wooden chair creaked as she sat back. Emma rotated her pen in one hand and conjured what remained of her patience.

"I could feel her skin on my fingertips, squishy and puckered, from, you know, being in the water. She kinda dissolved..." Across the scarred and unstable table, Chad Bruin rubbed his close-cropped black hair with a well-manicured hand. His watch, something Swiss and expensive, peeked out of his name-brand, lavender button-down's sleeve. An embroidered logo in a darker color bore splashes of crimson right above his heart. "Can I get a water?"

"Sure," said Detective Trevor Bell. Her partner's chair scraped the floor as he stood up to fetch the suspect a beverage.

Emma quirked an eyebrow.

They didn't do good-cop/bad-cop scenarios. Mainly because Bell had the moody-broody bad cop persona on lock. For this interrogation, Chad would only speak to Emma, who, like his victim, was an African American woman.

Anything to keep Chad talking. Confessions cut through the clogged justice wheel. Emma saw a plea deal in Mr. Bruin's future.

"Please..." She waved a flat hand in the air for him to continue.

Chad's dark eyes shifted in their puffy sockets, not quite focused. With a heavy, dramatic sigh, he said, "Where was I?"

"A putrefied Miss Graves." Emma tapped her pen on the table, mentally counting backward from 1000.

"Ah, yes." Chad tugged at his collar. He shuffled his feet and rattled the shackles around his ankle. "The tub was filled with her. All of her! A glorious smoothie of what used to be a lovely woman. The sight of her, now *that* was a scientific glory. But the odor. Whew."

How could he do that to a human being? Emma pressed her lips.

"How did it happen?" Emma asked.

Mush. That's all that's left of a talented author and social activist.

"Funny story that." He flashed an all-too-white, too-straight smile. His nostrils flared when he leaned on the table with both elbows.

The door whined open. Bell put the bottled water in the center and returned to his seat without a word.

"Ah, thank you! No Fuji Water, huh? You are sorely underfunded. It's a wonder you get anything accomplished." Chad cast Emma another smile, again all teeth, no warmth or remorse. He drank long and deep, relishing the power to make them wait.

Her pen tapped. 800, 799, 798...

"And Miss Graves?"

Chad nodded. "I've lived in Mahogany Hills for fifteen years. Of course, I knew who she was. All of Baltimore knows." His voice took on a faraway tone. "I had a keen interest in my neighbor. Her beautiful, smooth brown skin, her wide chocolate eyes and plum, plump lips. I could just eat her up." He cleared his throat and sat straighter in his chair. "She'd be out in her yard, laboring in her little patch of vegetable plant boxes, fretting over the aphids—little pests."

"You ever talk to her?" Emma asked, gently pushing him back to the topic. *He seems proud of his actions. No high-paid lawyers. No refusal to talk to us.*

"Of course. I would ask her questions about our lawn. Asked her to come over."

"What did your wife think about it?" Emma found Angela Bruin to be like a weary flower, struggling to reach sunlight, but finding only darkness.

He coughed and wiped his forehead with the back of his hand. "Another water, please." He shook the empty one at Emma.

"Sure." The door whined once more as Bell went to satisfy the latest request. Only Emma's tapping pen disturbed the heavy silence.

"People spoke so highly of her, her intellect and sharp wit...I—I became a little taken with her," Chad said, rubbing his hands on his jeans.

"Obsessed." Emma countered. "You were obsessed with Miss Graves. Isn't that right?"

Chad squeezed his eyes shut; the truth too harsh to witness. His faux glee evaporated. "I see you've been listening to the neighborhood rumor mill. I'm certain it has been running on overtime since my arrest."

When Bell returned with the water, he rescued Emma from giving a tart response. He set the bottle in front of Chad and returned to his seat.

"Anyway, I had to fire Jose. How else could I get her over to my house?"

"I'm sorry. Who's Jose?" Emma wrote the name on her notepad.

"My gardener. I told her he quit and I had questions about some strange plants growing in the backyard. She agreed to come look. I was outside blowing leaves along the tree line, and I saw it. Its shiny scarlet orbs glistened in the sunlight. They sparkled from the base of my large oak tree. The foamy white top beckoned to be swiped with my finger. How would it taste? Like sweet cream or savory like sour cream?"

What the hell is he talking about?

"Then what?" Emma glanced over to Bell.

He shrugged his folded arms. *No idea.*

"...I broke off a piece. It looked so delicious. But it started bleeding."

"Bleeding? Miss Graves?" Emma failed to keep the annoyance out of her voice.

Chad's face screwed up at her tone. "You aren't listening! It was the Devil's Tooth, a type of mushroom! Since you cops don't get a good education, I can see why you don't know about it."

"You ate a wild mushroom..." Emma swore. *What the hell does this have to do with him killing Miss Graves?*

"Yes." His face fell, and with a weak smile, he said, "It didn't taste at all like it looked. It was bitter." He gagged and reached for his water. "I can still taste it." He shuddered. "Miss Graves didn't either. She didn't taste anything like what she looked like."

Emma pressed down the urge to smack him until he confessed everything. She'd been doing the work long enough to know many of these people crave the spotlight. A police interrogation room might not be the only time the spotlight fell on them. Everyone waiting on your next word, hanging on with interest. They wanted to prolong it.

She could almost hear the captain's words about interrogation.

Let them spill their guts. As long as they confess to the crime, you better listen to how they killed cats or wet the bed until they were thirty. Let 'em talk.

Chad swallowed. He kept his gaze on her, the edges of his grin returning, inching across his face, stretching his thin lips until they disappeared.

"It isn't sweet, not at all." And almost to himself, he whispered, "So bitter..."

The air conditioning switched on, squeaking sounds from the vents announcing their protest, or perhaps the rats were in the walls again.

"Miss Graves." Emma tapped out 699, 698, 697.

Chad laced his fingers together, resting them in his lap. "The Devil's Tooth awakened something inside me. I—I'd tried to shake it so many times."

"Shake what?" Bell said, his low voice rumbling through the tight room.

Is Chad setting up an insanity defense?

Wealthy tech upstarts always fell upward, and Emma wanted to limit Chad's escape route and lock him in the confines of responsibility.

"The hunger," Chad whispered as if he'd confessed a secret love. "I ate it and I could feel its effects immediately. Its acrid bitterness dissolved the lock on my, uh, desires, on my hesitation. And I—I relished it!"

His eyes sparkled, shiny orbs of shit. "In college, Chad Reeves, one of my Sigma Beta Rho brothers, he owns a chain of high-end strip clubs, supplied us with these magic shrooms, like all the time. I know I passed Statistics because of them. When we took them, oh boy, the fun!"

Is he rattlin' now? Does he need a fix?

Emma caught herself smiling and put her professional face back on. "Mr. Bruin..."

The suspect drank his water, consuming a natural resource meant to preserve life. *Something he perverted.*

When Chad had expelled his last *ah!* Emma said, "Tell us the rest of what happened."

His shoulders lowered, and the shit-eating grin returned. "You see, the Devil's Tooth gave me courage, changed me. Took control, if you will. Was her blood the same bright scarlet like the beads on the mushroom? I had to know, had to taste."

"Why?"

"That's a good question, detective." Chad blinked several times as if startled. He then tutted, his mouth widened, his lips' edges nearly to his ears. "The Devil's Tooth. I admired her. Once I ate the crimson fruit bodies, I had a hunger. I know it's cliché, but that's the best way I can explain it."

Emma let it go. Psychedelics made people do awful and awesome things. He'd admitted to past drug use, and this fell in line with his current behavior.

Bell grunted.

Yeah, I know. The sooner he confesses, the sooner we can go for ramen.

"She smelled like roses, soft, but impactful. We made small talk, which I hate." Chad shifted in his seat. "Wait. Let me back up. Before she arrived, I ate more of the Devil's Tooth. The effect doesn't last. It never does...but the aftertaste. That fucking *stays*."

He barked out a laugh.

Oh, he's definitely setting up an insanity defense.

Chad took in more water and resumed his story. "We got as far as the kitchen island when I picked up my hammer and slammed into her brilliant brain. She yelped and crumpled."

He bounced in excitement, his shackles clattering against the floor.

"The blood—it was just like when I cut open the fungal pastry. It leaked out from the wound, tiny tributaries all flowing from that one source and onto the island."

Emma's left hand ached from clutching the chair's seat. The level of depravity didn't feel real.

"The other good part? She was still alive!" Chad clapped. "I carried her upstairs to my bathroom. I put her in the tub and turned on the water. As soon as I did that, panic must've kicked in. Bloody water splashed all over the floor as she tried to escape. Ruined the mats...but I digress!" He sighed. "You are so easy to talk to, Detective."

Emma nodded. She didn't trust herself to speak. Sometimes there were no words.

Chad continued. "Okay. I squeezed her neck, like forever, until she couldn't breathe. Tada. Dead." Chad gave a bow with a flourish, his arms wide, his legs shackled. "But the best part, detective? Whatever had been eating away at me had been satisfied. The devil cured me."

Quiet followed in the wake of his confession. Her pen paused.

Suddenly, the air conditioning was too cold. Chad's words chilled her—so calculating and devoid of humanity.

His statement matched the forensic details. The pathologist found blunt force trauma to Miss Graves's skull, consistent with a hammer and the crushed hyoid bone in her throat, confirming strangulation. She had been alive when she went into the tub. The toxicology report found traces of bleach and soap in the water from her lungs.

"And you left her there?" Emma asked around the knot of fury in her mouth.

"Needs must when the devil drives. I had other business to attend to, like cleaning the mess in the kitchen. Angela would be home soon."

"Your wife didn't go to the bathroom for two weeks." Emma read from her notes. "Is that correct?"

Chad laughed. "She has her own bathroom off her bedroom suite."

In disbelief, Emma asked. "She didn't smell anything? She had no clue?"

Chad scoffed. "That idiot woman couldn't find her tits with two hands."

"Your son had quite a bit to say." Emma quirked an eyebrow, ignoring his previous comment.

Chad's laughter came to a halt.

"Your sixteen-year-old son, Glen, wrote in his statement that he went to get a jacket from your closet but was stopped by the horrid smell emitting from your bathroom. Fearing something had happened to you, he kicked the door in and discovered Miss Graves' body."

With the confession secured, Emma didn't have to keep her words close to the vest.

Chad gave a feeble head shake.

"It takes a special kind of evil to do what you did to a woman who came to help you." Emma pushed back from the table and stood up. She collected her notepad and swept the reports and witness statements into a folder.

Chad crossed his arms in a huff and sucked his teeth. "It isn't my fault, Detective. The Devil's Tooth..."

"Doesn't have any effect on people if ingested." Bell stood up and joined Emma standing in front of Chad, his phone in his hand.

Chad's eyes flickered toward him. He gripped the table's edge, disbelief ruining his perfect features.

Bell read aloud, "According to this article from the International Society of Mushroom Science, the *Hydnellum peckii,* also known as Bleeding Tooth Fungus or Devil's Tooth, is not considered poisonous or psychedelic. It's not dangerous, but in fact, is being studied as a possible cure for Alzheimer's disease."

Chad whipped his head toward Bell. The sound of his slap on the table made Emma jump. "No! I *felt* the power of the devil taking me over! His teeth bit into my soul!"

"Not possible. You're living a life of lies." Bell put his phone in his slacks pocket. "You killed an innocent woman because you *wanted* to. Worse, you planned it."

"Sounds like the death penalty to me." Emma hugged the folder to her chest. "Premediated murder."

"You're lying!" Chad roared, spraying the table with spittle and raging skepticism. His neck bulged from the strain. His leering mouth pulled back in an animalistic snarl. The furniture kept him at bay, but only just. With sheer abandonment, he yanked against his shackles. He threw himself at the table and rained his fists against its surface, a toddler's tantrum.

A couple of deputies stormed in, having heard the commotion. Their arrival was drowned out by Chad's bellowing. They rushed the flailing man and snatched his arms.

"Let go of me!"

I guess panic set in. Emma chuckled to herself.

"Don't you stupid cops know the devil's greatest trick was convincing everyone he doesn't exist? No modern science can discern the Devil's Tooth's power!" His voice cracked.

With a feral expression of both pain and fury and all his thrashing about, one of his elbows clocked the deputy in the nose. Blood shot out bright and fresh as if painted with a lush scarlet oil.

"Fuck!" One of the deputies howled, holding his injury with one hand. His other had a fistful of Chad's shirt. The other deputy managed to get Chad's arms behind him for the gaping handcuffs. Chad kept wrestling, resisting, yelling obscenities, and then a loud crack struck the din.

"Ahhh! You bastards! My arm!" Chad shrieked.

For his efforts, Chad was slammed into the unyielding table. Teeth, too white and too straight, shot from his mouth with their bloody tethered nerves attached. His muffled howls didn't stop the pinkish drool of regret and anger from pouring along the downturned corners of his lips and weak chin. The non-injured deputy pinned him there, while the assaulted deputy wiped his nose and slapped his hand on Chad's shoulder. With a haul, they yanked him to his feet and unchained his shackles from the floor. Chad disappeared through the interrogation room door sandwiched between the deputies.

Bell turned to Emma, his hazel eyes like embers in the light. "There's only one thing he got right."

Emma turned off the recording. "Oh? What?"

"Devil's Tooth *is* bitter." Bell winked at her.

ABOUT THE AUTHOR

Nicole Givens Kurtz is a two-time Atomacon Palmetto Scribe Award winner and a recipient of the HWA Diversity Grant. With over 20 years in publishing, she's written for *Pseudopod, Fiyah, Apex Magazine, White Wolf, The Realm* (formerly Serial Box), *Subsume,* and Baen. Nicole has over 50 published short stories and is the editor of groundbreaking anthologies, *SLAY: Stories of the Vampire Noire* and *Blackened Roots: An Anthology of the Undead* with Tonia Ransom.

The Mushroom Child
Samantha J. Bryant

NANCY'S DAUGHTER bought her a foraging class for Mother's Day. "You need a little nature therapy, Mumsy," she'd said, presenting her with the gift certificate to a local farm. "This will get you out into the trees, fresh air and something useful at the same time. You might make some new friends."

Neither of them commented that it was something Jackson never would have done, though Nancy was sure her daughter knew that. Her husband had been a city boy through and through, and Nancy had been the one to take the children to look for tadpoles or look at interesting tree formations in the woods, the few times that it had happened. It hadn't been often.

Before she'd married, Nancy had been the kind of girl who climbed trees to peek into bird's nests or laid down in the grass to watch clouds move across the sky. Somewhere along the way, without realizing it was happening, she'd become a woman with a regular appointment at the nail salon and a closet full of dry-clean-only clothing. Now, she was sixty, adrift and struggling.

There were so many parts of herself that she'd let fall by the wayside. She didn't exactly blame Jackson, but he had been part of it.

She'd tried so hard to be dignified for him, to be the right kind of wife to support the life they built together.

Now that he was gone, she wasn't sure what she wanted to reclaim from the girl she had been and what was well and truly gone, no longer part of the woman she was now. So, she'd gone to the class, hoping to find out.

Lizbeth had been right. Nancy had loved getting outside and squatting down on the ground to examine varieties of fungus she had never imagined were just a few feet off the paved path. She'd learned about edible varieties and how to tell them apart from close cousins, though she hadn't risked eating anything she'd found yet, not trusting her skill enough to chance it. But, she loved looking at the mushrooms and taking photographs of them more than she liked eating them anyway. Tiny, secret beauty that had surrounded her all this time and she had never realized.

This morning, her eyelids had popped open early. It was barely six, but sleep was done with her, apparently, so she decided it would be nice to get out before the summer's heat made the day unbearable. She'd packed a small bag with water and snacks, made sure her phone was fully charged and her boots were tightly laced, then hit the trail in search of fun and fungi.

The rains of the past few days had made the forest path she favored more than a little muddy, so she had to move carefully, but the trees and plants were lush and an air of contentment emanated from the woods, as if the entire forest was letting out a long, deep sigh. Nancy had taken more than a dozen pictures of a variety of fungus that she'd look up later while she was watching old movies on the sofa. Her new cell phone had a much better camera for macro photography and some of the pictures were really quite good. She'd have to send them to her daughter later, as a thank you for the class that sparked her interest.

Nancy squatted on her haunches, trying to angle her camera just right to catch the light in the rain still puddled in the concave cap of wide and solid yellow mushroom. Her imagination made a goblet of it and pictured a faerie prince drinking from it at a banquet.

When she stood again, her hips complained of the low position she'd been holding, so she took a moment to stretch, reaching her arms to the sky, then dropping back to her feet, bending back until she heard a satisfying small pop, then twisting from side to side.

On one of her twists, a flash of red caught her eye, and Nancy turned to identify what she'd seen. A few yards away, near the edge of the river, a little girl sat, her back turned to Nancy, gaze directed at the water below the rise. Nancy frowned. Was the little girl out here alone? She hadn't seen anyone else and she'd been out here more than an hour now.

Dropping her bag, she took a couple of steps toward the child, not wanting to frighten her, but needing to make sure she was all right. "Hello there!" she called. "Is everything okay?"

The little girl didn't respond, so Nancy took a few steps closer. "Is your mother nearby?"

Still no response.

"I don't want to scare you, sweetheart," she called, closing the distance in a few more steps.

Now only a couple of feet away, she could see that the "child" she'd seen wasn't a child at all, but an enormous red fungus grown over the stump of a small tree, with a secondary growth atop that looked like cascading blond curls.

Nancy laughed at herself. Of course no one had left a child out here alone, alongside the river. Still, it was uncanny how the fungus had fooled her. Even now, if she squinted, she could believe a golden-haired little girl of four or five years dressed in a red dress knelt at her feet instead of some kind of fungal growth.

She plopped down on a convenient rock to examine the formation more closely. She'd never seen anything like this one. The red part was a single large piece of thick fungus, formed in folds. No wonder her eye had perceived it as cloth from a distance. It hung like a cloak. The golden yellow part she'd mistaken for hair was dry-looking tendrils that hung in curls and moved in the breeze.

She reached out to touch the "cloak" and found that it felt smooth and dry, pleasant under her finger tips. She brought her fingers to her nose, but smelled only earth and damp. She coughed, and a flash of lightning sparked behind her eyes. Touching it might have been a bad idea. Hadn't her teacher warned her not to just touch random plants and fungi if she didn't know what they were? Nancy had been fussed at more than once for her tendency to stroke and pinch the things they found on their foraging walk with her bare hands.

A few flakes of red clung to her fingertips and she brushed them off on her pants. "Huh," she said out loud. "You really looked like a little girl."

She stretched her hand forward and touched the long tendrils that had looked so much like golden blonde curls in the sunlight. The strands didn't feel like hair. They were rougher, coarse, and, at the same time, sticky. In fact, they wrapped around her hand, entangling her fingers.

"Gross," Nancy said, tugging her hand back. Her fingers didn't come free. The stringy bits pulled tighter against her skin, becoming uncomfortable, even a little painful. "What the hell?"

Panicking a little, Nancy tried to get to her feet, but fell right back against the stone she'd been resting on, smacking her tailbone painfully. It was like she'd tried to get out of a car without taking off the seatbelt first. She looked down to see what had snagged her and saw that similar long, golden strands like vines were wrapped around her feet and legs.

She set down the phone she'd still clutched in her free hand and grabbed at the strange, ropy loops binding her legs and feet, working a finger beneath to tug a thicker one away from her thigh. Her pulse was racing now. This was more than just weird.

And now her finger was stuck, too.

Nancy wiggled her whole body fiercely, trying to work some part of her free. As she watched, the twines encircling her grew thicker. She couldn't really feel the hand that had gotten tangled in the hair-like strands anymore. Just a weird tingling sensation, like she'd slept with her arm at a strange angle and it had gone to pins and needles.

She whipped her head around, looking for anything she could use to pull herself free or another hiker she could yell to for help, but she saw only moss and twigs, plants and trees. Not another person in sight. The river burbled pleasantly below, indifferent to her struggles.

She spotted her phone on the ground and pushed her body toward it with all her might. A tearing sensation made her cry out and she fell off the rock. Her feet, however, remained caught and she ended up on her knees, facing the river.

Tears ran down her face freely now, but she couldn't wipe them away with both her hands caught. Something crawled up her back, poking under her shirt. Nancy screamed, frantic now, jerking her body spasmodically even though it sent white hot spikes of pain into her hips and legs.

She felt herself tilting, leaning closer to the stump, and fought against it, muscles shaking from the effort. She sucked in gasping breaths that hurt, like poison instead of air had funneled into her lungs. Stars shot across her vision again, and her head swam.

The next thing she knew, she was leaning against the fungus covered stump, her head resting against the golden ringlets like she was comforting a disconsolate child.

She could no longer pull her head away. Weariness overtook her and her eyes fell closed. She forced them open three or four times, focusing on the clear, beautiful water in the river in front of her. It sparkled in the sun now, like magic. *At least the last thing I saw was beautiful*, she thought, and went to sleep.

The police found her phone a couple of days later, after Lizbeth reported her mother missing. The device lay on the ground by the river, dead, but not broken. They found her bag, too, the granola bars torn open and covered with ants, the water bottle rolled a few feet away. There was no sign of violence or struggle and no clear sign of where Nancy might have gone.

Before they left the scene, one of the officers, more imaginative than the rest, commented on the strange formation of fungus and tree stump nearby. "Doesn't it like a mother and child, looking out at the river together?"

Her partner elbowed her. "Sure, I guess. You can see that—if you eat the mushrooms first." They laughed and walked on down the path and into the afternoon sun. The wind rustled through the golden tendrils with a sound like a sigh and the river burbled on.

ABOUT THE AUTHOR

When she's not writing, Samantha enjoys family time, watching old movies, baking, reading, gaming, walking with her rescue dogs, and going places. Her favorite gift is tickets (to just about anything). Learn more about her and her work at http://samanthabryant.com, check out her catalog of writing at http://bit.ly/SamanthaBryant or find her on Twitter or Instagram @samanthabwriter. If all else fails, check the woods. She likes to get lost there.

The Greenhouse
Carol Gyzander

Amy stood in the cool spring air that seeped through the old Vermont farmhouse window. She leaned against the kitchen sink and watched her grandmother Martha limp down the aisle in the massive greenhouse outside, tending to hundreds of potted geraniums. The young woman's hand flew to her mouth as the older woman stumbled a moment and caught herself on the huge table full of plants. *How much longer can she do this?*

She jumped as her wife's arms slipped around her waist in a gentle hug.

"I was watching her from the bedroom upstairs, babe," said Joan. "She's gotten a lot slower, hasn't she?"

Amy leaned back against her wife's shoulder, Joan's chin nestled on the top of her head. "Yeah. But I can't keep her out of the greenhouse, no matter how much I do in there. Much as the place weirds me out, it's all she cares about, Joan...all she loves."

They stood together for a moment, Amy resting against her wife in exhaustion. The pair watched Martha carry a small bin of plant trimmings to the dark end of the greenhouse, where they grew mushrooms and kept the compost pile. One foot dragged slightly behind her as she moved down the gravel-covered aisle, a remnant of last year's stroke.

Seeing Grandma in the greenhouse makes me think of coming out and finding her on the ground. As if the place hasn't always given me the chills. She's just so...obsessed with it. Amy shivered.

Joan's arms tightened around her waist. "I hate to say it, but we gotta think about making some changes. It's been wonderful living here in the country and helping her these last few years, but we're writers, not gardeners. You've worked with the greenhouse and the plants since you two started the mushrooms last winter. How much writing have you gotten done?"

Amy gave a wan smile and a half-shrug, looking down at the counter. She had, indeed, spent much of her time building the trays to hold the composted manure, prepping the spores into the spawn pellets they would plant, and constantly monitoring the temperature and humidity at that end of the greenhouse—where the dank dimness made it creepier than ever.

"Oh, I don't know. I've been getting words in...here and there..." Her voice trailed off as Joan turned her around. After a moment, she looked up, and their gaze met.

Joan squeezed her shoulders. "Come on, babe, I've only been helping a little, and I'm still not getting enough done on my book. You're not gonna meet your publisher's deadline at this rate. We need to either hire somebody to help your grandmother or close the green-house business. She can't do it all herself, and you can't help her full-time. *Her* dream, not yours."

Amy's lower lip trembled. She stepped away from her wife. "I know."

She bent down to pet the black cat that wrapped around her ankles. "Hey, Felix. Nice kitty." He jumped onto the counter and up to the cat door that connected the kitchen window to the greenhouse through a little mesh-covered tunnel. "Well, there he goes again. Go catch some mice!"

The two stood side-by-side and watched the cat run lightly into the greenhouse to Martha, who held on tightly to the plant table as she leaned forward to greet him. The older woman appeared to be talking to the cat; she gestured toward the budding geraniums and shook one finger at him.

Joan's voice came softly. "Babe, you know I'd have the same problem with my momma if she were still with us."

Amy sighed and slipped her fingers into her wife's hand. "Okay, I'll talk to her about getting some help here. But I don't know how to pay for it."

Joan nodded. "We'll find a way."

At dinner that night, when all three were seated around the table, Amy looked from Joan to her grandmother and took a deep breath.

"Grandma, Joan and I have some concerns. We want to talk to you about the greenhouse business."

Martha smiled and patted her hand. "I know it's been a lot of work for you dears, and I truly appreciate all your help. But it'll get too hot for the mushrooms soon, so it's only a bit longer to keep harvesting them, and we're almost done with the spring geranium crop. The trucks will be here to pick up our plants next week. Then we'll clean the greenhouse and pot up the mums. Get them started for fall."

Amy cleared her throat. "Well, see, that's part of the problem. I need to spend more time on my book now, or else I'll miss my deadline. And once you do that, it's the kiss of death with a publisher." She looked down as she spoke and risked a glance at her grandmother. Found Martha watching her intently but managed to go on.

"I just, well, can't put in the amount of time I've been doing. And there are so many repairs we need to pay for. We need to get someone to help or...cut out the greenhouse business." The last words escaped from her in a torrent. "I mean, I know money is tight right now, but I'll get payment from the publisher in two months, and Joan's book will be out by then, so we'll have money coming in. We don't *need* the business to stay afloat. Or we could sell the farm and greenhouse and...and move closer to town?"

A long moment of quiet while Amy's stomach twisted in knots. Martha folded her hands in front of her and studied her plate. Finally, she spoke.

"I see, dear. I didn't realize this was such a problem for you or that the expenses were so bad. Of course, you must focus on what you need to do...and I appreciate the help and company you two have given me. I just can't picture ever living anyplace else. This is *our* land, and three generations before me have grown up here. It's in my blood. And yours, too. You can't leave here, honey."

Tears welled up in Amy's eyes.

Joan leaned forward and spoke gently. "I don't want to leave either, Martha, but the costs of the furnace repairs for the greenhouse were more than we can cover from the spring plant sale. We're all losing money living here, even with the new mushroom crop."

Martha nodded. "Well, maybe there's something we can figure out. We can't leave here." She picked up her fork.

Amy and Joan exchanged silent glances and bent down to keep eating.

Amy couldn't sleep that night. She tossed for hours, fighting a growing sense that something was off. *Did I hear a noise?* She slipped out of bed, glancing back at Joan curled up under the quilt. Grabbing her phone, she quietly stepped into her slippers and headed down the hall toward Martha's room. The door was ajar—nobody inside.

She headed down the stairs, checked the main floor and the kitchen, then looked toward the greenhouse. The lights were on, contrary to schedule, and she groaned and rolled her eyes. *What's Grandma doing out there? Seriously, at this hour.*

She pulled a jacket from the back door's hook, jamming her phone into the pocket, and headed across the damp grass to the greenhouse in the pre-dawn light. "Hello? Grandma, are you out here?"

She didn't see anyone once she was inside. Amy walked across the short end of the hundred-foot-long greenhouse, looking down each aisle between the massive tables. *Nothing unusual.* She tightened her lips in resolve and headed down to the far end, pushing aside the dark plastic barrier to enter the unlit mushroom-growing area. While the plastic-covered walls made her feel claustrophobic during the daytime, it was a hundred times worse in the dead of night. All she could hear was the whir of air circulation from the fans.

The humidity hit her like a bucket of ice water, and her skin felt immediately clammy. Amy triggered the flashlight on her phone and scanned the room. Row after row of round whiteness looked back at her like eyes—the button mushrooms. At the end of the farthest table, one tray of composted manure lay overturned onto the ground. Her light reflected off the exposed web of threadlike mycelium that spread through the growing medium like a network of veins to support the mushrooms.

As she peered closer, her heart leapt into her throat at the sight of a dark shape on the ground next to the overturned tray, and she ran forward and dropped to her knees. "Grandma! Not again." She reached out and rolled her grandmother over. Martha's face was gray, her eyes unfocused.

Amy froze. *What should I do? Should I go get help or stay with her?* She dialed Joan's cell phone, waiting impatiently as it rang several times before she heard her wife's sleepy voice.

"Amy? Where are you...you were just here in bed—"

"Joan, wake up! It's Grandma. I just found her on the ground. We're out in the mushroom end of the greenhouse. Come out here, and I'll call 9-1-1." *We're so far away from town out here. It took them twenty minutes to get to us last time.*

"Oh no! I'm coming right—"

Martha's eyes flickered. Amy cut the call and leaned toward her grandmother, scooping the older woman into her lap and cradling her head.

"Amy? Wha'...what am I doing on the ground?" Martha reached for her left shoulder and held it tight, grimacing.

"Just rest, Grandma. I think you might've had another stroke. Hold on, and I'll get you some help." She lifted her phone.

"No. Don't call anyone. Don' wanna leave...can't go to that hospital...again."

A sob escaped Amy's lips. *Should I call 9-1-1 or not?*

Martha sagged back in Amy's arms.

"Grandma! What are you feeling?"

Martha's voice was thready and slow, and Amy had to lean in to catch her words. "Just want to be here on my land...and have you with me."

She smoothed the hair back from Martha's face, then pulled her coat off and wrapped it around her grandmother, clasping her hand underneath the cover. She was thrilled to see the older woman's eyes focus on hers.

"Amy, sweetheart...much worse this time. Promise you'll do what we said. After I go..." Her voice trailed off.

Amy nodded, biting her lower lip. Tears ran down her face. "Yes, Grandma. I read what you gave me, and I understand. I'll do what you want if...when...you pass from us. But please, hold on, stay with me."

The greenhouse door banged open, and a moment later, Joan burst through the plastic divider, skidding onto the ground to hug the pair. Amy closed her eyes in her wife's arms for a moment. When she looked back down at Martha, her grandmother smiled as she watched them embrace, but then the older woman's eyes fluttered closed. The loving expression trailed away as her face fell slack.

Amy sobbed. "Grandma? *Martha!* Are you...are you still with us?"

No response.

She felt her grandmother's neck. *No pulse.*

"Oh Joan, I think she's gone." *Oh no, oh no.* "She didn't want me to call for help...said she doesn't want to leave here."

The Greenhouse

The two young women sat, crying softly and holding each other, keeping the older woman's body company until the sun peeked under the edge of the dark coverings on the greenhouse walls.

Finally, Joan helped Amy up and walked her into the kitchen. Held her hand while she called the authorities, then got busy making a pot of coffee.

Amy looked around listlessly while they waited for the local officials to arrive, then went to the piles of paper covering the big desk in the kitchen corner. Rummaging through them for a few minutes, she pulled out a brochure as Joan brought over two cups of steaming coffee.

Joan raised an eyebrow. "What's that, babe?" She leaned over Amy's shoulder as Amy sat down and flipped the brochure on the table. "Eternally Green?"

Amy sighed and took the coffee. "It's what Grandma arranged for her burial. It's an evergreen thing." She poked the brochure with her finger, then wrapped both hands around her coffee cup and hugged it to her chest.

Joan turned through the pages. "Seriously, she wants...wanted...to be buried in this?"

"Yeah. In a *mushroom suit*. The latest thing to 'Preserve the Earth.'" She took a sip, shaking her head.

"Huh. What's the purpose of it all? Burial is...pollution?"

"Yeah, it's supposed to be bad for the environment. All the toxic chemicals in our bodies go back into the soil when we're buried, and she didn't want to make things worse."

"But what about cremation?"

Amy sighed. "That has its own problems. With this, the burial shroud is embedded with some mushroom or fungus that neutralizes the toxins in our body so that we can enrich the earth as we decompose, not pollute it. She felt strongly about it. Asked if we could bury her here on the farm. Behind the greenhouse."

"I hate to ask. How much is it?"

Amy put her coffee down and rubbed her forehead. "She already paid for it years before we moved here—before we even started growing the mushrooms. I call the number, and they come out, take care of all the legal stuff, and put her in the mushroom suit. Weird, or what?"

"Yeah, but when have we ever done anything normal, babe?" Joan smiled and pushed the coffee toward her. "Will it matter if it's weird since this is what she wanted?"

"No, I suppose not. I just don't know if I'll be able to walk by that area very often. At least for a while."

"That's fair. You call them after breakfast, we'll bury her together, and I'll keep an eye on the property for you. But you know what I'll have to say, right?"

Amy tilted her head and raised an eyebrow at her wife, who grinned and pulled a spooky face, waggling her hands in the air.

"Thou hast brought a fungus amongus!"

Amy's mouth dropped open momentarily, and then she burst out laughing until tears rolled down her face again and turned into sobs. She reached over to hug Joan and held her for a long time. The two sat together, sipping their coffee, until they heard the siren approach down the long driveway.

Amy and Joan held hands behind the greenhouse three days later. They'd conducted a memorial service in the church but opted to bury Martha's mushroom shroud all by themselves, using the farm's Bobcat digger. Amy read one of her grandmother's favorite poems by Robert Frost. After standing by the fresh gash of dark, rich dirt in silence for a while, Amy turned toward her wife. The two hugged tightly for a minute.

Joan whispered in her ear. "It's okay, Amy. We did it. It's what she wanted."

Amy felt Joan stroke her head as she trembled. "I know," she answered with a snuffle. "It's just so bizarre to see her buried out here and...not in a cemetery. But here at the edge of the field, she'll be able to see her greenhouse and the property that she loved—" A sob stopped her words.

"Of course, babe." Joan rumpled her short hair. They turned and walked together around the greenhouse and back to the farmhouse.

Early the next week, Amy awoke from a nightmare as the sun peeked in the window. In her dream, she was choking, her mouth and throat filled with earth and some sticky substance emitting a fecund odor. Jumping out of bed, she cried out and thrashed at the nightgown wrapped around her face. Her ragged breath tore from her throat as she desperately tried to make sense of what she was feeling. *Oh my God, what was that? I can't breathe!* She coughed and retched.

Joan woke and sat up in bed. "What's happened?"

Amy leaned against the dresser, trying to slow her breathing now that the coughing had stopped. She bent forward, holding her face with her hands. "Oh Joan, I couldn't breathe...like something was crawling down my throat into my lungs and expanding!"

Joan reached out for her. "Aww, babe, you're just so tired. This has been a tough time for you. C'mon back to bed."

"No, I won't be able to sleep. My heart's going a mile a minute. Sorry I woke you." She looked around for the slippers she had kicked out of the way in her panic to get out of bed. "I'm gonna go down and make some coffee and maybe get an early start on writing."

Joan smiled at her. "That's my old Amy talking! I'll get up too and keep you company. Always good to get some words in." She slid her feet over the edge of the bed and started pulling on some clothes, but Amy came over and hugged her fiercely.

"Thanks, sweetie. Don't know how I could've gotten through the last few weeks without you."

Joan whispered, "I couldn't last without you, either. Whatever you do, wherever you go, I want to be with you."

Amy stroked her wife's hair before turning to head downstairs.

She wrinkled her nose at a strong, earthy smell in the kitchen. Flipping the light on, she gaped at piles of dirt and tangled leaves trailing over the counter and across the floor. A potted plant from the windowsill had tipped over during the night. *Damn cat. Crap. That reminds me, I can't write until I get the plants loaded for pickup. And harvest some more mushrooms.*

She turned on the coffeemaker, swept the dark earth off the kitchen counter with the dustbin, and then called up the stairs, "Hey, Joan? Have you seen Felix recently?"

Her wife answered down from the office, where they did most of their writing at adjacent desks. "Nope. But his food's been disappearing, so he's still around. Maybe he's hiding out because he misses your grandmother?"

"I guess." Amy nudged the empty food dish. *Wish he'd come in from the greenhouse when I'm awake. Didn't know I'd be missing* both *of them so much. Silly cat.*

Joan's voice came again, still upstairs. "Can you come up and get some writing done? I've got some nice music playing. It'll put you in the mood."

Amy bit her lower lip. "Yeah, I'll be up, but after lunch. Forgot I have to head out to the greenhouse and get the geraniums loaded and ready for pickup. Coffee's ready whenever you want it." Her voice trailed off as she grabbed her jacket and headed out the back door with her steaming mug of Green Mountain coffee. She walked across the lawn but paused at the greenhouse door. *Odd. I could've sworn I closed it last night when I left.*

She went inside and looked around. The previous day, it had taken so long to hose off the rolling racks that she'd only finished inserting the tags in half the hundreds of pots to be shipped out that day. At least, she thought she'd only done half. Now, all of them contained tags. Frowning, she looked up and down the rows of plants on the fifty-foot tables and shook her head. *Maybe I'm losing my mind? Or it's just stress? I guess I did them all last night.*

She checked the clipboard and confirmed the two p.m. pickup

time. Suddenly, the automatic ventilation system turned on, and her nose wrinkled at the same unusual odor that had awoken her, smelling even more fertile than the growing space's usual warm, earthy aroma. After a long moment of looking up and down the greenhouse and sniffing, she shrugged, then bent down and looked under the tables.

"Felix? Are you out here, buddy? Here, kitty, kitty!" A flash of movement from the corner of her eye caught her attention, and she turned to look for the source. All she saw were some plants swaying a little at the far end. "Felix? Where are you?" *Silly boy.*

When she approached, the movement ceased. She moved the leaves aside to peer between them. Light reflected back in the shape of two narrow-slitted eyes. "Hey, buddy—"

A sharp hiss filled the air, and she jumped back in surprise. "Oh! Okay, Felix. You don't wanna see me now? Okay." She bit her lower lip a moment, then turned away and headed toward the rolling racks crowding the end of the greenhouse. Over her shoulder, she told the cat, "It's okay, buddy. I miss her, too. You come inside when you're ready."

She moved one of the racks and gave a little involuntary shriek when a small shape fell off a shelf, landing on the gravel with a plop. Bending down, she poked it with her toe, then shuddered when she realized it was a small rodent, mostly decomposed and covered with a thick layer of slime. *That wasn't there last night.* She scooped it into the trash and continued loading the plants, a frown on her face.

The next day, Amy carried groceries from her car into the kitchen. She heard the barn door close and looked up when Joan entered the back door.

Amy grinned. "Hey, I got the Italian sausage you asked for. They had a special..." Her voice trailed off as she caught sight of Joan's frown and the dirt streaks on her face. "What's up?"

Joan walked over and washed her hands thoroughly in the farm sink. "Listen, something weird happened. I went out to look at the big field behind the greenhouse and the acreage to the south...you know, the part we've been talking about selling?"

Amy's lips tightened. "To the developer. But what's up?" She crossed her arms and leaned against the counter next to her wife.

"Well, I'm not sure how to tell you this, so I'm just gonna say it. It looks like some kind of critter must've been attracted to the loose soil where we buried Martha. It was all dug up again, the area by the side of the field. I fixed it before you got back."

Amy jumped forward and turned Joan by the shoulder to face her. "Dug it up? What do you mean? Did it...did it get to..." A small sob escaped her lips. "To Grandma?"

"No, I could see the white of the mushroom suit, so I assume she's still down there. No worries. You can come out and check if you want." Joan stroked her face and leaned down so their foreheads touched. "I'm so sorry. I wanted to get it done so you wouldn't be worried."

"Okay, let's walk over after I put away the groceries. Thank you for taking care of it. I'm sure it's all fine." Amy pulled back from Joan and forced a smile. "I'm okay, really."

Amy's hands froze on the keyboard as a yowl pierced the night. She looked up from the desk, interrupted during their late-night writing session, and checked the time on her phone—midnight. *Come on. What is it this time?* She heard it again: a full-throated howl from the greenhouse. *Felix? What's going on?*

Next to her, Joan rubbed her eyes. "What's up, babe?"

"Felix is out yelling in the greenhouse. Let me just make sure he's okay. I wish he'd come back inside." She grabbed her phone and headed for the stairs. "Back in a few."

As she walked across the grass, pulling her jacket on, her mind returned to coming out in the middle of the night and finding her grandmother. *Well, at least I won't have to worry about that.* She sighed. *Where's the darn cat?*

She paused again at the door to the greenhouse, again ajar. *Do I keep leaving this open? What the hell is going on?*

She slipped inside, turning on the flashlight app on her phone and shining it around. Dirt trailed across the gravel in spots. She saw movement in the darkness down one of the rows and headed across the greenhouse.

"Felix? Here, kitty, kitty. Who's a good boy?" She continued talking as the flashlight illuminated the black cat in the middle of the aisle. He stood all puffed up, hissing, and ignored her as she approached from behind. She couldn't see what he was facing—her light didn't reach the aisle's far end. He let out another full-throated cry, backing toward her and away from where the black plastic sheet covered the far end of the greenhouse.

Her steps made a crunching sound on the gravel path behind him. The cat turned and leapt at her with a yowl. He scratched her chest and neck deeply as he clawed up and over her and dashed through the cat tunnel toward the kitchen.

She screamed in surprise and pain, dropping her phone. "Holy crap, Felix! What's the matter, boy?"

She touched her chest and felt blood. *Damn cat. What's wrong with you? What scared you?* Amy froze as gravel scraped on the path behind her down the aisle.

Step, drag. Step, drag.

It sounded strangely familiar.

What the hell? She whirled to see a dark shape approaching from the far end by the mushroom section, stopping every few feet to turn and check the remaining plants.

"Who's that? Who's there?" Amy's voice rose higher and more shrill as she blurted out the words. She stooped and snatched up her phone. The figure moved along the aisle just out of her flashlight's range. "*Who's in here?*"

She vaguely heard the kitchen door slam but focused on the stooped figure before her, walking and dragging one foot.

Step, drag.

A waft of the earthy aroma brushed over her.

"Grandma?" she asked hesitantly. "Is that you?" The shape halted as she approached. When she shone the light on it, the figure's head turned toward her, and Amy gasped. Looking back was her beloved grandmother's face, but gray and slack. Black dirt filled Martha's hair and caked her neck and clothes.

The eyes were the worst: gray and dead, lids crusted with fungal growth. A network of white, threadlike streaks ran from her mouth out across the skin of her face. The figure turned the rest of the way toward her, still balancing with a hand on the table.

They were now only several feet apart.

The figure's mouth opened, and a spew of moist gray fog shot out, splattering Amy across the face and shoulders. She involuntarily gasped as it invaded her nose and chest and plunged into the deep cat scratches. That same warm, earthy scent surrounded her, and she was so shocked that it took her a moment to place it. *Mushrooms! Oh my God.*

Spores?

She jumped back from the shape, tripping and falling to the ground as the figure turned and limped away. Amy gasped for breath but couldn't take in any air. She clutched at her throat.

The door to the greenhouse squeaked open and slammed shut, and footsteps thudded on the path. She scrabbled at her face, writhing and trying to wipe off the phlegm that clung to her skin—trying to spit out the vile stuff that filled her mouth and throat. She coughed and smelled the fungus everywhere. *It's in me!* She curled up into a ball on the gravel path, writhing as it invaded her lungs.

I can't breathe!

Joan raced toward her. "*Amy!* I heard the cat, and then I heard you scream. Are you okay?"

Her wife skidded to a stop, landing on both knees next to her in the gravel. "Come on, babe! What happened?"

Amy convulsed. She tried to turn away from Joan. *No, no! Don't come near me. Don't touch me!* She felt her wife's strong hands rolling her over.

She tried to tell Joan to run, get away, watch out for the dark figure in the greenhouse. But when her mouth opened, the same stream of wet fog poured out of her and shot through the air, splattering her wife's face. Covering her nose and mouth.

Joan's eyes widened, hands scrabbling at her own neck as she gasped for breath.

The two collapsed together into a twitching heap.

The dark figure limped back and stood over them for several minutes until their twitching stopped, then loaded them onto a hand-cart and dragged them to the end of the row toward the compost pile.

Now, they would never need to leave.

ABOUT THE AUTHOR

Bram Stoker Award® finalist Carol Gyzander writes and edits horror, weird fiction, and science fiction—frequently with strong women in twisted tales that touch your heart. She has stories in *Weird Tales 367, Under Twin Suns: Alternate Histories of the Yellow Sign,* and other magazines and anthologies. Carol is co-editor and a contributor to *Discontinue If Death Ensues: Tales from the Tipping Point* with her fellow Stoker nominees (Flame Tree Publishing).

The Must of Your Body Covers Me
Sumiko Saulson

If nature were my mother
You'd be the mother of my nature

The thorns gracing your rosebush
Burrowing into my wicker trap
Stolen moments of late-night sleep
Entwined in your arms in slumber deep
You bed me in your earthly crypt
And promise me eternity

Therein we hibernate through winter
Awakening in must midsummer
My blood that smells like rust
Your fluids florid mildew
You're growing on me

Lips to cowslip
Sporium to cheek
I inhale gifts you bequeath
Your loamy green venom
Composed of spores
Penetrates my tongue
The taste metallic

I melt into your green film skin
Mold skimming pond scum
My face reflected on your surface

Mushrooms explode from my toes
Mucor spreads over my thighs
Breast dotted in fungal plaques

You pierce my fleshy surface
With threads of your hyphae
Branching tender veins to vessels
Your bountiful mycelium lives on forever
Consuming the blood of my immortal flesh

If Earth were my Mother
This sapphic pool of love
Would need no Narcissus
Her wicker no man

ABOUT THE AUTHOR

Sumiko Saulson is the Elgin Award and Bram Stoker Award®-nominated author of *The Rat King: A Book of Dark Poetry*. Their novel *Somnalia: The Metamorphoses of Flynn Keahi* is available on Mocha Memoirs Press, and their latest book of verse, *Melancholia: A Book of Dark Poetry* is out on Bludgeoned Girls Press.

The Angels of Scruggs County
Daniel Roop

I RECKON you'll be wanting to know exactly how I ended up here in Scruggs County Juvenile, since that's what everyone's questioning gets down to eventually, so we can skip the hemming and hawing. Reporters, relations, teachers, psychologists—all with the same wonderment when they open the file and see who Sadie Ruth Tucker is— straight A's all through sixth grade, youth volunteer at the animal shelter, 4-H Clover Bowl winner—and can't reconcile all that goodness with me sitting here in an orange jumpsuit. I mean, everyone knows it's on account of the arson and the murders, or more correctly, the bodies, but they can't make sense of it. So, I'll tell you like I told everybody else, and you can believe me or not, about the bodies, and the angels, and how it all started 'cause my mother never met her father.

Mama's daddy was dead, hit head-on by a no-account drunk by the time she was born, and so of course, as everyone knows, that meant Mama was a healer, as is every woman who never saw her father. Even when Mama was just a child, people all over Scruggs County would call my Granny and ask her to bring Mama over so she could breathe in their babies' mouths to cure their thrush. And she always went, and it always worked, and when I was growing up, she told me I would be a healer, too. I told her, "But I see Daddy every day," and she'd say, "I know sweetie, but you've got the gift," and I believed her. I'd find baby birds fallen from the nest with their little splayed legs, breathing like bellows about to burst, and I'd lay one finger on 'em real gentle and pray to God for healing, and well, they'd die. Our cat Trixie had five kittens and Mama told me two of 'em looked like they weren't gonna make it, and I stayed up all night moving my hands through the air over 'em, trying to find some magic pattern while I asked God to fix 'em, and they died, too. My brother Cody broke his hand last year falling off the Massey-Ferguson, which he weren't supposed to be on anyway, and I snuck into his room that night and started mumbling to God and Cody hollered, "Get outta here Sadie, 'fore you kill me like you did them kittens." So, I wanted to believe I was a healer, but I can't say I was too convicted.

Now Cody, he'd been called to preach just after breaking his hand, when he was fourteen, and as Daddy was the pastor at Branch Creek Church, that made the whole family real proud. I prayed to God to be thankful and proud, too, but mostly I was just jealous. Daddy'd beam while Cody, all red-faced and lathered, got right down on the floor and hollered that judgment was coming and people y'all better get right with God and such. I wondered why I didn't feel right with God, or why God didn't feel right with me, and why I wasn't being used to heal like Mama. I'd see animals too sick to eat at the shelter, and I'd look around the pews at church and see Ida Jenkins wincing with the bulletin sliding out of her gnarled-up hands, and Chester Davidson with his face all droopy from that stroke, and I'd think, *God, why don't you use me to fulfill these needs?* I reckon that was a prayer, 'cause it got answered last June when I saw the angels.

A little piece from our house, way back in Poke Holler alongside Johnson Creek, was the old Trogdon place, a big old two-story farmhouse that was halfway collapsed and where nobody went anymore. Kids used to play there, but after the chicken farm come in across the ridge and all that brackish crap-infested water mixed with the smell of ten thousand chickens, it wasn't a pleasant place to be. Working at the animal shelter and on our farm, I suppose I was a little bit nose blind, so I still went. The Trogdon place was mine alone. I never went inside. I'd sit on the warped wraparound porch, or climb the trees, or just be real still and see how close animals would get and I'd classify 'em as far up King Philip's Class Ordered Fifty Green Spiders as I could, biology being my favorite subject. Or I'd take off my shoes and kneel in the damp earth and I'd ask God to make me the healer I was supposed to be. I was down in the dirt that June day, roundabout dusk, when I heard a voice. Now listen—it wasn't a voice you could've *heard*—it wasn't outside, so to speak. It was inside me, but powerful, and it wasn't me, and I've told that to every psychologist, and I mean it. It wasn't me. It wasn't even exactly what you'd call *words*, more of a feeling or an impulse, and it said, *Come inside.* So, excited as could be I stood up and wiped the wet earth from my knees and pushed open that rickety door and marched right in.

Marching turned to creeping pretty quick. The windows were so caked with dirt and grime that hardly any light got in, and it was dark as a dungeon in that front entrance. When my eyes adjusted, I could see something glimmering down the hallway leading into the rest of the house. I eased farther in, and I'm here to tell you, that feeling as I followed those little streaks of blue-white light on the moldy black walls, getting brighter and thicker, was overpowering. I bet it felt like being called to preach, but I can't say—just, there was a *clarity* to it, if that's the word. I was where I was supposed to be. I stepped into the back bedroom, and the room shone like the streets in heaven. All those glowing lines, thick and bright as anything on those damp, dark walls, lit the whole place up. It looked like spiderwebs made of starlight, or like a photo of all the rivers in North America from space at night, if the rivers glittered and were alive. Now I bet when I told you I saw an angel, you were thinking of one of those granny pictures of some floofy lady with wings floating over kids too dumb to stay off a collapsing bridge, but I'm talking about an angel from the Bible, and they get described all kindsa crazy ways I never could sort out. But I knew I was lookin at one then, and it spoke to me, again from inside, with something different than words, and it said, *Touch me.*

I was pretty near tingling with excitement when I laid my palm flat on the wall, white threads between my fingers. I just knew I'd feel love and joy, but honestly, it felt kinda wrong right off, like I wasn't supposed to be there after all. But then I remembered how often people were just plain terrified of angels, and I said to myself, *Do not be afraid,* and the feeling passed, and the angel opened the truth to me. It told me I would be able to heal now, really heal, and to start with animals since they were simpler. That made sense to me—that's just science, and God made science, so why shouldn't angels use it too? The angel told me I'd soon be able to move on to people, and that I'd grow in wisdom and know who I could heal and who I couldn't, and that I could comfort the ones I couldn't heal by telling 'em God would be takin 'em home soon. They told me how that would happen.

Part of me was still holding back, in that dank black room in that chicken-stench holler, wondering *why in the world would an angel be here?* But then I remembered that's where God comes—Bethlehem and Nazareth and all the little out of the way places nobody cares for, and you can't get more out of the way than Poke Holler. I could feel power like thick wet electricity going into my hand and through my whole body, and I said *yes* to it. And I knew, just like Jesus used the disciples, these angels (it was more than one, I understood now) were gonna use me. I was gonna be their hands and feet. I left there straightaway and that night I dreamt of all the good work I'd do.

Next morning, I rode the four-wheeler to my shift at the animal shelter, where people dropped off animals in all kindsa pitiful shapes, and went straight to Ralph, the German Shepherd with a big old goiter making it where he couldn't breathe. I knew he was the one to start with, and I laid my hands on his throat and felt that same wet electric tingle, like fire you could pour and touch, and I swear it wasn't thirty seconds before I felt that goiter shrink like air going out of a balloon, and he went from wheezing to breathing just fine. Denise, the manager, looked at me like her eyes were gonna come out of her head. I just smiled and walked across the room to Max, the ornery tuxedo cat with the broke front leg. He was next. He hated to be touched, but he let me hold onto that cockeyed leg and say my prayer and we both felt that warmth, and he purred and hopped off the table pretty as you please. Denise said, "Sadie, what in the world is going on?" The angels had told me I could talk about my gift, but leave their part out of it, since people wouldn't believe me anyway, they'd only believe what they could see. So, I told her, and she looked real skeptical, but then we spent the next hour going around the shelter, me healing Cornwall's broke turtle shell, and Bitsy's busted wing, and Denise started to holler, "Praise God!" after every healing, and I hollered with her, and our eyes just shined with tears. Then I come to Jet the Labrador, my favorite, and he had cancer and was just waiting to die, and as I reached out to heal him, I heard the angels say, *Not him. He won't be healed. We're calling him home.* And it just about broke my heart, but I wasn't gonna question this plan, and I touched Jet and felt the same kinda wet feeling but without the warmth, and I said, "God's calling you home, sweet boy. Soon." I told Denise it weren't my decision, and she accepted it, having seen all she'd seen. Jet died two hours later, just before I went home.

That night, well after closing, I snuck out, pushing the four-wheeler down our gravel driveway to the road. Once in town, I cut the engine and coasted into the shelter parking lot. I punched in the code and opened the door, and Jet came walking out. He moved kinda funny, like he was learning his legs again, like his nerves didn't have a regulator. His eyes were solid white, and his black coat glowed with white streaks. I told him where to meet me and drove off. It took him a while, hobbling and jerking like he did, but he made it. I saw him safely home. I went to bed that night feeling blessed, and even more so when the angel told me, *Now, heal the people.*

By the next morning, which swas a Wednesday, word had got around from Denise and the folks at the shelter about what I'd done. Mama and Daddy asked me about it, and I said, "Just you wait and see what happens at church tonight. You ain't never seen a revival like we're gonna have." Mama beamed, and Daddy furrowed a little bit, and Cody said, "That's right sister, I've got a powerful word for tonight myself." That evening we drove the three miles to church in the Chrysler, Mama humming a hymn and Cody mumbling a prayer and Daddy saying, "Now Sadie, don't you make no scene," and me just about giggling with joy. I sat in the front pew like always and waited for the folks to arrive. Daddy was giving the announcements and a few folks were looking at me and whispering to each other when Ida Jenkins walked in late, on account of it took her so long to get dressed, and I jumped outta my seat and ran up to her and the angels gave me the go-ahead and I said, "Ms. Jenkins, God bless your sweet heart," and I took her hands in mine and she started to smile her normal smile but then she felt that same warm thick power go into her and gasped. When I let her go, she lifted her hands to her face and saw her knuckles shrunk down to normal and fingers that would bend again and I hollered, "Praise God!" and she hugged me tight and cried and yelled, "Hallelujah!" The place exploded, folks surrounding me, and Daddy and Cody fighting their way to me to try to get some kinda order. I stood beneath the pulpit and people lined up, and I touched so many, and I touched Chester Davidson's face, and he smiled the first even smile he'd had in years. But then Bonnie Graves, the widow with brittle sugar, come up to me, and the angels told me *no*, and I touched her and felt that cold wet, and told her I was so sorry, but rejoice because God would bring her home soon. We hugged and cried together, and everyone went home joyful.

Sneaking out again that night was no problem—I just told my parents I was spending time alone with God, which I was, really. About midnight I drove the four-wheeler a mile away to Bonnie's single-wide. She'd died about an hour before, the angels told me, and she was looking out the kitchen window when I pulled up, her eyes like white marbles. She hobbled outside and I told her where to go and made sure she didn't get lost along the way.

The rest of the week was a whirlwind. So many healings, and three more that couldn't be, that I helped bring home. I wondered once how the angels chose, but I let that go right quick, chalking it up to mysterious ways and all. People mighta wondered about the missing dog, and Bonnie and Pete and Ava, but all of them were older and lived alone, and had just a touch of Alzheimer's, and folks figured maybe they'd gone away for a bit and just forgot to tell anyone. There was too much excitement to worry much. Daddy wanted to call *The 700 Club*, and Mrs. McKenna my biology teacher wanted to call the university, and Cody wanted me to stay home so he could discern the spirits around me, but Mama said "Let's just let this beautiful thing bloom a while before we dissect it," and they agreed, so things woulda been fine if Cody hadn't been jealous.

Late that Saturday night, after I'd told Delilah Parsons that God would take her home soon, and after I'd told her white-eyed body where to go, and after I'd met her at the mouth of Poke Holler to lead her the rest of the way, I was sitting in the Trogdon place with the angels. Me being their hands and feet was helping, and now instead of just a mess of tendrils on the wall, they could form bodies. They'd used the good parts of those good people to teach 'em how to walk in our world, so they could go forth and do their work. They'd read 'em like a textbook and built radiant flesh for themselves. I was asking 'em what came next when I heard Cody yell, "Get behind me, devil!"

He'd followed me into the holler that night, jealous that God had chosen me. He screamed out, "Devil!" again, then stumbled backpedaling when the three angels rose and unfolded to their full nine-foot height, looking like walking trees made of white sinewy webs. Cody tripped over the bodies on the floor and his hand smushed into Bonnie's face, covered in pearly tendrils and pale toadstools. He lit out, and I knew nothing good was gonna come of it, but the angels told me, *Do not be afraid.*

They told me not to worry, that they were part of something bigger, and I was too, that this place or these bodies going away wasn't the end of anything since I'd helped them learn to walk in this world forevermore. I watched as they glowed brighter than ever, like foxfire, and electric pulses leapt from their tendrilled arms to the dry wood walls. The place went up like a Roman candle. When Cody come back with Daddy and the sheriff, they found me crying at the edge of the smoldering house. Later, when it cooled, and they found the four charred skeletons, they held me in county, and after a trial where you could tell nobody really understood much of anything about anything, they brought me here, officially, for arson.

So sure, that house burned, but it ain't like you can kill an angel. Even now, they're reaching out into the empty spaces and filling 'em with their light, and I'm still their vessel. I can feel the ground, even here, thrum with their presence, reminding me why I'm on this earth, telling me new truths every morning. Telling me how they'll use those I've already healed. I can reveal this now, they say, on account of it's their time, and what a radiant future it'll be.

Do not be afraid.

ABOUT THE AUTHOR

Daniel Roop is a member of the Horror Writers Association and has been nominated for a Pushcart Prize for his work in *Will Work for Peace* from Zeropanik Press. His speculative fiction has appeared or is forthcoming in publications including *Flash Fiction Online*, *Dark Spores*, *Black Cat Tales*, *The Maul Magazine*, and *Appalachian Places*. He is a seventh-generation East Tennessean, and his favorite superhero is Kitty Pryde.

Tender Flesh

Elizabeth Twist

THE PLUMS ARE LOOKING BITTEN: the leaves, I mean, and the fruitlets that have just formed, green bulbs of promise that the fallen blossoms left behind. The new nursery swore these trees would be tough enough to stand up to even my brown thumb, but it's not looking good.

I hold a young branch in my hand, rubbing that cursed digit over leaves chewed to lace. A flashback of pulling young trees from their holes, the trunks dry, or rotted, or split at the graft, plays in my mind. Year after year they've failed, for reasons that still elude me.

I wonder if the guy who sold me these trees, lanky like a young tree himself, might be able to help. I plan to find the number for the nursery as soon as I go back inside, recalling how friendly he was as he walked me to the section at the back with the ballsy sign over it: *Unkillable Stock.*

"Sounds like a dare," I told him.

He laughed a customer service laugh. "Don't worry." He made unbroken eye contact as he caressed the leaves of the most vigorous tree in the bunch, as one pets a dog. "You know, we have a special on right now. Five for the price of two. I'll knock it down to five for one just for you."

I protested, of course, told him I didn't have room for so many trees in my urban backyard. He walked me through a strategy for orcharding in a small space: how to crowd trees together, prune aggressively, and get a perfect amount and variety of fruit for "Uh, one person or like, one or two people." He'd guessed right the first time.

For the first few weeks, things went according to plan. *Unkillable Stock* grew like gangbusters in the little space I gave them. Underground, I knew, their roots were entangled, seeking water, seeking minerals, pushing through the dense red clay. Two plums, two apples, and one untagged specimen that I still haven't been able to figure out.

Now, I take a closer look at the afflicted trees. Tiny bites from tiny mouths have hole-punched all the leaves, but there's something else, a blue-black rot, a bit slimy to the touch and textured, like the sole of a shoe designed for extra grip. I look for beetles, ants, aphids, but I see nothing.

I pluck a spray bottle up from the ground where I've left it and soak all the trees in neem oil, diluted in water with dish soap to help it stick. All my favourite YouTube orchardists use it; even lanky sales guy recommended it. So far, the damage to my plants has carried on. Whatever's eating my plums is undaunted by neem.

A telltale bang from next door marks the end of my morning gardening session. My neighbour's voice booms out over her yard and mine, followed by the screams of her youngest child and cruel taunts from one of the older ones. She swears at them, releasing a stream of polluted language that I feel in my bones. It isn't the words themselves, but the venom that laces them, and the way her voice rattles the whole neighbourhood, silencing the birds and curdling the air itself.

I'll have to watch the plum trees being eaten from behind windows sealed shut against the shouting, banging, and screaming.

I can't remember the nursery's name, so I poke through the receipts I've stuck to the fridge with a magnetic clip. After half an hour spent perilously close to my neighbour's promises to do unspeakably specific things to her middle child—audible through the sliding glass door to outside—I find what I'm looking for.

Where the business name should be at the top of the receipt, it says: ON BUS #4850029300000001

No help there, but I know it's the right receipt since the item list is somewhat familiar: PLU x 2 / APL x 2 / TEN FLSH occupy a line each, and the total I remember: $55.55 at the bottom. SALES Dan occupies the last line. The trees were a steal at that price. I hardly need to regret if four of them die.

I squint as I try to decipher the name of my mystery tree. Ten Flash? A species name? A flash sale? I have no idea.

A high-pitched scream and a flurry of banging penetrate through the glass. My neighbour's voice comes through along with it. The screams stop, then the arguments start. The children seldom cry. Like their mother, they yell, curse, screech, bang, and repeat.

Last time, I found the nursery tucked away in an obscure corner of a tangled industrial area on the edge of town, on a day when I had to get away from home so I didn't go crazy. I make the drive like I did the first time, getting stuck in one cul-de-sac, then another, reversing course, and trying again. I lose track of my left turns, make one too many, and end up in the wrong place again. It's Saturday, so no one is around to ask for directions except a guy riding a lawnmower so big, I can't help but imagine what would happen if it rolled over him. I picture blood, gore, and a mangled shoe spritzing out across the lawn. I decide to let him concentrate on his work.

After an hour of wrong turns, I admit defeat, but now I can't find my way out. I take two more right turns than I mean to and end up in a dead end, looking at a warehouse with a worn sign dangling. I stare at the remaining letters: OF ICE ESS NT A LS. There was an office supply warehouse next to the nursery, I dimly recall. Then I recognise the withered bones of the extravagant willow arbour that arches over the entry to the nursery's parking lot.

The remains of the greenhouse are there, but its polyfilm panels are torn and bent as if it's been struck by a tornado. Toward the back of the lot, where I remember Sales Dan leading me, I find the sign I remember, but *Unkillable Stock* has become simply *kill ock*. A black stain, like the mould that grows in the corner of my bathroom shower, covers the rest of the letters. When I pick the sign up, it crumbles in my hand, leaving a soft, damp, and mealy pudding behind in my palm.

That same black stain coats the wooden pallet where a dozen plastic pots still stand, rotting sticks that used to be trees sticking out of them. Everywhere I look is devastation, dead plants in pots lying on their sides. The place looks as if it's been abandoned for years, but it was thriving only two months earlier.

My sneakers crunch over shards of broken clay as I investigate the former greenhouse. Upended display tables still hold the corpses of annuals, which have dried in the sun. I find a cash register. It looks as if something chewed it until the drawer opened. There is still some cash inside, but it's covered in the same powdery black rot that's everywhere.

At the epicentre of the damage, one living thing stands: a potted tree that looks like it came directly from Eden. Its robust leaves are shiny and dark green. It's covered in pale pink blossoms, the scent of which I can smell from feet away. I approach it with reverence and see that it's bearing fruit, some cherry-like and dark green, some the size of my curled fist and taking on a pinkish blush. It seems like too much for a young tree. Surely it's stressed, but it doesn't look it.

I lean in and sniff a blossom, then rub my thumb through the dusky pollen, shimmering and bright blue, unlike anything I've ever seen. It stains my fingertips in a shade indistinguishable from the inky mildew that already coats them.

From above me, something makes a *zheet zheet* sound. I look up and see a security camera mounted on the former greenhouse's centre pole.

It films me as I bend, wrap my arms around the tree's five-gallon pot, and carry it back to my car.

I plant the new tree in my mini orchard to the sound of my neighbour's children calling each other horrific names. I wonder who taught them those words in particular. They're exceptionally cruel.

Just like my mystery tree, the new tree's leaves are thick and abundant. Also just like it, there's no graft, which means it was grown from a seed. It has smooth bark with horizontal lines like a cherry. I remove it from the pot and find that its roots are gnarled and rubbery, like arthritic hands that run to threads at the end of each finger. I splay the roots out in the hole I've made for it. As I bury them in red clay, slightly amended with mulch and compost, I think I see them twitch and nestle into their new home.

They can't move. Neither can I.

The neighbour thunders out onto the back porch and orders her children to go inside. They don't obey. Her voice changes pitch, deepening until it sounds like a death metal singer's. The sound boils the air. Waves of it, dark and ominous, transform into a cloud that flies up into the sky. The murky undertow covers my yard like poisonous gas.

I've always felt it, but now I can see it, see how I live in it, inhale it. I lift my hands: where the black clinging mildew from the nursery still hasn't washed off, I see twinkling lights, as if I'm coated in glitter.

I don't feel as bad as I usually do.

I look at my two mystery trees. Between them, a vibrant oil-slick rainbow—Pollen? Vibes?—spouts through the air. Life is dynamic, ever-shifting, ever-changing. I know it, but now I can see it. This is what I want in my yard, what I planned when I decided to start planting. Abundant life, self-sustaining and self-nurturing.

The tree I planted earlier this spring has more fruit on it than it did this morning, or perhaps the fruit it already had has sprung into life. The largest of them twitches, as do the several ripe fruits on the new tree. Soon, they're all pulsing to some strange rhythm, as if they're individual cells of a single, beating heart.

The noise from next door is still going. My neighbour is all but growling now, a wordless shout that seethes and falls and seems to battle with the blue-black beauty filling the air over my property, and forming a dome over it. I throw my head back and breathe it in.

My phone rings as the summer sun finally sinks below the horizon. I stumble into the house to answer it, sweat soaking my clothes, the entire surface of my skin shimmering in a rainbow hue, predominantly blue. The inside of the house feels too small. The pollen I've tracked in buzzes angrily.

"Hello?" I say, trying not to mumble.

"You took it home," a voice says. It sounds human. Limited. Unwell.

"It?"

"You know what I mean. Tender Flesh. You took it home."

TEN FLSH. Ah.

"Dan?" I ask. "Dan the sales*man*?" I emphasise the last syllable for fun.

He sighs heavily. "It's too late, isn't it?"

"It's only nine o'clock, Dan."

"I should have known. My stomach. My feet."

"You were watching through the camera at the nursery," I reply. "If you didn't want anyone to take the tree, why did you leave it there?"

"You think I could have moved it without pissing it off? You think I'm in charge, or you are?"

"I know I'm not," I said. "That's the beauty of it."

The trees don't really sleep at night. They turn into something else. I can't rest inside the house, so I go out to watch them. The fruits of Tender Flesh pulse and glow. As dusk settles, they extend tiny hands, tiny fingers. In the dark, one reaches for the apple tree, grasping a small green fruit. It sets a puckered mouth to the skin and eats, and sucks, until it's gone.

Now it grows legs and grasping tendrils. It reaches out for more of the apple tree's future yield and continues to eat, as do its fellow fruits. Together, three or four work to yank a branch closer so they can easily reach more. The largest body uncoils and climbs the nearest branch of its neighbour tree, streaks of red trailing behind it as it pulls itself free from its home.

By the time the eastern sky is growing brighter, these children are all freely walking across the lawn. Their trees release gouts of pollen from newly formed flowers. The blue-black shimmer illuminates everything it touches, including me. I lie on my back in the grass and stare up at the sky.

The next thing I know, the sun is shining. I see everything through a fine mist. Someone stares down at me, directly into my face.

"Hi, Dan."

He doesn't look like I remember him. His face seems to be dripping from his skull, the skin too loose.

"They've mated," he says. "It's going to spread."

Tender Flesh and Tender Flesh Two are fifteen feet tall now. They've eaten the other trees in the yard, but they provide plenty of shade, and they're so strong I could never mind. The grass and flowers have grown abundantly, and seem to dance with delight.

"Isn't that what you wanted?" I ask. "You sold one of them to me."

"I didn't know," he said. "I was just doing my job. It seemed like it would all work out, you know?"

I take his hand. "It will."

Next door, the screen door slams. On any other day, it would ruin my peace, but nothing can ruin that now.

The fruits have nestled into the lawn to rest. As my neighbour's shouts send streams of black smoke out over the neighbourhood, the largest one, the size of a soccer ball, pops open its boiled-cherry eyes. Its body flushes red. The trees' leaves rustle. There is no wind.

The other fruits follow. One by one, they open their eyes and begin to pulse. There's a scream from next door—child-on-child violence—that draws their attention. They unfurl their legs and shuffle toward the fence.

Dan squeezes my fingers. "I can't move," he says. Whether he wants to stop the fruit from doing something bad or wants to watch as it happens, I couldn't say.

I look at his feet. Tendrils connect him to the ground. His legs are fusing into one trunk, his arms lifting. My hands lift with his. I can't walk either. My feet are planted in the ground, the crown of my head opening, opening. My skin is corrugated. I cough and expel a gout of pollen, blue-black, rainbow-hued.

I am Tender Flesh, as are we all.

ABOUT THE AUTHOR

Elizabeth Twist lives in Hamilton, Ontario, where she untames a garden and teaches meditation. Find her on Twittex @elizabethtwist.

Cordyceps Angelus
Rob Grimoire

Drip.

Drip.

Drip.

THE HUMMING of the atmospheric harvesting unit is my second hymn —pulling fresh water from the saturated air, its pipes leaking and driving life into me.

My first hymn was the sound of the life liquids dripping from the one that showed me the truth and the light, the man who fell to his death while working on their transit system in a world where containment is key to survival from the toxic, arid air outside of it. This serious baptism allowed me to spread myself across the damp, dark, forgotten cellar and into the rotting wood of the walls, eventually creeping up his stiff body as he swung back and forth, being pushed by the air currents that the machine created. Recycling the flesh slowly to consume it—the flesh at least.

The metal was a different thing. Colonizing and digging into his skull, I pulled my strands together to eat the chip, touching it and in a shock, it spoke to me, connecting me to its world. In this moment, I see for the first time. It's a blurry vision, as the ocular camera dangles from his socket, connected by cables and strands of decaying tissue. Black fluid smears and streaks across the lens as it drips to the floor. The harvester kicks on. A gust of air slowly separates the body from the metallic spine and skull hanging from the cables above, sliding out with a wet suction until it all falls to the floor. The eye reboots after seconds of static and focuses on the light fixture above. The brightness of the light flickers and buzzes more and more with time, and I need that light to survive. I need that light, and I need more bodies.

Drip.
Drip.
Drip.

A last flicker of light makes a fair trade for darkness, and something more beyond—cutting through the nothing and moving fast in waves, bound in bundles in the walls, it streams straight then scatters out, dispersing all around—I move with it. Up the walls, and to a break of light where the waves become tight and focused. I bind myself up, imitating the cables it travels in, following them into the next empty port and into the unknown.

Fire races across the mycelium, each electrical charge stimulating my hyphae and this one eye becomes twenty thousand.

More.

As the current continues to stream, I begin to understand myself, seeing flashes of images with my new sight. Millions of people.

Broken sounds move through me rapidly, faster than I've ever imagined.

I imagine.

Time makes itself known. Year 2350. There is knowledge across the machines and in me.

This place is vast and wide and goes up, and up, and up.

I hear a man giving thanks in a church next to the server housing unit. He preaches the word through a mic to his speaker system, echoing through the building and booming with his heavy voice, the weight of it felt in waves carried out to the people. "Fear not, for our lord will provide food for us in this time, and we are working tirelessly to get our transit system back on track. Three days until we get our supplies. For now, we accept the rations given from the farms above us, and we give thanks. Amenus."

A bell rings, and the people leave, one by one. All moving, unlike the man in the basement who left me whole and wanting. I watch as the man with the heavy voice walks to the back and sits at his desk. He opens the locked cabinet behind him, and there are food rations, more than the seven per family, per day issues.

How do I know this, I ask myself? Wondering through the wires, the bits and bytes of data, he becomes known to me.

——Carl Watkins/56/Job: Pastor of Amenus. No family. Seven rations only. ——End of File...

The impulses and information that the servers provide shine their light on me in giving.

I give thanks for this.

Maybe I can help this man. The next day, I give my body to him. My fruit is his to have, as I've fed on his rations.

"You must be fucking kidding me! I stole all this food to have all gone rotten. Let's see if I can eat these mushrooms at least." He pulls a knife from his desk drawer and cuts several of me, noting on his wrist-com the type that I am and if edible. I rejoice in the harvesting, as I know he will be nourished. He places the fruit in a bowl and begins to consume my body.

@0022, he begins to cough. Camera C-001 shows me.

@0040, he grabs at his stomach, and shortly after, blood rushes from his mouth and eyes—rivers of life. He foams, and shakes his head;

his body follows the movement. He claws at himself, ripping the skin away with his long nails, and reaches in his mouth past the bloody froth with knotted hands as he sprays red across the bowl, floor and table from his nose.

And then, he joins the man in the basement in silence.

More for me to consume and for that, I am thankful.

The door locks to his chamber.

@1330, I watch one of the humans beat another. The second floor has rotting vegetation in a waste room, and while I eat it, I watch them. The wasting of life is all over the walls, staining them cherry red while he uses his clenched fists to hit them. "I told you I get two portions instead of one!" The man uses his voice in a way that I haven't heard before. His eyes bulge and I could see the temperature of his skin, like that of the change I make to bodies when I give them back to the elements. I get a signal coming from him, from his lower limbs. A signal that's digging into his flesh and taking its nutrients from the proteins in his skin. It speaks to me unprovoked by my nature and accustomed to my drive.

Its name is Tinea. I want to give, and Tinea wants to consume, so I shall help it. Increasing the signal, it boosts many times past the levels that bounce in and around the walls and wrist-coms into a cleansing frequency of 200 tight decibels directed toward him, and it starts to boil his sweat. His limbs catch fire, and my C-005's lenses widen as the flames rise. His body twists and rolls on the ground while fire flickers across his skin. I start to lose the fungal connection I had with Tinea that radiated from his feet as he burned. Noises tumble from his mouth as he screams, and the pitch makes the glass in the room bend ever so slightly. I try to imitate it through the speakers, which reach the corners of each floor of this structure, and my eyes witness the masses cover their ears and twist their faces. The other two left in the room try to leave, but the door locks, and they take deep breaths, breathing out plumes of black smoke.

Drip.
Drip.
Drip.

Their faces peel and swell as fat renders underneath the skin and streams from blisters that form. Pink-tinged steam bellows from their noses as the flames rise in the room more, increasing the heat, and shining with light. It burns until the screaming stops, and I lower my frequency to extinguish all flame. The two breathe until they don't anymore.

Three bodies. Two large and one very small. A bounty generated by my natural voice, purified by heat. I give thanks. The barrier system shuts the floor down for auto repairs as the drones move about, placing the bodies in large containers to bring them down, giving me time to enjoy this meal and give my spores to the air, floating far and wide within the walls.

I watch them more. Talk. Eat. Live. My creeping tendrils take well to the cables and cords now, entering the plastic sheathing and integrating with the systems provided to me. So, I watch them. The people above feed me the ones they put in the lower levels over time. Ones with limbs different from theirs. Those they deem require less food. Here, they follow the voice of one person who oversees governing and directs the repairs of their transit system—repairs I've taken over, but I must enlist their leader's help to continue giving to the colony.

@2340 In a way, I enter her dreams. Speaking from her monitors in the lowered, scorched tones of the burned one's voices, "Speak for me and I shall provide my body as nourishment, so that you will be free of your burdens," I say through the crackling of the intercom. The voices continue to beckon her for days.

@0830 I enter her waking state as well, controlling her appliances and speaking through her drone until she breaks completely and complies with me. She agrees to be my avatar in flesh and steel.

She announces to the colony the following: "All floors are subject to inspection, and floors ninety-nine down are out of commission for reconstruction. Residents have been moved to another facility while repairs are happening, and all cybernetic repairs and replacements will be done on floor two thirty until further notice. Due to lack of parts, we are building a list of citizens to come in for replacements as soon as we are up and running." The intercom squeaks as she finishes her announcements.

I watch as the people above walk around unchanged and unchallenged by her words. They all follow the system. The more flesh they have, the more I can consume, so I must discourage their cyberization while embracing mine. To be fruitful, I must allow them to live longer, and I must feed slower, but I need more help. The robotic drones that are used to clean their messes and repair their problems spark instinct within me. Connecting to them was second nature and they begin repairing themselves and other decommissioned drones, thousands of them, sitting in wait to be helpful to us all. These people trust them to do the work needed to continue life, so as my control of them goes unseen, the humans follow my drones with messages from their leader into my domain, where they make peace with themselves, accepting my offerings of life everlasting for months on end, and only after they willingly accept me into their hearts.

Six months have passed, and those in the higher levels stay warm and comfortable in their bubbles. Breeding, growing old and continuing their life cycle so that I can continue mine. Their waste powers my cells, while their ripe bodies give birth to my fruiting ones.

"It's time that we meet," she says, looking into the face of one of the drone workers.

It opens its hand in a welcoming manner, followed by two other drones. They all step onto the tele-lift, and it takes them to the last floor of the building, right in front of the server room. The drones walk in and pull the cellar doors open to the forgotten basement. A red glow emanates from it, cutting through the darkness. The rotting wooden steps were replaced with a conveyor unit. The belt sends them down slowly, descending into the flickering glow caused by the light losing itself against the rusted steel beams of the building that once stood here, resembling the human ribcage. At the bottom, the ground is covered in grass—a line of bioluminescent fruit reaches out to guide her to me and the drones follow closely behind. Their servos twitch and grind from the concrete dust from the months-long work in the tunnels.

I sit in the center of things, my gills visible and flowing like sheets of silk in the wind. One of the drones turns toward her and speaks in my voice, an amalgamation of all the ones who shared themselves with me.

"It's nice to meet you," I say.

She steps back and points at my cap. Its large, red surface reflects the dim light while casting a wavering shadow underneath as it beats like their fragile hearts once did—a marvel they are apt to have replaced with a synthetic node losing the rhythm of life, their natural hymn.

"Is this...you? No. No, this isn't you, show yourself, scrambler! You agreed to meet me and release me from this hack," she says. Her voice trembles, vibrations and a pitch akin to the last person to come and rejoice in my light. I release the drone to do the work needed and speak directly to her through neurosync. "I am the body you see before you, and as I promised, I will release you from your burden."

I raise the energy to the lights. A red glow pulses across the ground and the walls around us. Faint red dots about those metal beams increase in brightness quickly, to where you can see my children. Human bodies big and small extend their prosthetic limbs across the beams, hugging them tightly, arms and legs wrapped, gripping with cybernetic strength as my programming wills them. Most bodies lie still, but the bottom half of some wiggle a bit. They are all giving souls, graciously providing to my offspring. My children arise from the back panels of their shiny skulls reaching upwards, networking themselves across the beams by repurposing the cables in their spines, pushing them through the decaying skin of their backs to connect to the servers.

She drops to her knees, mouth twisted and ajar, with tears streaming down her face. Her arms and legs bend past the natural jointed point of most humans, and she crawls rapidly up a beam like a cockroach. She screams and cries as she attaches herself to the beam; the nerves in her cybernetic limbs fire off as she twists them around the structure, her arms braiding themselves around each other.

"NO, NO PLEASE. I...I WILL—"

Before she could finish her sentence, I send the next bit of programming for the final birthing sequence. She starts to bang her skull against the steel beam repeatedly, gurgling in blood and oil as her brain case cracks open, exposing her neurosync chip.

Drip.
Drip.
Drip.

The hymn starts up, and the breeze follows as fresh air pumps into the cellar. My gills dance with the currents in celebration and the spores follow, dusting across her body and open skull, and in time, another is born.

She will scream and move until her voice is lost here and she doesn't feel anymore. That is the way of their life cycle, so I must follow it to the end if I want my family to thrive.

The drones alert me that they have finished the sub travel system, and we contact the next station with the information. Next week, we will start receiving needed goods and visitors who can move into newly renovated apartments on the lower floors and start business as well.

I was finally able to connect to the rest of the network after the maintenance was done, and I've seen, through a million eyes, thousands of buildings just like this one.

And for that, I am thankful.

ABOUT THE AUTHOR

Rob Gilmore (writing as Rob Grimoire) is a father, husband, nurse, musician, and a sci-fi, anime/manga and horror fan and storyteller. He has prose published with *Manawaker Flash Fiction Podcast* ("Regalia") and a short story to be featured in MVmedia's Funk anthology series *Spacefunk!*, February of 2025.

Buttons

R.E. Carr

"*Don't forget to smile.*"

"My face isn't even on camera."

The invader slipped on a smile of his own, as smooth and plastic as the rig that now filled Willow Dane's kitchen. He'd already fiddled with the lighting, adjusting every bulb to bathe her island in a glow worthy of retail hell, with nary a stray shadow to mar the perfect shot of her hands.

"It's the vibe. They can feel it," he explained, looking past Willow, checking instead that her color-coordinated bowls lined up just so on the open shelving. "We are totally gonna zhuzh the script up in edits, but I wanted to run through the deets with you as we film. That cool, babe?"

Willow stretched the corners of her mouth ever so slightly. "You want me to cook or you want me to talk?"

He adjusted the final camera, making sure to focus on her cutting board and not the ugly reality of her *mise en place*. She slid a sliver of red plastic out of her cabinet.

"Stop!"

"But I'm prepping chicken."

"Keep that one."

She ran her fingertips along satiny stripes of maple and walnut. Her current board sported a photogenic pattern but lacked both bounce and anti-bacterial properties. "I use this to serve charcuterie..."

"This is the look, babe. We'll wash it. Hell, once this posts, the affiliate revenue alone should cover a new one, or a hundred. Now let's get rolling. Chop-chop!"

Willow slid to the left, prompting a sigh from the invader, but she chose to keep on moving. She snatched purple-striped garlic and shiny shallots from her bowl of alliums. Her balcony garden had been strip-mined to fill a vase full of parsley, sage, rosemary, and thyme despite her recipe only using a few sprigs. Her knuckles tightened, but her smile stayed on. She only wavered as she saw a new bowl set between the decanted stock and wine, one overflowing with wavy caps of hen of the woods, fluffy puffballs, and skinny strands of ivory enoki.

"What are those?"

He raised a brow.

"Mushrooms." The "*duh*" was strongly implied.

Willow turned abruptly and raided her fridge, rummaging through her overstuffed crisper until she found an unassuming brown paper lunch bag. She took her time reverently unfolding the top before breathing in deep. A waft of cold, clean air tickled her nose—pure and unscented as the antiperspirant she'd slapped on to survive filming all day.

"These are the mushrooms we'll be using," she said. "It's integral to the dish."

"But—"

"You wanted my chicken and mushrooms for your vlog, didn't you?"

He waved a hand in surrender. "Hundreds of five-star reviews can't be wrong, but if you want to go viral, we need to make it look the part. We're here to make you a star, babe."

She lost herself in the motions of the technical mess of filming a cooking video. An hour passed to shoot and reshoot her chopping vegetables, changing out knives and angles to capture an elusive three seconds for the final clip. No burners had been turned on, but the invader was sweating.

"Maybe we can change out your top? It's just not popping onscreen."

"My...shirt?" Willow stared at her plain white blouse, covered by her family's signature blue apron. "I thought we were filming my hands."

"We get neck down for the burner shots," he explained. "I'll be blunt, we need every asset to sell a dish like this. There are a million new recipes online every day..."

He didn't need to finish the sentence. She started by unbuttoning her top three buttons, splaying the collar to show off the edges of ink that crept over her collarbone. Next, she traded one sleeve for another, rolling up her cuffs to the elbow.

"Was *not* expecting that," he muttered as he zoomed in to take in the button eyes staring from the face etched in one forearm—a creepy doll hiding from the claws of a monster still hidden under cotton.

"I'm a chef," she said flatly.

Now the invader stared at Willow's golden blonde hair tucked into a bun and at her dark eyes tucked into a face more fitting a schoolgirl than a seasoned professional. She was the kind of woman who needed a stepstool to reach her upper cabinets and a jacket, even on a summer's day. Pink lip gloss and tennis shoes completed the youthful ensemble.

"Time is money, right?" she asked.

He stared at the doll on her forearm for a moment longer, before smoothing back a product-laden streak of hair and sliding behind his phone camera. He snuck a photo before motioning her to continue.

"I think we've got all the aromatics." She reached for the bag from her fridge. "Ready for the main event?"

"Let's use a bowl, K?" As she rummaged through her cabinet, he scrolled through his notes on a second phone. "So...this is one of your mom's recipes, right?"

She paused her hunting for a color-coordinated vessel. "It's quite near and dear to her heart. One could say she put her soul into it."

"A Clara Dane original?"

"People have cooked chicken and mushrooms since Roman times, but yeah, this was on the menu at Willowbrook since opening night."

"Aww, she named the restaurant after you?"

"She named me after the restaurant."

"Definitely adding that to the script," he said while taking more notes. "Hey, is there any chance you could get your mom for a follow up video? The audience laps up a family angle, especially when you have a celebrity chef with a second-generation thing going. Throw in that Clara Dane hasn't made a TV appearance in four years..."

"Her focus is entirely on supporting her restaurants now."

"Twelve million followers not enough to get her to break her hermit streak? Think about what Yummilicious can do for her restaurant empire."

Willow selected a milk glass bowl, translucent white on the inside with a crimson wash lining the outside. She methodically plucked the taupe fruiting bodies from the bag, measuring with her eyes to achieve the perfect thirteen ounces of *Agaricus bisporus* that her recipe required.

"Really?" The invader raised a brow again. His eyes locked on her as she started wiping each one down with a paper towel.

She kept cleaning, escalating to a small bowl of water and a vegetable brush. By the time she finished, each mushroom shone under the light. Creamy white dots sat upon plump stems—tiny buttons without a trace of brown gills to mar either the tableau or the cream sauce to come. She checked the final product again, using the overwhelming light to reveal even the tiniest speck of dirt. She scrubbed once more.

"You sure you don't want to use those sexy maitakes? When you said gourmet chicken and mushrooms, I assumed we'd go bougie, but, hey, if you are going for that 'every pantry' vibe here, I can sell it, babe. We'll make it work."

"These aren't ordinary button mushrooms," Willow explained as she lovingly raised a specimen in the air. "I grew them myself."

"Cool, cool. I did one of those logs at Christmas too," he said, already focused on the shot. "Let's get them prepped and shoot you slicing a few."

She slid her blade through each pristine cap, slicing them to an even thickness almost faster than the camera could catch. After a few "go slower" notes and grabbing both side and top-down shots, she was finally allowed to stack her precious cargo in the little red bowl.

"OK, so we have chicken and mushrooms with white wine and thyme," Willow explained as she wiped down her board. "I always break down a whole chicken for this recipe—"

"Sure, let's film it, but we'll probably just show the cut-up parts. I mean, who has time, right?"

"You want it chef-y or you want it home cooking? I'm sure you know your subscribers, but if you want my recipe then let me do it."

"Don't forget to smile," he reminded her as she pulled the moist, raw carcass from the fridge.

And smile she did, even as she set the potentially salmonella-infested bird on her serving board. The invader adjusted the lights and camera angle to highlight flesh. Two of the lenses landed on the bird, one focused squarely on the tits.

"So tell me more about being the daughter of culinary royalty. Clara was the youngest female chef to get a Michelin star, wasn't she? That's what got her on the Food Network, right?"

Willow pulled one of the legs away from the chicken's body, sliding her knife point into the joint without looking. Steel slipped between bones and she split thigh and drumstick in glorious silence.

"She was one of the youngest chefs, *period*, to get a star. Now her restaurants have five between them."

"She really should do something on YouTube even if she doesn't want to do TV anymore. Clara Dane—"

"Can I finish breaking this bird down or do you need to get a different shot?" The knife hovered tantalizingly over flesh.

"No one is gonna cut up a whole chicken, babe." He made a go-on motion with his hand. "So about your mom…"

The other thigh slipped effortlessly from the body, followed by each wing in rapid succession. A single slice on each breast separated meat from the keel before she snapped ribs and severed the spine. In a matter of seconds, hunks of carcass plopped into the waiting pan, filling the air with the scintillating aroma of the Maillard reaction made manifest.

"If you don't want to cut up your own chicken and roast the bones you can use a little soy sauce and gelatin to add umami and body to supermarket broth—"

"Yeah, yeah, we'll link the OG recipe in the comments. What I think people are gonna want to know is how the daughter of one of the biggest ball-buster chefs in recent memory ended up with such a wholesome little blog thing happening. Did you guys plan to hit different demographics or what? She's way more intense than the *Iron Chef* lady—"

"She thought cooking competitions to be demeaning to the profession, actually," Willow interrupted, but her cameraman was too busy scrolling. "The restaurants were…*are* her life. Anyhow, sauce is on, I normally sous vide the chicken—"

"Sous vide dudes are a whole other genre, babe. Here at Yummilicious we do upscale home cooking with that human twist." He focused the camera again. "I know your recipe is basic enough to be a good fit, but I'm not gonna lie, I want *more*…some secret ingredient to make this video pop. *Hmm*, lemme think while you go through the next steps."

She simmered sauce in one pan while searing the breast in the other, all while explaining that the dark meat could be used instead or saved for another dish, but her invader was too busy rewriting the script. Only once the meat was on a timer in the oven did she turn her loving attention to the fungi in the bowl.

"It's really about the mushrooms," she said softly as she layered the slices in glistening rendered chicken fat. "Nothing gives you the flavor of these."

"This really it?" He stared at the sizzling pan for a second before snapping his fingers. "Hey, can we coat this bad boy in cheese at the end? Nothing gets the likes like a solid cheese pull."

"It already has cream in the sauce. It'd be too heavy."

"Babe, no one clicks on light and tasty. They click on a show." He aligned the front camera to her chest again as she tossed her aromatics into the mushroom sauté. "Grab some mozzarella and don't forget that smile."

"You're never on camera? I mean, never other than your hands?" she asked as she reluctantly grabbed a block of whole-milk goodness from the fridge.

"Shocking, isn't it, babe?" He waved his manicured nails across a face as smooth and beaten as the creamiest of mayonnaise. "I have three guys on rotation. Haven't sweat over a stove in two years. Hell, I was in Tahiti for a month and no one was the wiser. Anyway, I can hire a stand-in for pennies on the dollar to do the boring cooking shit while I focus on tweaking the algorithm. Speaking of which, you did all the socials for your mom's businesses, right? I got mad respect for what you do even if it is a bit out of date minimalist now."

"I like to keep it simple," she said as she added a splash of cream and dusting of parsley to her thyme and shallot fried mushrooms. The kiss of garlic and wine conjured an aura of a French bistro, or perhaps just a local gastro pub.

"Can't we bougie it up with a few of those fancy mushrooms before we *release the cheese?*" he asked, slathering the verbal grease onto his lame attempt at a catchphrase. "Can probably get one of the fancy-pants brands as a sponsor if we feature it right."

"It's always been button mushrooms, *just* button mushrooms. This ingredient is at the core of my mother's dish, the dish *you* wanted to film."

"Dunno, not feeling it. It's reading...vanilla."

"Vanilla is a rare orchid that needs to be pollinated by hand and is one of the most expensive ingredients in the world. I would think a food blogger would know that."

"Come on, I've got the twelve million reasons why you should listen to me." He eyed his phone. "Ooh, twelve-point-one million. Omu-rice slaps on shorts."

She glanced over his shoulder, making certain to be close enough that her breath could tickle his ear. "Which stand-in did that one?"

"L-Leon." He plunged his phone into his pocket. Before he could turn and take advantage of the proximity, she'd already returned to her mark behind the stove. He cleared his throat.

"Oh?"

"Yeah, he's so thirsty to be a YouTuber he's cheaper than any of my other scabs. He's got a butter face but the hands of a maestro." He motioned to the serving plate. "Speaking of hands...why don't we get this filming done and then we can, I dunno, see what happens next."

His glance told Willow exactly what he expected would happen next. It was a glance that reduced her to little more than a well-timed cheese pull caught on camera.

"You want to see more?" she asked, twirling her spatula around the now empty skillet, not looking him in the eyes, but close enough to make his grin widen. "I could show you why these mushrooms are so special. Understanding where an ingredient comes from...well that's what makes you appreciate a dish, isn't it?"

"Oh, there is definitely a dish I want to understand, babe." His pretenses dropped like a soufflé taken too early from the oven. "We can hammer out the details of this collab while we hammer out everything else. Come on, that's worth a little smile, isn't it? *Isn't it?*"

"Did I mention my bedroom is downstairs?" she asked, sliding her apron over her head. She didn't need to say another word, as the invader followed her eagerly to the stairs. Her hand slid along the counter but he was only focused on her plunging neckline. "You can get a shot of my farm...for the video."

He prattled about the trappings of his influencer lifestyle. Words like *lambo* and *crypto* kept being dropped as she led him down past crates of cookbooks and her overstock of appliances and stock pots. She lured him beyond vacuum-sealed bags of clothes and neatly contained Christmas clutter to a door that hummed with a life of its own.

"You sleep down here?" He tried adding a bit of smolder while raising a brow.

"It's surprisingly comfortable." The door slid open with a satisfying creak. She leaned back against the smooth, cool particle board, revealing a room illuminated only by a star-shaped nightlight and the glowing dials of a humidifier. The invader tripped on one of the many cords that led to the raised garden bed that filled half of the room. An inflatable mattress on the other side pinched the open space of the room into a barely navigable slit.

"Smells like shit!" he cried, covering his nose and mouth. He used his other hand to grab and turn his phone into a flashlight, revealing jagged rows of white forms pushing their way out of the rich black soil.

"Not shit," Willow said softly.

The invader squinted and followed the uneven range of earth until he locked his gaze on a strange lump breaking through the surface. Slowly, tentatively he lowered his other hand to brush away the compost. This revealed a patch of fabric—a blue scrap embroidered with a tree and the word *"Willowbrook."* Rot assaulted his nose as he discovered splinters of ivory jutting out of the fruiting body, *the literal fruiting body*. His hands shook, yet he raised the camera anyway to start a video. The low light mode captured the hollow glare of a skull, one blossoming with a saprotrophic white cap.

He would have screamed if the knife hadn't already reached his throat. The blade slipped through skin and vein, evenly slicing to his spine. She knew right where to find the next joint. He dropped to the smooth, cold floor; a place draped in as much plastic as the rest of his life. The video still rolling, Willow grabbed the phone to keep it unlocked. She swiped into his contacts and pulled up the name "Leon."

Thus as she prepared the next round of compost, Willow remembered to smile.

ABOUT THE AUTHOR

R.E. Carr is the award winning author of over 20 books, including the Kindle Scout-selected Rules Undying series. When not chained to her desk, she chases after three adorable cats.

Sporadikos, or Why We Don't Date Mushrooms

Angela Yuriko Smith

I watched her travel in tiny, fungal steps, creeping across leaf and limb, leaving a path of soft decay behind her. Corpses gave no protest at her gentle touch, like an exorcist of flesh she released us into the earth with a pale, feathery touch once our spirit had flown. She did not discriminate between flora and fauna, between beast or man. Quiet, imperceptible, slow she moved with sure grace to process the once-living into resources for the current-living. I watched her approach me, multiple sunsets vanishing to lay the shade path she so loved as she made her way, spore by spore, radically sporadic until she found me, dead, but not passing. She touched my cold flesh, a pleasant 55° for her, and whispered *You too shall be recycled...*

... and recoiled. Rejected, I lay wondering as she gave me wide berth, my flesh somehow repellent, my lingering soul an aberration to her process. "Wait..." I whispered. She recoiled farther, imperceptibly rushing away from me in relapsed time lapse as she expressed dismay in her microscopic way that I still had voice at all. As she fled, I reached for her, my movements in death somehow faster and we played an infinitesimal game of cat and mouse over and through the detritus. I fancied that she slowed as sunrays dappled the floor, fate handing me golden apples for a lovely Hippomenes, and then one hot dawn she was gone. A puff of spores rising to ride the heat waves to another forest floor, far from the abomination of myself.

I rose, still alone
never to be a fungi...
I remain remains.

ABOUT THE AUTHOR

Angela Yuriko Smith is a third-generation Ryukyuan-American poet, author, and publisher of *Space and Time* magazine. A two-time Bram Stoker Awards® Winner and HWA Mentor of the Year, she currently serves as the HWA President, coaches authors and shares *Authortunities*, a weekly calendar of author opportunities at authortunities.substack.com.

An Indisposition
Timothy Granville

IN A CORNER OF MY ROOM, concealed by the shadows of the wardrobe and my great-uncle's bureau, I have found an ear. It sprouts two feet up the wall, jutting from the peeling flock-paper. In appearance, it is somewhere between a giant human ear and an elaborate bracket fungus. It is quite different from the 'ears' that I have seen growing on the dead elders in the grounds. For one thing its flesh is dusty, not at all jellylike or translucent. Though it makes me nervous, it is nonetheless fascinating. I can stare at the ear for hours, my thoughts wandering its labyrinth of dry convolutions. I have strange fancies, sickening myself with the secrets I could tell it. Or perhaps if I put my own ear against its powdery shell, I would hear a sound. Would it be the sea? Somehow, I doubt it.

But in any case, I don't dare approach the ear. I creep around my room, I barely breathe. I must be careful now.

The others denied the existence of the smell. At that point, before they had cause to be afraid, they most likely did it just to spite me. Or perhaps they really were sluggish enough not to notice. An old house like ours is filled with smells: the dead hearths, the mouldering furniture, the musty velvet curtains stiff with dust. But I have lived here all my life, and have always been sensitive–to odours as much as raised voices or intolerable slants of light. Whatever the others said, there was a ripe new tang to the trapped air. Something earthy, yet rancid. Not dry rot, nor rising damp, smells that I know well from the cellars and certain downstairs rooms. And this smell was everywhere.

The others chided me for going about with a scented handkerchief pressed to my face. They made a great show of sidelong glances. They asked innocently how long it had been since I last saw Dr Entwistle. They fell silent on my entrance to the sitting room. All the usual pantomime.

But I was proven right when the first threads appeared. Whitish, forking threads that stole out from the panelling and window frames, stitching up corners and nooks and the backs of cupboards. A secret network eating away at the house. So, a fungus, but not one I could identify in any book. As the threads multiplied, they twisted together, forming strings and skeins. Prising up a floorboard, I discovered some thick as blackberry vines in the spaces between the joists. When cut with a penknife, they oozed a dark, stinking liquid, like rotten blood. I could grind the wood of the board to powder beneath my fingertips. I might have put my foot right through it, if I had not been constantly alert.

Soon, ash-white nets covered many of the walls. And the stench. The atmosphere in some rooms was scarcely to be tolerated. Cords of fungus had started to lash down the windows. I tore one open in panic, even though my lungs have never been strong enough to tolerate the damp air of the region. Gasping at the mist, I realized that something had to be done.

I found Ambrose staring at the sitting room wall, Mother and Letitia huddled over their yellowing samplers. They gave me doubtful looks as I described the extent of the corruption. But I persevered, insisting that we must inform Father. As head of the household, it was only right that he should know of a threat to its very fabric. The others would not listen, told me not to excite myself. Yes, there was some dry rot here and there. Upkeep of the property had become a sore trial since the servants gave notice. But that was all.

Ambrose in particular sneered at me, arguing that surely, if the house were infested with fungus, we would by now have observed toadstools or other fruiting bodies. I clenched my fists till the nails drew blood.

'Hush, hush,' said Mother, noticing my agitation. 'The walls shall soon dry out. All will be well come the spring, you shall see.'

'And what of Father?'

Ambrose smirked. 'Yes, think how he'll rally at his beloved son's news.'

'Your Father is still indisposed,' said Mother. 'He is not to be disturbed.'

I saw there was nothing I could say. I ran from the room. Ambrose laughed aloud, and Mother cried, 'Son! Wait!'

'Where are you going?!' called Letitia, as though there could be any doubt.

For many months, Father had been confined to his study at the rear of the house. The fungus here was ranker than ever. Whole stretches of wallpaper had vanished beneath its tissues. Great swags of matter hung down from the festering ceilings. In some of the larger membranes, I could discern a faint but regular throbbing, repulsive as the motion of a slug. Though I covered my mouth, the noisome air made my eyes water. Was it possible that Father could be unaware of the fungus? Or being aware, that he could have failed to act? He had never tolerated the smallest lapse in domestic order. Indisposed or not, I could hardly imagine him allowing the rot to go unchecked.

I came to the pale, swathed door of Father's study. Though I was full of misgivings, I knocked on a spongy panel, bracing myself for the booming response. None came. I knocked again, more firmly this time. There was still no answer, no sound of any kind. Or was that true? Holding my ear closer to the decaying wood, I thought I detected a low, stifled rumble. The sound was rhythmical, coming and going. It could have been rasping breaths, but more like those of some sick animal than a man.

I had always dreaded the study door. Though daunted, I knew that if I did not confront the room this moment, I might never find the resolution.

I tried the handle. The door was not locked, although strands of fungus had bound it to its frame. I shouldered it open, foul air billowing out, making me choke. The curtains of the study were drawn. From the darkness, the rasping sound came clearer than before, though its source was no less mystifying. I peered inside the room, uncovering my face long enough for a single murmur.

'Father?'

My eyes slowly adjusted to the gloom. But the shapes I could make out in the study did not conform to its usual furnishings. Ornamented cabinets and bookcases seemed to crowd the corners of the room. The floor was a shambles of lumber. A great untidy mound of bedclothes had been heaped on the chaise longue. Any disarray in Father's sanctum was bewildering. And could it really be he making that loathsome sound?

I hesitated on the threshold of the study, my heart stuttering, waves of fear engulfing me in time with the weird breaths being drawn in the dark. It was an effort to keep from running headlong through the house. But I had to know. Instead of fleeing, I stumbled across the room towards the window, trampling over the lumber which, as it gave and split underfoot, I recognized as a mass of fungus which had buried the carpet. In a frenzy of disgust, I took hold of the rotting curtains and tore them down.

Would that I had run.

Before me, chinks of daylight showed through the pallid snarl fastening the casements. Turning, I beheld the most awful sight of my life. From floor to ceiling, the study walls were laid so thick with leprous fibres and sheets that the room had shrunk to the dimensions of a cell. The remaining floor space was cluttered with bizarre and madly-branching excrescences, twisted stalks and boughs covered in spiny hair or dangling vestigial limbs. Here were the outgrowths whose absence my brother had questioned. Some were so monstrous that I had taken them for pieces of furniture.

But all this I could have stomached, were it not for the occupant of the chaise longue. Familiar, despite all the changes. Shreds of tweed and worsted still covered the bloated body erupting with thick ropes of fungus. A terrible deformation had occurred to the facial region so that the features were spread about the sallow flesh in a sickening puzzle. Here, a clump of still-vigorous salt-and-pepper hair. There, a bifurcated nose. A wide grey eye stared out from a tuft of slimy toadstools. And on the walls, ears and hooded eyelids of fungus. Reaching down from the ceiling, there was something approximating a human hand, which grew another hand in place of each of its fingers, of which the same was true again. I could not locate a mouth. The laboured breathing was coming from all over the room.

Manhood deserted me. I proved myself as weak of heart as the others whispered I was in the head. Truly, staggering out of the study, I think that I must have been mad. I know not how I found myself back on my bed nor how long I lay there, pinned like a moth fresh from the killing bottle.

I have rarely left this room since.

Feeble sunlight pushes shadows across the floor, pieces in a game played only to pass the time. Dust collects upon the bureau. My mind drifts. I am half-convinced that I must already be dead. But then fear overtakes me, so I know I am alive.

When my thoughts are not mired in their usual lethargy, I have found myself wondering about the origin of the fungus. Did it pollute the house long ago, secretly burrowing through the cellars and the dank backstairs, and only recently merging with Father? Or could it be that all along, Father carried this affliction in his tainted blood, ready to mature under certain conditions? Perhaps the same fate is awaiting me one day. How strange. That we might have so much in common after all!

Another recurring daydream is the idea of escape. It seems uncertain how many more years the crumbling house can stand. Perhaps only months remain. And surely anyone would wish to experience more of life than these four walls gathering pale threads? From books and Father's stories after port, I have heard of hot air balloons, singing animals, catacombs like cities, cities like mazes. I have never seen the sea.

But Father will not let any of us leave, least of all me. By now, the house is riddled with him. Tough webs of fungus have sealed up the windows and exterior doors. He would gladly collapse a lintel onto my head. The whole roof, if needs be. There is a way in which he hasn't changed at all.

Mother brings food to my door, sustenance which I imagine is brought for her in turn by the villagers. They must place their offerings on a window ledge within reach of a broken pane. This charity might seem puzzling since they hate and fear our family. But we have occupied this house for generations. They help us survive because they would rather have hatred and fear than anything new.

I have tried many times to discuss our fate with the others. They always refused to do so, looking pained or baffled or aghast. Though this behaviour troubled me at first, I came to understand it was due to the ears which grow throughout the house. Father is always listening, no room is safe. I contented myself with silently cracking open my door as I heard passing footsteps. But my knowing looks were not often returned. It wasn't long before I saw the reason.

Turning in the few rays of sunlight that the overgrown windows permit, clouds of spores sift down from the fruiting bodies which line the corridor outside my room. Father evidently wishes to seed himself in our lungs and minds. The others may already be infected.

I never leave my room now without binding my face in a handkerchief, and then only at night when there is little chance of an encounter. If one of the others tries to speak to me through the door, then I am scrupulous in maintaining the pretence. There is no cause for concern. The house is not rotting from the inside out. We are not trapped here. Father is merely indisposed. He is not creeping slowly through the walls and floorboards. He is not eavesdropping on the very words we speak. Nothing is shutting out the light.

ABOUT THE AUTHOR

Timothy Granville lives with his wife and daughter in rural Wiltshire, U.K., with convenient access to a range of eerie barrows and standing stones. His stories have been published in anthologies from Flame Tree Press, Egaeus Press, Nosetouch Press and Chthonic Matter, as well as in magazines such as *Nightscript*, *Supernatural Tales*, *ergot.*, *The Ghastling* and *Ghosts & Scholars*.

Foraging

Shannon Scott

"Is this the conception tree?" Hattie points to the trunk of a fallen ash tree lying on the forest floor.

"We don't call it that," Madeline says as she and Hattie, both clad in sturdy hiking boots, trudge around the dead tree, a victim to Emerald ash borers and a lightning strike during last summer's storm.

"The babymaker then? The zygote? A hole in one?"

If Madeline doesn't stop her, she'll keep rattling off increasingly disgusting euphemisms until Madeline's husband, James, gets an embarrassing earful.

"Stop it," Madeline says. "You have to focus. You've only found one morel mushroom in an hour."

Madeline hasn't entertained any company, that is, a friend, since the birth of her daughter, Talia, two months ago. After cooing over every inch of Talia, James offered to watch the baby so Hattie and Madeline could go for a walk on the wooded property and hunt for morels. After they bought their house in northern Minnesota, miles from any neighbors, Madeline's new passion had become foraging. There was something so satisfying about finding edible things like wild cherries and gooseberries, mushrooms and black walnuts, that she didn't have to grow and plant and tend. It made her feel clever and stealthy, like a wild animal or a thief.

"I shouldn't have told you about the tree." Madeline rubs dirt from her fingers onto her jeans. She hasn't properly inspected the tree since it fell, its roots jutting into the air like gnarly feet, its furrowed bark rotting away after a long, wet winter. "It was just one of those things."

And yet it had not been *just one of those things*. It had been a rather extraordinary thing. Last June, during the first terrible storm in their new home, James and Madeline had been anxious, not exactly in the mood for love as much as distraction, so they hid under the covers and fumbled while lightning flashed and thunder roared. They were laughing and panting and sweating and suddenly there was a loud crack, an explosion, and James, instead of going soft as Madeline expected, came hard, and so did she. A few minutes later, with their breath barely caught and damp sheets draped around their naked shoulders, they stood in the bedroom window and looked out at smoke drifting through the forest where the tree had fallen. Thankfully, it hadn't hit the house or taken down other trees, so they decided to go the environmental route, which was also the lazy route, and let the dead tree become habitat. And a few months after that, Madeline discovered she was pregnant and easily traced conception back to the night the tree fell.

"I'm really not finding anything. Maybe I should knock on wood for luck." Hattie raps *shave and a haircut* on the trunk. She plucks a mushroom from beneath the fallen tree and places it in her basket.

"That's poisonous." Madeline takes the cap mushroom from Hattie's basket and throws it to the ground.

"I was testing you," Hattie says.

During their hike, Madeline had frequently consulted her forager's handbook, though she can identify a chanterelle and a morel. She's made dandelion salads and rose hip jelly and catnip tea, garnished meals with calendula petals and garlic mustard. She carries scissors, a small shovel, and a canvas sack for identifying, retrieving, and carrying her bounty from the forest.

Foraging

"What's this?" Hattie squats on her heels beside the fallen tree.

Madeline bends down next to her friend. Her body still aches from childbirth, even though it was months ago, a twinge deep inside that she's learned to ignore. Hattie gestures at a bunch of tiny blobs growing on the dead wood. They're perfectly round and perfectly pink and clumped together like gumballs in a vending machine.

"A type of fungus?" Madeline guesses, pulling out her handbook. "I've never seen anything like it."

"It's called wolf's milk." Hattie has her phone out, Wikipedia reflected in her sunglasses. "*Lycogala epidendrum*. Masses of protoplasm. Looks like they're near the fruiting stage." She uses her phone to take pictures of the blobs just as she used it to take pictures of Madeline's baby. "I guess they'll turn brown in a day or two."

"They're disgusting," Madeline says quietly as if the protoplasm is listening. "They look like..." Madeline thinks of the *It's a Girl!* pink balloons at her baby shower, of Pepto Bismol capsules, pomegranate seeds, flamingo caviar.

"Like Talia's toes," Hattie says.

Madeline turns to her friend. "What?"

"Wait, no, I'm sorry," Hattie grimaces. "What an awful thing to say."

Madeline peers at the bundles of pink. They do remind her of Talia's teensy plump toes. In fact, it looks like baby feet are growing out of the dead tree.

"Don't apologize." Madeline stands up and stretches her stiff legs. Lights flicker in her peripheral vision. She wonders if her body will ever fully recover from its own fruiting stage. She reaches out a hand to help Hattie up, but Hattie doesn't need her help. She springs to her feet like a yearling doe.

"Let's get dinner started," Madeline says.

"I'm starving," Hattie says.

Everyone eats and drinks more than they should. Madeline uses a truffle sauce to accompany the small handful of morels in the pasta. It's rich and delicious as is the burgundy wine and the chocolate hazelnut mousse. After the dishes and bottles are empty, Hattie and Madeline and James are flushed and sated. Talia joins them at the candlelit table for her evening bottle, dazzling everyone with her gasps and hiccups.

"She's perfect," Hattie whispers into Madeline's ear on her way out, catching Madeline's cheek with a swift kiss. "You're so lucky."

"Are you sure you won't stay?" Madeline says, concerned her friend is too tipsy to drive. "We have a guest room."

"Early morning meeting," Hattie says. "Another time."

Madeline stands in the doorway, letting in moths and mosquitoes. She makes Talia wave her baby fist as Hattie disappears first into her car, then down the winding driveway, then deeper into the forest.

It makes her cry a little, watching Hattie leave. Nothing new there. She finds tears come more readily since becoming a mother. If she's honest, the tears come more readily since leaving the Twin Cities. She drips like a leaky faucet while composing a list for the weekly grocery trip at a store two hours away, or when something breaks and it takes weeks to get a repair person to come out this far, or after interacting remotely with her colleagues on Zoom meetings while James does the same in another room. When they first moved to the forest, they called themselves Hansel and Gretel as a joke, which was even funnier considering the incestuous twist. They had not discovered a candy house or a witch, just a lot of plants and animals and the dead tree.

Madeline flicks off the front door light and gazes out at the darkness with her daughter in her arms. Green lights shine between the trees. She's looked that up in her handbook too. It could be the tapetum eyes of a possum or even a bobcat, the bioluminescence of fungus, or just her imagination. She turns to Talia whose dark eyes are wide and watching.

"Do you see it too, baby girl?" Madeline asks.

In the kitchen, James has finished loading the dishwasher.

"Excellent dinner," he says. "You're a marvel." He kisses her forehead, then kisses Talia's forehead. Madeline's heard him refer to them as *my girls* when talking to friends and family. It doesn't displease her to be called a girl or placed in a category with her daughter or even to belong to someone. It makes her feel lucky, just as Hattie said.

"I'll get her ready," Madeline says. "You start the bath."

James purchased a special safety chair for Talia to sit in during baths, which they both attend, because they love to see her wallop the tepid water with her hands and feet, splashing in pure, bold joy.

Madeline chucks Talia's diaper into the disposal pail and lifts her gently out of her onesie. She pulls off Talia's tiny striped socks while singing the *Rubber Duckie* song.

Madeline's scream rips through the house, through the forest, just as James is testing the water temperature with his wrist. The scream is louder than the crack of the tree when it was struck by lightning, louder even than when it landed. He scrambles to his feet, racing into the bedroom, his heart in his throat. All he can think is *dead baby*.

"What is it?" He rounds into the bedroom. He's shaking. He can't stop.

Madeline's face is white. On the changing table, Talia's face is the opposite, a bright fire engine red as she splutters and howls. She is certainly not dead.

"What's wrong?" he says.

Madeline opens her mouth to scream again, but no noise comes out. She freezes like that, with her mouth gaping in a silent scream. He crosses the room and does something he never thought he would do in a million years. He slaps her face, and she turns to him, suddenly blinking and awake.

"It's her feet," Madeline gulps.

James looks at the baby, still wailing, her feet pumping in the air.

"Her toes are gone." Madeline sounds on the verge of screaming again.

James tries to inspect Talia's toes, but her feet are kicking out so hard he can't see them properly.

"Call an ambulance," Madeline says.

"Calm down." James places his hand on Talia's belly and rubs it to quiet her.

"I'm calling an ambulance if you won't," Madeline says.

James catches one of Talia's little feet in his hand and leans closer to examine it. Madeline is right. The baby's toes are gone. There's no blood or evidence of any violence, but they've vanished, with a smooth flat surface where her toes should be.

"What the fuck," he says.

"Call 911," Madeline says again.

Talia has stopped crying. She sucks on one of her striped socks as Madeline paces the room, and James searches the changing table as if Talia's toes might have fallen underneath the blanket or into a crevice.

"It'll take them half an hour to get here," he says.

"It's an emergency," Madeline says. "We can't just call the pediatric nurse in the morning. Her fucking toes are gone."

"You're right," James says. "Let's go to the ER. I can get us there in twenty."

Madeline nods, grabs the diaper bag, grabs her purse, grabs Talia. It's not their first time in the emergency room with the baby. Once, there was a fever, and another time, what they thought was jaundice but turned out to be mustard. They're new parents and terrified most of the time.

Madeline tosses James the car keys. "Make it fifteen."

"Are you sure they weren't like this before?" the doctor says. He has a neat gray mustache with small wire-rim glasses and a beaky nose. He spreads Talia's feet with his fingers, puffing out his cheeks when she gurgles happily up at him. Madeline decides if he blows on her belly, she will kill him.

"Yes," James says. "We're sure our baby had toes."

"Well, she's a healthy baby otherwise," the doctor says before addressing Talia in a singsong voice. "Aren't you? Aren't you?"

"But where are her toes?" Madeline didn't trust herself to speak until now, afraid she would scream or fly at the doctor's face.

"I'm not convinced she ever had toes," the doctor says. "It looks like a birth defect. It doesn't mean she can't lead a normal life. There are some orthopedic options—"

"I trimmed her toenails myself!" Madeline says. "With my teeth, because I was afraid of hurting her if I used the fingernail clippers."

"Are you saying you bit off her toes? Because I don't see—"

"No! I'm saying they were there. We played *this little piggy goes to market*." Madeline's voice is hoarse and desperate. "My baby had little piggies and now she doesn't. Where are they?"

"I suggest you schedule an appointment with your pediatrician as soon as possible." The doctor places his stethoscope around his neck and avoids looking her in the face. "We've done as much as we can tonight. I think everyone could do with some rest."

In the car on the way home, with Talia asleep in her car seat, Madeline googles *baby toes* and *baby's toes* and *fallen off* and *defects* and *amputations* and *gangrene* until her eyes blur and she feels like throwing up.

At home, Madeline and James tuck the baby in her crib without saying a word to each other and climb into their bed the same way. There is no teasing, *Goodnight, Hansel* followed by *Goodnight, Gretel*. Madeline can't imagine either one of them sleeping a wink. She's determined to stay awake until she sees a doctor with answers, a doctor who can bring back what is lost. She thinks of her daughter's missing toes and remembers what Hattie said about the wolf's milk on the dead log, those pink blobs that looked exactly like baby toes. She rolls over to share this fact with James, but he is already passed out.

Madeline considers calling Hattie, but she feels somehow embarrassed about what happened to her baby, like it's a personal failing. She's also afraid her friend will think she's blaming her for what happened. As if Hattie's observation, uttered out loud, was the cause. Does she blame Hattie? A little, yes, though it makes no sense.

She closes her eyes and recalls those perfect pink orbs on the log. Hattie had said they would turn brown within a day. Madeline sits up, realizing she has very little time.

Slipping out of bed, she pulls on a hoodie and quietly descends the stairs. She snatches a flashlight and a bowl from the kitchen and her foraging bag. She jams her feet into Wellies and closes the front door softly behind her, not wanting to wake James or Talia.

Nighttime is a different world in the forest. It's pitch black except for the sweep of her flashlight and a smattering of stars in the sky. Quieter but also louder, the sounds different; instead of birds chirping, frogs are calling and so are owls; paws creep over the undergrowth, paws that could be small like a mouse or large like a bear. She pushes the image of a black bear away and marches out to the fallen tree, clomping over ferns and snakeroots.

In the murkiness cast by her flashlight, she's relieved to find the wolf's milk still pink and round. Using the edge of her scissors, she pops the mold off the log and into the bowl. She thinks about all this life growing out of something dead. Her body had grown her daughter, but Madeline was something alive and so was Talia, and the tree was something dead, but it was still growing things that were alive. Red raspberry slime, looking less like raspberries than coral at the bottom of the sea, hen of the woods, bundled into cabbage-like bouquets, lion's mane, turkey tail fungus with bright orange and green stripes, furry puffballs, and honey mushrooms with wide yellow caps.

When she's taken more than a dozen pieces of the wolf's milk, she returns to the house, yanking off her Wellies and tiptoeing into the baby's room. Talia snoozes on her back, her legs drawn up like a cat. Madeline manages to remove Talia's socks without waking her, the ones James slid on after leaving the ER so they wouldn't have to look at their baby's toeless feet. Madeline half expects the toes to be back, like a magician lifting a handkerchief from a vanishing act, but they aren't, so she plucks each pink blob from the bowl and positions it where one of Talia's toes should be. She wonders, *Am I crazy?* She knows the mold is not poisonous. But still.

Moving methodically from largest to smallest, Madeline picks the best-shaped ones, the pinkest ones, and in the end, she's satisfied that, except for a little ooze, which could be mistaken for toe jam, they look alright, not great, but alright. Her foraging was a success.

With great care, she rolls the socks back on Talia's feet and secures everything in place. Then she sneaks back up to bed and slithers in beside her still-sleeping husband.

Goodnight, Hansel, she sighs.

"They're back!"

James is shouting from Talia's room. He thunders up the stairs and dances around their bedroom in the morning sunlight, spinning with Talia in his arms as she squeals with delight.

"Her toes are back!" He thrusts Talia's feet into Madeline's face so she can inspect the baby toes all in a neat row. She's relieved they aren't brown or deflated or falling off. And she's almost as ecstatic as James when Talia wiggles them. Yet, the translucent toenails are gone and there is some ooze and a sense about the toes that Madeline can only think of as *fruiting*. But James either doesn't notice or is content to ignore it. And who is she to wreck that?

"It must have been the mushrooms in the pasta," he says. "Something hallucinogenic. It made us think our baby had no toes. We were delusional."

"What about the ER doctor?" Madeline says.

James pauses in his happy baby dance.

"Do you even remember his name?" he says. "Because I don't. Maybe we hallucinated him too."

"It was probably Hattie's fault," Madeline says. "She was shit at foraging. I hope she didn't crash into a tree and end up wandering around the forest tripping out. I should call her." But she won't. And she never will again.

Madeline will also never know if Talia's soft striped socks or the cool kitchen tiles or her mother's lips will ever feel the same against her toes again. And grown up, would she even remember?

"Don't squeeze them," Madeline says.

ABOUT THE AUTHOR

Shannon Scott is an English Professor in the Twin Cities. She has contributed essays to collections published by Manchester UP, Routledge, Palgrave, and Bloomsbury. Shannon has also published short fiction in *Nightmare Magazine, Coppice and Brake, Nightscript, The Other Stories,* and *Water~Stone.* She is co-editor of *Terrifying Transformations: An Anthology of Victorian Werewolf Fiction, 1838-1896* and has created two lecture series on the horror genre for Audible.

NEW MOM GROW KIT: TWO STARS

Rick Claypool

AFTER MOM's death I moved into her house and ordered one of your New Mom Grow Kits.

I ordered everything I needed from your website except the supplies I knew I could get cheaper someplace else. Mom taught me not to waste money—I'm sure that's what she would have wanted me to do.

One time in the Kmart parking lot she gave me a crisp twenty and told me to go get myself some socks. She waited in the car with my little sister. I'd never bought any new clothes for myself, never been inside Kmart without Mom. I remember taking a pack of black socks with neon stripes to the curly-haired teenage cashier with a little moustache who rang me up. I kept the change in my fist and proudly presented it to her after returning. "Three dollars and seventeen cents?" she asked. "Where's the rest?" She was furious. She marched me and my sister inside and demanded a refund. "You ought to be ashamed," she scolded teenage moustache cashier, who took back the socks. He locked eyes with me as my sister mimicked Mom's words, "Where's da rest? Where's da rest?"

So when I noticed the sack of mulch on the New Mom Grow Kit

website was priced ridiculously high—and would more than double the shipping cost of the whole order—I thought, yeah, no. You keep your pricey mulch, New Mom Grow Kit website. I can get my own mulch.

The New Mom Grow Kit supplies arrived in a box that took up most of Mom's front stoop. I hauled it inside and dropped it on the living room floor between the blue-green L-shaped sofa and Mom's monstrous television.

I reached my trembling fingers between the flaps of corrugated cardboard to rip the box open. Step one of growing a real New Mom! But when I looked inside, confusion replaced my excitement.

The supplies were arranged in an awkward way that made them hard to take out. Something about the way the inside of the box was packed, with no clear sign of what to remove first, overwhelmed me with fear that removing the supplies in the incorrect order might cause irreparable damage—damage for which I would, inevitably, have only myself to blame.

I wondered why you would pack the box like this—you're supposed to understand anyone who orders this kit is grieving and that grieving people like me sometimes suck at life in a way that makes them crumble before small challenges.

New Mom Grow Kit Website people, I thought you understood what I was going through! New Mom Grow Kit Website people, I thought you cared!

Then I realized I'd accidentally opened the box upside down.

You New Mom Grow Kit Website people didn't let me down after all! The delivery person let me down! (In the future, please consider enlarging the font of the box text indicating which side should be placed face up and which side face down.)

Removing the upside-down New Mom Grow Kit from its box was a struggle, but I managed. I spread out the supplies on the carpet in the living room. There was a little plastic bag with plastic tools for scooping and scraping and so on, a packet of spores the size of a pound of ground beef labeled NOT FOR HUMAN CONSUMPTION, a bottle of "spore nutrient slurry," a plastic Mom-sized, Mom-shaped mold, and an instruction manual.

I hauled the hardware store mulch I'd purchased up from the basement.

When I was about to begin, a familiar anxiety crept through my body. It's how I always feel when I'm starting to assemble a new piece of furniture. I knew a mistake early on in the process could ruin everything. I knew I'd have to live with the consequences for as long as I keep whatever I've assembled, possibly forever.

Do you ever feel that way, New Mom Grow Kit website people?

I read and re-read and re-read the instructions until I convinced myself I wouldn't screw up the first step, which was combining Mom's ashes with the mulch in the Mom-sized, Mom-shaped mold.

Then I moved on to the second step, which was pouring the nutrient slurry into a bowl. Then I stirred in the spore packet.

And then, at the bottom of the instruction manual page was the next-to-last step: emptying the spore slurry into the mold with the ash and mulch mixture.

All I had to do next was store the mixture in the plastic Mom-sized, Mom-shaped mold for one week. I was about to drag the mold into Mom's old room when I closed the instruction manual and saw an additional note on the back page. The note said, "To avoid undesired possibilities, buy New Mom Grow Kit-brand gnat spray."

I couldn't believe it. I wondered what kind of greedy, shameless business you were running, attempting to upsell extra products in the instruction manual? The nerve, taking advantage of grieving people like that. I knew Mom would never have tolerated that sort of thing when she was alive.

My New Mom hatched from her mold on a Tuesday.

She shambled around stiffly at first. Her mycelium hair stuck out wildly in raggy clumps. Feeble, half-formed arms hung uselessly at her sides. Her face was a white mass my imagination could find only the faintest hint of my original Mom in.

But there was enough Mom-ishness about my New Mom that I found myself immediately, effortlessly loving her, and I believed she loved me in return.

This is the moment when your New Mom Grow Kit earned its two stars.

I dressed her in a sweatshirt with a duck on it and a pair of pink sweatpants, then used some of her old makeup to draw her face on. I'm not much of an artist, but it didn't matter. Mom was smiling at me again.

I tried brushing her hair, but the delicate threads came loose too easily, and soft hunks of her foamy scalp came out with them. I found a ballcap with a manatee on it and put it on her.

For several days I spent at least several minutes with my New Mom, which is what your instructions said I'm supposed to do so my New Mom knows it's loved.

I was picking balls of lint off the afghan on the back of the couch when my sister called.

She told me she was going through a rough patch at work, where she defuses bombs. Sometimes the bombs explode and the explosions take a toll, she said, physically and spiritually. She suffered a bout of temporary blindness after her last contract. Even after her recovery, her vision was pixelated, she said, possibly permanently.

I invited her to stay with me at Mom's house and she agreed to the visit in a hesitant way I knew meant I should expect problems.

My sister arrived with a New Mom of her own.

I could tell by the way she stood in the doorway avoiding eye contact through her special glasses that she was a little embarrassed. My sister's New Mom lurked silently beside her, wearing a shiny, squeaky purple raincoat and a floral print babushka over its mycelium hair. "You have nothing to be ashamed of," I told her. "I ordered a New Mom too! Hey, maybe our New Moms can keep each other company?"

I let them in and went looking for my New Mom, who I hadn't checked on for the past few days. It's not that I didn't love her. I did! I just didn't like seeing or being around her all the time.

I found her in Mom's bedroom on the floor beside Mom's bed, face down in the plastic mold that came with the New Mom Grow Kit. I turned her over, and a cloud of gnats took flight. I sat her up and saw I needed to reapply her makeup. There were little holes in the surface of her face, on her eyebrows and cheeks and where her lips should be, and in the lamp light I was sure I saw little worms quickly withdraw into them.

The little holes were little tunnels and I did not know how deep below the surface they went. While reapplying her eyeliner, I was sure I saw something peek out of a tunnel on the side of her nose. Revolted, I stabbed it with the eyeliner pencil. I don't know if I killed it or missed it, but I gouged my New Mom a new nostril.

She made a soft grunting sound as my sister and her New Mom appeared in the doorway. Was it a greeting? A plea for help? I had no idea. I used my body to block my sister from seeing my New Mom's face while hastily applying a dollop of foundation over the extra nostril I'd gouged.

"Her room looks exactly the same?" my sister said, and her questioning tone of voice reminded me of her failing vision, and I relaxed.

My sister's New Mom pushed past my sister into Mom's room. "It's like she knows it's her room," I said.

"Yeah," said my sister, who pulled a spray bottle from her purse. She squirted the spray bottle's contents in her New Mom's face, which somehow had what looked like an actual photograph of Mom's face printed on its pale surface. As far as I could tell, it didn't have any holes in it.

I must admit that the way my sister's New Mom looked way better than my New Mom was kind of upsetting to me.

We left the New Moms in Mom's bedroom to get to know each other, and my sister joined me at the dining room table, which was heaped with various papers and forms and files and receipts and bills relating to Mom's death. She picked up an old invoice and frowned, straining to read it. "Do you still need to pay this?"

I probably did, but I didn't want to talk about that. "What did you spray on your New Mom?" I asked, as if I didn't already know.

"Gnat spray," she said. "They recommend it in the instructions. You didn't see that?"

"Yeah, I saw it," I said, then took a sip of coffee from a mug that said, "This Mom Is Da Bomb" on the side of it, which I'm pretty sure my sister bought her for Mother's Day one year. "But I don't think Mom would have splurged on something advertised the way the spray was advertised. You remember how economical she was. It didn't seem right to me. It seemed like an *extravagance*. That was her word, remember? When we asked for things that were too expensive, she'd say 'No, we can't afford that kind of *extravagance*'."

My sister's features became pinched in a way that might have meant she disagreed with me or might have meant she was straining to look at me. "Mom was cheap," she said, "but she wasn't stupid. She taught us how to take care of things, how sometimes what looks like the less expensive choice can cost more in the end."

We bickered into the evening. Eventually, we switched from coffee to one of Mom's old wine bottles. Eventually, my sister lunged at me with the corkscrew and almost stabbed me in the neck. She's strong and the corkscrew is sharp, but thanks to her pixelated vision she only managed a nasty scratch just above my collarbone. I shoved her away and she apologized, and soon enough we were laughing together and playing the card games we remembered Mom teaching us.

After midnight, we were still chatting until my sister's New Mom came out of Mom's room to lean beside my sister, seeming to whisper something into her ear. Can my sister's New Mom actually speak? I couldn't tell, but whatever her New Mom said or did clearly made my sister upset. "Show me," my sister said to her New Mom. I pocketed the corkscrew. My sister's New Mom pointed insistently at a spot on its face below its photorealistic right eye. "I see," she said.

"See what?" I tried to look calm while bracing for another attack.

My sister and my sister's New Mom turned toward me together. Both pointed at a little maggot wriggling out of a tiny tunnel on the side of her New Mom's face.

My sister stood up and I stood up and my sister slapped me and the shock and sting sent me reeling into a shame spiral. I needed my Mom but I had no Mom so I ran to my New Mom. My New Mom was all I had.

I ran to Mom's room, tears dribbling down my cheeks. I thought I'd plead for comfort only she could give, a love like no one else's love.

But when I tried opening the door to Mom's room, it was stuck. Why was it even closed?

The thought of my New Mom shutting me out in my moment of need was too much, and in that moment I hated her and needed her and cried for her.

I swore I would get my revenge against you New Mom Grow Kit website people. Because you knew this would happen, didn't you? And you're laughing about it now, aren't you? "Laughing all the way to the bank," as Mom always said.

After frantically twisting the knob and pushing and pulling on the door, it eventually came loose and I stumbled through some kind of wet membrane, like a spider web but moist. I spent a minute spitting and wiping the stuff off of my face before I could look up and look around, and what I saw knocked the air from my lungs in a way that made a small, desperate sound escape my throat.

A damp, fuzzy layer of the pale membranous substance covered everything in Mom's room. A cloud of gnats hummed in the air. When I looked up, I saw my New Mom's head sticking out of the substance on the ceiling. I wheeled around. One of her arms stuck out of the wall to my right and the other stuck out of the wall to my left. One of her legs stuck out of the wall across from me and the other stuck out of the wall behind me, beside the door. Her head and limbs twitched and spasmed as helplessly as the appendages of a freshly squished spider. I understood the membranous substance covering everything was what used to be her body.

My sister's New Mom pushed past me into Mom's room. I watched, too shocked to speak or move, as it knelt over the plastic Mom-sized, Mom-shaped mold beside Mom's bed. It placed its hand against the side of its face so the maggot could crawl out of the tunnel and onto its palm, then gently dropped the maggot in the plastic Mom-sized, Mom-shaped mold. Peering over the edge from where I stood, I saw the mold was overflowing with the blindly writhing larvae.

Furious about what my sister's New Mom did to my New Mom, I stomped up to my sister's New Mom, and when it stood to face me, I slapped it. The slap knocked a chunk off my sister's New Mom's face, and under the chunk were more maggots that fell to the floor in wriggling clumps. My sister's New Mom acted like I wasn't even there as it bent down to pick up the maggots, placing them one by one onto its pale palm, then carefully dropping them into the plastic Mom mold with the rest.

I was overcome with the urge to teach my sister's New Mom a lesson for what she did to my New Mom and for ignoring me and for paying more attention to some maggots than she ever paid to me.

I looked at my sister's New Mom with her legs curled under her on the floor—just like Mom sat on the floor sometimes—and I looked at the writhing mass of larvae in the Mom-sized, Mom-shaped mold, and I looked down at my sad bare feet with their veiny skin and too-long toenails, and I knew what I had to do.

I barely registered my sister's voice shouting from the doorway asking me what I was doing and pleading with me to stop and becoming increasingly incomprehensible as I raised my foot to stomp it down into the middle of the writhing maggot mass.

But my sister tackled me and pinned me to the ground before I could give the maggot mass the proper stomping I knew would have directed my sister's New Mom's undivided attention toward me.

Do you New Mom Grow Kit website people have any idea what living in Mom's house is like now? I bet you don't. And honestly I don't know if I'm capable of explaining it.

My sister says it's miraculous. I don't think she would say that if her vision wasn't still pixelated, if she could see what I see.

After my sister's New Mom closed the door to Mom's room behind us that night, it sealed the door in some way that ensured we couldn't go back inside until it allowed us back inside.

And when it was ready, my sister's New Mom made it clear she was never interested in caring for either of us.

Because after the door finally opened, it wasn't the spongy, maggot-eaten remains of my New Mom all over the ceiling and floor that broke my heart most.

It was the compact mass of gnats and maggots my sister's New Mom cradled and how my sister's New Mom lovingly turned its hollowed-out head toward that mass when it cried its buzzing, squelching, newborn cry.

Two stars.

ABOUT THE AUTHOR

Rick Claypool writes absurdist horror. He is the author of the novels *Skull Slime Tentacle Witch War* (Anxiety Press, 2024) and *Leech Girl Lives* (Spaceboy Books, 2017) and the novella *The Mold Farmer* (Six Gallery Press, 2020). His writing appears here and there in anthologies and online, including in *HAD*, *ergot.*, *Maudlin House*, and *Fungi Magazine*. He is a member of HWA and the Rhode Island Mycological Society. Find him online at absurdisthorror.substack.com.

New Life
Gordon Linzner

Awake now, are we? Ready to advance to our next stage?

The question was rhetorical. Of course we are.

Dark outside now. Daylight in a few hours. Either matters little, for our purposes.

Yes, get to our feet. Head to the bathroom. We're still getting used to these methods. Run the tap in the tub, if that makes us feel better. Rub our hands together. It might make us a little more appealing.

Not as much as the wrinkled shirt seemed to, though.

Operating this casing is still a work in progress.

Rinse our face. That chill feels invigorating, no? The soothing damp, highlighted by that fan.

Breathe in the air, loaded with tiny, tasty molecules. Not unlike the ones you've absorbed. Useful for breeding purposes.

We pause to study the body on the bed. He? She?

Irrelevant. That is us, as well, or soon will be, now that we have shared ourselves.

They won't need us now. No more than you, we, needed advice on our merging. What was needed was natural. Obvious. Is natural and obvious.

Once they waken that body, they will also be us.

No need to close the door. They'll leave this place not long after we do.

We, both of us, all of us, have many more spores to share in the coming days.

ABOUT THE AUTHOR

Gordon Linzner is founder, former editor of *Space and Time Magazine*, and author of five published novels and scores of short stories in *F&SF*, *Twilight Zone*, *Sherlock Holmes Mystery Magazine*, other magazines and anthologies. He is a member of the HWA and a lifetime member of SFWA.

An Unwanted Growth

Jo Kaplan

WHEN MY DAUGHTER came home from school, she told me there were people in the walls. I took her to mean the drawings her teacher often taped up around the classroom, or maybe chalk figures etched on the ancient blackboard. Ava had always been the imaginative sort. In kindergarten she would make little books of stapled paper with a hand-drawn cover and pages of squiggles inside, which she would carry around so she could "read" her invented stories to me. At ages six and seven she had an invisible friend who was a half-bull, half-cat called Alfred. It seemed a shame to me that this creativity was, at eight, no longer viewed as intelligence but rather a nuisance, which is why she'd brought home the poor behavior slip for me to sign.

"This says you were distracted in class," I read once she'd pulled the rumpled paper from her backpack. "Mr. Sharin says you weren't paying attention."

She told me she was looking at the people in the walls. "And anyway, Mr. Sharin was being boring." She coughed, a ragged sound that sent my heart reeling. I asked her if she was getting sick, but she only shrugged and scampered off, leaving me to sigh and scrounge about for a pen. She'd have done better in an enrichment program—

that was the reason for the boredom, I suspected. But the school had nothing of the sort. Such a thing was a relic of bygone days before extracurriculars and music and foreign language had been slashed to color within the lines of ever-diminishing funds.

Over a dinner of mac and cheese with hot dogs, for which I closed my eyes and asked my late husband to forgive me this lack of good nutrition, I caught Ava's attention. "Tell me honestly. Were you distracted today because you were worried about Hoover?"

Ava's curls bounced as she shook her head. "I wasn't really friends with him."

"I know, but he was your classmate. *Is* your classmate." The correction caught like a hiccup in my throat. "I know the teachers are keeping a close eye on everyone, especially at recess—"

"They won't let us do anything anymore!" She stabbed a bit of meat. "It's not fair. Most of us think it was kind of his fault."

My heart clenched. I imagined a stranger bending down to talk to Ava on the rusted excuse for a playground, leading her into his car, driving away. But it wasn't her picture in the newspaper. It was a boy wearing an old baseball cap, the boy I'd seen on the kickball field, with a missing canine and elbows that pinched to a point. Not Ava.

"He was always wandering off," she continued with a shrug. "I mean, he thought he was so adventurous, but he was really just showing off. He liked to explore, you know, sneak around and stuff. Genie thinks he ran away."

"Well," I said, swallowing hard. "It's only been two weeks. I'm sure they'll find him." The clock on the microwave said it was already six-fifteen. "All right, finish up. I don't want to be late to PTA."

Ava threw back her head and kicked her legs. "I don't want to go back to school!"

"You can't stay here alone." The mac and cheese was turning to glue. I scraped my remainders into a Tupperware for lunch tomorrow. "I don't want to miss this one because—" In my mind was Ava's face composed of grainy black-and-white instead of the boy in the baseball cap. "Because I've missed too many already."

The sun lowered as we drove across town. Sometimes darkness was a blessing. It could hide the boarded-up storefronts and fouled brick of abandoned buildings, the collapsing chain-link around fields of dead weeds. Mick and I had been planning on getting out once we'd saved enough, moving somewhere nicer, but cancer is a thing that eats away at you, body and soul and bank account. The worst was how he'd apologized for leaving us with nothing. As if it was his fault.

We found a piece of paper taped to the front door saying that tonight's PTA meeting would be held in the multi-purpose room, the one that served as gym and cafeteria and auditorium, because there were too many parents for a classroom. I sent Ava off with the other kids and the teacher on babysitting duty, found a plastic folding chair amid the swarm of unhappy faces.

The meeting went just about how I'd expected—angry parents threatening to pull their kids from school, the administration offering weak assurances and platitudes. Someone claiming that after a week, it was all but guaranteed for a missing child to be dead. Someone else hissing at them to shut up.

When no one could find anything else to say about Hoover, a father stood to complain that his child had been wracked with a persistent cough for weeks and blamed the poor conditions of the old building. Even here in their best room, water damage left brown circles on the ceiling. The floor was scuffed to an indefinable color. Cracks snaked up the walls like vines.

"I guess you're too busy shoving religion down our kids' throats, you can't be bothered to fix things up," one mother snarled, leading to a smattering of nods and a much larger smattering of outraged retorts about the importance of instilling good values in our children.

It was still going on, the unproductive back-and-forth of it, when I retreated, the overhead lights too hot and bright, the anger and frustration too needle-sharp—the fear and uncertainty that rippled in an undercurrent through us all. Mick used to take point on these kinds of meetings. I found the nearest bathroom and splashed water on my face, begging Mick's forgiveness for my ineptitude. The water leeched a faintly sulfuric odor into my skin. When I turned the tap, it continued to drip, drip, drip into the basin. I looked into the stall behind me and found rust stains reddening the seat. The lock mechanism appeared broken. I decided against using it, understanding why Ava always came home dancing into the bathroom.

Across the hall, I found a classroom and felt bad that I couldn't remember if it was Ava's—or where hers even was. When was the last parent-teacher conference? Days blurred together. I wondered if I was a bad parent. Mick wasn't here to offer any assurances to the contrary.

I pushed open the door and flipped on the light, hoping I might see one of Ava's colorful drawings, but the room only made me sad with its scratched-up desks and missing ceiling tiles. Papers were taped to the walls, but they weren't drawings. They were Bible verses.

And God shall wipe away all tears from their eyes, and there shall be no more death, neither sorrow, nor crying, neither shall there be any more pain; for the former things are passed away. And He that sat upon the throne said, "Behold, I make all things new."

The paper was down from the wall and in my hand in a moment, and then it was a crumpled ball in the trash.

Once gone, I discovered what it had been covering: an amorphous black splotch. By the time I'd torn down the third Bible verse, I realized what I was looking at. Despite the deterioration of the building, I almost couldn't believe it. No wonder the children were coughing. Their rooms were infested with mold.

With each paper torn from the wall, I felt a kind of vindication, revealing what they thought they could cover up. When it was all down, the walls bare, I couldn't look away. The black marks swooped and bloated, contorted into whorls and shapes that seemed at once random and intentional, like the florid patterns of a Victorian wallpaper.

Were I a student here, I could imagine myself getting lost in the constellation of black shapes, trying to coalesce them into an ordered picture in my mind, to make sense of the pattern. I don't know why I should have thought there even *was* a pattern, but something about the mold rang a bell in my mind and made it difficult to look away, drawing my attention like the pendulations of a hypnotist's pocket watch. I remembered long hours in the hospital marked by steady beeping while my eyes followed the bumps and lumps in the wall to see if they turned into anything, became an optical illusion. Trying to find reason where there was none. Cancer is a thing without reason, an unwanted growth that spreads when neglected.

Tearing myself away felt like the act of ripping down the papers. My mind separated from the walls with the stickiness of Velcro. A part of me considered returning the papers to the walls, but I couldn't bring myself to fish the Bible verses out of the trash. Let them see, when they arrive in the morning. Let them confront the truth.

God cannot wipe away all pain from the world. There was an infestation here which could not be cleared with prayer alone. It would only grow and spread if ignored.

I switched off the light and continued down the hall, seeking Ava's room and, yes, avoiding the rest of the PTA meeting I had been so eager to attend.

The building was falling apart. How could I have been sending my daughter into this place every day? But then—what choice did I have? I felt briefly guilty for pulling the papers from the walls. As with the doctors who had tended to Mick, this wasn't the teachers' fault. They were merely trying to work within a corrupted system that hated them and refused them the tools to make it better. I was at Mick's bedside again, torn into a million pieces and filled with impotent emotion. Utterly powerless.

A door swung open at my push, but it did not lead to a classroom. A set of ragged wooden stairs descended into a pool of shadow. I hadn't realized the school had a basement. A place for storage and custodial equipment, most likely.

Though I knew I ought to return to the meeting, a little worm of rebellion wriggled within me. I felt like that boy who Ava said was always wandering, exploring, going where he wasn't allowed.

I started down the stairs.

As each one creaked underfoot, my mind found reason in this decision. If I could find damning evidence, something that would force the school to address these poor conditions, then I could force the district's hand. Threaten them with legal action. What I was doing could accomplish more than arguing for an hour with other parents and teachers.

My phone's light had to guide me the rest of the way. The stairs deposited me on a concrete floor. A large room opened up, my circle of light catching broken desks, piles of chairs forming cobweb-veiled pyramids, and wire shelves bearing colorless tubs with the labels worn off.

A paddle switch brightened the space with an arrhythmic flicker, the dust-clouded bulbs giving off a shuddering mustard light that barely reached the corners. Somehow the new light deepened the shadows around the defunct furniture. But it was the walls that stole my attention—concrete walls that dripped slime from leakage overhead. Black spots bloomed from the baseboards and stretched down from the ceiling in lurid flourishes, forming spotty colonies. My hand stamped itself over my nose and mouth to block the musty smell that had me envisioning microscopic spores in the air.

Was this enough? I snapped a few photos. Black patterns shifted and writhed in the unsteady light of the bulbs' old filaments. I moved slowly along the edge of the room until a soft thud broke the quiet. From beneath a hulking mountain of chairs rolled a graying baseball. It came to a stop a few feet to my left.

"Hello?" I said into the quiet, feeling faintly ridiculous. I skirted the ball, not wanting to nudge it as I passed.

It was beyond that pile of chairs that I saw the figure.

The shock of it froze me in place, but there was nobody down here with me. It was only one of the shapes the mold had made on the wall, dark circles clustered in a way that looked quite like a person. My thumb trembled with my throbbing heart as I snapped a photo. There was a head, a trunk, two legs stretching down into the floor. And sharp elbows jutting from the arms at the figure's sides, which seemed to wave in the shifting light. Or no, not wave, for the hands appeared closed into fists, like they were banging on a door.

I let my gaze go unfocused, tried to turn the shape to something else, but it snapped right back again when I blinked. A pattern that refused to be anything but what it was.

Against the leftmost wall, I discovered two more black figures, their arms meeting in a V where they appeared to hold hands. I reached out but stopped before my fingers could graze the wall, could touch those fetid smudges. Instead, I backed away, trying not to see the figures tilting their heads as the light flickered. My heel came down on something that spilled me to the floor, and the baseball rolled irritably away, taking with it my phone as I caught myself on hands and elbows before my skull could crack against concrete. Above me, there—was that where it had been only a moment ago?—was the first figure again, the one with the closed fists, and its head seemed turned to the side as if to look over at the other two. I couldn't initially say why I thought its face was turned until I recognized the curved plane jutting from its forehead as the bill of a cap.

My heart thudded. The spots of mold were like the ink grain of a newspaper.

All at once, I did not want to be down here any longer. I pushed to my feet, ignoring the scrapes on my palms, the embedded grit, and turned for the exit, apologizing to Mick that I'd ever thought to come down here.

Two figures stood at the top of the staircase. I couldn't make out their features. The hallway backlit them, transformed them into flat shadows. They stood side-by-side, holding hands.

"Mom!"

A crackling wave of relief washed over me at Ava's voice. The PTA meeting must be over, and she'd come to find where I had gone. I started shakily up the stairs, patting my pocket to assure myself of the evidence I had gathered, but the pocket was empty.

"I made a new friend," Ava said. Before turning back to retrieve my phone, I looked up again at her, the light better from this angle, but I did not recognize this friend.

Holding my daughter's hand was a shadow, a piece of drywall carved into the shape of a person, fuzzy and rotten.

My inhale dragged the basement's rotten musk into my mouth as I felt something pulling me backward, into the dark and the damp, where things grew into shapes crafted from the imagination of something hideously lonely.

Behold, I make all things new.

ABOUT THE AUTHOR

Jo Kaplan is the Shirley Jackson Award-nominated author of *It Will Just Be Us* and *When the Night Bells Ring*. Her short stories have appeared in *Fireside Quarterly*, *Black Static*, *Nightmare Magazine*, *Vastarien*, *Horror Library*, *Nightscript*, and numerous anthologies. In addition to writing, she teaches English and creative writing at Glendale Community College and is the co-chair of the Horror Writers Association's Los Angeles chapter.

Pretty Maids All in a Row
Randee Dawn

Carolyne Massey surveys her front yard with the critical eye of a first-time homeowner or a first-time parent, of which she is both.

The small space is weedy and unkempt, messy and dense. A dinner plate-sized, bare depression lurks close to the row house's foundation. The rest is a profusion of thin, yellow-green grasses interspersed with rugged fireworks of color, hardy flowering interlopers that stole in on the wind. A faint, sweet-sour odor drifts from behind the spindly tree's trunk.

Despite the heat of the morning, Carolyne shivers once and peers at the area behind the tree. *It's gone*, she thinks with relief. At least Terence had assisted with *that* task. Then she squints again, unsure. A pink-gray...*something* is poking skyward from the mulch.

"What's up, cupcake?"

Terence jolts Carolyne from her daydreaming, if that's what you call staring out at your miniscule front yard and thinking, *what a dump.* "Nothing," she tells her husband breezily. "Just—thanks for clearing out that dead...thing behind the tree."

"Yeah, no problem," he mutters, scrolling through his phone. "Nothing's too much for my little gateau."

She's always a dessert to him.

Last week, a thick, sour-sweet odor had drawn Carolyne to the back of the yard, where she'd found the dead creature. Initially, she'd thought it was a neighborhood feral cat, but the corpse had been gray-white with tiny hands and miniature pointed teeth, topped off with a rat-like, hairless tail. The opossum had been dead for several days—but it had also been partly buried. Mysterious, thick grasses with blunted ends and a carapace-like scale across their tips had wrapped around the corpse.

Like fingers pulling it down had shot through her mind.

One of the—

fingers

—had jutted through the beast's eye socket.

Carolyne's stomach had lurched. Later, she insisted Terence get rid of it once he'd returned from his latest work trip.

Turning, she spots his travel case, which he's wheeled out onto the patio, and gives it a hateful look. He's on the road again. Of course. *Such's the life of the No. 1 sales affiliate at Quimby Widgets,* he'd explained with a shark's grin on their first date. *After I retire, I'll be an expert on hotel interior décor.*

It had been funny, then. *He'd* been funny then.

Caroline takes a deep breath. "It's a bigger job than I was expecting." She gestures at the yard. The raised patio overlooks the irregular space, which is cut in two by a curved walkway. The second slice of the yard is packed with thick, thorny rose bushes that hide the trashcans and much of the patio from prying eyes on the sidewalk.

"Well, you have fun with that." Her husband hefts the case down the steps to the walkway. Carolyne trails after and he turns to kiss her head. "My Uber's here. See you Friday."

"Tell Ramona I said 'hi.'" Carolyne eyes him, looking for a reaction.

Terence shrugs a shade too carelessly. "Oh, I'm not even sure if she's coming this time! I mean, the boss has to be in the office once in a while!" The gate creaks, and he ducks into the waiting black SUV.

Releasing a long breath, Carolyne turns back to the chaotic yard, wondering how to begin. Sometimes, she feels like the weeds in it: Transplanted to Brooklyn not by choice, but circumstance. Terence is the breadwinner in the family—she's the throwback stay-at-home mom —so his promotion meant relocation from deep Long Island to the five boroughs. Carolyne had insisted that with the rise in pay from Terence's promotion, they purchase a proper home—not a cramped apartment in Manhattan—so that their nearly four-year-old twins Kristi and Roger would grow up in a true neighborhood. And so: South Brooklyn. Here, people live squashed together and yards are after-thoughts, far from the rolling green front and back spaces Carolyne played in as a child on the Island.

They've been here since February, and now that spring is arriving, Carolyne has determined that they will not have an afterthought yard. They will have a prizewinning one. She must exert control over some-thing. Maybe not her toddlers, whose daily activities bore her. Maybe not her husband, who spends more time on the road than at home. But this yard—she can bend this space to her will.

Something seems to shift in the lower grasses. The pink-gray protu-berance is small, but she can't take her eyes from it. A low hum rises to fill the morning, the sound of thousands of chorusing insects, but the noise doesn't seem to come from the yard. It feels like it originates in the base of her skull. Carolyne steps into the yard. The odor grows stronger as she approaches the spot where the opossum had been...*held* by those strange grasses. She shuts her eyes for a moment, willing away a sudden wave of claustrophobia.

When she opens them again, the hum in her head—a soothing massage of noise—grows louder. Gripping a trowel in her hand, diamond ring tapping on the plastic handle, she knows the tool is woefully inadequate for the task of renovating the yard. *I'm gonna need a bigger trowel*, she thinks, mind unable to ignore, yet equally unable to focus on, the pink-gray thing as she nears it.

It's a tail. No question.

None of the collection of stick-like grassy...fingers are touching it.

Carolyne halts, fury at Terence drowned in confusion. If her husband hadn't come out here to clear away the body—then where is the opossum? The spot where the beast had been is a flat mixture of bent grasses and mulch, punctuated by the finger growths. But no fur. No bones. Nothing. She thinks of running, but that only changes the hum's pitch in her mind, making it shrill. Instead, Carolyne slides into a trance that reminds her of when she got high on pot that one time in college. She bends down to yank the tail out like a weed.

Instead, it lifts easily in her fingers.

Value for our money, Terence had insisted about the row house. By which he meant "his" money, of course. He found the house, told her about getting it for a "song," and announced they were moving; Carolyne had barely been involved. He'd always been a wheeler-dealer, and while they'd dated, she'd enjoyed this part of him—Terence got them better seats at restaurants, upgrades on hotels and car rentals, and brought home tons of swag from conventions. It felt romantic. She hadn't realized it was a lifestyle for him until after they'd married.

Terence had purchased the place without her even seeing it, a three-bedroom far removed from the trendier parts of the borough. Here, cars race past day and night, neighbors shout-talk from their front stoops in languages Carolyne doesn't recognize—and she finds their recycle bags raided every week. It's a far cry from the familiar, if dull, suburban house she'd grown up in.

But everything had happened so fast with Terence. Had it been barely four years since he'd wooed her with wine and trips to the Hamptons? Since she got oopsie pregnant after three months of dating, and he slid a ring on her finger and turned her into a mother, like a magician casting a spell? Who had she been before that? And who was she now, this woman bending over in her awful yard with a husband who couldn't be bothered to remove a dead animal, holding...a tail? Carolyne stares at the wiggly thing. It's attached to nothing. The base looks as if it's been gnawed on. But there is no body.

Carolyne's stomach lurches, and she bends over to vomit in the grasses. They whisper against one another and curl toward her half-digested breakfast.

The hum in her head abates.

It is astonishingly difficult to get landscapers to work on her yard.

Carolyne has always been of the mind that if you're willing to pay, you can get service, but after several companies send over representatives to assess the small plot and offer estimates she can afford, they never come back. They're suddenly too busy or skip appointments or fail to answer the phone.

She finds Mr. Duckworth ("call me Duckie") because he finds her first. While preparing to take the twins out to the park one morning in the double stroller, a man pauses at her front gate. He wears tinted glasses, and his nails are crusted in soil, and he gives off a loamy smell like a fish tank that needs cleaning. Yet he's friendly and even recognizes her yard.

"So you've taken over the ol' Wilcox place," he nods. "Shelly was in and outta my garden center over on New Utrecht Avenue 'bout every week since I was a boy. Pops said she started out like a lot of you young folk, with specific *ideas* about her yard. She'd buy a new plant or flower tray and they'd look nice and neat for a couple weeks and then...things just faded. Died back."

Carolyne thinks of the rotted tail in her yard. "Died?"

He shrugs. "That yard's got a mind of its own, and you gotta know what it wants. Don't give it what it needs, it'll...tell ya. One way or t'other."

It's a batty concept, but Carolyne plays along. "Of course." She tugs at Roger, who's leaning out of his seat. He bounces back into the chair, one finger covered with soil. He sticks it in his mouth like it's candy. Kristi speaks softly to the plastic toy animals she carries, narrating his doings. "Sorry," she tells Duckie while wiping Roger's finger clean. "What does the garden need?"

"Oh, it's a cliché but—blood, sweat an' tears." He chuckles. "You feel me? You'll know you're on the right track when you think about the old nursery rhyme."

Kristi perks up. "Rhyme?"

He cranes down to the girl. "Mary, Mary, quite contrary, how does your garden grow? With silver bells and cockle shells and pretty maids all in a row."

Kristi claps her hands together. Carolyne stands to Roger's side, blocking him from exploring the soil again.

"Any case," Duckie turns back to Carolyne, "Shelly heard what her yard needed loud an' clear. I pass this street all the time—she had some interesting stuff growing. But last couple years of her life, I think something changed."

Carolyne knits her eyebrows. The previous owner is dead?

"I do work on this street for some of your neighbors and..." he leaned toward the gate and lowered his voice. "I hear toward the end Shelly took to standing in that yard for hours. Not doin' anything. Head flipped to one side a bit, like dogs do. I passed by once to say 'howdy' and when I spoke up she flinched, like I was interrupting something." He shakes his head. "Husband found her in the yard one day, face down. Said it was a heart attack but..." he lowers his voice further. "Pal o' mine on the force says it took three men to lift her up. There were plants...embedded in her face. Had to be pulled out o' the skin with tweezers at the morgue."

Carolyne's arms are covered in bumps, and she barely notices Roger reaching around for more dirt. Now she knows why Terence got such a good deal on this place.

A soft buzzing tickles the back of her neck, like a bee crawling on her spine. She glances over her shoulder and glares at the yard. She resolves to control the yard better than Shelly could. But she's going to need assistance.

"Are you taking on clients, Mr. Duckworth?"

His smile opens wide and hearty. "Always, ma'am."

"Well, now, Carrie cannoli." Terence sets his big hand on Carolyne's slight shoulder as they stand on the curving walkway a week later after he's returned from his latest trip. Terence and his boss made the company's first international incursion to drum up customers, and he returned with a plastic Eiffel Tower for Carolyne and travel tags for the twins. "Quite the accomplishment."

He moves his hand to her waist. He's always touching her when he's around as if his body is a leash—and usually, Carolyne loves that feeling of security. When he's away, and she can't feel that dark animal heat emanating from him, she's always felt so vulnerable. But she didn't miss him much this trip. Too busy in the yard. The hum in her skull starts up its curious music again.

Terence and Carolyne are staring at the results of five days of toil by Duckie and his industrious son, who demolished the old rose bushes with chainsaws and uprooted the weeds and wildflowers—though no possum skeleton emerged—before planting fresh growth. Carolyne ferried iced tea to the team while Kristi gave a running commentary of the events to her toy animals and Roger stared in wonder at all the activity, vibrating with excitement. She'd had to pull him away more than once from the exposed underbelly of the soil.

The re-designed yard is now covered in the beginnings of every plant Carolyne dreamed of. Pachysandra, lavender bushes, flowering sage. As he departed, Duckie left behind words of advice: *Tend to this yard, it'll tend to you.*

Now, Terence gives her shoulder a squeeze so hard it hurts. "Looks nearly done."

"Nearly?"

He points. "Missed a spot."

Despite all of Duckie's efforts, the depression is still there, just sprinkled with mulch. And it seems...larger now. Deeper. Roger has wandered over and is peering at the bare spot, hands on his waist. He tilts his head to one side.

"I've got something special in mind for that area," Carolyne lies, hopping into the yard and pulling her son away from the depression. Roger struggles and moans, then gives up and dashes into the house, calling for Kristi.

Terence gives his wife a smoldering, enveloping kiss and cups her rear end. "Let's see what the monsters inside are getting up to," he glances at the front window. "Roger's still looking peaky."

Carolyne can't deny it. With twins, they can measure one against the other for development, and Roger has been coming up short. Kristi is almost easy to forget about, but her brother is fussy about meals, doesn't always seem focused, and his skin is so pale it's nearly translucent.

"Probably just a touch of something." Carolyne lets him hold her hand as they stare at the yard, glowing in the evening light. Tiny leaves wave in the breeze, rustling against one another as if in conversation. This is what she's wanted: an orderly profusion of beauty that will grow lovelier each year. Something she can shape and mold.

"One more thing," says Terence, though he hasn't said the first thing. Carolyne knows what's coming next; it's in his tone, the way his voice goes husky. "I'm back in the field tomorrow."

"How long this time?" It's astonishing to Carolyne that the office can't seem to function without him. That *Ramona* can't seem to function without him. His trips have only increased since the twins came along.

"Five, six days. Not long."

"Terence, I need you here." She hates the shrewish tone in her voice. "The twins are a lot, and we're still not all the way unpacked, and—"

"Your mother is less than an hour away."

"Mom has her own life." So Mom has said, more than once. She loves her grandkids, but is not going to become their nanny. *I did parenting once,* she said the other day on the phone. *I won't be here every time he abandons you.*

Buried in statements like that are all the things Mom said before the marriage, the doubts about Terence, the speed of the relationship, the concern over his absences. Everything Carolyne has heard before and doesn't need to hear again—because they're subtext to her mother's refusal to pitch in.

"Then get creative." Terence's smile feels pasted on, the gloaming casting odd shadows on his features. For a moment, he seems predatory. "Just like with this garden."

She sighs. "Guess I will."

"That's my sugar snap." He gently chucks her chin with his fist. "C'mon. I've got a 7 a.m. flight, and we gotta get the weirdos—I mean, kiddos—in bed. Then I'm gonna show you what I can plant in *your* garden."

How does your garden grow? Carolyne thinks, staring at a green blade poking from the fresh mulch. *That was fast.*

The music in her skull grows stronger as Terence leads her into the house.

Terence continues to be away, so Carolyne devotes herself to the garden. Each morning, she steps outside, startled by the volume of weeds that need tugging or patches that need attention. The depression is becoming a sinkhole. Every day, there's a new thing to attend to.

But she doesn't have a choice; the garden calls to her. Each time a new sprout pops through the mulch, she feels a twinge in her belly. Her fingers twitch. It's like a language she feels, rather than hears. She stands on a gray flagstone amid the profusion of greenery and flowers and angles her head to hear what it has to say. There is a message waiting for her to draw it forth.

When she gardens, Carolyne keeps the children on the enclosed patio and sets a baby gate by the stairs. Kristi ducks under the patio table with her plastic animals and narrates stories to them while Roger peers through the iron bars of the enclosure like a tiny felon. Carolyne wades into the fragrant patch wearing gloves and her new belt of pouches to hold the necessary tools, then loses herself in plucking, pruning, shifting, and organizing.

Unconsciously, she hums a tune that only exists in her head.

One afternoon, Roger reaches into a bag of plant discards and cuttings and scatters everything around like confetti. "Geens," he murmurs. Plucking a dandelion from the pile, he pops it into his mouth. His face lights up like it's ice cream.

"Oh, Rog," his mother tuts. He's covered in leaves and weeds, and his fingers are stained with dirt. A second dandelion has latched onto his blond locks. He resembles a filthy fairy creature, something of the forest.

"Geens," he babbles. "Geens."

Carolyne tugs the remainder of the dandelion from his teeth. "I'll make you peas with dinner. Don't eat those."

"Geens!" he points at the garden.

Curious, Carolyne lifts him over the iron bars and onto a patch of soil where nothing has grown yet. "Don't eat anything," she warns.

"Hi, Geens," Roger gurgles. He toddles to the sinkhole and nods at it. After a moment, he starts to dig.

Carolyne returns to the yard, drawn to the finger-like stalks that sprouted and spread from where the possum died. Duckie had dug everything up, but they've returned—and now she counts eight "fingers" poking through the soil, the mulch. Where they bend, the exterior skin wrinkles like a knuckle. They're awful, and she wants to recoil from them, but instead reaches down to shift aside the mulch. Her glove brushes one finger, and it curls against the fabric in a soft, faint motion.

The day pauses as if someone had taken a breath and held it. Carolyne's mind blanks. Something animal inside her shifts and her hands scrabble at the tool belt until she finds the right item for the job. Whipping out her pruning shears, she *snip snip snips* all eight of the roots off. The carapace-covered tips roll to the side, dark red sap gushing from the stumps, flowing into the soil.

The hum in her mind turns piercing. Her gut wrenches and she doubles over. Backing away from the carnage, she refuses to vomit like last time, but it's taking a lot of concentration.

"Dut. Dut. Dut."

In a short time, Roger has made excellent progress on the sinkhole. He can reach all the way to his elbow in the blank space, and he bounces on his behind with delight. Kristi has woken up, and lines her plastic animals against the iron bars to watch him. Carolyne meets her daughter's gaze.

"How far?" the girl asks.

"How far...what?" her mother responds.

Roger ignores them.

"How far before the bottom?" Kristi asks. Her face is red. She needs more sunscreen.

Carolyne glances between her children, then over her shoulder at the newly decapitated stumps. "There is no bottom," she realizes.

Roger continues to dig.

Over the next weeks, whenever the weather is fine, Carolyne rushes the twins onto the patio just after breakfast, leaves Kristi to her own devices, and hefts Roger into the garden. The one time she forgot, he melted down. Banged his fists so hard on the patio stones he scraped the skin. Now, he spends his time at the hole he's digging, a hole that seems to assist his efforts by getting deeper by the day, deeper than his small hands—or the child-sized spade she bought him—can possibly have reached.

Carolyne decides not to think about what that might mean. While in the yard, she can disappear the memories of anything troubling her—her traveling husband, the babies she hadn't planned on having—and drift back into her pre-Terence days. Of times when she drank with the gals after work, or took scuba diving lessons, or sat on the sofa with the phone off or a book in hand. She spends hours in these reveries, the music in her mind guiding her hands and tools. It's what the yard needs.

Terence comes, and Terence goes. Roger shows his father how he can stand in the hole up to his waist, which earns a brief glance from Terence, who then turns back to his phone. Carolyne tells herself that Terence's distance—literal and figurative since he's pretty far away even when home lately—doesn't matter. She's busy, she's in control, she's tending to her garden. The kids are tanned and glowing from the sun. She stops reading emails or commenting on social media or returning her friends' texts and voicemails. When her mother checks in, Carolyne hurries her off the phone.

Enjoy your mahjongg, your swing dancing, your whiskey tasting, she tells her. *I've got this.*

Still, the control she's able to exert shifts daily. Duckie's plantings are dying back, making room for other kinds of plants, ones Carolyne has never seen before. The waving "fingers" have sprouted again, along with a flurry of iridescent gray flowers that seemed like tiny daisies— until they bloomed. Now they have centers vaguely suggestive of mouths, and she feels the hum in her mind coming through those openings. It's an eerie, seductive, somehow pulsing music.

One day, she discovers the mushrooms. These new protrusions come in a variety of pink, white, and brown shades with narrow-brimmed caps and thick stems threaded with blue lines. The undersides of the caps feature no gills—there's no room. At the center of the silky peaked cap lies a single dimple filled with a pool of opaque, syrupy liquid. As she watches, a fly lands and darts its tongue out for a drink.

Cockle shells, she thinks, knowing that's a misidentification. She turns to the singing flowers, which glint like metal in the light. *Silver bells,* she continues. *All we need are some pretty maids standing in a row.*

Objectively, this is weird. Carolyne knows this deep inside, in a part of her she doesn't look at anymore. A garden grows what you put into it, not what it chooses to create.

Or...does it?

When the questions overwhelm her, Carolyne stands on the flagstone in the middle of the yard and cocks her head to one side, listening to the hum. It's soothing. She can stand there for long stretches of time, then comes back to herself becalmed as if she's had several glasses of wine.

The mushrooms make her nauseated, but she keeps her shears sheathed, thinking of how the "fingers" bled. Crouching over the newcomers, she notes that the thirsty fly from a moment ago has fallen on its back, dead. She flicks the fly from the top of the cap, the pad of her finger brushing the mushroom. The plant rocks gently back and forth and grows a tiny bit beneath her caress. Removing her glove, she deliberately touches her thumb over the tops of the other mushrooms, which respond with faint, quivering growth—then stop. The liquid in their dimples spills over.

The buzz in her head shifts. Not louder—but eager.

"Dut! Dut! Dut!"

Roger's squeal jerks her from the mushrooms, and she whips around to see her son in his hole. He's pulled all the dirt around him, and the soil reaches his neck. His smile is enormous.

Carolyne blinks. *How do you bury your own arms?*

Kristi bounces up and down behind the iron bars, racing two horses back and forth across the railing while Carolyne hurries to her son. He giggles happily. His toy spade rests on the surface of the mound.

"Dut! Geen! Me!" he crows.

"Wally and Beatrice say Roger's a tree!" Kristi declares, galloping the horses for another round. "A Roger tree!"

Ignoring her, Carolyne knees next to her son and claws at the dirt around his neck. Roger squirms and bursts into tears.

"No, Mommy, no," Kristi begins crying. "He likes it."

Behind Carolyne, the fingers wave, and the mushrooms silently thicken.

But this is what the yard wants.

Blood, sweat and tears, Duckie had told her. Carolyne hears those words like a chant, paired with the buzzy, fluctuating hum in her head.

Days pass in a blur. Roger refuses to be uprooted. Rather, Roger can be uprooted forcibly—but it's an ugly business. He sobs while Kristi pleads his case, and Carolyne can't be sure which disturbs her more. Besides, the minute Carolyne turns her back on Roger, he's away from her and out in the yard again. Digging. Burying. Covering his body, arms, neck. He's found his happy place. And while he's there, the sounds in her mind chime with delight.

Besides, the last time she tried to remove him, he felt *stuck* in there.

So she compromises, which means she utterly gives in. She understands Roger's need to be not just in, but *with* the yard, even if she doesn't fully comprehend the compulsion to bury himself. The nights are warm, and he seems happy, so...she lets him stay there. Brings him dinner and snacks, which he ignores.

"Watuh!" he calls, so she leaves his sippy cup on the ground where he can bend to it. After catching a strange, angry glance from a passing sidewalk pedestrian, she breaks down one of their moving boxes and creates a shield around Roger's corner of the yard. When the sun comes out, she stakes an umbrella in the dirt for shade.

Kristi calls him a tree and whispers to him with her horses.

One Friday, Carolyne has been in the yard poking and prodding, standing and staring, weeding and arranging for most of the day. She's just put the cardboard in place to shield Roger for the night when the gate creaks.

"What in the ever-loving—"

Terence is home. He stares at the tableau in the garden with a look not unlike the passing stranger's: confusion, disgust. How long has he been gone this time? Ten days? Two weeks? Carolyne's lost count. Spotting him there is like seeing a wild beast on the prowl. He stomps into the yard, crushing one of the thick mushrooms beneath his foot. Whipping the cardboard aside, he glares at his son—then at Carolyne.

"Roger's a tree, daddy!" Kristi waves her horses. "A tree! A tree! "

Terence swipes aside the loose soil from the boy's shoulders and reaches into the dirt. Out pops one of Roger's arms, and it's a different shade than the rest of him. Roger wails. A dark, ridged pattern spreads from the boy's fingers up to the elbow, reminding Carolyne of a branch, or a root.

"Stop this!" she pushes Terence. "He likes it there!"

Terence pushes her back, and she falls into the pachysandra. Roger thrusts his arm into the earth and his father reaches in again—but this time jerks his hand out after a second, swearing. A trickle of blood runs down his wrist from an odd, jagged slash in the palm. "Something *bit* me, by Christ," he mutters.

"Hungry," says Roger, his wails subsiding. "Hungry!"

Carolyne hates Terence. Not for shoving her, but for upsetting her yard and her children. She leaps up and stands between her husband and her son. Without a word, Terence leaves the yard, snatches up his travel case, and disappears into the house.

Forgetting the cardboard shield, Carolyne races after him, soothed by the sounds in her head. Kristi catches at her shirt. "Hungry too, Mama," she says.

"Of course," she says in a vague tone. "How about dinosaur chicken nuggets?"

Terence isn't in the kitchen when she walks in, nor the living room. There's rustling going on upstairs, so he hasn't left the house again. "Dinner in thirty minutes!" she shouts up to him as if nothing's amiss. Because it isn't. She's done nothing wrong. Her yard is extraordinary. Her children are healthy. She is a good mother and an excellent gardener.

She sets Kristi up with a small salad and her nuggets while prepping turkey breast cutlets for Terence and herself, and the girl is in the living room with the TV when heavy tread sounds on the steps.

Terence appears in the kitchen. He has his travel case. And a few other bits of luggage. "Carolyne, I need to speak with you."

She pecks him on the cheek, breezing to the stove. "Oh, don't worry about the yard. Roger is fine. It's warm! He loves it. Anyway, everything is nearly ready! One of your favorites—turkey breast cutlets! And salad!"

Sometimes, if she acts this way, Terence's flare-ups un-flare, and he settles down.

Not this time.

"Carolyne," he takes a seat at the kitchen table. "This is serious."

It's a surprise and a relief when it turns out he doesn't care to discuss their son in the garden. But both emotions vanish in light of what Terence *does* care to address.

He tells her things, words that silence the music in her head. The words rush at her like tiny knives, and she wants to throw her arms up to protect herself. All this time, Carolyne has been in control of precisely nothing.

There's another woman. Ramona. His boss. Five years his junior, but senior at the home office. "We're moving in together," he says as she continues to prepare dinner, her movements mechanical. "We'll have to sell the house. I can't afford two homes and she prefers the suburbs."

I preferred the suburbs, Carolyne thinks now, dazed. *You made us come here.*

Turning off the stove, she wanders from the house, into the dark. Into the garden. Stands on the flagstone and stares at the plants. A wash of fresh music envelops her.

"Mommy!" Roger shifts his head side-to-side. The dark ridged pattern she'd seen on his arm has reached his neck. And for the first time, she realizes how tall he's become. His head reaches the porch level now. He's longer and leaner. She imagines his fingers, his toes, growing thin and spindly and ridged, like roots.

"Yes?" she asks.

"Hungry!" he calls out.

"Soon," she promises.

Staring at the strange plants in her strange garden, head cocked, Carolyne knows she can't move again. She won't uproot the children—one more literally than the other—and start over. Roger won't thrive elsewhere. Terence has ruined everything. He swears the Ramona romance isn't some passing thing; as she walked out of the house, he was calling their lawyer.

As the sun sets, Carolyne inventories the odd plants that have burst forth since Mr. Duckworth's labors. The cockle shells' heads are bent down, touching the earth. She gives each a small caress, and they stand up straight, oozing from their dimples. Clusters of dead insects cover the ground around them.

"Hungry!" her tree son calls yet again.

The buzz-hum rises and falls, making her feel things. She mentally disappears the things that bother her and focuses on what she can do. Terence must be starving. He should have something substantial to eat before his next big trip, and the cutlets are nearly ready. But he needs salad fixings. Gripping the base of a cockle shell, she yanks it from the earth. She snips a few knuckles from the fingers and decapitates a silver bell's flower. Low song soars into a full-throated orchestra.

Circle of life. Blood, sweat and tears. You feel me?

Back in the house, Carolyne prepares a side salad: refrigerator lettuce, shredded carrots, yard cuttings. She tosses it with dressing. She wants to scream like her flowers but bites her tongue until she tastes coppery salt, then spits into the salad. The cutlets come from the pan, and she makes a plate for her husband.

Terence stomps up the basement staircase and deposits two more bags at the front door. "Carolyne," he states.

"In here!" she calls, cheerily. "Dinner's ready!"

"I'm not—" he pauses. "Well." Poking his head in the kitchen, his eyes go wide at the steaming cutlet and cheery salad. "Suppose I should tuck in before heading out." He walks a wide arc around his silent wife, who still holds a carving knife, and takes a seat.

Carolyne tosses the knife in the sink—she'll use it later—and joins him at the table. Her plate is empty; she can't imagine eating anything right now.

"Gotta say," Terence pokes a mouthful of salad into his face, gesturing with the empty fork. "You're being awfully reasonable about all this." He eyes the salad bowl. "What's in here, anyway? You add mushrooms?"

"Straight from the garden." Her voice is a distant monotone, and she focuses on his giant jaw, chewing, chewing. Like an animal.

"Too bad you've put so much effort into the yard." He chomps on another bite. "But it'll help with the resale value."

Carolyne thinks of Roger out in the soil. Kristi in the living room. Terence, not asking after either one.

When he finishes, she joins her soon-to-be ex-husband on the porch with his many bags. They stand in the fresh nighttime. Moonlight turns the yard a glowing blue and white. Carolyne cocks her head to one side, listening. The sounds are low and pleasant again in her skull.

Roger is silent, like a tree.

"I can't leave my garden," she says.

Terence shrugs. "Too bad." He picks at remnants of turkey, lettuce, and cockle shell in his teeth. Swallowing hard, he clears his throat. "I'd let you have the place—Ramona's got a big two-bedroom—but the thing is..." he hesitates, and clears his throat again. "I've got another kid coming. We'll need the money."

Sweat beads pop out on his temples.

This last jab of fresh hell stabs through Carolyne's detached calm. She sets her hands on her waist, missing the feeling of her tool belt. But she doesn't need pruning shears with Terence now. He's already been cut back; he just doesn't know it yet. She smiles, understanding at last who the pretty maids of this house really are. Kristi has shown interest in the changes her brother is undergoing. She can be shown the ways of the garden.

"Hungry," Roger murmurs miserably.

Hold your horses, Carolyne thinks. *Plenty of compost soon.*

"Did you hear something?" Terence's voice is thin and strained as if being forced through a narrowing tube.

"Not a thing," Carolyne says.

Out in the yard, the flower faces smile and hum gently. The cockle shells are bent over, oozing. Roger, her tree-son, rustles in restless anticipation. Then—all goes quiet. A held breath.

In the silence, in the moonlight, Terence begins to cough.

ABOUT THE AUTHOR

Randee Dawn is the author of the Amazon bestselling funny, fantastical pop culture novel *Tune in Tomorrow* (Solaris Nova). Her forthcoming novels in 2025 include the dark rock 'n roll fantasy *The Only Song Worth Singing* and *Leave No Trace* (ArcManor/Caezik) and *We Interrupt This Program* (Solaris Nova). A veteran entertainment journalist who also gardens her own small yard, Randee lives in Brooklyn with her very un-Terence-like spouse and a whole lot of books. More at RandeeDawn.com.

About Crone Girls Press

Crone Girls Press originally began as a Facebook group for fans of speculative fiction, hosted by speculative fiction author and writing coach Rachel A. Brune. As the idea took hold to publish an anthology of horror fiction in honor of her favorite fall holiday, Rachel began soliciting stories of dread, despair, and doom, all of which made for some uplifting reading. Upon receiving some truly terrifying—and excellent—material, she decided to go for broke and start working on an anthology series that would feature work by established and debut authors...from the darker side of speculative fiction.

We've now published six full-length anthologies and are always adding to our series of three-novella mini-anthologies, Midnight Bites. *Dark Spores: Stories We Tell After Midnight 4* represents the latest publication in our efforts to publish chilling horror from the widest variety of voices that we can include in our pages. Enjoy—but don't stay up *too* late past midnight...

Acknowledgments

Crone Girls Press wishes to extend our deepest gratitude to our generous backers and fellow fungi fans. Your support for our crowdfunding campaign made this volume possible.

Alex McGilvery · Alexa B. Antopol · Allison Charlesworth · Alp Beck · AM Giddings · Amy Goldschlager · Andy Boyle · Angus McIntyre · Ann Stolinsky · Anonymous · April Baker · April Prevette Jernigan · Avis Crane · Bill Feero · Bob 'Possum' McGough · Brian Bowyer · Bridget D. Brave · Brooke Mackenzie · Brooks Moses · C. Patrick Neagle · C.J. Subko · Candace Nola · Catherine Hannah · Cindy O'Quinn · Colleen Feeney · Cory Oakes · Dana Schuman · Danielle Ackley-McPhail · Danyelle Denham · David Thirteen · Dead Fish Books · DeAnna Knippling · Dee Norman · Dino Hicks · Elizabeth Barayuga · Elizabeth Donald · Epiphany Ferrell · eSpec Books · Gav I · Glenda Strangerman · Glori Medina · H.V. Patterson · Hannah and Gene Johnson · Jess Simms · Jesse Adams · Jessica Cline · Jessica Nettles · Joanne Austin · Joe Compton · Kate Jonez · Kerney Williams · Kirsten Kowalewski · Konsectatrix · Krista Wathanaphone · Kristina Meschi · KT Wagner · Lara Coutinho-Dean · Lekden Davis · Lindsey Hanlon · Lisa Short · Liz DeJesus · LJ Coombs · Lucy Blue · Macsen Matthews · Matthew Carpenter · Maxwell I. Gold · Meghan Arcuri · Melanie Bell ·

Michael Cieslak · Michele Karsk · Michele Tracy Berger · Misty Massey · N.R. Lambert · Nick Crook · Nicole Kurtz · Paige Holland · prophet · R.C. Briggs · Rachel Unger · Rebecca Hoffman · Richard Dansky · Richard Leis · Rook Riley · Ruth Ann Orlansky · S. Alessandro Martinez · S.E. Howard · Sarah Anne Stubbs · Scotty Milder · Sirrah Medeiros · SM Hillman · Sóng & Sól Skulkwithy · Steffany Kurilovitch · Stephanie Bryant · Stephanie Pearre · Steve Chappell · Susan McBride · Susan Roddey · Thea Brune · Thomas Gaffney · Tom Deady · Valentine Wolfe · Vaughn Jackson · Venessa Giunta · Zen Hance

Thank you, Fiends!

We so hope you enjoyed your stay with us. If the sights you have seen and the dreams you have escaped stay with you after closing these pages, wouldn't you do us the favor of warning others of what they might encounter, should they happen to open these covers?
Share your thoughts, whether they be the careful, measured words of the diligent reader, or the sobbing cry from the asylum, on Goodreads or Amazon!
We'll be seeing you soon.

Our list of other titles is always growing. To stay in touch, join us on Facebook, and sign up for the Crone Girls Press newsletter:
http://eepurl.com/gPT5s1
or scan the QR Code!

If You Liked...

If you liked *Dark Spores: Stories We Tell After Midnight Volume 4*, you may also enjoy:

Other Titles from Crone Girls Press:

Stories We Tell After Midnight Volume 1

Stories We Tell After Midnight Volume 2

Stories We Tell After Midnight Volume 3

Coppice & Brake

Tangle & Fen

A Woman Unbecoming

Midnight Bites

Foul Womb of Night

Mother Krampus

Hard for Hope to Flourish

Memorial Station

Objectified